CARRIE DALFONSO
D1359093

ALSO BY ERNEST BRAWLEY

The Rap
Selena

THE ALAMO TREE

A NOVEL BY

ERNEST BRAWLEY

SIMON AND SCHUSTER NEW YORK

This novel is a work of fiction. Names, characters, places and incidents are either the product of the author's imagination or are used fictitiously. Any resemblance to actual events or locales or persons, living or dead, is entirely coincidental.

Copyright © 1984 by Ernest Brawley
All rights reserved
including the right of reproduction
in whole or in part in any form

Published by Simon and Schuster
A Division of Simon & Schuster, Inc.
Simon & Schuster Building
Rockefeller Center
1230 Avenue of the Americas
New York, New York 10020

SIMON AND SCHUSTER and colophon are registered trademarks of Simon & Schuster, Inc.
Designed by CHRISTOPHER SIMON
Manufactured in the United States of America

1 2 3 4 5 6 7 8 9 10

LIBRARY OF CONGRESS CATALOGING IN PUBLICATION DATA
Brawley, Ernest.
The Alamo tree.

I. Title.
PS3552.R356A78 1984 813'.54 84-1337
ISBN 0-671-45088-3

For Lucia, with love . . .

"Francis Kevin O'Hare, who was trainmaster of the American-owned and -operated Colima Pacific Railroad line in the years before the Mexican Revolution, had a wife he couldn't control," the lady said, seated like an ancient queen mother in a thronelike wicker chair on the veranda of the tropical hotel where she had made her home for the past forty years. "She claimed that she had a 'weak disposition' and made him keep a mestiza mistress in Manzanillo. And yet every night he either dreamed or (he was never quite sure to the end) actually *heard* her moving the cotton sheets under the mosquito netting in a highly suspicious way.

"O'Hare was a small man," the lady said, squinting out over her lawn and flower gardens and the shacks of squatters on the hillside toward the bright-blue waters of Acapulco Bay, "but he cut a fine figure, and if you caught him sitting he seemed a much larger fellow. He wore a thick blond mustache. His hair was straw-colored and thin and hung over one eye, and he'd developed the correct nervous habit of brushing it back with his hand. He had a fine nose, pale-blue eyes, almost no eyebrows or lashes, and absolutely noble features. His face, his bearing and manner, his attitudes and Back Bay accent, were those of a Boston Irish gentleman of the highest rung of Roman Catholic Society. Yet in fact he was the black sheep of a family of sober, respectable railroad men, trainmasters, yardmasters, civil engineers and such, and there wasn't an aristocrat in the lot.

"Apart from the fact that O'Hare was a fraud, and something of a snob, he had a cruel streak, which he displayed by treating his wife—a girl young enough to be his daughter—abominably in public. Society in that place was dominated by the creoles, who were as you know landowning aristocrats of pure Spanish extraction, and by members of the large foreign colony—wealthy North American, British and German entrepreneurs, for the most part—who dominated local industry, commerce and shipping. At fandangos in the creole community, or at soirées in the foreign colony, O'Hare would make sport of his wife's gay and amusing little puns and anecdotes. He made fun of her intelligence, her taste, her breeding, and even of her 'weak disposition,' to any of his fellow railway officials or club members who would listen. They, and their wives, called it his 'little man thing,' behind his back, and wondered out loud how she put up with him. She never seemed to care about defending herself, as far as they knew. When he subjected her to the most horrid public scenes, she'd never utter a word. The poor thing would go off like a ghost. All the light would leave her eyes and she would simply become absent.

"But as soon as they got back home, he'd come to her on his knees and beg forgiveness and swear to Jesus and Mary and all the saints that he'd never do it again, didn't know what evil seed inside him had made him do it in the first place. Of course, his promise would only last until the next time they went out, or only till the next day at home, when he would ruthlessly attack her for no reason, or pooh-pooh her accomplishments at the piano, or even go so far as to actually *strike* her when she spoke admiringly of another man—for he was insanely jealous and he never left her a moment's peace though she told him again and again that she could not endure his touch.

"But don't take me wrong. I don't mean to imply that there were no moments of ease in their marriage, no fleeting joys, no small rewards. On the contrary, when all is said and done, their life in this imperfect world was steady and respectable and comfortable and they had plenty of time to do as they liked.

"O'Hare liked to go prospecting and exploring, panning gold and looking for oil, and every time he had a week or two off he'd tramp into the Sierra Madre with a native guide, or ride an Indian canoe through the mangrove swamps, mapping the delta of the Río Coayuayana for Royal Dutch Petroleum.

"His wife, on the other hand, very much preferred to stay at home.

"At home the O'Hares liked to read. It was the one thing they had in common. They would dine latish, after the mestiza nanny had put their little boy, Brian, to bed. Just the two of them. Dressed. With candles and imported California wine, and two Nahua maids serving. And then they'd settle in for the evening on the veranda, behind the mosquito screen, O'Hare with his pipe and whiskey, his wife with a glass of Agua Tehuacán, indulging their opposing tastes in literature. O'Hare liked to read anthropology, etymology, geography and history. He kept a great fat journal full of facts and maps and dates and graphs and origins of words. His wife liked to read poetry and romantic novels, especially the French. She liked Stendhal best of the novelists, and Rimbaud, whom she often read aloud, to the extreme distraction of her husband, was ecstasy itself.

"Late one evening while she was reading some Hindi poetry in translation she came upon something quite wonderful, something about *'The one who waits and does nothing is the one who wins in the end. . . .'* She was so struck by it that she read it aloud to her husband and said, 'That, my dear, is precisely what I've been doing all my married life—waiting and doing nothing.'

" 'Bullshit,' said O'Hare, and went back to his Thucydides.

"Every evening he would start to nod over his book and his bottle of booze at about nine o'clock and by ten he would drag himself off to bed half-drunk. His wife would go on reading till she was sure he was asleep, then she'd pull out her notebooks from their hiding place in the linen closet and indulge herself in her secret vice.

"She was an incurable scribbler. Had been ever since she was a small girl. She spent all her free time dreaming up the most implausibly wild and romantic short stories and novelettes, typing them up when her husband was out at work, and sending them off to be instantly rejected by popular women's magazines in England and America. The heroine was always someone very much like herself: young, married to a much older man, living in some exotic locale . . . when a tall, dark, handsome stranger comes upon the scene. . . .

"Then, hours after her husband had turned in—even after the insects had gone silent and the long blue frogs by the Río Colima had stopped their strange, purling night whistle—she'd creep into their bed and he'd be awakened by the sound of her body moving in that unmistakable fashion, faster and faster against the sheets, and her breath coming harder and harder, until finally she would finish, with a loud sigh, and sleep peacefully the rest of the night.

"O'Hare had the patient, methodical traits of a trained engineer. He executed his purpose very carefully, over a period of many months.

"Five times, at precise intervals, he reacted. 'Retreating in the face of overwhelming force,' I believe the maneuver was called. Must've picked it up in the Spanish-American War, or somewhere. But if he was more and more desperate in his actions, then, I can assure you, it was a tightly controlled desperation.

"The first time, he pretended to lose control of himself. He mounted her and tried to take her by force. But she fought him off, and shamed him by declaring herself, as one said in those days, 'shocked and scandalized.'

"He confronted her point-blank the second time. She replied that he must be mad, or suffering from some rare tropical infirmity, with such 'lewd and vagrant' notions rattling around in his head, and he'd best toddle off to see the company doctor post-haste.

"The third time he cried out 'Stop, stop, oh please stop, I beg of you!' as you might cry 'Stop thief!' to someone who'd run off with a dearly beloved possession. She just rolled over and ignored him.

"The fourth time he gave himself up to despair, weeping his eyes out all through the night, imploring her to stop it, crying out, 'You have killed me!' many times.

"He listened quietly the fifth time till the thrashing and moaning were over and she appeared to be resting peacefully. 'So be it!' he said, praying she'd hear it, and relent.

"He lay back with his eyes wide open," the lady said. "I can picture him now, the poor soul, waiting all through the tropical night, till the last nightbird and the last cicada gave up and the sun came up above the banana trees. Then he rose, dressed himself in his working clothes, his jodhpurs and pistol and Sam Browne belt, his pith helmet and his knee-high lace-up boots, walked to the railroad terminal, ordered a large Mexican breakfast of huevos rancheros, tortillas, frijoles and café con leche, fired up one of his own locomotives, and, leaving no note or word of farewell, at ten o'clock in the morning, November 20, 1910, drove it off the Sayula Grade and fell three hundred feet to his death.

"His wake and funeral were attended by the entire foreign colony, and no one could imagine what had ever possessed him to leave his lovely young wife, especially in such desperate straits. As it was discovered, he'd not a penny's worth of insurance, and he'd not been employed by the railroad long enough for a pension. A collection was taken up for his widow. She was the beneficiary of several church and club raffles as well. When it was determined that she still felt a deep attachment to Mexico, and intended to stay on, several influential members of the foreign colony chipped in as silent partners and helped her make a down payment on a small hotel in the central plaza. For years, while the Revolution raged across Mexico, and the creole community and the foreign colony got smaller and smaller, she devoted herself to her business and the raising of her child. She entertained no suitors, had few callers, and spent most of her free time reading in her room.

"It was assumed that she was pining away for her dear, departed husband, when actually it was a bit more complicated than that. Though she'd been relentless in battle with O'Hare his defeat brought her little satisfaction. She'd never imagined that he'd go as far as he did. She kept telling herself that all she'd meant to do was teach him a lesson, to give as good as she'd got. 'Ah, but vengeance is mine, saith the Lord' kept running through her brain. And all her Catholic training came to the fore. Suddenly she found herself in a crisis of conscience. And it was seventeen years before she could regain a measure of perspective on herself, or recover the courage of her own convictions. Then one morning in May of 1927 she awakened with a sweet and gentle man in her bed and it came to her in a flash: O'Hare had dreams of empire, she thought, and he deserved everything he got."

It was fifty-five years later—at about the time that President López Portillo nationalized the banking industry—that Merle Carrizo heard this story from the redoubtable Mrs. O'Hare's own charming lips. The two of them, drunk as lords on cheap Baja California wine, were lolling abandoned on the veranda of the nearly empty off-season Tropicana Hotel. And though he'd known the lady since he was a boy of three, this was the best story he'd heard her tell yet. He could picture her perfectly in her company-owned tropical bungalow with her imperialist American husband in those remote years before the Mexican Revolution. With a little help from the lady herself, he could picture her even before that, in the ludicrously long-ago year of 1895, when she was nothing more than a little Irish immigrant girl, as she said, with something of the "magic" about her, something of the ghost, that her husband, poor dear, had never learned to appreciate.

"If not magic, then what was it?" she demanded of Merle, rising imperiously from her wicker chair and shaking her puffy little hand in his incredulous face.

What had compelled her all alone on that foggy winter day eighty-seven years ago to walk like a tiny sleepwalker from Tehama Street to Third Street and then all the way down Market Street to McAllister and the brand-new San Francisco Public Library where, in time, and after repeated visits, she discovered the existence of art, science, music, literature, philosophy, history, all by her little self, eh? And what made her scrimp and save and sew clothes and take in laundry and scrub floors till she had enough money to buy one fine lady's dress when her stepmother had said, in her unspeakable accent, "Tha' sor' a fing ain't fo' our class, is it? Puttin' on bleedin' airs, are yer? Yer'll turn out like yer dir'y mum oo's on the gaime, yer will. Mark me words!" And what made her send herself off to the St. Anne's Academy, then, she asked, her gray eyes blazing, when nobody else in the neighborhood went and she had to win herself a scholarship to do it, and she had to walk two miles over Nob Hill and Russian Hill to the Western Addition in all sorts of awful weather to get there? And what made her beg and wheedle Sister Michael Archangel the grammar teacher to spend extra time with her after school to improve her horrid, slack-jawed Shanty Irish elocution, and what made her try so hard and persevere, and manage to ward off Sister Michael Archangel's mannish advances, yet coyly, in her cunning Celtic way, keep her just enough interested to continue teaching her until she'd gotten it down perfectly and could put on her lady's dress and promenade into posh shops in Union Square and inquire about this or that and not be stared at like a parlor maid out of place? And what, the lady persisted, waving her stout marbled arms in the air before the smiling, paralyzed Merle Carrizo, what made her run away to San Diego, to the Coronado Beach Hotel, when she was only fifteen and charm her way into the heart of a gentleman's gentleman waiting at the coastal steamer slip with his employer, who gallantly paid her way to Long Beach, and then on to fashionable Santa Barbara, where, after adventures too varied and numerous to relate, she met and, shamelessly misrepresenting herself, married the dashing Major Francis Kevin O'Hare, lately retired from a twenty-year career in the United States Army Rail Transport Corps?

"And what," the lady repeated, "what made me ignore the insults of his family in Boston when they refused to accept me and called me 'beneath him' and threatened to disown him? And what made me persuade him to thumb his nose at the lot of them and accept a position on the Colima Pacific Railroad in deepest Mexico where no one knew us and we could make a fresh start? And what made me go on and on, becoming a real *person,* despite all the obstacles?"

She knew, she said, in a way, and in another way she hadn't a clue. But she did know that she had been rare; she was sure that she had been *something,* something real, something special, something not at all commonplace, something—she didn't think it vain if she said it herself, she was too old for that now—something beautiful. She'd often looked at herself naked in the mirror. But not out of vanity. She'd been too sure of her physical beauty for that: "My long slender legs," she said, rising coolly, demonstrating—while Merle looked on in horror—"my lovely rounded hips, my hourglass figure, my perfect derrière, my two little handfuls, Mick Prides, Irish Apples," she said, giggling, "and my face, not at all wide and peasant, nor thin and Protestant either, but for my coloring, which was English Country Beauty, peaches and cream. . . . My nose," she said, "might have been Classic Greek. No! I did not look into the mirror for vanity's sake. I looked, and I still look now, to see if the magic is still there.

"And by God, after ninety-eight years, nearly a century of life," she said, and paused, as if shaken by this reminder of her own extreme antiquity in a swiftly changing world, "I defy you to say the magic isn't still there!"

Merle Carrizo believed her. Indeed it was magic the way, like a great queen bee, she had lasted . . . *waiting and doing nothing* for five generations. And he could not defy her to save his soul.

PART I

CHAPTER 1

Above the green furrows of the irrigated river valley rose the elegant parish church of Huentitán—stone-walled, baroque, permanent—on its austere desert hill, surrounded by the gray, squalid, temporary digs of the poor. On Sundays Father Dowd used to walk into the city after Mass. It was a beautiful old pink-volcanic-stone-and-red-tile colonial city from the seventeenth century, sliced through at angles by grand elm-lined boulevards in the style of Baron Haussmann. It was a city of taxicabs: yellow and black, red and orange, blue and green, Ford Model Ts and ancient Renaults, twisting and turning in the traffic of taco wagons and hot corn carts, donkeys and mules and yoked oxen, high-wheeled carretas and decrepit American streetcars all going around and around the statues of dead generals in the glorietas.

On the first day of the rebellion the taxis disappeared. They stole away to the barracks in Zapopán and picked up the Olimpia Battalion and drove back into Guadalajara in the middle of the night. The battalion, which was in reality little more than a band of thieves and cutthroats left over from the Revolution, occupied the cathedral and the headquarters of the Diocese of Jalisco and hanged six young militant priests from the streetlamps in the Plaza de la Liberación.

In Huentitán the people allowed themselves to be incited by an agent provocateur in the service of the army and gutted the rectory and shot Father Sabadell and Father Galardi against the bougainvillea in the central courtyard. Father Dowd locked himself in the bathroom with his friends Father de Falla and Father LeFevre. The mob came around and started beating on the door with sticks and stones, laughing and making fun.

"Come on, padrecitos, it only takes a minute. You won't even know what hit you and you'll be on your way to paradise."

The priests jumped into the darkness from the narrow second-story bathroom window. They could see nothing. They flung themselves down the hill to the river, stumbling and falling over rocks and garbage and animal bones. They threw themselves into the black water and quickly became separated in the darkness. Father Dowd floated and crawled down the shallow sewage-ridden stream for a mile or more. Then he slithered up a dry, dusty riverbank under an ancient stone bridge and limped into the city alone. There were laughter and dancing in the streets to the light of burning Catholic mansions. He made his way to the Plaza de Armas and hid in the attic of a Spanish anarchist friend till he heard shooting in the courtyard below. He leaped to the rooftop next door, ran down to the ground floor, and fled in a panic over back fences and kitchen gardens toward the United States Consulate. When he was still three blocks away he could see that it was surrounded by troops and armored cars. He hid in a back doorway and prayed for his life. In the morning a woman came to the door and, taking pity on him, brought him into her small room in the servants' quarters of a rich Freemason's house. She was a widow, she said, and she offered him the clothes, peddler's license and road kit of her late husband, who had been a traveling salesman of anti-lice shampoo.

On the third night of the rebellion Father Dowd darkened his face and hair with dye. He dressed himself as a peddler and set off for the port of Manzanillo. The woman started to laugh as he was leaving, and he picked it up for a little moment while they stood shaking hands at the gate. It was the nice dry laugh of two conspirators in a losing cause. He gave her his blessing and slinked off down the Calzada Independencia like a pariah dog. From the Colima Pacific Railroad station he could hear them shooting Catholics against the cathedral wall.

It was May 1927, and the Church and State were locked in a battle to the death.

It had begun the year before when President Calles decided to enforce the anticlerical clauses in the new Mexican Constitution. Hundreds of foreign nuns and priests were deported. Parochial schools were shut down. Priests were ordered to register like street vendors at local city halls. The Church responded by announcing that it would go out on strike rather than comply. The government refused to back down; and on July 31, 1926, every priest in the country walked out of church. For the first time since the Spaniards landed in Vera Cruz over four hundred years before there was not a Mass performed anywhere in Mexico. In retaliation, President Calles confiscated all Church property and handed it over to elected committees of local citizens. Most of these committees decided to keep their churches open; and this was the undoing of the strike, for the peasants discovered that they had no need of priests. Like most Mexicans they were devoutly religious, but their religion was more pagan than Christian and they had always distrusted priests as white men, foreigners in league with the oligarchs and landowners. Rapidly the country polarized, with the radicalized peasantry and working class on the side of the government and the reactionary white "creole" aristocracy and the mestizo middle class supporting the Church. Rebels known as Cristeros, organized and led by militant priests, formed in the mountains of west-central Mexico to ambush federal columns. Then toward the end of April 1927, the Cristeros came out of the mountains, blew up the Mexico City–Guadalajara express train and massacred the survivors. Over a hundred innocent people were killed, and it was proved that a score of disaffected priests, if not the archbishop of Guadalajara himself, were immediately involved. The archbishop, who made no secret of his sympathies for the rebels, refused to place himself under house arrest, as ordered by the government. Instead, he joined the Cristeros and took a leading role in their rebellion, anointing the knightly standards that they carried into battle, saying Mass and offering the Holy Eucharist before each military skirmish, and leading his men in their infamous war cry, "Viva Cristo Rey—Long Live Christ the King!" At the most solemn moment of the Mass, the Elevation of the Host, it was said that he ordered his men to present arms as to a military commander. And he took no prisoners, though he permitted federal soldiers the comfort of a final Confession before they were shot. The Calles government, which had no love for the Catholic Church in the first place, responded by exiling all the remaining bishops of Mexico and sending the federal army out on a holy war to exterminate the Cristeros. Only after the first military engagements, in the month of May, did the government see fit to give an official name to the insurrection. They called it the Cristero Rebellion. From the perspective of a fugitive foreign priest, a "pacífico" caught in the middle of two outrageous extremes, it was like a walk through the valley of the shadow of death.

On the morning of the fourth day of the rebellion, Father Dowd sat, small and tight and wiry, hunched up like an Indian on the station platform of a village on the high western plateau of Jalisco. His train had been commandeered by federal troops a few miles outside of Zocoalco and he'd spent the night in the open. Now there were flowers and Mexican national flags all around him. A ragged brass band inside the station played martial music, loud. An old red wood-burning steam engine came rolling up. "San Francisco, 1899," it said on the boiler. Father Dowd took it as an extraordinarily good omen, as that was his place and year of birth.

A fat priest stood near him waiting for the train, guarded by a soldier with a Mauser. The priest was the kind of fellow, Father Dowd reflected, whose plump poised little fingers made him look as if he was just about to pick his nose or his ass. When the train arrived another priest with a soldier escort got off to meet him. This priest was tall, slender and scholarly-looking, with a carefully trimmed Vandyke beard flecked with gray, and swift ironic eyes behind thick wire-rimmed spectacles. It was Father de Falla, his friend from Guadalajara. He spotted Father Dowd on the platform, but betrayed his recognition only by the merest shadow of a sardonic smile. Then he shook hands solemnly with the smaller priest, with whom he appeared to be acquainted, and they gave each other the abrazo. They linked arms and with the soldiers following slowly started for the village. During the entire ceremony neither priest showed the slightest flicker of emotion. Yet their encounter was charged with unmistakable secret meaning. In a few moments they would dig their own graves, perhaps, and be shot together against the wall of a church.

Father Dowd got on the train and paid the fare with his last thirty pesos. It would be easy to telegraph ahead and stop the train, he thought, should Father de Falla decide to betray him. He pictured his friend before the firing squad, his El Greco face raised to God, and comforted himself with the notion of martyrdom, toward which de Falla on at least a dozen occasions had confessed to yearn.

The train began climbing into the mountains as soon as it left the village. Every seat was taken. Peasants and army men rode on the tops of cars and on the engine. Father Dowd stood for two hours. Then he sat down in the aisle. In the next car the army had a number of Cristero prisoners under guard. They were Catholic Action youth cadre, and most of them looked like little boys. Every few minutes word would come back that another one had been thrown over the cliff.

The train labored up the first cordillera of the Sierra Madre, going through tunnels and galleries carved out of the sheer volcanic rock, going around bare windy faces that looked back down on Zocoalco and the Lake of Atotonilco, twenty miles away, going up and down and back and forth on spectacular switchbacks hanging hundreds of feet above the river gorge. At Diablo Canyon the train stopped briefly and he saw five small brown bodies hurtling through the white mist toward the river.

Yet through it all Father Dowd remained curiously detached. His years in Mexico had made him cynical, perhaps. Nothing was quite real down here. You could never trust your own senses. Everything was in doubt or open to personal interpretation. Even the most sacred Commandments. The places were like comic-opera places, and the people were the same. The political landscape resembled nothing so much as the Italy of the condottieri. The states of Mexico were governed neither by the central authority nor by their elected governors but by regional caudillos, wealthy and greedy generals who had seized power during the Revolution and functioned as warlords, with their own private armies and their own networks of political patronage that extended through their caciques or straw bosses right down to the level of the village and barrio. These caudillos were reknowned for their cruelty, treachery and rapacity, and the commander of the garrison in Guadalajara, General Saturnino Sánchez, was no exception. A wily old full-blooded Tarascan Indian from the shores of Lake Pátzcuaro, he had started out as a populist leader in the early days of the Revolution, with a rallying cry of "Land and Liberty!" He gathered a small army of peasants and marched to join General Emiliano Zapata in Morelos. After the first round of the Revolution, he betrayed and rejoined Zapata several times and was eventually involved in the plot that resulted in Zapata's death. During the course of the Revolution, in fact, General Sánchez had been a leading figure in countless plots and intrigues with and against one faction or another, and he had unexpectedly switched sides so many times between the Maderistas, Zapatistas, Villistas, and Constitucionalistas that he had grown enormously rich from bribery.

More recently, he had secretly aided and abetted the Cristero Rebellion, currying favor with the archbishop as well as the federal government, specifically in order to afford himself new opportunities for rape and plunder. Yet, shockingly enough, General Sánchez was not disdained by the Mexican people. On the contrary, he was admired for his sagacity, his bravery under fire, and the nepotism and political payoffs with which he pampered his friends and relatives. And it was he whom the government had entrusted to carry out its war against the Church in west-central Mexico, on the grounds of "corruption." Ironically, like all things Mexican, the Church really was corrupt, from top to bottom. The bishops were in the pay of the landowning aristocracy; their "Cristero Rebellion" was little more than a brazen attempt to forestall the distribution of land to the peasants according to the terms of the agrarian reform. The native clergy was riddled by vice, and village priests lived openly with their concubines and bastards.

What could you do, what could you say about a country such as this? Its barbarity defied description. When Father Dowd wrote letters to his grandma in Turlock describing conditions here, he imagined her sitting by the fire in her parlor above the Merced River, sipping tea with the neighbors, and he wondered how they could ever believe what he said. They must have thought he'd taken leave of his senses. He wondered about that himself at times, as the cardinal rules of Mexican life, so far as he could tell, were: (1) everything is in question, (2) all is deception, (3) passion rules, (4) trust no one, not even yourself.

In short, Father Dowd could barely believe he was the same bright-eyed young cleric who had come down here in 1923 fresh from a California seminary filled with immense fervor, inspired by a clear and constant sign of vocation from the Blessed Virgin to do God's work among the poor and wretched, the sick and hungry and oppressed of the world, to awaken sleeping minds and win souls for Christ. The Great Popular Revolution had just been won, the Mexican Senate had ratified one of the most liberal and enlightened constitutions in the world (albeit with certain regrettable anticlerical clauses), it was a great time to be alive, and Father Dowd was bursting with energy, instilled with a great desire to participate in the bold new experiment in social and economic progress that was taking place south of the border. The Mexican Revolution, the first great popular revolution of the twentieth century, had flared across the country for ten years, from Arizona to Guatemala, destroying the old order of hacendado and péon, white man and brown, and raising up in its place a new nation, a new and uniquely Mexican man: the mestizo, a dynamic fusion of Spanish and Aztec race and culture, the physical embodiment of all the egalitarian aspirations of the Revolution. But the climate of Mexico is brutal, and things there tend to corrode, or to burn out quickly and crumble into dust, even the fondest hopes and dreams of mankind: Within a very few years the mestizo was stiffing his brothers in such novel and inventive ways that the hacendado himself would have blushed with shame.

Father Dowd's religious faith, and his faith in humanity, had therefore been sorely tried long before the Cristero Rebellion. If he remained steadfast in his loyalty to the Church, and true to his Holy Orders, it was for other more personal reasons than absolute conviction or devotion. Exactly what those reasons were, even he could not say. Sometimes he thought it might be force of habit. Sometimes he thought it might be that he was slowly becoming a Mexican. Whatever, he felt himself strangely willing to follow his predestined course where it might lead him, even into the darkest and most unexplored regions.

At the summit there was a small town and a station. Solemn peasants stood around on the platform and on the railroad tracks, celebrating the defeat of the local Cristeros. Some of them were playing trumpets and guitars and tubas and other European instruments, but the sound they made was like nothing Father Dowd had ever heard. A young blond North American was swinging upside down from the spout on the railroad tower. And he was such a superbly rawboned American, a midwestern type. He looked like a Baptist preacher or a young politician. Yet somehow you knew that he was a priest. His left arm was tied up behind him. The other had broken free. It looked as if he were waving. Father Dowd was a bit shocked at himself for not pitying his countryman, his fellow priest of God, for not even bothering to say a prayer for his soul. The only thing he felt was a kind of mild astonishment at seeing him hanging that way. There were two reasons for Father Dowd's astonishment. One was that priests from north of the border were extremely rare down here, because of the Church's sensitivity to charges of "religious imperialism." And the other was that he had comforted himself till now with the wishful notion that the Mexicans would not dare to harm a United States citizen for fear of provoking armed intervention.

Everyone on the train was suspicious of everyone else. Father Dowd decided that if someone spoke to him, he would pretend that he was mute. His accent in Spanish was not particularly North American, but they would know he was foreign. He computed his chances of escape again and decided they were as slim as ever.

How should he try to go? Should he skirt the flanks of the Volcán de Colima and go by way of Atenquique, Tonila, Cuauhtémoc, El Trapiche and then down to the coast from Colima? Or should he go by way of the Sayula Grade to Zapotiltic, Tuxpan, Taximixtla, Pihuamo and Trapichillos? Such barbarous names, such barbarous places. . . .

The coast was mostly tropical jungle and it was still a no-man's-land. General Sánchez had permitted the Catholic rebels to flourish in Manzanillo in order to prolong the conflict and obtain more funds from the federal government, funds that he intended to promptly expropriate for his already sizable bank account in San Antonio, Texas.

Maybe there was some hope after all.

But who ever heard of a mute peddler?

A pair of policemen wearing holstered .45 caliber pistols and little red ribbons stuck in their caps came walking down the aisle selling cigarettes, newspapers, and refreshments, and checking documents. Father Dowd ignored them when they tried to sell him chewing gum, but he reacted quickly when they asked, in more severe and official tones, for his papers.

In Mexico every adult male was required by law to carry on his person at all times a voter's registration certificate and his record of, or exemption from, military service. Father Dowd handed them these documents along with his peddler's license. They scanned the papers carefully, but it was apparent from their effort that neither of them read very well.

"Donde vas?"

He pulled out a pad and pencil and wrote out in perfect Spanish that he was a mute peddler and he was going to the market in Zapotlán to sell his lice shampoo. He rolled his eyes at them. They laughed and continued down the aisle.

I think I'm going to be sick, he thought. What is it?

Father Dowd was having a crisis. In Guadalajara he had been known as a social democrat. Jesus was the first radical. The True Church will be the militant voice of the people. No one had suspected his secret and ever-growing cynicism. He and Father de Falla had been alone among their colleagues in welcoming the social programs of the revolutionary government: the agrarian reform, the guarantees of the rights of workers and unions, the expropriations of the great private landholdings, the literacy campaign and the secular school program. They had marched with the peasants in the streets of the capital, demanding Land to the Tiller. They had supported the communists in their clamor to expel the foreign oil interests, and other exploiters of the mineral wealth of Mexico. They had spoken out against the conservative hierarchy of the Mexican Church, the most reactionary in the world, and they had been censured by the archbishop for their opposition to the clerical strike and to the formation of clandestine military units led by priests. But now all of their efforts on behalf of the Mexican people were to be counted as naught. Now they would be stood up against the adobe wall, the paredón where there is never any pardon, and they would be shot, right alongside the rightists and militarists. Why? Father de Falla had probably already played his role in their revolution, their rebellion, their passion play. What was Father Dowd's role to be?

The lamb, he thought.

And all of his bones, muscles, joints and his testicles began to ache.

In the morning Father Dowd found himself in Zapotlán, an ugly, desolate little place near a wide sick-looking lake full of water lilies. The lake was white, white as the sky in these parts, white as the hard clay walls and dusty streets of the town, white as the skeletal cattle that waded up to their white eyes to nibble on the lilies while tall white herons rode between their long horns, picking at the insects in their hides.

Hungry, ill, demoralized, Father Dowd stumbled through the crowded streets to the market plaza. There he engaged the services of a young mestizo by writing him a note explaining that he was a mute peddler and needed someone to make his sales pitch for him.

The mestizo turned out to be quite a good pitchman. A large crowd of peasants gathered around them. The mestizo gave a peso to a dirty ragged little Indian boy with an Eskimo face. Father Dowd took out the peddler's road kit that he'd borrowed, opened up a bottle of lice shampoo, poured it into the boy's hair and rubbed it in. It got into his eyes. He grimaced and began to cry. The peasants laughed, their mouths flying open but their eyes not laughing. Father Dowd scrubbed the boy's hair and rinsed it. He combed the dead lice out and displayed them on the tips of his fingers. The peasants seemed impressed. They bought forty pesos' worth of the shampoo in less than five minutes. The mestizo collected the money.

Then a drum and trumpet marching band came around the plaza with union pennants flying. A Model T truck drove slowly behind them loaded with Catholic merchants and gentlefolk and a single forlorn priest. They were on their way to the municipal slaughterhouse, where they would be shot against the wall of the meat market. Father Dowd watched the parade until it had disappeared, and when he turned back the mestizo was gone. Sadly he walked to the outskirts of town, where he spent the rest of the day sleeping in a cornfield. He broke the yellow stalks and the brown ones and covered himself. The brown ones kept the insects out.

When the evening came he got another mestizo to help him. This time Father Dowd ran away with the money.

That night he caught the train for Tuxpan. When the police came around selling refreshments and checking documents he said to hell with it and stopped praying for deliverance and bought himself a bottle of beer and again they accepted his story. After that he quit praying for things.

In Tuxpan he went to the plaza again to sell his lice shampoo. But the plaza was deserted. He walked the single dirt street of the town, mutely peddling to passersby. No one bought. He had spent all his money on the train fare. He was very hungry, very tired. He found it extremely difficult to get around, on account of the pain of his muscles and joints. The dye on his face was wearing off. It looked as if he had some kind of skin disease. He didn't worry about it. He wanted to look as disreputable as possible. But the dye in his hair was coming out as well. He walked down to the bottom of the deep barranca on the edge of town and caked his hair with thick, gooey black mud from the little stream that flowed there.

Father Dowd's spirit was weakening. He felt like lying down and giving up.

The next day he fasted. He spent the entire morning washing his body and hair and clothes in the barranca. The dye in his hair and on his face came completely away. He hid under a rock near the stream until dark, then limped into town and loitered in the deserted plaza till it was closing time at the general store. He waited till the last customer came out, then he walked in and hit the pudgy Syrian proprietor in the mouth with his fist. The Syrian fell, striking his head on the potbellied stove.

Father Dowd had hurt his hand. He was surprised at his own strength. He had forgotten he was still a young man.

He tied up the Syrian with a length of twine, stuck a gag in his mouth, and blindfolded him. Then with shoe polish and clothes dye he redarkened his own face and hair. He stole all the money in the shop, seventy-five pesos, along with a kilo of cashews, a straw sombrero, a purple bandana, a pocket knife and a woven hemp carry-all. He put out the lantern and slipped out the back door. He walked through the dark streets to the suspension bridge, then across and out of town.

There was no train till morning. He sat down and waited for a truck or a mule-drawn cart to come by. The moon came out. He looked back across the chasm at Tuxpan. The town was white. It went up the base of a towering volcano with twin conical peaks, one spouting fire and smoke, the other covered with snow. The mountain blotted out half the night. Above it, white cumulus clouds rose in the starry sky. Music from the cantina drifted across the barranca in the wind. A dog barked.

"I'll never see that place again," he said.

He got a lift on the first vehicle that came along, a big Reo lumber truck headed for Pihuamo. On the dashboard the thin little driver had constructed a candle-lit altar to the Virgin of Zapopán. A pretty Indian woman in native costume with a two-year-old child that kept eating its own snot rode between them. When the woman stepped out to urinate the driver nudged him and said, "Oye, compañero, I been trying to make that bitch ever since Zapotlán. Why don't you give her a try? Then when you get in, I just climb on afterward. Once they been breached, they fall like sand castles."

Later, Father Dowd talked with the woman quietly and told her about the driver's plan. They laughed together. And suddenly he realized that he was no longer a mute. The woman wore a black-and-green rebozo and a straw man's hat and her serape was blue with orange tassels. The child sucked snot contentedly in his sleep. The woman said, "Well, hombre, I tell you what, we better smooch or he's gonna guess what happened."

In Taximixtla they were having a fiesta in the plaza. Peasants stood in long lines with crossed arms, moving and swaying in no apparent relation to the music, dancing the Mescalito under the colored lights in the tamarind trees. Drunk, the peasants danced, sipping mescal, pulque, tequila, sotol and a raw sugar-cane liquor called aguardiente, their eyes glazed over, dead in their heads. The driver wanted to have a pulque beer. The woman took Father Dowd out for a turn on the floor. She wanted to dance European-style. There was a ragged, barefoot band playing guitars, drums, flutes, harps and cornets in an unearthly cacophony. Father Dowd and the woman danced for a long while. The driver didn't seem to mind the wait. Some of the dancers weaved and lost their balance and fell to the dirt. The others paid no heed. The woman gave Father Dowd mescal to drink. His tongue went numb and then his eyes and his head. He wondered if he now had her eyes. She came to him under the lights and kissed him, licked his mouth like a cat or a dog, and his eyes and his ears and hair. He liked it. He liked her smell too, an aromatic mix of cornstarch and cactus and urine.

A man got up on the bandstand and started to deliver a speech. He said the Cristeros were defeated in Michoacán, Nayarit and most of Colima. That left only certain pockets in the mountains of Jalisco, the city of Manzanillo, and its surrounding jungle areas in subversive hands.

"Viva el presidente Calles! Viva la Revolución!"

Father Dowd knew this man. He was a very small, very oily, olive-skinned mestizo. Chinless, long-nosed, low-browed, he spoke with a slight lisp and affected a kind of sleazy Spanish look—black hat, black boots, black vest and long dirty fingernails. He had often come sniffing around the rectory in the days of the clerical strike. He said he worked for Railway Express but he never seemed to have anything to deliver. Gallo Carrizo was his name.

Father Dowd was afraid of this ferret-faced little fellow as he had not been afraid of anyone in his life. He could not think what he would do if he was recognized. He could make no plans. He was overwhelmed by the unreality all around him. At the same time, he was terrorized by his own feelings of guiltlessness, and by his extraordinary success in excusing mortal sins on grounds of survival and self-defense. "It's not like me," he kept telling himself, "it's not like me," despite growing evidence that it was indeed very much like him—a side of him that he'd never seen before.

Father Dowd started to have trouble breathing. His heart commenced to palpitate violently, and again his muscles, bones, joints, testicles, even his eyes and teeth began to ache. He went weak at the knees and sagged in the woman's arms. She let him go. He fell to her feet, but she never even lost the beat. He was only another borracho now, a drunk lying in the dirt. Yet his head stayed remarkably cool and precise, and his life ran by him in hallucinogenic detail.

He remembered the little workingman's Victorian house on Telegraph Hill where he was born. The endless hum of the trolley cable that ran under the Union Street tracks. The fog horns on Alcatraz and Angel Island, and walking down the Filbert Street steps every day with his mama to take his dad a hot lunch on the Embarcadero. And then the earthquake of 1906. The rumbling noise as it approached. The cracking sound when it hit. And the chandeliers swaying, the bed jiggling, the crockery jumping up and down, the furniture falling over, the windows breaking, the walls shaking, splitting, tumbling down. And then the darkness from which he thought he would never waken. The sound of diggers above him. His tomb suddenly flooded with light. His mama and dad and baby sister laid out in a neat row on the cobbles alongside a dozen neighbors. And then the Red Cross. The Catholic Charity. The orphanage. The stern-faced Sisters of Mercy. His kind-hearted Grandma Mary McCracken who finally tracked him down. And riding the San Joaquín Daylight to her turkey ranch in Turlock. His first view of the ranchhouse, long and low, with a veranda that went all the way around, and flower trestles full of purple wisteria. Her rustic kitchen festooned with strung tomatoes, onions, garlic and hams. The woodstove, the hand pump, the rough pine table carved up with the initials of departed menfolk: a son dead in the Spanish-American War, three husbands laid to rest. And the old bunkhouse. The Mexican farmhands. The turkey hutches. The wire-mesh fencing. The Merced River a half-mile away through the almond orchard. Watching the sun come up out of the Sierra Nevada while he was scattering feed to the gobblers. Star of the Sea, the beautiful Spanish Revival Marist school he went to in Turlock. His devotion to the Holy Mother that grew stronger with his multiplying blessings. The headmaster, a blond, bearded young Marist named Father Blau. The stories he told of his years as a missionary in South America. Falling in love, very briefly, very secretly, with Father Blau. Declaring his intention of entering a seminary at seventeen. The clear and wonderful sign of vocation he received directly from the Blessed Virgin when she came to him as a Mexican farmhand's daughter while he was baling alfalfa and told him he was destined to do God's work among the poor and wretched in the far places of the globe. Kissing his sweet Grandma Mary goodbye and riding the Daylight and the Lark down to the seminary in San Luis Obispo. . . . He remembered the ten short years that were all he was ever to know of bliss. He remembered them so vividly, so intensely, that memory was everything, and this barbarous fiesta under the tamarind trees, with an immense and indifferent emptiness just beyond the circle of light, was no more than a dream of perdition.

When Father Dowd reached Pihuamo, seven days after the rebellion began, he went to visit its celebrated church. Its walls were pocked with bullet holes from the insurrection, but inside it was untouched. Its gold and silver furnishings were exactly as they had been two years before when he had visited to pray with his friends Father de Falla and Father LeFevre. He found its familiarity extremely comforting now. The riches of the church had not been looted because the local peasants were devoutly religious, in the sense that they worshiped the Virgin of Zapopán as the Mother of All Things and revered the Christ of Esquipulos as the Lord of Miracles. Priests they traditionally loathed. Apparently they considered them larcenous.

The church was made of heavy tezontle stones taken from a pre-Columbian ruin, and its style was Churrigueresque, with fantastic stone carvings, huge gargoyles, Moorish arches, Gothic domes, Baroque altars, Byzantine saints lined up along the wall, and primitive sleeping Jesuses lying in glass and hammered-gold caskets and bleeding from their wounds horizontally, from forehead to chin.

A pair of dirty little mestiza girls with black feet and torn skirts grabbed at Father Dowd's hand, begging for a tostón, a fifty-centavo piece.

"Por favor, señor, por favor," they said. They were an appealing little pair; with a bath and a few good meals they might have even been called pretty. "We are the Mescalero sisters," the eldest one said beseechingly. "I am Ramona, and this is Carmen. Our mama died a month ago. Our papa died in the Revolution. We're on our way to our sister in Manzanillo, and we've walked all the way from Michoacán."

He went to a little side chapel and tried to pray, or at least reestablish some rapport with his past, his vocation. The little girls followed him closely and watched. He was afraid they might see through his disguise and report him to the authorities. When he came out of the church they went down and got him around the knees.

"Propina, propina, una propina!"

"What have you done to earn a propina?" he asked them. And then, alarmed again that his conscience had deserted him so completely, in these times of stress, he showered them with coins and mea culpas.

It was in Pihuamo that Father Dowd began to feel dirty. He decided to risk getting a hotel room for the night. He went to the lowest-class place he could find, the Hotel Juárez in the Coyotl Quarter. It stank of feces in the hallway. He asked the pock-faced man behind the counter if there was a bath, and was shown a water trough for donkeys and mules and oxen in the inner courtyard. He got a bucket and filled it with muddy water and took it up to his room. He stripped and sponge-bathed quickly. He had expected to be surprised when he saw his own white skin. Even the expectation did nothing to diminish the shock. He had begun to think of himself, in spite of himself, as Indian-brown.

In the morning he was awakened by a loud knock at the door.

"Policía!"

A tiny smiling mestizo with a pencil-thin mustache and a six-shooter stuck in his belt stood in the doorway and asked Father Dowd how he had slept. He was wearing a black gypsy hat, black vest, black boots. He was either that same Gallo Carrizo who'd given the speech in Taximixtla or his twin brother. But it was a common type in Mexico, Father Dowd thought, and they were all brothers. They were all either secret agents, informers, pimps, purveyors of dirty pictures, taxi drivers or marimba players. They came in only one size, one color, one shape, and their oily qualities rendered them effectively ageless. This one could be anywhere from twenty to fifty, and he would look the same till the day he died.

Father Dowd said that he had slept very well.

"Why do you speak with a foreign accent?"

"Why do you ask me questions? You are not a local policeman, or you would be wearing a blue uniform."

"Railroad police," he said. He was still smiling when he said it. And Father Dowd believed him. The railroad was run by a consortium of American oil interests, with nominal participation of the Mexican government. It was a law unto itself in this part of the Republic, where it owned virtually everything. And its directors in New York and Dallas were said to be militant Protestants, as they so enthusiastically supported President Calles in his war against the Cristeros. It was probably just a matter of expediency, however, for the railroad had been similarly cooperative with the Cristeros in parts of the country where they held sway. The situation in Mexico was now so complicated that foreign investors found themselves playing both ends against the middle as a matter of course. Sometimes, it was said, they even found themselves fighting against themselves.

"I am a North American," Father Dowd conceded.

"Passport?"

"It was stolen in Zapotlán."

"What is your business here?"

"Tourist."

"Where are you going?"

"I wish to return to my country as soon as possible."

"Are you a priest?"

"No, why? Do I look like one?"

"What do you think?" the little man said in English.

Father Dowd tried to laugh. He was watching the mestizo's slanted, lizardlike eyes. They never blinked.

"Do you mind, padre, stepping down to police headquarters for a moment? It is only a formality."

"Why do you call me 'padre'?"

The little man pushed past Father Dowd. Quickly he looked around the room.

"No luggage?"

"Stolen at the same time as the passport."

Father Dowd could not produce his passport because it listed his occupation as "Cleric."

The mestizo started poking around the dresser in the corner. He bent over and stuck his hand in the bottom drawer. Father Dowd had hidden the carry-all with his passport in there. He lunged, kicked the drawer shut on the man's hand and smashed his head against the heavy oak paneling. He slipped the man's pistol from his belt and struck him on the crown with the barrel. He hit him again and again. He dragged the body (was it alive or dead?) across the room and hid it under the bed. He went through the mestizo's pockets and stole his money—five hundred pesos, more than he could have come by legally—and ran to the rear window and dropped to the courtyard below, scattering chickens everywhere. He climbed over the rear wall without looking back, flagged down a mule-drawn wagon loaded with rice and asked the driver where he was going.

"Trapichillos," he said, and Father Dowd laughed and climbed aboard.

"What's so funny?" the driver wanted to know.

Father Dowd wondered about that himself.

"I guess I'm just happy to be alive," he said.

The wagon climbed upward for several hours, winding around spectacular drops and chasms. Then it reached a kind of narrow tropical plateau with intricately cultivated fields of lush green cane and yellow corn. In the middle stood a little thatch-and-mud village. Banana trees grew in and around the village, and palm trees and century plants lined the adobe walls along the road. High, high above the village, looming over it as if it might topple and destroy it, the mighty twin volcano of Colima, ominous yet implausible concoction of fire and ice, split the sky. At the far end of the mesa the land fell away almost perpendicularly into an immensely deep canyon or barranca choked with tropical vegetation. At the bottom of the barranca another swift brown river ran over black volcanic rocks, and another steep jungle cliff rose to the next green-and-yellow cultivated mesa, which contained another little mud-and-thatch village much like the one the wagon had just passed. It was no more than a mile or two away, but the driver said they would not reach it before nightfall. For nearly forty-eight hours the wagon went up and down the barrancas and across the mesas. At each village the driver would drop off a little more rice and take on another passenger or two. After two nights had passed the rice was nearly gone and the rear of the wagon was full of silent vacant-eyed Indian peasants.

The rainy season had begun on the first afternoon. The rain slanted down through the holes in the covered section of the wagon and soaked through Father Dowd's coat and then it went into his trousers and through his underwear and seeped into his boots. It was not a cold rain, but at night in the higher elevations a wind came sweeping down off the snowfields on the volcano, chilling one to the bone.

Father Dowd rode that whole eternity of two days and two endless nights feeling the sickness come stealing into his body like death. He thought of hot summer days in the San Joaquín Valley when he was a kid working on his grandma's turkey farm, and the smell of new-mown alfalfa, and the look of heat waves rising off the tomato fields, and then death himself came creeping all done up like Dorothy's scarecrow with corncobs sticking out of his ears yet smelling of frijoles, tortillas, tamales, pulque, mescal, sotol . . . the fruits of the Cactus Kingdom. Father Dowd's limbs were not numb. They tingled. His head often felt unbelievably light, filled with air or helium. Once he even saw it detached from his body, lying by his side under the almond trees of Turlock while the turkeys gobbled around him, plucking at it.

In the morning they came upon a roadblock on the precipice. The tall, handsome young officer in charge was quite intelligent and polite, and he had a very nice smile, but he did not believe that Father Dowd was a peddler.

"First Captain Raúl Mondragón, at your orders," he said.

Then he took Father Dowd off the wagon and waved it on.

The rain had finally let up. But it was a windy morning. The wind came straight down off the volcano, and once the wagon was gone all Father Dowd could hear was the sand blowing across the dirt track. The captain searched him and found the five hundred pesos in his shoe.

"Where do you think you're going with that kind of money?"

Father Dowd had heard it said that when you are in a really tight spot, when your life depends on it, you can always come up with a ready lie, a quick line, a story to save yourself. But all he could do was smile.

"No answer?"

Father Dowd, knowing that only words could save him, remained silent.

"You know what it means that you don't answer?" the captain asked. His voice registered little more than mild irritation. Father Dowd felt only a kind of embarrassment.

"I'm tired of fooling around with you," the captain said wearily, and made Father Dowd take off his socks so that he could light a flame under his feet to make him talk, and discovered that he was a white man. He put out the match and, in a much softer tone, said, "So that's all you were then, a little padre?"

Then Father Dowd heard himself, all in a rush of words, admit in detail everything he had done since he left Guadalajara. He realized that he was making very little sense, but he could do nothing to stop himself. Most of all he was afraid the captain would think he had no personal dignity.

When he had finished, however, and the captain said, not unkindly, "Padre, I am not your confessor," Father Dowd felt something that was more than half pleasure.

Just then a half-ton Ford truck came rolling up. The captain stopped it and ordered his men to give it a thorough search. In the wheel well beneath the frame they found another white man, obviously an educated person from the city. He was small and plump, about ten years older than Father Dowd, with fine brown hair, wide yellow eyes, soft and pampered white hands, and a tiny pursed mouth. It was Padre LeFevre, with whom Father Dowd and Father de Falla had taken refuge in the rectory bathroom in Huentitán. The captain motioned for him and the driver of the truck, a young peasant with a sly nervous grin, to be brought forward. The captain too was grinning, and he had very pretty teeth, and he invited them all down the road with him for a little parley. After they'd gone about fifty yards, he motioned them to sit under a small pepper tree that grew by the side of the precipice. He was standing over them now and in a mock-stern voice he motioned off toward the mountains and said, "All this belongs to us." And the white men and the little driver all quickly agreed that sí señor this certainly did belong to the Mexican people, all of it! Then the captain asked them what their politics were. Father LeFevre said that he was a liberal; he lied. Father Dowd said, truthfully, that he considered himself a social democrat. The driver said he didn't know nothing about politics, he could not read or write or sign his name, he'd never voted in his life, and he'd never laid eyes on this creole white man who'd sneaked a ride on his truck.

Then the captain became very serious for a moment. He warned them that they were in a very ticklish situation here because his men were Indians from the mountains who had been swindled by the priests for many generations and several of them had lost compañeros in the dynamiting of the Mexico City–Guadalajara Express and they were out for blood. But the captain was sick of bloodshed, he said, after fourteen years as a soldier. He did not approve of the shooting of unarmed civilians, no matter how venal or exploitive they might be. Nor had he ever been the type to lead a firing squad. And he would not like to see his prisoners in the hands of these unfortunate but brutal men of his. So it might be better if they went through a little charade. He would tell his men that he would handle the affair. He would ask his prisoners to cross over the road and get down on their knees beside the ditch. He would fire a shot into the dirt and as he did each of them in turn would fall forward and play dead until his men and he were gone. He told them sincerely that this was their only chance of survival. They all agreed that perhaps this was the wisest course, considering the circumstances, and thanked him for his kindness, generosity, and humanity. The captain said it was nothing, and would they please march ahead of him. He stopped briefly on the way, called to his men, and ordered them back up the road toward the mesa. Then he walked his prisoners single-file to the edge of the ditch and ordered them to kneel there together while he simulated the placement of a neat hole in the base of each of their skulls.

All the way across the road Father Dowd was thinking that the captain could not possibly mean to spare his life after his confession. What a sadistic son of a bitch the captain is, Father Dowd was thinking, playing cat and mouse with our lives like this. And yet, on another level of consciousness, he was thinking how unreal death is. He simply could not accept the notion that soon, instantly, he would cease.

And then he thought: There's no one on earth or in heaven . . . there's no one to stop it but me.

And he felt his scrotum swinging in his pants.

He screamed and pointed up the mountain, and when the captain looked he ran out over the edge of the cliff. He fell about fifteen feet and landed in soft dirt and kept rolling and stumbling and skidding toward the bottom with the bullets hitting all around him. But now there was the certitude that nothing as little as a bullet was going to stop him. Then he leaped into the river, into the brown water, with the soldiers firing at him, little spurts of white kicking up around him, and he went under, holding his breath as long as he could. He could hear the stream rolling underwater rocks, and he could hear the scraping noise they made against the volcanic bottom. He tasted mud. And then he was out of their range, he judged, and around a bend and banging up against half-submerged boulders in the swift current, bruising his body, cutting himself on the sharp edges, and then he found himself a piece of driftwood, clung to it, rode the wild river down the rapids for what seemed like hours till he heard the sound of a waterfall ahead and got himself to shore.

He rested for a time, and then he saw a trail high above him. He pulled himself together and got up and struggled toward it, scaling huge black rocks in the sun, digging his fingers into tiny crevices, teetering over chasms, losing his balance at times, taking chances, panicky at times, ripping his flesh on the shale. If there is a trail, he thought, they will know about it. He clambered over the edge and started running down the barranca. His bare feet quickly bloodied. He ran for an hour without stopping until he saw an Indian woman coming with a load of firewood on her back. The woman smiled, bowed humbly, said "Buenos días, señor," and slithered by him at a wide spot in the trail. Father Dowd thought for a moment, She will tell. He crept up behind her, grabbed her by the scruff of the neck, and flung her over the side. If she screamed Father Dowd did not hear her. He was running down the canyon.

That wasn't me, he thought he said. That wasn't me.

But all he could hear was his own breathing.

The trail crossed the stream on a suspension bridge made of heavy vines. He scurried across, almost upsetting himself in his haste. He was exhausted now. He was choking on his own breath. He took out his pocket knife, laboriously cut through the vines, and dumped the bridge into the river. Then he rolled into the shade of a boulder. He had rested perhaps ten minutes when he heard someone coming up the trail from Colima. It was another Indian. He had a baby goat hung over his shoulders, its hooves tied together with twine. Father Dowd stood up. He opened the knife in his pocket, taking care to unfold the blade that was not dull from cutting through the vine. The Indian saw him and looked at the fallen bridge.

"Why you cut the bridge?"

Father Dowd said nothing.

"I got to cross that bridge and now I can't."

"How do you know it was me that did it?"

"It is clear that it is you."

"I had to do it. I am being chased by bandidos."

"For sure not by bandidos but justly by the federales."

"No, no, that is not true. I am an agent of the federal government myself and I am on my way into Colima. Can you tell me if the Cristeros have been driven out yet?"

"I don't know, cabrón, but how am I ever to get home to my old woman? She has already gone over the bridge."

Father Dowd said she probably wouldn't miss him. The Indian went for his machete, but he was clumsy. The little goat was wriggling on his shoulders. Father Dowd whipped out his pocket knife, swung, and hit the Indian on the side of the head, slicing off the top of his ear. He went down. Father Dowd put his foot on the Indian's arm and sawed at his wrist with the pocket knife until he dropped the machete. He picked it up, swung it with both hands, with all his force, missed the Indian and killed the goat, nearly shearing its body in two. The man was squirming on the ground trying to get to his feet, but the dead weight of the goat slowed him down. Father Dowd swung again and sliced his face in half. He was still alive. He lay in the dirt with his eyes open. They were like the goat's eyes, wide and brown.

Father Dowd stooped over, gripped the Indian's thick black hair, pulled his head back onto the dead goat, exposing his jugular vein, and while the man watched him, sliced it through.

Father Dowd lay down to rest. A few minutes later he got up and untied the goat from around the Indian's neck, removed the Indian's serape, his trousers, his shirt and huarache sandals, rubbed the serape in the grass to blot out the bloodstains, removed his own clothes and replaced them with the Indian's things. He sat down and washed his feet with saliva, bandaged them with strips of material from his shirt, and put the Indian's huaraches on. Without them he could not have continued. The rock had stripped his feet of skin. He dragged the man and the goat into the brush and covered them with his clothing and a few leaves. He set off again down the canyon, looking at everything. And he loved what he saw. All along the river it was green and brown and black. Green shoots and brown roots and black volcanic rock. Green cactus and palmeras and chirimoya trees with black moss on their brown branches. Mahogany water in the river below. Green moss on damp stone.

The path narrowed. It hung five hundred feet above the churning water. Several times Father Dowd almost fell. Once the trail crumbled away beneath him. He started to fall. He gripped a vine. The vine began to give way. He managed to scissor over and hang on to a rock, his legs flailing in midair. He managed to scale the rock with his hands. He slipped and fell perhaps four feet. He reached for a little yucca tree. It held. He gripped it with his life. Slowly he worked his way up, looking at everything, the moist brown clay in his fingernails, a shiny red beetle, each blade of green-and-yellow grass, the mottled rock. He reached the trail again. He was spent. His limbs were battered and numb, dead. Only his eyes were seeing, seeing, seeing. The canyon began to widen, and then he was walking between wide fields of yellow corn and green pastureland surrounded by tropical forest. There were goats feeding there: black, red-brown, gray, spotted. The path became a road with high adobe walls on either side. Father Dowd was on his way into Colima.

Then he heard the church bells ringing the hour. There are very few clocks in provincial Mexico.

Now all he had to do was find some way to bypass the town and he would be safe for the time being. He was elated and full of hope, and he had only one worry. It was a fear that had haunted him all the way down the trail. But it was very closely related to another fear that had been growing inside him, like a hairball in the belly of a fretful cat, for a much longer time. What if there were, after all, and despite all the evidence to the contrary, a God? What if heaven and hell actually existed? What if everything that he was really seeing seeing seeing right now was merely the moss, the clumps of grass, the mottled stones, the trickling water, the crawling insects of various sizes and shapes and colors that distinguished the rock and earthen embankment where he knelt in the ditch with the others, waiting for the shots?

Suddenly the level of Father Dowd's anxiety rose infinitely higher. Just when success was in reach it had been snatched from his hands. By now he was out on a muddy flat near a lake. He felt naked, exposed, utterly alone. The mud sucked at his feet, holding him back. His heart beat faster. His breath came harder. He began to hyperventilate. He reeled and fell on his back in the mud.

"Yes, this is the way," he cried aloud. "This is the way I pay."

But God would not listen, and his body would not die.

When he came to several hours later he discovered that the mud flat was being used as a staging area for trucks and wagons and livestock. The trucks went by him, backing up, gearing forward, some of them barely missing him, splashing him as if it made no difference if they hit him. Animals and Indians nudged up against him and stepped over his body gingerly, as if he were mere rotting meat, carrion for the great shrieking black zopilote birds that flapped and clamored in the surrounding trees. At first Father Dowd was not terribly concerned by all of this. In fact, he felt rather relieved to find himself still breathing. Then he realized that he must be dreadfully ill, and he would probably not be getting up again. He began to weep. To die an anonymous death, he thought, an anonymous animus dominus animal cracker death. The wind started to blow again. It blew mud and spray into his face. He screamed.

At another point he found himself surrounded by Indians in black hooded ponchos that made them look like gigantic crows. And he believed that the carrion birds had come down from the trees to pick at his corpse. He screamed. The Indians just stood over him staring. He cried out in Spanish. They did not understand. He stopped his bellowing and began planning for his own immediate demise. Just then he heard the Indians speak their language, which seemed to possess no vowels. It was guttural talk, inhuman talk, the talk of demons.

Father Dowd awakened, to his surprise and delight, in a clean room with a red-tile floor. A white woman came into the room with a tray of hot food. She was tall and red-haired and full-bodied. She wore a long, thick single braid that went all the way down her back, and a kind of modified native attire—huarache sandals, a white embroidered peasant blouse, a wide red skirt—which on her looked rather bohemian. She smelled of beef broth, hand lotion and soap. And there was something oddly familiar about her, though he'd never laid eyes on her before.

He asked if it was she who had saved his life.

"It is not saved yet," she replied.

"But why did you take me in?"

" 'A stranger might be God,' as the Mexicans say."

She spoke with a lilting foreign accent.

"Are you Irish?" he asked.

"By way of Brooklyn and San Francisco," she said. "I was born in Cork."

And Father Dowd, seven thousand miles and three generations from the Ould Sod, began to cry.

"Go on with you now, Father, and eat your supper."

Her name was Maureen O'Hare, she said. She had found him on the mud flat while out for a Sunday buggy ride with her devoted doctor, a bald, dyspeptic little creole named Bermúdez. The rain had washed the dye from Father Dowd's face and hair. She could see it through the caked mud and guessed most of the truth. She swore her frightened but loyal doctor to secrecy, and they carried him back to the small pastel-yellow, Moorish-looking hotel she owned on the central square. She hid him in a secret attic room with a trapdoor that opened onto her own on the second-story arcade. Dr. Bermúdez gave Father Dowd all the assistance he could, but there was little that he could really do, he said, besides feeding him lots of liquids and trying to keep his temperature down. He had contracted double pneumonia. He was delirious for three days. Then his fever abated and Dr. Bermúdez could drain his lungs.

When Father Dowd awakened, Maureen sat by his bed all day, every day, and half the night, nursing him and feeding him by hand. To help pass the hours, she told him the story of her life. She was an Irish romantic, she said, who had married into a family of proprietous, middle-class railroad men. She was educated in the Church and her stepmother had meant her for the veil, but she was a bit wild, and she ran off at seventeen with a man already twice her age. His family never forgave him, for they considered her beneath him. So he accepted a position in Colima, running the local railroad line. Maureen found Mexico "quaint and charming," and full of "local color" that she liked to put in the stories that she wrote, and after her husband's death of a liver complaint some years back she had decided to stay on. "Here," she said, "a person such as myself is *somebody*. I hobnob with the highest aristocracy of the district, and maintain the kind of respect I feel I deserve. If I'd stayed on in San Francisco, as you know well, I should have held a far less exalted position in society.

"And besides," she said, "we Irish have always had a rapport with the Mexicans. During the War of 1848 a Mexican priest convinced several hundred Irishmen in Winfield Scott's army that as fellow Roman Catholics they were fighting on the wrong side. They deserted, the Yankees won, and the Irishmen were hanged. But you can still find heroic statues and mural paintings dedicated to them all over Mexico. . . . Nowadays," she said, "you will run into persons like myself—Europeans, North Americans—in the most remote and unlikely locations in the Republic. Before the Revolution there were tens of thousands of us in every walk of life. But then they slanted their laws against foreigners. It's illegal for us to own property within fifty kilometers of the sea, for example. Now there are only a few of us left. Don't ask me why we stay. I suppose we're all a bit touched."

She often sported native garb, she said, and she admitted that the townspeople, who were on the whole rather provincial and conservative, found her something of an eccentric. But she'd been living in Colima for nearly twenty years and she'd owned her little hotel across from the cathedral for seventeen years and she'd never had a moment's regret about staying on, even during the darkest moments of anarchy, in 1913 and 1914, which happened to coincide with a catastrophic eruption of the volcano. "You can't imagine the 'local color' that I collected in those times!" she said, laughing. "Not that it's done me any good. I still remain sadly unpublished."

Because of its remote location—cut off from the rest of Mexico by a rugged range of mountains and several active volcanoes—Colima had little communication with the outside world, Maureen explained. It had been passed over by most of the currents of Mexican history, including the Reform, and it had retained its colonial charm and its feudal land system virtually intact. Its venerable university was medieval in both physical aspect and curriculum, and it resembled the crumbling seat of some obscure, atavistic religious order rather than a modern institution of higher learning. As a fallen Catholic, she fit right in, she said, and she couldn't imagine living anywhere else.

Though Maureen had spent long years as a widow, she still thought of herself as a . . . *woman*. Her life with O'Hare had been comfortable, but aside from the first giddy hours of her elopement, the notion of romance had not really been a part of her experience.

Only after Maureen had fallen irretrievably in love with Father Dowd, she told him later, did she allow herself the exquisite pleasure of contemplating the possibility of his priesthood.

She was aware that he was in mortal danger. If they caught him they would shoot him. They would shoot her too, probably. This danger she accepted with something very near ecstasy.

Within a fortnight she had seduced him. She was only slightly disappointed, she said, that Father Dowd had not resisted. Not at all.

She kept him in bed long after he was well. She admitted that her feelings toward him were not a little incestuous. Her son, Brian, who had followed in the family tradition and worked for the railroad in Manzanillo, was nearly his age. And they had remained close. More like brother and sister than mother and son. Brian visited her several times a year, riding one of his cabooses to Colima on inspection tours, bearing gifts from "civilization." He spent the night in her hotel and then returned to the port city the following morning. In fact, he had just left her on that very morning when she found Father Dowd on the mud flat.

The padre had confessions of his own to make. She forgave him everything, even murder. "It was a matter of survival," she said. "You had no choice."

"I am damned!" he cried.

"Then we both are," she said, and fell to her knees before him to beg forgiveness. "Father, I have sinned. I have lied. I was never meant for the veil," she said, with searing self-derision, "and my husband did not die of a liver complaint."

She confessed that she had teased Mr. O'Hare to his death in 1910 by means of the most shocking self-abuse, and portrayed in vivid fire-and-brimstone detail the guilt that had consumed her ever since.

"If we are to burn, then let us burn together," she said.

And kept the padre locked up in her hotel far too long for his own good.

The servants became suspicious, whispering among themselves in the kitchen and on the stairs. It was clearly only a matter of time before the authorities came for him. Yet still she hesitated. She could not believe that their idyll must end so soon, she said. All it would take was a letter to her son, a tacit admission of the situation, and Brian would be on the next train to Colima. Father Dowd could hide in his caboose on the return trip. But she could not bring herself to admit to her son the circumstances of her relationship with Father Dowd. And yet, if she did not tell the truth, she was afraid that Brian would guess it. He was no prude, she said, but he was still a Catholic in his soul.

She was afraid of what her son might think of them.

Father Dowd assured her that there was no reason to apologize. He understood perfectly.

Actually, he had no wish to meet this "incestuous" son of hers, nor had he much reason to trust anyone connected with the railroad. And besides, he was quite happy right where he was. Here in the señora's hotel he was no longer responsible. Not even for his own fate. And he could think no farther ahead than the next time that large freckled woman entered his bed naked and her bountiful white breasts with their soft pink nipples were again touching his hairy chest.

One morning Maureen came in from the market plaza with the news that the police were planning to search the hotel. She decided that he must go as soon as night fell. There was no other choice. She gave him half the money she had hidden, five thousand pesos. He did not protest. He would dress as a peddler again and blacken his hair and skin. He would make his way into Manzanillo by road. On no condition must he try the river route, for it emptied into a treacherous mangrove swamp inhabited by unfriendly Indians. Once he had reached the port, he could book passage to San Francisco on the monthly United Fruit Company steamer, which was due to depart in three days. Maureen would join him as soon as she could sell the hotel. They would start a new life in America. They would buy another hotel, perhaps, or at least a rooming house. They might even have a child. She was only forty-three, and she felt years younger. And she was healthy and capable and more than willing to take the chance.

Maureen quickly shed her dress. The silk made that unmistakable slithering sound as it went down around her hips and buttocks. She slipped again between the starched sheets. He loved it. And he loved the carrot-red hair that ran penciled-in from her Irish rose to her belly button, and he loved her great pink nipples and her cool, cloudy, complicated gray eyes. After their lovemaking, as they lay exhausted and sweating on the bed, there was no question in either of their minds that they had conceived a child. Maureen was so sure that she even professed to know the sex. "It's a boy, I feel it here," she said, patting her pale, round, soft belly. She insisted that he think of a name for the child, "just in case." So she'd have something to remember him by. He chose the name Christopher, for luck on his journey. She was overjoyed; it was a name she might have picked herself. They slept enfolded till nightfall, when Father Dowd leaped from the bed, throwing his peddler's clothes between his skin and hers. He ran from her out the door. She tried to hold him, to stop him. She got down on her knees again and begged him to stay. She would write her son, she said, she would enlist his aid in an escape attempt. He could hide the padre in his place in Manzanillo till the steamer came again next month. Bursting into tears, she swore she could not live without him. She clung to his pantleg, pulling him back. Her sudden and unexpected compulsion made him stronger, because it faintly repelled him. For the first time he saw her as a cloying older woman, sucking his youth away. He allowed something of this to cross his face, and at last she let him go.

He went down the marble stairs and across the courtyard and out onto the pink tile of the central plaza under gaslight. Soon lost in a maze of dark cobblestone streets, he followed the pale stucco wall of an enormous shadowy shoe factory made of black volcanic stone that looked like something from the early Industrial Revolution. He tiptoed past the sleeping Indian soldiers at an army roadblock and skirted the edge of a deep barranca that fell abruptly away at the edge of town.

I'll never see that woman again, he thought.

An ox cart appeared at the crossroads and he flagged it down. By the time the sun came up in the morning he could see the blue Pacific spread out a thousand meters below him and forty kilometers away across a green panorama of rolling hills, winding rivers and flat coastal plains, rain forests, coffee fincas, canefields, banana plantations, mangrove swamps and palm-fringed black sand beaches.

He slept until dark in an orchard by the Río Coayuayana, and awakened to the scent of early evening: ripe mango and mashed chirimoya fruit, wet palm and bamboo, cooking tortillas, wild green chile sauce, frying beans and bananas, avocado, chocolate, the smell of fresh goat entrails being cleaned in the river, the smell of fertilizer, guano and nightsoil; and, from the village nearby, the smell of putrefying human flesh.

In Mexico, Father Dowd reflected, one is never far from death.

And then rising up from where he lay in the grass he nearly stepped on a hissing five-foot fer-de-lance and was chased panting and sweating from the orchard.

He walked into a little riverport town called Boca de Pascuales which was constructed almost entirely of bamboo and palm thatch and entered one of the few permanent structures in the place, a dirt-floored restaurant and bar owned by a smily toothpick-sucking Chinaman with nicotine-stained fingers. A meal of shrimp tamales, two eggs, and an avocado was soon set before him. The only other customers in the joint were a pair of handsome young Negroes, a man and wife, who were engaged in a game of cards with each other, fighting and cursing like troopers: "Herculano, you sonofabitch, you are cheating now." "Why, Eulalia, you lying whore, it's you who've been cheating on me, all of our married life. . . ." A crowd of ragged dirty mestizo children with distended bellies gathered in the doorway to stare at Father Dowd. Flies buzzed, clinging to his skin and clothes. The air was hot and unbelievably humid. The table was sticky with spilled fruit juice. Father Dowd's bare elbow stuck to the wooden top. Two dogs came in and began to fornicate near the bar, the bitch yelping in pain. Outside someone was playing a chirimía, a kind of pennywhistle. Another person, a woman, was singing, perhaps to the music. The sound was high, rough, primitive, unutterably sad. An Indian came in and ordered a pulque beer while his skinny little pink sow squatted on the floor waiting for him. The Chinaman called him Pedro Martínez, an unremarkable name in Mexico. "Pedro Martínez," he said. "Como te va?" The sow had a leash around its neck and it was clever as a little dog. The man was an Indian from the mangrove swamp, a shrimp fisherman, dressed in traditional coarse white cotton calzones—pajamalike trousers tied with twine at the waist and ankles—a collarless, loose-hanging shirt made of the same material, and a pair of muddy huaraches cut from an old rubber tire. His narrow-brimmed little straw sombrero with a red-and-green band and a yellow tassel signified that he was married. He was very grave. He had a wide, round, almost black face, and he kept spitting on the floor at his feet. His forehead was extraordinarily low; his eyes, wicked, slanted, glittering; his strong white teeth appeared to have been sharpened with a file. Nearly overwhelmed by his distaste for the man, Father Dowd paid the bill and left. Walking across the muddy field that passed for a plaza, he felt he was going to vomit. He went down the bank to the river. The river was wide and brown and navigable here, and the Indian's dugout canoe waited on the bank, unattended.

"Forgive me," Father Dowd said aloud. And on an impulse he ran down and pushed the canoe into the gentle current. He paddled out to the middle of the river and stopped. It had grown dark, and the lights from the village followed him. The sound of the pennywhistle had a metallic ring to it, when it came at him across the silence of the water.

He struck out into the night.

In the morning he judged himself to be nearing the end of the mangrove swamp. The trees rose in a solid thirty-foot wall on either side of him. The air assailed him, heavy and damp, alive, vegetable rather than mineral. One almost needed gills to breathe it. The channel, narrow and muddy, clogged up with water lilies, weaved in and out among mangrove islets where drifting logs and bamboo poles from flash floods, cyclones and tidal waves lay caught in the tangled roots, bleaching in the sun like bones. Father Dowd had expected to hear the clamor of millions of birds and even monkeys in the swamp; yet there was no sign of animal life. He was dumbfounded by the immensity of the swamp, the profundity of its silence. All day he perceived not a sound, not a movement, save, toward midday, a solitary pair of white herons, fishing daintily in the shallows.

By late afternoon, when he came to the great maze of sloughs and islands and false rivers where the Río Coayuayana delta merges with the Pacific, his spirits had risen considerably. He figured the mouth of the river to be about thirty-five miles from Manzanillo. Once he had reached the ocean he planned to simply paddle up the coast till he saw the lights of the city. The current ran north here at about three miles an hour. If he paddled all night, averaging another three miles an hour, he ought to be in Manzanillo harbor by morning. He wouldn't need anything to eat. He wasn't hungry. If he got thirsty he would have to endure it.

Just then he came around the corner of a mangrove islet and nearly ran into the village of the shrimp-fishing Indians. It was no primitive thatch-walled place, but a permanent adobe brick town like a tiny Venice, or a miniature version of ancient Tenochtitlán, the capital of the Aztecs, with canals for cross streets and one wide, circular water avenue marking its circumference. Though Father Dowd could see a church steeple and a couple of red-tiled roofs, the place looked as old as time. Nearby were other circular islets upon which Father Dowd could see corn, beans, chiles and maguey growing. He even passed what was apparently a cemetery islet, with a multitude of crude wooden crosses shaded by a great, vase-shaped alamo tree that looked as old as the town. A tall tree with thick green leaves, open spreading branches, a warty grayish bark and witches' brooms of tangled twigs, the alamo was related to the American elm, Father Dowd knew, and it was more common on the high central plateau of Mexico than on the coast. Yet it had thrived somehow in this humid swampland of the Tierra Caliente, and it soared, mysteriously, a hundred feet into the air, towering above everything else in the delta.

Hastily Father Dowd turned around and paddled into another, narrower branch of the river, hoping the Indians hadn't noticed the stolen canoe.

That night before he reached the ocean he got lost in a false river. He thought he could follow it out again to the main channel. He'd done it many times before. Yet the silence now was hot and palpable as breadfruit. He felt he could have squeezed it between his fingers. And creeping lianas, cobwebs, tree ferns, clammy mangrove roots dangled before him, dragging in the canoe, across his body and his face, spooking him. The water got shallower all of a sudden. Someone was watching him. He could feel it right between his shoulder blades. He got tangled up in an impenetrable thicket of water lilies. He managed to back the canoe around and start off again in the opposite direction. There was no moon. His breathing, and the sound of his paddle, were the loudest noises in the universe. He paddled harder. His wake heaved water lilies onto the mud. Then from beyond a mangrove islet arose the first animal sound he'd heard in hours: It was the low murmur of many men working at night. He came out onto the main channel and found himself drifting toward an apparition that he would take with him to the grave: a hundred shadowy Indian canoes, their ghostly oarsmen invisible save for glittering eyes and sharp flashing teeth, afloat amid thousands of tiny lights that hovered just above the surface of the water like fireflies.

Father Dowd did not pray when they captured him. He did not cry when they bore him away to their island village. He thought of the son that he was sure he had left behind, and took comfort that his blood would flow on after he was gone. He made his confession to the confraternity of fishermen at large, excluding no sin large or small, and expressed his heartfelt contrition. He asked nothing of God. At dawn when the Mexican sky was an empty and pitiless red above the mangrove swamp and the afternoon's rainclouds were merely a line upon the remote horizon, the Indians dressed him for burial and carried him to the cemetery island in a long procession of black canoes. There they sang songs of the bravery of the white man, the stranger, the thief. They nailed him up in the sacred alamo tree in the center of the island and made their final request.

"Our church has stood empty for seventeen years," they said. "The bishop of Manzanillo has forgotten us."

"I am no priest," he said.

"Your life as a man is over," they said. "What remains you must give to us."

"I am no priest," he said.

"You must fill our church," they said, "or we shall eat of your flesh, according to the old rites."

"I am no priest," he said. "I no longer belong to the Church of Rome."

"We know nothing of Rome," they said. "And we have our own ways with God."

"Then cut me down," he said, rejoicing, "for I shall embrace you as my brothers."

CHAPTER 2

The pregnancy was a nightmare that Maureen thought would never end. All of her normal courage and sangfroid deserted her, and she let herself dissolve into such a state of wretchedness and hysteria that she doubted she'd ever be the same. Due to her age, and a weak mucous membrane, she was made to spend her last six months in bed. In the humid climate of Colima she developed painful rashes, bedsores and hemorrhoids that made her life a torment. Her muscles sagged from lack of exercise and her body turned to jelly. From morning to night she had the maids running up and down the stairs bearing trays full of antojitos mexicanos, panes dulces, cactus candies and a sweet curdled milk called chongo zamorano. She gained so much weight that she felt herself flowing out of the bed and onto the tile floor . . . felt herself begin to reek of her own milk, and the baby inside her. Dr. Bermúdez warned her about her eating, but she protested that it was the only way she could relieve her severe anxieties. She was plagued by such fears, worries, doubts and inner conflicts, she said, that at times she doubted her own sanity. She feared that Father Dowd had been killed. She worried that he might have escaped to America and forgotten her. Her son Brian had chosen to ignore her existence ever since she turned up *enceinte,* and now she doubted that he would ever forgive her for her peccadillo, as he refused to answer any of her letters or telegrams. She trembled over the possibility that her mortal sin of fornication with a priest of God would result in her eternal damnation, or that the progeny of her sinful union would be some sort of devil. She fretted over the statistical chances that her advanced age might cause her to bear a mongoloid idiot or some other kind of monster. And finally, she said, she felt guilty because she had turned down Dr. Bermúdez's kind proposal of marriage; she had done it out of loyalty to Father Dowd, but the result was that her child would be born a bastard.

At the same time she clung desperately to life and to hope. She imagined that she would soon receive a letter from Father Dowd, from some safe haven abroad, begging her to join him there after the baby was born. She invented scenes in which Father Dowd died heroically in the jungle with her name on his lips. She dreamed his son would be born as sweet-tempered, poetical, and handsomely Black Irish as he, a constant and lifelong reminder of her one grand amour. She hoped that Brian would someday find it in his heart to forgive her and accept the child as his own blood.

Dr. Bermúdez decided that she was suffering from delusions, a result of her prolonged hysteria. As a case in point, he said, he had never in fact proposed marriage to her. And indeed if he had it would have set the whole town laughing, as he was the most infamous pederast in Colima State. He prescribed baths in Epsom salts for Mrs. O'Hare, massages and tincture of opium three times a day. But nothing helped. She continued to gorge herself, getting fatter and fatter, more and more frantic, till at last her water broke and the delivery began.

A child of sorrow, then, Christopher O'Hare was born out of wedlock in a Colima hotel room while skyrockets celebrating the end of the Cristero Rebellion flared overhead and dogs howled, Indians chanted, and insubordinate soldiers fired their Mausers at the moon. A blue baby, female, she came into the world with the umbilical cord wrapped tightly around her neck, and with webbed, batlike little fingers that would have to be surgically separated, the doctor said, at the age of five. During the difficult delivery, Maureen bucked and fought and cried out loud, shrieking the name of the fugitive priest who had seduced her, abandoned her, sentenced her to eternal damnation, and cursing the name of this blue-faced little devil who was living proof of her mortal sin, divine retribution for all the world to see.

The instant she saw it was a girl she prayed it would die. But Dr. Bermúdez saved the infant's life by snipping off the umbilical cord in two places simultaneously and smacking her soundly on the bottom several times. She began to wail, she turned a normal red color, and at last Maureen came to understand that Chris was the cross that she would be made to bear.

She asked the doctor if it wasn't true that blue babies were sometimes born with brain damage. He said it was true, but that Chris had not been deprived of oxygen long enough to be in danger. She displayed no signs of arrested cerebral development, he said, and she should grow into a healthy, normal girl. But Maureen could not, for some reason, accept his opinion. And she spent the first years of her daughter's life suspecting, despite all the evidence to the contrary, that the child would soon show certain telltale signs of mental retardation, or some exotic, possibly terminal, hereditary disease.

Chris's first memories were of being hauled down to Dr. Bermúdez's clínica once a month. There she would get thoroughly pawed and probed and inevitably pronounced "fit as a little bow fiddle," only to hear her mother protest that he must be mistaken—"Haven't you noticed that her webs are thickening, Doctor?" or "I believe her eyes are starting to cross" or "I'm afraid her growth isn't progressing normally" or "She isn't learning quickly enough" or "I'm afraid this lump on her neck is possibly cancerous. . . ."

Finally one day when Chris was nearly three the doctor threw up his hands in disgust and said, "Maureen, why is it that you continue to view this innocent little child as a symbol of everything that's gone wrong with your life?"

"Because, very frankly," Maureen said, making no allowance for Chris's presence in the room, "that's exactly what she is."

"One would almost be led to conclude that you actually *wanted* something to be wrong with her," the doctor said. "And I've noticed that you are entirely too lax about her safety around the hotel. She's allowed to play out on the terrace despite the fact that she could go right through the railing. There's always some sort of cleaning lye or rat poison lying around within easy reach. I mean, really, my dear, is there nothing I can do to provoke you, to make you care?"

"Yes," she said. "Bring me her father."

"How can I do that? He was never anything more than a figment of your imagination, the daydream of a lonely widow."

"But you saw him."

"Did I?" he said. "I still think he was too good to be true. My advice is to forget him and concentrate on someone who really needs you, right here and now."

"If only I could."

"You must."

"I'll try, Doctor, I promise I'll try. . . ."

Chris could not begin to comprehend this conversation, which was carried on in the coolest, most detached tones, but its general meaning was clear: Her mama didn't love her, and probably wanted her dead. Yet Chris was far too young and clever and too resilient by nature to allow herself to be defeated by this knowledge. Instead, she initiated a program designed specifically to win her mother's attention, and eventually her love. If her mama didn't like her, didn't want her around, there must be some reason. It must be something about Chris herself, something she had done, or not done, or something about her that her mama found unattractive. In the following weeks Chris tried to be as sweet and cute and cheerful and obedient as she could be. In her frenzy to please she leaped to do her mama's will. She groveled at her feet. She built her up into a great good queen and cast herself as her most despised and abject slave. She anticipated Maureen's every whim and desire, bringing her water when she wasn't thirsty, spectacles when she had no intention of reading. She refused to ever be tired or hungry or cranky or cloying or craving of affection. She ignored cuts, bruises, insults and blows from her contemporaries in the plaza, and all the other hard knocks of a small girl's life, presenting a constant, preternaturally bright, alert and smiling face to the world. And for a while it even seemed to work. Her mother tried to spend more time with her. She tried to touch her and kiss her and fondle her more often. But the effort showed on her face. And soon she was locking herself in her room again, reading books and scribbling notes to herself and typing for hours on end.

When after several weeks of application, and the passage of her third birthday, Chris's program showed only these very modest and temporary signs of success, she conceived a brand-new strategy. Overnight she turned herself into a spoiled, contrary little creature, jealous-hearted and impossible to please, sniffling, whining and complaining all the time, prone to day-long crying jags and sudden murderous conniption fits during which she attacked her mestiza nanny with her teeth and nails, tore at her own face and hair, and broke much crockery.

It was about this time also that she began to have trouble sleeping at night, and to be set upon by vicious animals in her dreams, and the Mean Queen made her first appearance in her fantasy life.

The Mean Queen lived in a gingerbread house and she had a voice like honey and she attracted children like ants. But once she got them inside she stuck them in her oven and served them up with mole sauce and green chile. Chris spent much of her time trying to figure out some way she could trick the Mean Queen into looking inside her own oven, so Chris could shove her inside, lock the door, and turn up the gas.

A year went by, and Chris's naughtiness seemed to have as little effect on her mama as her sweetness had. In the end she felt she had no alternative but to give herself up to despair, hoping that at the very least she might inspire her mama to pity. She stopped eating. She started wetting the bed again and shitting her knickers. She let her mouth hang open and she refused to focus her eyes. She unlearned how to talk and then she unlearned how to walk. She resisted every effort to get her out of bed, and she made no attempt to recognize the existence of the people around her. In the end she was sleeping sixteen hours a day and staring listlessly up at the ceiling fan for the remaining eight.

Yet even this plan went astray. Instead of inspiring her mother's pity, as she had hoped, it apparently inspired her delight.

Triumphantly, almost gleefully, it seemed, Maureen appeared above her one evening with Dr. Bermúdez at her side.

"Look at her," she said, in supreme vindication. "What did I tell you?"

The doctor examined Chris. "Such a shame," he said, shaking his little bald head. And he picked her up and sat in the Spanish rocking chair, rocking her gently. "Such a shame. . . ."

Now there were only two courses left open for Chris. She could remain in a state of suspended animation for the rest of her childhood, and gain nothing for it, or she could revert to the cunning, malicious little monster, hoping that sheer incorrigibility might one day force the issue.

Once her decision had been made, she reacted instantly. To Dr. Bermúdez's utter dismay, and Maureen's ill-concealed disappointment, the child suddenly came alive in his arms. Violently she began to flail about on his skinny lap, wailing at the top of her lungs, kicking at his tender old flanks with the sharp little spurs of her heelbones, making him wince with pain.

Within a month after the doctor's visit Chris had transformed herself into a creature a hundred times crueler and more devious than before.

Here at last was a strategy that began to pay dividends. After each of her brutal, premeditated acts of cruelty toward the family dog, the cat, the insects she trapped in jars, her poor harried Mexican nanny, her smaller playmates in the plaza (whom she tortured without mercy, slyly ensuring that she left no telltale marks upon their little bodies), she could observe her mother's attention growing, until at last she was rewarded with her frank, active, yet guilt-ridden loathing.

Slender, raven-haired, with big melting gray eyes, skin like ivory, a cute little button nose and a voice full of sugar and spice, Chris became the terror of the barrio by the time she was four. None of the mothers would allow their children to play with her. "La bastarda," they hissed at her as she pulled at her nanny's hand on the way to the zócalo. Or "la murciélaga," the bat, they would call her, and remark to each other aloud how she sent shivers up their spines.

And there had always been a good deal of whispered speculation in the marketplace as to the identity of her father. The more humble women claimed that her mother'd had congress with the devil. The more cultivated ladies said it was probably worse than that, and spoke of rumors that she had seduced a priest of God.

Chris didn't know what to make of all the talk she heard in the plaza. Unlikely as it might seem, she had always thought of her mother as essentially good and noble, her haughty disdain being a simple consequence of Christopher's extreme unworthiness, and her inherently despicable nature.

Maureen had never volunteered the name of Chris's father, and now Chris was afraid to ask, for she half believed that he might truly be some kind of devil. She had forgotten much of what had happened during her second and third years, and it seemed to her that she had always been the naughty, horrid little creature that she was today. She was at a loss to explain her own behavior except in terms of what the women said in the plaza. They called her an imp, a monster, an hija del diablo, and she supposed it must be true. But if it was true, what did that make her mother?

Maureen was at this time a hefty, handsome woman in her late forties. And her body had recovered from the ravages of pregnancy to the extent that it, along with her perennial freckle-faced good looks, her long flaming red hair, and the low-cut peasant blouses and long silver earrings she wore, drove the machos of Colima half to distraction. In polite society, of course, she had been persona non grata since the birth of her bastard daughter. As she had nothing to lose, she occasionally let one of her admirers in the back door of her hotel. Over a period of years, however, the list of her current and former admirers grew to such a length that half the gentlemen of the town had been through her bedchamber. These assignations were no secret (nothing was secret in Colima), nor was it a secret that several of her amours—including the mayor, the chief magistrate, and the commandant of the local army garrison—were married men. For causes such as these, Maureen's reputation—never good—deteriorated eventually to the point of infamy. Dr. Bermúdez, whose notoriety nearly equaled her own, was her only friend in town. She was still estranged from her son. Her daughter was a terrible trial. And two of her admirers—the mayor and the military man—were even threatening to fight a duel over her. She felt lonely, beleaguered, distraught, and she had thoughts of moving on.

Shortly after Chris's fifth birthday, in February 1933, her mama took her to Manzanillo to consult a German surgeon of Dr. Bermúdez's acquaintance. They caught the United Fruit Company banana train which departed daily from Colima station for the port. They rode with Manola, the nanny, in an old-fashioned first-class Pullman carriage with plush reclining seats, walls of padded velour, polished oak paneling, and an ancient corroded silver samovar for the making of coffee and camomile teas. Second-class passengers rode on the tops of freight cars, up where it was cool and breezy. Third-class rode inside the stifling banana cars, where, occasionally, they were bitten by tarantulas. A barefoot conductor in a dirty tattered blue uniform and a striped engineer's cap wandered from one end of the train to the other, inside and topside, up and down the ladders, braving death on the sharp curves, stepping gingerly over sleeping Indians, drunken mestizos, blankets and baskets and bundles full of peasant produce—tomatoes, squash, beans, rice, mangos, nespuras, chirimoyas, chickens, goats, pigeons and piglets.

It was fifty kilometers to Armería on the coastal plain, and the entire route was downhill on a winding narrow-gauge line with bent wavy rails, unsettled roadbed, rickety vine-choked wooden bridges and dark dripping tunnels that seemed to be propped up with soggy toothpicks. The grade was so steep it was unsafe at any speed. But the engineer kept his rusty little woodburner going full-steam the whole way, with the black volcanic dust flying out behind him, the smoke billowing, the soot settling in the cars, the whistle echoing shrilly down the arroyos and canyons.

At this velocity, and from the perspective of an overawed five-year-old, the scenery from Colima to Armería consisted of a nearly uninterrupted procession of coffee trees and telegraph poles. Once the train reached the coast, however, it slowed to a crawl and chugged along for hours on an immense palm-fringed, black-sand beach with the blue Pacific on one side and a dark forbidding mangrove swamp on the other. Fishing boats were pulled up on the beach, each with an evil eye painted on its prow. In the shade of fishnets, little brown men were sleeping beneath their straw sombreros. The villages in this locality, under tall swaying coconut palms, appeared to be constructed solely of bamboo poles and palm thatch. And the whole look of the place, with the ominous smoking volcano always looming in the background, was to Chris like a picture of the South Seas that she'd seen in one of her mother's *Vanity Fairs.*

Riding into Manzanillo along a fetid brown lagoon, she was struck by how very different it seemed from her hometown. If she had had to describe Colima in a few words, she would have called it high, cool, quiet, clean, full of Indian peasants in straw hats and immaculate white calzones who came down from the Sierras to sell their wares. Manzanillo, on the other hand, she would have described as low, hot, loud, dirty, full of mestizos and Negroes, sailors and stevedores, fishermen and foreigners, and not an Indian in sight. There were flower stalls and vendors selling tropical fruit on every corner, and the place smelled of rotting fish and processed sugar cane. Everywhere you could hear music, laughter, raucous human voices. With the exception of its low stucco public buildings the town was constructed all of rough unpainted wooden planks, two stories high, and it had a temporary frontier look about it, whereas Colima was made of cut volcanic stone plastered over with pastel-colored mortar and seemed finished and permanent by comparison. Though Colima was the capital of the state, there never seemed to be much happening there. Manzanillo was the place where the army and naval bases were, and where most of the business seemed to go on. Colima was situated on a great, gently sloping plateau, and was graced with wide elegant cobblestone streets and spacious parks, but it had a tight closed-in feeling about it and the people were dour and mean. Manzanillo, on the other hand, was built on a narrow neck of land, hemmed in by high green jungle hills on the east and west, the Lagoon of Cuyutlán to the south, the Bay of Manzanillo to the north, and its streets and its single plaza were narrow, muddy and cramped, its homes were small and humble, yet it had an open free spirit and its people were lighthearted and generous by nature. In Colima the people stayed locked behind heavy wooden doors, taking the air in the privacy of their marble courtyards. In Manzanillo all the doors and windows were left open to the air, and you could look right through the houses to the courtyards in the rear. In fact, you could look from one house into another and another and another and see dozens of people in dozens of homes sitting, standing, lying in hammocks, eating, sleeping, scratching, washing, laughing, crying, carrying on their lives as if they were alone in the world.

When Dr. Weber examined Chris's hands that afternoon he announced that surgery to remove the unsightly membranes should present no undue difficulty. Nor did he see any reason for delay and he offered to perform the operation the very next day.

"Now," he said, "I should like to explain the procedure to Christopher in simple terms, so she will not be startled or frightened."

Maureen agreed that surgery should take place on the following day, but she prevented Dr. Weber from explaining it to Chris on the grounds that it might upset her and make her "unmanageable."

So it came as a complete surprise the next morning when the strange big man with the monocle and the fierce black mustache strapped her down to a hard leather bed, clamped a foul-smelling rag over her nose and attempted, for all she knew, to suffocate her. Chris cried out and struggled for a moment, but soon she felt herself growing drowsy. And then she was falling, falling, into a sad dark place full of loudly lamenting adult voices and the screams of tortured children . . . where she saw her daddy at last. He was dressed all in black. He had a red goatee like Dr. Bermúdez, yellow cat eyes like her nanny Manola and little horns like a goat. She could have sworn he even had a tail with an arrow-shaped tip like a manta ray.

Nevertheless the operation was a complete success and within a fortnight she had taken on the appearance of a normal child.

Since Chris's birth, the only contact that Maureen had maintained with her son, Brian, was a yearly exchange of cards at Christmastime and birthdays. Maureen's sense of shame was such that she had always hesitated to reestablish a more personal contact. And Brian had seemed perfectly content to keep a discreet distance between himself and his scandalous mother. Maureen was so encouraged by the result of Chris's operation, however, that now at last she decided to approach her son. But before the meeting took place she rehearsed it carefully for several nights, staying up till the early hours, imagining that her little daughter was sound asleep. Anxiously, obsessively, she rehearsed it, using Chris's groggy unresponsive nanny as a kind of sounding board.

"What shall I do, Manola? Shall I take him by surprise or shall I phone for an appointment? I think I'll take him by surprise. That way I'll retain the initiative and he'll be the one who's off-balance. . . . Do you like the gray dress or the red? The gray makes me look too matronly. I must look very stunning and very young so I don't appear ridiculous with a five-year-old child. . . . How should I approach him, do you think? He's got two sides to his character. A practical side and a wild side. The Yankee and the Celt. But he does command a certain amount of respect. And he's got so much power for a man his age. Why, people are afraid of him around here, Manola. Not me, though. I'm his match. You'll see. . . ."

In the end she settled on a prudent approach. She spent hours primping, perming and preening herself to look as youthful, beautiful and seductive as possible without appearing vulgar. Then with her freshly scrubbed, shampooed, pigtailed and pinafored daughter in tow she surprised him at noon in his sooty little office in a wooden tower above the railroad yard.

"Adelante!" he shouted, when they knocked at his door. Yet when they came inside, he was turned away from them, seated on a high, backless draftsman's stool, gazing out over his domain.

"Gallo Carrizo, Gallo Carrizo," he was saying to a shifty little gypsy-looking mestizo who was standing behind him. "Now where have I heard the name before?"

"I used to work for the railroad, chief," the mestizo said. He was fluent in English, but there was a shallow cleft in his fleshy upper lip and he spoke with a slight lisp.

"What'd you do?"

"Railroad dick."

"No kidding?"

"Naw."

"When was that?"

"Well, I signed on in 1918, just after the Revolution. And then . . ."

"You didn't get fired, did you?"

"No sir. Got a brain concussion in May of 1927, in the Cristero Rebellion. Renegade priest snuck up and hit me from behind," the mestizo said, tipping his head and spreading his hair to show the dent in his skull. "Railroad give me a cash settlement."

"So what's the problem?" Brian demanded. He had not bothered to look at the mestizo's wound, which was really quite impressive, Chris thought.

"Well sir," the mestizo said, "I took my family up to Texas to start a new life. But the Depression come along and ruined us. Now we're starting up a laundry business, with free pickup and delivery, and we sure would appreciate your patronage."

"Always do what I can for an old railroad man," Brian said. And then he let it be known that the audience was at an end. During the entire conversation he had not once turned from his perusal of the railyard to look the Mexican in the face.

"Thanks, chief, thanks a million, you lemme know when you want it picked up," Gallo Carrizo said, and scurried out the door, leaving Chris and Maureen alone in the room regarding Brian's broad, hairy, muscular back and the shiny black straps of his shoulder holster through his sheer white tropical shirt.

Chris would never forget this first vision of her brother. Indeed, from the moment she first fixed on him it was like a flash of lightning before her eyes, with Brian in the middle, enshrined in the fire and ice of a soaring volcano, a cathedral of ashes.

On the whole, she decided, this great big adult male looked far more like a daddy than a brother. It was a notion that would have long-lasting effects on her life. She would never quite get over it, and in later years she would often conjure up an idealized picture of herself and Maureen and Brian in the railroad tower: Mama, Daddy and Daughter together. Daddy with his back turned, looking out over all that chugging, steaming, whistling industry that he controlled.

"Qué quieres?" Brian inquired, in the gruff familiar tone that one employed in Spanish with male inferiors.

He was still staring out over the railyard, the machine shops and the roundhouse, absorbed in the movement of trains, the unloading of boxcars, the humping of tankers, reefers, hoppers and flats, the switching of engines, coal cars and cabooses.

"Long time no see," Maureen said huskily. But her long freckled fingers tapped nervously on her handbag strap, and her voice cracked at the end.

"Maureen?" Brian said, and his voice was higher and younger than before. Then he jerked up straight on his stool and swiveled smoothly around to face them, smiling widely but uncertainly.

He was a stocky middle-sized man of about thirty. He had curly straw-colored hair, a large thin-lipped mouth with a comical gap between his two front teeth, a flattened off-kilter nose and tiny hazel eyes with droopy wrinkled lids. Yet there was something warm and humorous in his expression that Chris responded to immediately.

"How can it be that you never change?"

"Are you married yet?"

"Are you?" he said. And leaped across the room to embrace her. It was a prodigious leap, a single graceful bound, and it left Chris wide-eyed with admiration.

"I'll never marry again," Maureen said.

And when they kissed, they whirled around the room like husband and wife, with the husband just home from the wars.

"This calls for a drink."

"Let me look at you," she said, laughing, holding him out at arm's distance, "before I burst into tears."

"Darling," he said. "How long has it been? I hope you didn't get me wrong."

"Oh, I didn't get you wrong, Brian."

"I didn't want to embarrass you," he said.

"How *does* one explain such things to a loving son?"

"One doesn't."

"Suffice it to say that I . . ."

"Slipped?"

"I fell," she said flatly. "And this is the result."

"Pardon me?" he said. Her method of referring to her daughter seemed to have taken him aback.

"Dear," she said, grabbing Chris by one of her little gloved hands, "I want you to meet your brother."

"No," she said. And she was about to say: "He's my daddy." But instead she just said, "Pleased to meet you, señor."

He bent over and winked at her extravagantly. "So this is my new little sister, eh? Well, you know what? I don't even know your name yet."

"Christopher," she said in a tiny voice, playing with the lacy hem of her pinafore. For the first time in her life she felt shy. His breath smelled of cigar smoke, tequila and lime. She liked his smell.

"Christopher?"

"She was meant to be a boy."

"If you'll remember," he said, throwing his mother an irritated look, "I was meant to be a girl. You had me in long curls till I was seven."

"Anything," Maureen said, grinning unrepentantly, "to make you less like your dad."

"He was nothing but a bore, you said."

"That's right, and a coward to boot. Look how he died."

"Oh well," Brian said cheerfully, turning back to Chris. "I've always preferred little girls anyway. Why don't we just have us a nice big hug and a kiss, sweetheart, and make friends, huh?"

"Yes," she cried, and flung herself into his arms.

"What a big girl you are!" he said, lifting her lightly off the wooden floor to gaze with him out of his tower window.

"Please don't put me down," she said.

All the while holding her aloft, he pointed out to her alone every landmark of his domain beneath the volcano. And she felt as if she reigned over every bit of it with him until at last he put her down beside her mother again.

Maureen was adjusting her handbag, her hat, casually preparing to take her leave, when she snapped her fingers and said, "Say! I almost forgot. I need your advice about something, dear."

"Glad to oblige."

"Well, I've got a buyer for my hotel."

"I didn't even know it was on the market."

"It's a deal I just can't pass up, Brian. Dr. Bermúdez has decided he needs a property investment. . . . Yes," she said, "and my hotel happens to fit his requirements exactly. He can hold his office hours in the library and keep an eye on the place at the same time."

"I see," said Brian. "So what have you got in mind?"

"I'm thinking of throwing in with a partner," she said, "and buying another place in Manzanillo. That is, if it's possible, what with the fifty-kilometer law and all."

"Oh, it's possible."

"It is?"

"Sure, with friends in the right places, you can get a special dispensation."

"On what grounds?"

"Well, for example, with a hotel you could prove that you're performing a needed public service."

"Really?"

"Of course," he said. "What kind of place are you looking for?"

"A much larger place. I'd like to refurbish it as a modern hotel, with a restaurant, a ballroom . . ."

"What? Catering to tourists? We haven't got any tourists all the way out here."

"No. It would be a sort of commercial establishment, but first-class, catering to businessmen and local society."

"I thought you were on the outs with society."

"That was in Colima. Manzanillo is a much more freewheeling sort of place, don't you think?"

"Well, maybe," he said doubtfully. He seemed torn between resisting and succumbing to his mother's designs. His evident indecision threw panic into Chris's heart.

"I hate Colima!" she cried.

"Do you, honey?" Brian said, bending over to examine her closely and register his concern. "Why is that?"

"Nobody likes me there," she said. "I'd rather come here and live with you."

"All right," he said. He seemed touched by her sincerity, and her emotion. "I'll see what I can do."

"Yes," Maureen said, pleased with her daughter's unexpected success. "Do keep an eye out, won't you, dear?"

"I doubt if I'll find anything very interesting," he said. "I'm not making any promises."

Yet only three days later he showed up at their lodgings with plans to go in with Maureen as a partner and purchase the old Hotel Colonial.

"We can pick it up for a song," he said. "And it's bound to be a winner."

"And the official dispensation?"

"It's in the bag," he said. "The governor's arranging it as a special favor to you."

"But I don't know the governor."

"You will soon," he said. "We owe him ten percent of the receipts."

"I see. Well, I can't imagine a more substantial investor."

"In this region there is none."

"None but General Sánchez."

"General Sánchez doesn't invest," Brian said. "He possesses."

The Hotel Colonial, where Chris would spend the next eleven years of her life, was situated on the main plaza of Manzanillo, the Jardín Obregón, which fronted on the Muelle Fiscal, the railroad terminus, customs office and deep-water port where large foreign vessels docked and loaded the mineral wealth of west-central Mexico directly from American-owned hopper cars. An old fortresslike four-story building with a terra-cotta façade, a red-tile roof and enormously wide Tuscan eaves that kept out the seasonal rains, it boasted marble floors, blue-and-white-tile wall paneling with colorful Aztec patterns, massive oaken doors and exposed ceiling beams. The large dining room on the first floor was completely open to the air, with great Moorish arches and ornate wooden grillwork in place of windows. A breezy vaulted lobby opened directly onto a tropical garden and patio in the courtyard. Guests' rooms were arranged around the courtyard in three tiers of high open arcades. From the upper floors there were unparalleled views of the jungle mountains, the busy harbor, and the plaza with its ugly little brick cathedral on one side, its equally undistinguished palacio municipal on the other, and its astonishingly exquisite wrought-iron Victorian gazebo in the middle.

Maureen fell in love with the old place at first sight. She imagined flowers in the windows, hanging plants, antique Mexican furniture and silverware, native Indian rugs, blankets and crockery, imported linens, a modern stainless-steel kitchen, impeccable room service, and efficient American management.

The next day they engaged a Mexican lawyer and drew up a contract incorporating themselves as equal partners in an enterprise known thereafter as the Hotel O'Hare.

When Chris and her mother closed up the hotel in Colima and moved permanently to Manzanillo, the nanny, Manola, stayed behind. She had an ancient mother to look after, she said, and she could not abandon her. Actually, she had no such mother, but Maureen accepted her excuse in good grace. "I know what Chris has put her through," she told Dr. Bermúdez when after weeks of browbeating he reluctantly took possession of her hotel, "and I can't say as I blame the poor thing."

On the train back to the coast she sat her daughter down and gave her a good talking-to. She spoke frankly, female to female. "Chris, we're two of a kind," she said. "We're both incorrigible, I suppose, but there is one difference between us. I have an awareness of what's right and wrong, yet I often find it difficult to resist temptation, and afterward I always feel guilty. Apparently you have no sense of right or wrong whatever, and you simply go about doing as you please with no regard to the consequences. But don't take me wrong, now. I'm not setting myself above you. We have both made our mistakes."

"What kind of mistakes?"

"Well, for one," she said, "I was not married to your father, which is a sin."

"Who was my father?"

"His name was Dowd. He came from California."

"Where is he now?"

"I don't know."

"Why did he go?"

"He was fleeing for his life."

"What for?"

"He . . . he had done something wrong," she said. "I don't know what exactly. But he was very sad, very frightened and alone. At that time in Mexico it didn't take much of an excuse to hunt a man down and shoot him like a dog. And I thought that I could give him some comfort, some rest."

"Was he nice?"

"He was a lovely young man, but he was weak."

"Was he handsome?"

"As handsome as a prince," Maureen said. "So you see, Chris, we have both been naughty girls, perhaps. But now we have a chance to make a fresh start. Nobody knows us in Manzanillo. No one knows what we might have done in the past. They will accept us as we appear to them now. If we impress them with proper manners and ladylike deportment, they will like us and respect us and we shall never have another moment's trouble. But if we make a bad first impression it will remain with us as long as we live there."

It was at about this time that the Black Prince entered Chris's fantasy life. The Black Prince was a kind and handsome young knight who had been bewitched by the Mean Queen into leading children astray, getting them lost in the forest by dropping candy along the trail. In this way he brought them to his consort, who put them in her oven to bake.

After they moved into the Hotel O'Hare, Maureen was as good as her word. She called herself "twice widowed" and everyone deduced from the age of her young daughter that her second husband had recently passed away. If rumors arrived from the direction of Colima they were ignored or discounted. As she had said, it was an open town, a port town here, and nobody's closet was without its skeletons. Some of Manzanillo's finest families had been founded by pirates, slavers and bandidos, and several of its larger fortunes were based on gunrunning, bootlegging, dope smuggling, counterfeiting and worse.

Maureen was introduced into local society, which was made up of fourteen families of landowning "creole" Mexicans of pure Caucasian blood—the Herreras, the Castañedas, the Arciniegas, the Amados, the Negretes, the Bordas, the Galindos, the Ichigarays, the Ballesteros, the Hinojosas, the Cuevas, the de Benitos, the Rabagos and the LeFevres—and eight families of foreign traders, professionals, plant managers and engineers under contract to local industry—the Hollisters, the Whitlaws, the Calvins, the Wassons, the Kellys, the Webers, the Jeffers and the Zimmermans. Maureen took care to make friends with all of the creole ladies and the foreigners' wives, she was invited into their homes, and if there were flirtations with macho admirers they were very rare and exceedingly discreet.

But Chris's behavior improved not a whit. If anything, it grew worse, and within a month she was the talk of the plaza.

"Why, Chris, why?" her mother cried out in despair, after she'd come very near to poking out little Billy Whitlaw's eye with a sharp stick.

"I don't know why, Mama, I don't why I wanna do those things!" she cried. And in the very strictest sense she was telling the truth. She went out to play in the plaza with all the best intentions. She loved her mama dearly and she wanted to do everything she could to please her. But she was constantly being thwarted in her ambition by the naked aggression that boiled up out of her from some deep inner source. Though Chris could no longer identify the origin of her aggressive instincts, she knew that at one time they had been somewhat justified. But she could no longer remember her justification.

After the episode of the sharp stick, Maureen had a talk with her son.

"I've given up on finding a nanny who will take her abuse," she said. "Why don't you try to do something, Brian?"

"Why don't you try treating her like a human being once in a while?" he said. "I've been watching you at work, dear, and it's not a pretty picture."

"Brian, I have tried, believe me," she said. "But all she does is turn my kindness around and use it against me."

Then one Sunday morning a few weeks later Brian was making his way home from a night of gambling and carousing on the waterfront with some railroad friends when he stopped by an adobe wall, in the shade of a chirimoya tree, to watch a pair of mestiza women and a little boy of about three on the banks of the Río Cuyutlán.

The "río" was in fact a kind of fetid slow-moving creek at the bottom of a shallow ravine. It was used by the city as tap water, washbasin and general sewer, and it was renowned even in Mexico for the number of infectious microbes it contained. All of the stray cats of Manzanillo seemed to have taken up residence on its banks, and they grew fat and sleek on the rotting fish heads and other stinking ordure that the housewives pitched at them from their windows on the far side.

The little boy was olive-skinned and naked and painfully thin, with the protuberant belly of chronic malnutrition. Yet he seemed lively enough, playing with an old rusty soup spoon, throwing black sand in the air and laughing delightedly when it unsettled the circle of spotted cats around him. The women knelt in the wet sand with their skirts hiked up to their shapely thighs, scrubbing some laundry on a large volcanic rock, rinsing it in the río.

It was only after having viewed the charming scene for some time that Brian recognized the distinctive gray-striped shirting pattern of his own Mexico City tailor, and realized that their "laundry" consisted of several of his finest English linen shirts, which looked considerably worse for the wear. Infuriated, he vaulted over the wall, charged down the bank, grabbed the astonished women by their shoulders and flung them around to face him. He had intended to ask them what in God's name they thought they were doing with his shirts. But the moment he saw them his words stuck in his mouth. They were, he said later, absolutely the most beautiful creatures he had ever seen. Tiny, slender and girlish, no more than twenty, with curved Aztec noses and huge, upswept black eyes, they were perhaps even more beautiful in their surprise and fright. Of the two, he decided that he preferred the elder. She was taller, frailer than the other and her features were sharper, more defiant.

"Perdóname," he said, far more courteously than he had intended. "But may I ask where you have acquired my shirts?"

They peered at him quizzically for an instant, then sat back on their haunches to laugh. It was a lovely purling laughter, and, as he said later, he thought he could listen to it forever, even if it was at his own expense.

"Gallo Carrizo, Gallo Carrizo," the younger girl said, loudly enunciating her syllables, as if Brian were some kind of silly foreigner. "Gallo Carrizo, comprende?"

The elder girl had a more sophisticated look. And to Brian's astonishment she composed a perfect sentence in English.

"You gave your laundry to Gallo. We are the sisters of his wife, María."

She had just the softest edge of a Texas drawl, which charmed him fatally. There was also something about her bare, copper-colored throat, and the way her small round breasts rose up when she drew in her breath to speak. "I am Ramona Mescalero," she said gravely. "This is my sister Carmen. And that," she said, turning her exquisite head and nodding toward the little boy, "is my nephew Merle."

"Merle?"

"I was born in Texas," the child said, looking up from his digging.

"He's an American," said Carmen, in English only slightly less fluent than her sister's, but much less pleasing to the ear.

"We call him Hijo del Viento," Ramona said.

"It means Child of the Wind," said the boy.

"I know what it means."

"We call him that because he was born in a whirlwind," Ramona said. "It blew off our roof but it never touched him or his mama."

"Oh yeah?" Brian said. He was not used to being manipulated in this way.

"Yeah," the boy piped up. "That's why they call me that."

"He really is amazing," Ramona said, gazing fondly at him. "Why, just the other day—"

"Hey, what're you trying to do?" Brian said. "Sell him to me?"

"No, we just—"

"If it's the shirts you're worried about, forget it," he said. "You're still going to get paid."

"Really?" Ramona said, as if she had considered such a possibility highly unlikely.

"Of course," he said. "I might be mad at Gallo, but believe me, I've only got the tenderest feelings for you."

"Ay ay ay!" Carmen said, rolling her eyes.

Ramona blushed.

And little Merle stood up and did a perfect cartwheel into the water.

"Say, where'd you learn how to do that, boy?" Brian hollered, running over to catch him around the waist and pull him out of the river.

"Taught myself," he said. His voice was surprisingly mature for a child his age. And his eyes were a remarkable, glacial blue. But he couldn't have weighed more than a child of two.

"Did you teach yourself how to swim too?" he asked, holding him high above his head.

"Naw," the boy said, arching his back, kicking his feet. "My Aunt Carmen taught me. You oughta see me at the beach. I can ride the waves."

"Can you?" Brian said, laughing, setting him down in the sand.

"Oh, he can," said Carmen.

"He can indeed," said Ramona.

"Ramona, Ramona, Ramona," Brian sang (the effects of last night's mescal having yet to wear off), "what a beautiful name!" And grabbed her around the waist and reeled her about in a wild, cockeyed little Irish jig on the sand. "What a beautiful name! What a beautiful girl! What a beautiful day! How can it be that I already love you so?"

"Perhaps it is the sun, señor," she said in Spanish. "It is often unkind to North Americans."

On that same Sunday, after Mass, Brian persuaded his mother to interview Ramona for a job as nanny. And that evening after siesta he went to seek her out. He found her with her family near the squatters' encampment where they lived. They were strung out along the railroad tracks, collecting firewood and soda bottles to turn in for the deposit, and they'd not had the best of luck. Their feet dragged, their eyes were hollow, and the black dust clung to their ragged clothes.

"Looks like you caught me with my pants down, chief," Gallo said, when he saw Brian approaching across the ties.

"Incredible," Brian said, noticing for the first time the large dent in Gallo's head, and wondering how that renegade priest in the Cristero Rebellion had found occasion to put it there. "But I've come for something else. My mother needs a nursemaid, and she would like to see Ramona."

Gallo exchanged a rapid feral glance with his outlandish-looking mother—the dark-skinned, blond-haired descendant of a shipwrecked Swede and a native girl—and Brian understood that they believed he was making an indecent proposal.

"This is an honorable proposition of employment," he said sternly. "She is to work for my mother and sleep in the nursery with the child." Then he turned and strode away, leaving Gallo to scurry along behind him.

"Wait, wait, chief," he called, making a motion as if to pull at his sleeve.

Brian, who knew his Mexicans, stopped suddenly and wheeled around. Ignoring Gallo and his mother, he made straight for Ramona, pulling a hundred-peso gold piece from his watch pocket.

"Take this," he said, pressing it into her small, warm, dirty hand. "You will have to visit the public bath. You will have to get your hair done. You will have to buy yourself some suitable clothes and shoes. My mother expects you tomorrow evening at five, for tea."

Brian said later that he only hoped she would give a good account of herself. He had no idea if she knew how to behave in polite company. But he needn't have been so concerned. She had worked as a housemaid and child-minder in El Paso since she was thirteen and she was perfectly at home in an Anglo household.

She appeared at the hotel the next evening promptly at five, freshly bathed, manicured and lightly scented with cologne, wearing newly bobbed hair, faint lipstick, a pleated, low-waisted brown cotton dress and matching brown leather shoes with French heels, looking very much as if she'd just stepped off a plane from Mexico City or Cuernavaca.

"Mrs. O'Hare?" she said, clicking across the tiles of the lobby to shake her hand. "I'm Ramona Mescalero."

"Why, how do you do, my dear?" Maureen said. Ramona had the kind of erect carriage, the quiet dignity that she looked for in a Mexican girl. "Why don't we step out into the patio and have some tea?"

Ramona smiled calmly and allowed Maureen to precede her. "Ah," she said, "is this the little girl?"

"Yes, this is Christopher," Maureen said. "Chris, come meet Ramona."

"No!" she said. "No!" And commenced racing furiously around the patio with a little digging stick, tearing up flowers and scattering them everywhere. "No, no, no, no!"

"You see?" Maureen said, sighing. "I hide nothing from you. This is what I have to contend with. Her brother was the same way when he was little. But you expect such things from boys, I suppose. And then he turned out all right, didn't he?"

"Mr. O'Hare is a fine man."

"Yes. Well, do you think you're up to it?"

"I believe I am, señora."

"I don't mean Brian," Maureen said. "I mean the girl."

"Of course."

"Brian is off limits, I'm afraid."

"I understand," Ramona said firmly. "Now, about the child. It's just the age, I think. The little boy I used to watch in El Paso—he was difficult too. It's a stage they go through."

Maureen smiled skeptically.

"Is that where you learned your English, my dear? In Texas?"

"Yes," she said. "I attended school there for five years. I even got a diploma." She reached into her handbag. "I've got it here somewhere."

"Oh, that won't be necessary," Maureen said, patting Ramona on the hand. "I already noticed your class ring. Is that a sapphire?"

"Yes," she said, holding it up to be seen. EL PASO HIGH SCHOOL 1932 was inscribed around the small blue stone.

"You're a nice, clean girl, Ramona. I think you're going to work out just fine. And now perhaps I'll manage to get my books unpacked."

"Books?" said Ramona, as if she'd never heard of anything so exotic. "You have books, señora?"

"Why, of course, my dear. I have an enormous library full of books. And I'm sending off for new ones all the time. Would you like me to lend you some, after I've got it all set up?"

"Oh, señora," Ramona said, "there's nothing in all the world I'd like better."

On Ramona's first day as nanny she dressed Chris up in her frilliest pink frock, her shiniest white patent-leather shoes, her most spotless white knee socks, and took her out to the squatters' camp to show her off.

It was a shocking lapse of judgment. Maureen had even warned her specifically against it. But Chris found it endearing. No one had ever shown the least bit of pride in her before. And she was not averse to seeing her mama disobeyed and defied from time to time.

The next day, however, when Ramona suggested that they spend the morning in the Jardín Obregón, Chris did not hesitate to threaten her with blackmail if they did not immediately return to the squatters' camp.

And thereafter Ramona found herself obliged to go there nearly every day, rain or shine, regardless of the danger of discovery, and despite the extra trouble it cost her: She had to remove Chris's fine clothes the minute they got there and let her run around naked in the dirt with the Mexican kids; then, just before they left, she had to give her a thorough washing in the ocean.

Chris was fascinated by the Fifth of May Encampment, where Ramona's family lived, because it was so vastly different from anything she'd known before. It had been thrown up willy-nilly on a low flat expanse of miasmal black sand between the lagoon and the sea, and it consisted of little more than a collection of forty or fifty small huts, called jacales, made of cardboard, scrap tin, cane and bamboo, with palm thatch roofs. There was no road, no sanitation, no running water or electric light, no foliage except for a few bedraggled coconut palms and thorn trees.

The property belonged to the railroad. In fact, it was directly adjacent to a rail spur containing no fewer than a hundred LQCs (Living Quarters Cars) that had been standing there apparently abandoned by the Colima Pacific—complete with functioning woodstoves, attachments for running water, tin sinks, bunk beds, closets, windows, even flower boxes—for the last ten years. The residents of the camp were called squatters, Brian had said, because they were squatting on the land illegally, and he was always being prodded by his superiors in Guadalajara to evict them. But he knew better, he said. They were prepared to fight eviction with arms, if necessary, until they were given land under the terms of the agrarian reform. Also, they had threatened to "liberate" the LQCs the minute they were molested in any way. Meanwhile they'd been squatting there for years now, and it looked as if they'd be squatting there a good deal longer.

Because Ramona's family were newcomers, their hut was built on the edge of the camp, nearest the railroad tracks. You approached it on a winding path through the city garbage dump, with chickens, piglets and filthy naked babies underfoot. Outside the jacal a campfire always glowed, and inside it seemed rather cozy and romantic to Chris's mind, like the inside of a wigwam in one of her picture books. Straw sleeping mats called petates covered the hard-packed sand floor. And jars, gourds, Indian blankets and articles of clothing hung from pegs on the bamboo poles that held the roof up.

To her nanny, Ramona, however, the place was an abomination, and she hoped to get her family out as soon as possible. Centipedes, scorpions and tarantulas lived in the thatch, she said, and sand and soot from the railyard sifted endlessly through, covering everything. In the daytime a scorching wind blew off the hot coastal plain, driving even snakes and iguanas inside for shade. In the hours before dawn a cold night wind would sometimes come whipping down off the snowy volcano and straight through the tattered blanket that served for a door, chilling everyone to the bone. And just outside the door, twenty-four hours a day, switch engines and boxcars would go hooting and rumbling by, making sleep impossible.

One time when Chris was sitting inside the jacal with the entire family, sheltering from a thunderstorm, she noticed a big double-barreled firearm hanging by its trigger guard from one of the bamboo pegs.

"What's that?" she asked.

"A shotgun," Gallo replied.

"What's it for?"

"For shooting things."

"What things?" she wanted to know. She was at the stage where she never stopped asking questions.

"That depends," said Gallo, grinning like a fox, reaching up and dropping the gun into his lap. Then he broke the barrel and peeked through it at Chris.

Ramona instantly changed seats and placed herself between Chris and the gun. Gallo sniffed derisively at her overreaction. But Chris was touched by the gesture, and laid her head in Ramona's lap for a moment to let her know how she felt.

"We brought that gun with us from Texas," said little Merle, who was the matter-of-fact member of the family.

"Right," said Grandma Carrizo. "But believe me, we been tempted to pawn it on a number of occasions."

"We kept it though," said Merle.

"Why?" Chris wanted to know.

"Because," said Gallo in English, pantomiming a hunt, a kill, a feast, "in a pinch, a shotgun is eats."

"At night," explained Carmen, "we can go outside and jack-shoot the varmints that come around."

"What varmints?" Chris persisted.

"Oh, jackrabbits, coyotes, iguanas, rats, moles, bats, mice, owls, ocelots, polecats," said Gallo. "We'll try anything, if the going gets rough enough."

"Yeah," said Ramona, making a face, "but usually we only try it once."

"De vera!" they all shouted at once. "It's true, it's true," they went on laughing delightedly, until Chris wondered if they weren't having her on. But later she discovered that they often laughed this way, over little or nothing. It was their only form of entertainment. Most of the time they were just laughing at themselves.

Gallo's fat little pregnant wife, María, was the only shy or taciturn member of the family, and she was the most "indigenous-looking" one of them. The rest of them—Grandma, Gallo, Ramona, Carmen, even little Merle—were all very lively and voluble and mestizo in appearance. In Grandma Carrizo the mestizo look was extraordinary. She had very dark, almost black, wrinkled skin with startlingly blue eyes and wild kinky blond hair.

The boy Merle was obviously the pet of the family, and they all bragged upon him outrageously. The kid was amazing, they said. He didn't walk till he was nearly two years old. Didn't even learn how to crawl. Then one day he just up and took a stroll over the International Bridge to Juárez and back. He never talked baby talk either. Cut his teeth on full sentences, in Spanish and English. "I want to be a girl" was the first thing he said. And they all had to laugh. Because, as Gallo pointed out, with four women around the place and only two masculinos, he probably thought he'd do better with the ladies.

By the time Chris met little Merle, he could swim like a fish even in high waves. He could do a front flip in the sand from a standing position. He could count to a thousand. He could read, write and spell the words El Paso, Texas, America, Manzanillo, Colima and Mexico, not to mention his own full name. Chris could do none of these things. Merle's physical prowess and his easy self-confidence never ceased to amaze her, for she was riven with morbid fears and physical debilities of every kind. She suffered from asthma, hay fever, tonsillitis, nearsightedness, hypertension and chronic diarrhea. She got seasick and carsick, and was allergic to cats, dogs, flowers and even straw furniture. She was afraid of the dark, of heights, of small rooms, of strangers, of sleeping alone, of deep water. Most of all she feared poison in her food and murder in the streets at the hands of unknown assailants.

Displeased with the unspoken comparisons between Merle and herself, Chris made a point of gaining ascendancy over him through her native cunning. At first she started with little things. "Merle," she would say, "could you please carry these rocks over to the beach for me? We're gonna use 'em to make a wall for our sand castles." Then her demands grew: "Come here, Merle. Get a stick and pick up this scorpion I found and put him in a jar for me." He was such a good-humored, simple-hearted little fellow, he never thought of resisting even her most capricious orders: "Merle, go steal my panties from Ramona and put them over your head like a mask." "Okay, okay," he would say, smiling beatifically, and set about doing her will.

In this way Chris discovered her one great advantage in life: She was born to be a leader.

Yet she was always on her best behavior when the adult Carrizos were near, and in time they nearly accepted her as a member of the family. Ramona gave her the run of the camp, and Chris quickly uncovered all its hidden marvels. She scampered over stinking mounds of garbage in the city dump, making friends with the filthy lice-ridden children who lived there, seeking treasures and curiosities amid the refuse: headless dolls, broken dishes, the maggoty corpses of cats and dogs, the residue of a home abortion. She tumbled with little Merle and the tiny neighbor girl, Delia Nieves, over the black dunes and out onto the beach and right into the foamy brown waves, treating the two little ones more as creatures of her own invention, or fabulous new discoveries—broken toys or thrown-away dolls—than real human children like herself.

Then suddenly one day she was no longer welcome at the camp. She bawled and screeched and threatened blackmail—"I'll tell my mama on you, Ramona, I'll tell!"—and she had a conniption fit right in the middle of the Calle Juárez, but it was no use.

"We can't have a bunch of kids running around the jacal when María has her baby," Ramona said.

And as it happened she was right. It was a breech birth that went on for twenty-four hours. María nearly died in delivery, and the baby—a little girl—was born with a slightly misshapen head. But Grandma Carrizo, who had acted as midwife, assured everyone that it would pop back into shape in no time.

"Go on, son," she said to Gallo. "Take off. Nothing you can do around here anymore."

Gallo whooped it up and lit out for the cantina to celebrate, taking little Merle along with him. He deposited him at the Hotel O'Hare, despite his mama's protestations that he'd be perfectly all right at home.

But he'd left him off at the hotel several times before, at Maureen's insistence, and there had never been a moment's trouble. Maureen, who made no secret of her preference for boys, liked Merle so well she gave his daddy a peso every time he brought him over. "He's a real little charmer," she said. "Look at those eyelashes. And he's a good influence on Chris; he's the only kid she can get along with."

Actually Merle was just an exceptionally good sport. He never tattled when Chris threw flaming garbage on him in the city dump, or rubbed sand in his eyes at the beach, or rolled him over in the cactus garden at the Hotel O'Hare. Even at that young age, it seemed, he knew instinctively where his bread was buttered, and he was already willing to go to considerable pains to keep it well spread.

This time however—because Merle was getting even more attention than usual on account of his mama's new baby, and because Maureen was just doting on him, laughing and clapping her hands and shaking her head in disbelief at his precocious antics—Christopher was provoked into taking her wickedness a long step further than ever before.

She timed her attack to coincide with Ramona's daily trip to the marketplace. She made sure that her mama was busy for the moment, overseeing the replastering and repainting of the hotel. Then she enticed him into the toolshed with tamarind candy and got him down on the floor. Got his kneepants and knickers around his ankles and started tickling him. Then, while the boy still laughed, she swiftly worked her vengeance upon him with a weapon she'd concealed there an hour before.

Strangely, after it was done he did not cry out. It was she who was horrified by what she had wrought. Merle, it appeared, did not quite understand what had happened to him. He seemed more surprised than hurt or alarmed, even when a pool of blood formed beneath him. Neither of the children made a sound for the longest time.

Then her mama materialized in the doorway.

"Mother of God," she cried. "I knew it would come to this."

Her face went chalk white, her eyes bright red.

"Aaaiiieee!" Merle screamed. He screamed so loud it carried all the way into the marketplace, all the way to the railroad yard, all the way into his own future, and Chris's too, and gave them both nightmares for years to come.

Frowning, whacking Chris out of the way with the back of her hand, Maureen bent to examine the Mexican boy.

"Aaaiiieee!"

He'd been cut with the rusty tin top of a can of imported Del Monte peaches. The wound was not grievous, just barely deep enough to lay open his little scrotum. But it was very long, running the entire length of his underbody from the upper end of his rectal crack to the tip of his uncircumcised penis, and it would leave a scar that would remain for the rest of his life.

"Holy Mary," Maureen said, raising her eyes to heaven. "What have I created?"

And dragged Chris out of the shed by the hair and locked her in a hot, airless little closet under the stairs.

"This is the end," she said, from outside the door.

The instant Maureen was gone a host of spiders, centipedes, scorpions, beetles, hornets, army ants, mice, rats and tiny bats came shrieking out of the dark, banging into Chris, knocking her down, creeping up her legs and under her dress, stinging her, biting her, crawling into all of her orifices. She screamed at the top of her lungs, but no sound came out. She lost control of her bladder. She rolled herself up into a tiny ball to protect herself, but they were inside her now, like little demons, eating at her lungs and entrails and heart. Her heart leaped out of her chest, nearly breaking her ribs in its frantic effort to elude them. And she knew that she would die now, in a state of mortal sin, and go straight to hell. Maybe she was already *in* hell, and this was what it was like. Yet even in the midst of this horror, from which Chris knew she would never, ever recover, a faint, rosy tinge of pleasure glowed just where her consciousness went over to the night.

A thousand eternities later, a knock at the closet door seemed like a hammer beating on her own skull, splitting it. And when she heard a deep, rumbling male voice outside, she assumed it was the Evil One in person, come to take her away to his fiery bed. And then suddenly she was in his arms, in blinding light, kicking, biting, scratching, howling, "Mama said she wanted a little boy! Mama said she wanted a little boy! Mama said she wanted a little boy!"

What finally revived her was the smell. The smell of tequila, lime, salt, cigar smoke and male sweat. It's Brian's smell, she thought, and at last she could hear his words.

"Don't worry, honey, don't worry. Merle's gonna be okay. Merle's gonna be okay."

"Okay?" she said. And finally she could see his face. He wore an anguished expression, and there were tears in his eyes.

"Daddy, I'm thirsty," she said.

"What would you like?"

"Guava juice?"

"All right," he said, smiling, carrying her toward the hotel bar. She could feel the tension in his great, hairy arms, and his strength.

"I wanted to turn him into a girl like me," she sobbed, burying her face in his chest. "I wanted to turn him into a girl like me."

That night when Gallo came in he forgave Maureen and Ramona and even little Chris and took all the blame on himself.

"My mother told me," he kept crying. "She told me she had this feeling. 'Leave the boy at home,' she said. But I wouldn't listen."

Then he spoke with Dr. Weber, who had attended to the child.

"Be frank with me, Doc," he said. "What is gonna happen to my little boy?"

"Physically he's going to be perfectly all right; but mentally," the doctor said, "there's a chance he might have some problems later in life."

And all night long while his newborn baby daughter wailed in the cane shack and the ocelots growled in the thorn trees and the engines hooted in the railyard and the wind rattled through the coconut palms, Gallo rocked back and forth by the campfire with his hurt little strangely silent boy hugged tightly to his chest, crying out, "My son, my son, how will you ever forgive me?"

The next day there were birth complications because of unhygienic conditions in the Carrizo thatch hut and a lack of nearby emergency medical facilities and María died of a hemorrhage while softly calling out her husband's name.

And the baby was not long in following her.

Gallo was sick with grief for several days. When he recovered, he spoke with his mother. They agreed that he'd made a dreadful error in judgment, a result of his overwrought state, when he absolved the O'Hares of blame in the mutilation of his son.

That afternoon they paid a call on Mrs. O'Hare. Spoke right up to her in her own language, English. Alluded delicately to her grave liability as a foreigner under Mexican law, and to their own severely straitened circumstances. They let it be known that they weren't looking for any legal trouble, or any handouts either. They assured her that there was no one so honest or hardworking as they, and represented in some detail their desperate need for permanent employment and a permanent dwelling place.

Maureen was feeling just guilty enough at that time, and just vulnerable enough, and she cared for Ramona and little Merle enough, to consider the Carrizos' request in a favorable light. She conveyed to Gallo and his mother her profound sympathy for their plight, and declared that she was ready to do anything within reason to remedy it. She suggested that they leave their temporary abode in the squatters' camp and move into the servants' quarters at the Hotel O'Hare. When her renovations were completed there would be work for them as clerks, maids, cooks, waitresses, bellboys, busboys, launderers and bartenders. Maybe Brian could even get Gallo a job on the railroad eventually. Meanwhile, she said, they would receive room and board, and she would be happy for their assistance in feeding her construction crew and keeping the place tidy during its refurbishment.

The Carrizos said they would do exactly as she suggested, and they would be delighted to be of assistance. They departed her presence bowing humbly, and repaired instantly to the Fifth of May Encampment to collect Carmen and little Merle. They were back at the hotel in an hour with all their possessions. By evening they'd settled into the servants' quarters. Within a couple of days it seemed they belonged there. And before the month was out they could barely remember having lived anywhere else.

CHAPTER 3

It was some months later, on the Hotel O'Hare's grand opening day, that Brian was notified by telegraph of a rail accident at Kilometer 51. A gang of train robbers—bandit remnants from the Cristero Rebellion—had gotten their timetables mixed up, it seemed. Instead of derailing the 5:05 Guadalajara express, which was carrying a quarter-ton shipment of silver bars, they had inadvertently run the 4:05 local freight off the Tecomán Curve.

When Brian reached the scene, at midday, the locomotive and the coal car were resting at the bottom of the gorge along with the engineer, the fireman and the head brakeman, and it looked as if they were going to stay there forever unless somebody figured out how to get down a two-hundred-foot vertical cliff with a cutting torch and ignite it under five feet of silty swift-running water. The rear brakeman and the conductor, who had already crossed themselves devoutly and prayed for the souls of their sadly departed compadres, were sitting calmly on the track in their untouched caboose, brewing a pot of coffee and cooking up some beans. The train's cargo—three cattle cars and an empty hopper—lay overturned and astraddle the main line to Colima, blocking traffic in both directions. The cattle themselves were either dead and stinking to high heaven amid the debris or had taken to the jungle to rejoin their wild relations.

Normally, in a situation like this, the line would have stayed closed for three to four days until a crane rig could be summoned by telegraph, fitted out, and humped over the mountain from Guadalajara. But Brian was not the kind of man to simply accept this as a fact of life. Before his promotion to trainmaster he'd been the most renowned railroad mechanic on the west coast of Mexico, and he had been called all over the Republic to unsnarl some of the worst train wrecks of the era. It was said on the Colima Pacific that he could splice a broken switch or a split rail junction with baling wire and a soldering iron, that he could fire up a cold engine boiler with a cigarette lighter, that he could set a thirty-ton boxcar back on the rails with saplings he cut down by the side of the track, or construct a shoofly—a temporary bridge—out of scrap railing and cannibalized flatcars.

Brian's reputation on the railroad was exaggerated, perhaps. But he had no intention of leaving his main line shut down for half a week, in any case, and he set right to work clearing it. He tied onto one of the overturned cattle cars with his light yard engine and a length of bridge cable, sprayed the track with oil, and highballed it back down the hill. The cattle car slid sideways over the slick rails, screeching and throwing off sparks, bursting into flames. Then, when it reached the next curve, it swung out over the precipice and tumbled spectacularly into the canyon. It might have taken the engine right along with it had not Brian, at the very last instant, signaled the engineer to let up on the throttle just long enough to slip the cable off the coupling and let her go. He did that with all three cattle cars and the hopper, and by the end of the day the line was free and two hundred feet of fresh track had been laid. But the river was a disaster area, dammed up with splintered wood and the rotting corpses of beef cattle, flooding the Indian corn and cane fields on its narrow banks, littering the scenery with a mass of twisted metal.

All of which was highly illegal, of course: The cattle cars and the hoppers were in theory salvageable, and railroad directives specified that they be dragged into the shop for repairs whenever possible. And the Mexican Forest Service and the Secretariat of the National Patrimony might well have something to say about what the Colima Pacific had done to the Río Colima watershed. But Brian did this kind of high-handed thing all the time. He was convinced that it was the only way you got things done in this country. What the Mexicans respected most was a man of decision, even if his decisions turned out to be wrong. What they appreciated most was impetuosity, audacity, the grand gesture that threw caution to the wind. Down here you had to accept certain risks as a matter of course, risks you wouldn't dream of taking had you been employed by, say, the New York Central or the Santa Fe.

Take the matter of bribery: In theory it was just as illegal in the Republic as anywhere else. But Brian earned a major portion of his income, and had become a leading light of the local commercial establishment, by using the power of the railroad—the power to deliver, the power to deny—to generate kickbacks, payoffs and special favors. Basically, Brian maintained this power by ensuring that all regular service was substandard. In order to obtain ordinary service, the customer had to pay extra, under the table. And in order to obtain superior service, the customer had to pay a very great deal under the table. In the passenger section, for example, second- and third-class rolling stock was kept in such poor condition that first class became a necessity of travel. As a consequence it was always overbooked, and passengers were willing to pay enormous sums merely to obtain standing room. Likewise in the freight section. If a merchant wished his products to arrive on time, undamaged and unpilfered, he had to pay a fee far above that listed on his waybill. Farmers and finqueros with perishable crops were especially vulnerable, and paid accordingly high bribes. Yet Brian was not resented by his customers. On the contrary he was greatly respected, inasmuch as his modus operandi was known to be general practice throughout the Republic. Indeed, he would have been considered suspect if he acted otherwise, as nothing in Mexico was appreciated less than a do-gooder. The attitude of Brian's customers reflected a fundamental understanding of the Mexican political system, which differed from the Anglo-Saxon system in that only the *appearance* of democracy was maintained. In reality there were no system of checks and balances, no parliamentary debate, no minority rights. The actual political structure had remained unchanged from the time of Montezuma through the Spanish viceroys to the present era, in that *only those with power had rights,* and all the real decisions of government were taken by certain rich and well-connected men, behind closed doors. The rest of the population had no rights whatever, except those they begged, bribed or demanded as a favor from those in power.

Or take the matter of social appearance. Every once in a while Brian liked to go out on a three- or four-day binge, a real corker, just to let off steam. Had he been employed by some railroad north of the border, such intemperate behavior would never have been tolerated. Trainmasters, upon whose sobriety so many passengers' lives depended, were expected to be pillars of bourgeois respectability. But down here Brian's bad habits were not only tolerated, they actually added luster to his reputation as a macho, a rounder, a man's man, even among the foreigners of the town. Mexico had a way of bringing out every gringo's latent anarchy, and they all found themselves doing things they'd never dream of doing at home. It was as if things didn't *count* the way they did in the States. And nothing was forbidden, apparently, if you just had the guts, or the unmitigated gall, to pull it off. It was as much for his reckless qualities, therefore, as for his acquisitive and organizational abilities that Brian had recently been elected board chairman of "the Company," a clique of fourteen rich creole planters and eight foreign traders and plant managers—corresponding exactly to his mother's social list—which functioned locally in lieu of a chamber of commerce.

After Brian had cleared his main line, he tied onto the caboose with his light yard switcher and burned the rails back for the roundhouse, sitting up in the cupola with the train crew and a couple of cronies, sipping tequila with salt and lime, swapping railroad disaster stories—with which Mexico abounds—and singing old revolutionary songs while the ties went clackety-clack, the crew of section hands snored in their bunks below, and the big dark jungle trees fled by in the twilight.

"Yo tengo pistolas con mangos de marfil," he sang, *"para matar los gringos que vienen por ferrocarril. . . ."*

And then he did a dance.

Their tequila gave out about halfway back to the terminal, so they decided to stop off for a quick mescal at a little riverport town called Boca de Pascuales.

There were three of them that night, besides the train crew and the gandy dancers. There was Brian; there was Gallo Carrizo, his greasy little dent-headed mestizo batman, majordomo, chauffeur, armed bodyguard and all-round gofer; and there was the assistant trainmaster of Manzanillo Yard, a lanky lugubrious New Englander named C. J. Hollister who complained all the time about his kidney ailment but drank more tequila than any man Brian had ever known.

They left the crew behind to hold the fort and headed for a little clip-joint on the wharf where they could hear the cries of a monte dealer calling his cards in Spanish and English—"El Rey Rojo! The Red King!

Hombre a Caballo! The Man on a Horse!"—and the sound of a marimba band playing bambas and sambas in the jarocho style.

The instant he hit the door, Brian found himself going around and around with a big black barefoot whore from the Costa Chica, the coast to the South where a Spanish slaveship once went aground on the rocks and the niggers ran wild in the jungle. She wore a ragged orange-and-purple cotton mammy dress and a red-and-green bandanna tied around her enormous elongated head, and she got so raucous doing the bamba that little Gallo, who usually figured things out pretty much in advance, lost control of himself for once, ran up onto the bandstand, shoved the marimba man off his instrument, and started beating it like a pro with the sticks going pinga-ponga-pinging up and down while the sallow-faced C.J. grudgingly coughed out a giggle and swilled another at the bar and the crowd of sailors, gamblers, prostitutes, stevedores and tuna fishermen laughed and cheered and hollered and Brian got caught up in it as he always did—against all rhyme or reason, to the detriment of his dignity as a white man—beating time with his railroad boots while the black girl heaved and humped and sweated and groaned and glistened under the colored lights.

And then a Norwegian seaman from off a motor ship in the river walked in and without a word cracked a full liter of rum over some other Norwegian's skull and the man dropped like a light and everyone except Brian and his negracita figured he was dead for sure but inside of ten minutes he was up and around and drinking rum at the bar and there was only this little bitty lump upside his ear and broken glass scattered all across the floor. Brian and his great black banana danced through the entire ruckus, lost to the music, the Latin rhythm, their eyes rolled back in their heads. And it was the samba down the length of that smoke-filled room and the fandango back and the bamba up close to the cleft of those fat black melons . . . and only after the longest while did the crowd notice that the floor was turning red, that neither of the dancers realized it but the lady was cut and bleeding bad on the pink-skinned soles of her black feet and the blood was trailing behind her. The crowd tried to stop her but she just kept right on shuffling back and forth across the floor, so Brian figured he had no choice but to join her and he kicked off his railroad boots in an act of machismo that raised a great hurrah and he continued to do the bamba with her across the broken glass feeling it crunch under his feet and cut through his skin, watching his blood stain the wood-plank floor in the shape of his big gringo footprints.

And then the next thing that happened there was this fight. They were outside in the dark on the muddy street and Gallo had insulted Brian's nigger. Exactly how he'd insulted her Brian would never know and C.J. would not remember, but it seemed that somehow they'd had some truck in the past. Curses were flung back and forth in rapid argot and there were accusations of double-dealing and betrayal. "Pela me la berga! Me cago en el coño de tu puta madre! Hijo de la gran puta negra! Traicionero! Engañador!" She smacked Gallo in the face. He hit her back. And then her pimp—another coal-black nigger from off the Costa Chica—appeared from out of the shadows and jumped in and they got Gallo down on the ground and they were knocking the shit out of the poor skinny little bastard, hollering, "Now we got you, cabrón! Now we got you, you double-crossing, pig-sucking little sonofabitch!" or words to that effect, while Brian and C.J. tried frantically to pull them off.

And then, just as the pimp pulled out a wicked-looking stiletto and looked as if he was going to use it, Brian got a bright idea. He reached in his wallet and pulled out a wad of greenbacks and started waving them around in the air, screaming, "Here, here, stop, stop, I'll pay you in cash, American dollars!"

And they climbed up off of Gallo all smiles and Gallo got up panting, sweating, spitting blood, and pulled out a snub-nosed .38, and started waving it around in the air, shouting, "I'll kill you this time, Herculano, you black motherfucker, I'll kill you!"

"Easy down, now, Gallo," Brian said, patting the Colt .45 that he wore in a shoulder holster under his shirt. "The whole point was to avoid violence, here."

And then the next thing Brian knew he was alone, incredibly, with the black whore. It was part of the deal, she said. And they were stepping gingerly out across some narrow wooden catwalks to her little tin-roof cane shack built up on stilts above the river and then she was washing their feet, pouring rum on their wounds, while a baby cried softly in the next room, and she was wrapping the wounds in torn sheets and then she was doing her stuff, man, doing shit to Brian naked on her bed, black on white, that he didn't even know *happened* before. She must have been some kind of fat acrobat the way she did those things—standing on him, squatting, sitting, spinning on him—and then she finished him off and she said, quite matter-of-factly, in her Trade English, "Hokay, babee, thaz all," and went in to attend to her infant.

And then the next thing Brian knew he was up and stumbling around alone in the dark on the catwalk with his feet wrapped in torn sheets and he tripped over a loose board and pitched headfirst into the black water and he heard the splash but he didn't feel anything—not fear or wet or cold or anything—because the water which had suddenly enveloped him was exactly the temperature of his body, and as comforting as the womb. But then he panicked. He recalled that he couldn't swim a stroke. And he was fighting to stay up, flailing about, but it all felt too unreal and he knew that he would die of drowning. Then damn if he didn't spot his great black madonna above him on the catwalk, strip-ass nekkid, shining like an eightball in the moonlight, hauling him out of the stinking river.

"I don't even know your name," he sighed, when she landed him on the boards.

"Eulalia," she breathed, and disappeared into the night.

Then C. J. and Gallo figured out where he was at, some way, and they got ahold of him and escorted his ass back to the caboose and poured three fast Mexican coffees down his gullet and his head snapped clear and it was then that he looked at his pocket watch and discovered that it was 9:32 P.M. and he was late for his mama's opening-night party and he'd better get home to the Hotel O'Hare before she had a fit. . . . A new military comandante was to take up his post in Manzanillo, and Mrs. O'Hare, at the Company's behest, had timed her grand opening to coincide with his arrival. A dazzling welcome reception had been arranged for tonight, during which Brian, in his capacity as chairman of the Company's board of directors, would bestow upon the new comandante his traditional first bribe, a brand-new American automobile.

So on the way home he had himself another snifter or three of the dog that bit him and he got his second wind and then he did another kind of dance. He bailed out of the caboose at Independencia and Juárez, with Gallo right on his tail, while C.J. and the others rode into the station to tie up the engine and write out the accident report. Then he stumbled across the sleepy dim-lit town to the back door of the hotel, singing softly with Gallo: *"God save me from this affliction, I feel like I'm going to die, the Virgin of Mescal and Tequila is the only thing that can save me now. Cabrón what a hangover! And nothing to drink in the house. . . ."* And he slipped off his boots and tripped up to his room on the second floor, tracking mud and bloody water, listening to the dull murmur of a hundred decorous voices speaking genteel Spanish and

English while an orchestra played waltzes and boleros quietly in the background. He had himself a quick shower and then let Gallo wipe his feet with alcohol and cotton and dress them with sticking plaster. He felt nothing, certainly no pain. Felt a bit distant, perhaps, conversing with his man about this and that.

"Sometimes I think I was cut out for better things, no?" Gallo said, cynically, with a little coyotelike snicker of sly self-deprecation.

"Oh yeah? What makes you think that?" said Brian, barely listening. He often found himself having half-conscious conversations with Gallo. There was something about the mestizo's hoarse, lisping, conniving little voice that slid right off his back. Why he kept him around he couldn't say. Maybe it was precisely because he was such an unsavory little sonofabitch. Maybe it was because he didn't presume to judge, since he was in no position to throw stones. Maybe it was because he spoke English and understood the foibles of gringos. Maybe it was because his presence was somehow reassuring, since one always came out so much better in a general moral comparison. Maybe it was because of his sister-in-law, Ramona Mescalero.

"I got talents," said Gallo. "You'd be surprised."

"Like what, for instance?"

"Hell, I know a damn sight more than C. J. Hollister about running the Colima Pacific."

"That wouldn't take much. He's married to the division chief's daughter."

"I want you to tell me something frankly, chief," said Gallo, on his knees at Brian's feet, laughing at the absurdity of his own situation. "Am I gonna be doing this kinda thing forever or do I got a future on the railroad?"

"That depends."

"I know."

"What does it depend on, Gallo?"

"On my sister-in-law, I think."

"I'm beginning to wonder if you're not trying to keep them both for yourself."

"Hey," said Gallo, raising his little yellow hands off Brian's big white feet, "that's family, chief."

"Then what's the problem?"

"No hay problema," Gallo said. "It's just that . . . hell, I ain't no slave driver."

"You mean she won't do it."

"She got a mind of her own."

"Saving it for her husband, I bet."

"That's up to you, boss."

But Brian had spent so much time around whores that he was shy with virgins. And there was something about Ramona, a straitlaced dignified air, that precluded the possibility of an ambush on the stairway, or a furtive grope in some dark corner of the nursery while Chris and little Merle were taking their naps.

"That's enough on the feet, Gallo," he said. "I could dance all night on them now. Just polish the black-and-white wingtips for me, will you?"

Then he got up, went into his blue-and-white-tile bathroom, shaved very carefully, and trimmed his brushy British-style blond mustache. Cleaned his furry teeth. Brilliantined his curly hair and slicked it down, combing it straight back with a part in the middle. Gallo helped him into his navy-blue silk shirt, his shoulder holster, his .45 that he never went without—it was a matter of status, locally—and his white linen suit. And by the time his man got him up to the ballroom on the third floor he seemed a model of decorum.

He hesitated for a moment before he made his entrance, surveying the provincial crowd. Slight swarthy local gentry for the most part. Enormous three-generation families of them. With a smattering of stout, florid foreigners, their dull-looking adult offspring and bottle-blond wives. All of them well dressed in the fashions of ten years before, standing around striking interesting poses with drinks in their hands, or taking a turn on the gleaming red-tile floor, under imported candlelit chandeliers from the days of Maximilian. Near the door, Don Cruz Herrera, patriarch of the most respected local creole clan, stood in a huddle with three other silver-haired latifundists, Don Miguel Castañeda, Don Enrique Aciniega, and Don Carlos Rabago. Out on the dance floor, the German surgeon Dr. Johann Weber waltzed about with Eleanor, the young and pretty wife of the elderly United States Consul Robert K. Jeffers, while the dashing young landowner Emilio Ballestero whirled around with tall, horsy Hariett Whitlaw. Over near the stage where the orchestra was playing, Mrs. Whitlaw's husband, David, the rich banana plantation owner, was deep in conversation with his general manager, brawny, low-browed Frank Kelly. By the window, between a pair of potted palms, Brian's lawyer, Licenciado Aquilino de Benito, appeared to be discussing a pending court case with his arch enemy, State Prosecutor Pancho

Cuevas, while their fat middle-aged wives flirted with young Pablo Zimmerman and Buddy Wasson, the sons of local shipping merchants. . . . It was an ossified, ingrown society, for the most part. Cut off from the rest of the world by geography, underdevelopment, and its own exaggerated fear of change, prevented by an almost pathological racial prejudice from accepting new blood from the lower orders, it had grown stale and stagnant over the years, and from Brian's point of view it was a crushing bore. Apart from his fellow railroader C. J. Hollister, who shared his disdain for local society and his preference for the low life of the port, Brian had no real friends in the set. But the room abounded with his old romantic rivals, political enemies and business competitors, including Emilio Ballestero, with whom he had once come very near to having a pistol duel over the favors of Eleanor Jeffers, and David Whitlaw, who was at present engaged in a brazen attempt to outbribe him in obtaining a lucrative government silver-mining concession, and Pancho Cuevas, the gringo-hating state prosecutor who had mounted a vicious campaign of character assassination to prevent Brian's election to the chairmanship of the Company. . . . If life in Manzanillo was insular and stifling, it was not without its little excitements, and these were what Brian lived for.

"I feel like bringing this bunch of stuffed shirts back to life!" he stage-whispered to Gallo, and launched himself into the ballroom.

"Go get 'em, chief!" said Gallo, slinking back into the shadows.

Yet the crowd was not so staid as Brian liked to pretend, and they were "stuffed shirts" perhaps only in comparison to the denizens of Boca de Pascuales. To the unaccustomed eye they might have appeared a reckless, rough-edged, rakish lot as they waltzed about the room in their sideburns and moustachios, their unplucked eyebrows and unshaven legs, hooting and stamping their feet to the music. They all went armed, even on the dance floor. Duels and vendettas were still commonplace among them, and their code of honor—*He who insults me, I will strike; he who strikes me, I will kill,* and its corollary, *He who refuses to fight like a man I will kill like a rabbit*—had led to much unpleasantness over the years, aggravated by the fact that the disputes of gentlemen were settled more often by jungle ambuscade than meetings at dawn, and one's seconds were more likely a band of hired assassins wielding Mausers and machetes than unarmed caballeros of one's own rank. This raw frontierlike atmosphere existed in astonishing contradiction to the fact that the city of Manzanillo was nearly half a millennium old, and had been in direct communication with the Orient for more than three hundred years when the first China Clipper set sail from Boston Harbor.

Little Carmen Mescalero was the first person to catch Brian's eye, as he drifted out onto the ballroom floor. She was dressed in peasant fiesta costume and looked surprisingly adult, and stunningly pretty, as she passed out drinks and hors d'oeuvres to the chattering guests. On an impulse he strode to her side, plucked the silver tray from her tiny hands and, despite her frantic whispered protestations and the raised eyebrows of his mother's guests, whirled her out on the floor to do a bolero that she would never forget, that would set the tongues wagging in Manzanillo for months to come.

"But señor, we shall make a spectacle!"

"Then a spectacle it shall be!"

It was an act of pure will, contrived to shock and subdue the creoles in the crowd in a show of public defiance. Again and again he led Carmen around the floor—her black hair flying, her wide skirts rising up to display her comely brown legs and thighs—compelling them through sheer bravado to swallow their prejudices and acknowledge her surpassing beauty, and his own indisputable superiority. They were a soft, malleable race, despite their habits of violence. Their culture was old but it was not strong. They were decadent and inbred. The Revolution had sounded their death knell, and they knew it: It was only a matter of time. They looked for salvation to the Republic of the North. But they were unsure of their origins; they were afraid they might not be Europeans. They suffered from a national inferiority complex that rendered them defenseless against intimidation based upon an assumption of moral ascendancy.

The bolero ended with a flourish of drums, a fanfare of trumpet and violins. The crowd parted. The creoles bowed and the gringos clapped politely as Brian, flushed and excited by his triumph, conducted his panting, perspiring young partner back to her silver tray.

When at last he thought to pay his respects to his mother, he found her fanning herself near one of the open archways. Mrs. O'Hare was seated with a group of creole ladies of about her own age, and she was conspicuous not only for her freckles and red hair; the others seemed withered and old by comparison. She was dressed that night in concert with conservative local tastes. But the effect was rather daring, since the styles of the flapper era still prevailed in Manzanillo, and skirts were worn that year six inches shorter than in Paris or New York: a fact that was all to Maureen's advantage, for she had the longest and best-kept pair of legs in Colima State.

"Did you enjoy your little fling?" she asked, rising to receive his kiss.

"I did indeed, Mama."

"But now you smell of cheap perfume," she said. She had ambiguous feelings about the Carrizo clan. "They're like cockroaches," she said of them. "You let them in and suddenly they're everywhere." But she had to admit that they were dependable workers, and they had made themselves indispensable in the running of the hotel.

"The cheap perfume was acquired earlier in the evening, I'm afraid."

"Oh dear," she said. "When am I ever going to settle you down?"

"When you find me an acceptable mate."

"Do such things exist in these parts?" she asked, switching to English.

"Possibly," he said, stroking his mustache.

"I wouldn't set my hopes too high," she said, glancing around at the thin hairy legs (in provincial creole society the women refused to shave their legs, so all the world could see that they were unpolluted by indigenous blood) of Mari-Eugenia Ichigaray and Melinda de Benito.

"They ever get around to enforcing their laws against alien ownership of property, down here," Brian said to his mother, while smiling and nodding politely at Señoritas Ichigaray and de Benito, "and a native wife might come in handy."

"I wonder which is the lesser evil."

"Come on, Maureen," he said, seating her among the grinning, uncomprehending creole ladies again. "You're an old Mexico hand. You wouldn't be worth a damn anywhere else, and you know it."

"Unfortunately," she said, sighing, "I suppose you're right. And that's why lately I've made some attempt to conform to local customs. It might behoove you to do the same."

"It might," he said. And then something moved him to add, spitefully, "But you have more reason to be concerned with convention, haven't you?"

Why he had chosen precisely this moment to allude, however elliptically, to Maureen's seven-year-old indiscretion, he couldn't say. But he could see that his words had reached their mark, and it made him perversely glad. At the same time he felt sorry for her, because he knew they were two of a kind. The problem was . . . she was a middle-aged woman, after all. She had no business looking so youthful and long-legged and sexy. She was his mother. He had always hated it when she displayed traits of his own dissolute character. Yet on another level he had spent his entire life proving to her that he was a chip off the old maternal block; and he could barely remember his self-destructive little swillhound father.

The instant he left her he found himself avoiding all his acquaintances and marching defiantly across the room to Ramona. He caught sight of her behind the punchbowl, where she had been pressed into service alongside Grandma Carrizo. She was wearing the same peasant costume as Carmen and Grandma, with the addition of a pair of large gold earrings, and she looked, as he expressed it to himself, "hauntingly beautiful." Meaning that there was something in her that at once aroused his protective instincts and produced in his belly a sense of profound and constant loss.

"You're trembling," he said, after he'd overwhelmed her serving maid's obligatory defenses and swept her out on the floor to dance. "I thought you might be expecting me."

"Yes," she said. "I was afraid you might do something like this."

"You don't like to dance with me?"

"I don't think it's right."

"It's the first time I've touched you since the day I saw you at the river washing my shirts," he said, not listening, feeling her hips sway lightly to his command, searching those great dark eyes for a glimmer of the emotion that had engulfed him the moment he pressed her into his arms.

"I don't like to be made a fool of, Don Brian."

"Any man would want to touch you."

"Any?"

"Even him," he said, tossing his head at the handsome young comandante, who stood near the stage, head and shoulders above a circle of fawning sycophants and ardent female admirers.

"Colonel Mondragón doesn't even know I exist," she said, blushing. "And you have barely spoken to me since my family moved into your hotel."

"Your beauty is daunting."

"Or familiarity breeds contempt."

"You've got me wrong, señorita," he said, and fell to brooding over her sanguinary reaction to the mention of Colonel Mondragón.

It was not the first time that he had brooded over the comandante in the past few days. Aside from his dashing good looks, and his obvious appeal to the ladies, the man had enough theoretical power to make life exceedingly difficult for the Company. After all, no one knew enough about him to be sure who he really was, or what he represented. He had been out of the country for several years, it was said, as an embassy attaché in Paris and Moscow. And his politics were a matter of some question. He was believed to be a protégé of General Sánchez, the military caudillo of Jalisco and Colima, under whom he had served in the Revolution, and during the Cristero Rebellion. This was thought to be a good sign, as the Company had been paying off General Sánchez on a monthly basis for years, relying on his puppets, State Governor Nacho Ibañez and Mayor of Manzanillo Tito Bejár, his corrupt chief magistrate, Pépé Calderón, and his bloodthirsty captain of police, Vasco Camacho (the only representatives of the mestizo race to be invited here tonight) to keep a restive peasantry and proletariat in check while it consolidated political and economic control of the state. On the other hand, Colonel Mondragón was also known to have served with General Lázaro Cárdenas, and to have maintained ties with him ever since. And General Cárdenas had just been elected President of the Republic on a platform of agrarian reform, wholesale nationalization, and flagrant anticapitalism.

Brian remained moodily silent until their tango had come nearly to an end, and then he said suddenly: "Why do you suppose a distinguished officer like Mondragón has been sent to a provincial backwater like this?"

"I can't imagine," she said. And then: "They say he's an honest man."

"If so, he's a rare breed," Brian said. "But, you know, General Sánchez might have appointed him for more devious reasons. He might have sent him out here to kill two birds with one stone. Figures he'll placate Cárdenas and the socialists while he scares us out of more bribery money. See what I mean?"

"I'm afraid you've lost me, señor," she said. "But the colonel seems a long way from political intrigue tonight."

"He's been kept in the dark," Brian said. "He's a fall guy."

"For a fall guy," Ramona said, "he seems to be doing all right for himself."

Something in her tone made Brian turn again toward Mondragón. And he discovered that the comandante was no more insensible to Ramona's charm than he. At any rate, he seemed patently more interested in her than in anyone nearer at hand. Brian also noted that the interest was possibly mutual, though it is always hard to tell what lies behind the veiled glances of a beautiful young girl.

It was precisely because Brian cared so much for Ramona that he suddenly felt compelled to prove his worst suspicions, and break his own heart. He continued to watch Ramona and Mondragón very carefully, and then after one particularly exuberant Argentine tango he left her off in front of the comandante.

"Andale pues, mi coronel!" he shouted, with frantic gaiety. And there was nothing the colonel could do but take Ramona into his arms and waltz her out onto the floor.

He seemed delighted to stretch his legs with a pretty girl again. And Ramona entered into the spirit of the dance boldly, following him with her head held high, her red mouth laughing, her heels clicking, conveying to the crowd, and to her mistress who stood tapping her fingers tentatively on the sidelines, an air of the most glittering conquest.

Never, never, never again in her life would Ramona be quite so young, quite so radiant, quite so happy and hopeful and intoxicated with herself. Somewhere inside she knew this. And it added a certain pathos that Brian found enticing.

The magic ended all too soon, however, when little Chris and Merle came running out on the floor in their nightclothes and Ramona had to take them back up to the nursery and read them to sleep.

When the time came to make the presentation to the new comandante, Monsignor LeFevre, bishop of Manzanillo, rose and went to the stage, accompanied by Brian, Colonel Mondragón, Governor Ibañez, Mayor Bejár, Chief Magistrate Calderón, and Captain Camacho.

The monsignor, who came from a fine old family of these parts, had been posted to the papal nuncio's office in Mexico City for a number of years, and had only very lately received his purple biretta and returned to his native place as bishop. And apparently he could not resist showing off the vestments of his new office to his friends and family gathered here tonight, for he was wearing his traditional white tropical cassock, purple sash and biretta in defiance of the federal laws against the wearing of priestly garb in public.

As soon as he reached the podium, he blessed the crowd and turned to the colonel, who stood beside him.

"My dear comandante," he said. "I wonder if you recognize me after all these years."

"I . . . I believe I do," said Mondragón, his momentary confusion revealing a more sensitive side of his nature than his fierce slanting green eyes, his hanging black mustache, his bridgeless hawk nose and extreme pallor had suggested.

"Ladies and gentlemen, señores, señoras y señoritas," the bishop intoned, "I owe my life to your comandante. . . ."

And then he proceeded to recount a hair-raising tale of the Cristero Rebellion, in which a young first captain in the Federal Army, Raúl Mondragón, had to face down his own men to save Padre LeFevre's life. It seemed that they had become infuriated when another priest, a Father Dowd, escaped their captivity. And they were about to summarily execute Padre LeFevre and his driver when Captain Mondragón ordered them up the road at gunpoint. Then he went through the charade that had been arranged beforehand. He pretended to shoot his prisoners, and he left them lying in a ditch. When the soldiers were gone, Padre LeFevre and his driver simply got back into their truck and drove away.

"For this humane and courageous act," the bishop said, "I shall always remain indebted to our new comandante, and I wish to take this opportunity to welcome him to our beautiful city of Manzanillo."

Among the crowd of politely applauding guests, Maureen O'Hare stood out in her son's eyes for the extraordinary way she reacted to the bishop's speech. As the story unfolded she seemed to grow more and more restless. She appeared to lose her breath for a moment, then she blanched and clutched at her throat.

What's the matter with her? he wondered. Can it be that she's finally getting old? Suddenly she reeled and lost her footing. And Consul Jeffers had to support her till Brian could reach her from the stage.

"It's just the heat, the heat . . ." she gasped, as he conducted her to a chair.

But Brian feared she was withholding something from him. Perhaps even some kind of mild stroke. And he sat fanning her briskly till her color came back.

When Brian's turn at the podium came, after the mayor and the governor, he made it quick. He was not a public speaker, certainly not one in the florid Mexican style, and his mother's discomfiture had left him flustered and preoccupied.

"As a token of our esteem for your distinguished office, mi coronel," he said, in stiff formal Spanish, "we have arranged to make available for your disposition a modern means of private transport that we trust will be of service in the discharge of your public duties. If you will be so kind as to step out on the terrace and look below, I think you will not be disappointed."

Whereupon the loud honking of a large American motor car could be heard in the street, and the crowd smiled knowingly.

Colonel Mondragón declined the invitation, however, causing an uneasy rustle in the audience, and in an unusually deep and resonant voice, began his own speech. He had prepared it beforehand, and he read it with great expression, even passion, looking up frequently from his text to convince Brian and the audience of his sincerity.

"I appreciate the sentiment behind your gift," he said, "but I must very humbly decline it, with great thanks. For I firmly believe that such harmless displays of goodwill lead inevitably to corruption and bureaucratic incompetence, and it is my task, as outlined by our new president, to root out these vestiges of the Porfiriate wherever they may be found. Moreover, I must tell you in all frankness that I have been conjoined to strictly enforce our Constitution in Colima State, including those articles pertaining to agrarian reform, workers' rights, economic exploitation, foreign ownership of property, and the role of the Church. . . ."

Neither Brian nor the rest of the audience had expected their worst nightmares to be confirmed so swiftly or forthrightly. And the effect of the comandante's speech, which went on in the same vein for another twenty minutes, was to leave them all dumbfounded. There was such an appalling silence when he stepped down from the stage, in fact, that Maureen felt compelled to rouse herself from her swoon long enough to signal the orchestra to strike up a gay Strauss waltz, so the colonel could at least withdraw in peace. Which he had the decency to do forthwith, disappearing down the stairway shortly after having paid his final respects to the hostess, and to the surprised and delighted Ramona who received him with awkward curtsies behind the canapés.

Only when the colonel had departed did the crowd come back to life, breaking up on the dance floor into loudly conversant groups of five and six irate gentlemen, while the ladies were left to twitter excitedly among themselves on the sidelines.

Brian avoided Don Cruz Herrera and old Sol Zimmerman, who clamored for his attention in the name of the creole planters and foreign traders, of whom they were the most respected and powerful representatives, and gained admittance into a pretentious, self-conscious little group of their hired mestizo lackeys, including Governor Ibañez, Mayor Bejár, Chief Magistrate Calderón, and Captain of Police Camacho.

Chief Magistrate Calderón, who was a great fat man with kinky white hair and thick negroid lips, was quoting Colonel Mondragón, scathingly.

" 'Now, I expect that some of you may face certain temporary difficulties as a result of our new policies,' he says."

"What he doesn't seem to realize," said Governor Ibañez, a tiny, elegant old fellow of nearly pure Tarascan blood, "is that the economy of this state is a very fragile thing."

"He'll destroy the economy," Brian said. "It's as simple as that. He'll harm the very people he means to help."

"Then it's unanimous," said big, pockmarked Captain Camacho, and his sinister undertone left no doubt as to the subject of their unanimity.

"Now hold on a minute," Mayor Tito Bejár, a bespectacled, serious-looking young man who was renowned in Manzanillo for his remarkable record of attendance at church (it was said that he had never missed a daily Mass in his life). "Surely he deserves another chance. Let's send someone over to explain how it is. Perhaps we could even send Bishop LeFevre. He knows how we do things here."

"And if he persists?"

"We'll go directly to General Sánchez," Brian said, "and seek his dismissal."

"And if the general refuses?"

"Why, that's simple; we'll bribe him to change his mind."

"Of course," said Mayor Bejár.

"Why didn't I think of that?" asked Governor Ibañez.

"It takes a gringo," said Chief Magistrate Calderón, in a typically Mexican blending of sarcasm and self-mockery, "to come up with the humane solution, no?"

And they had a nice long laugh of nervous appreciation all around their circle of sweating, white-suited conspirators, after which Brian returned to his own set and left the mestizos to chat among themselves.

Next day, despite all of Monsignor LeFevre's most noble efforts on the Company's behalf, Mondragón refused to see reason. It quickly became apparent that he was deadly serious about "cleaning up" the state of Colima, starting with the police, the judiciary and the state government, and finishing with the planters and hacendados, whose great landholdings he intended to purchase in the name of the government and turn over to the peasants as collective farms. The "bonds" with which he proposed to acquire these properties were not worth the paper they were printed on, as everyone in Mexico knew. In addition, the bishop said, Mondragón was resolved to begin immediate proceedings, as a friend of the court, against the foreign domination of local commerce. Not to mention the bishop's clerical garb, which the comandante had as much as threatened to tear off him bodily, if he ever saw him in it again.

The Company was thrown into a panic by the bishop's report, which he delivered at their weekly Wednesday meeting of the Club de Leones, in the private dining room at the Hotel O'Hare.

"Gentlemen, gentlemen," Brian said, pounding his gavel on the table. "Please be calm. Don Carlos, Mr. Kelly, Dr. Weber, take your seats, please. If you think about it, this was not exactly an unexpected occurrence."

"He's right," said Don Miguel Castañeda. "We have only ourselves to blame. We've been spoiled, out here."

"Spoiled?" shouted David Whitlaw angrily. "I don't feel in the least bit spoiled. I've put my life into my plantation, and I don't intend to see it lost to some tinhorn . . ."

"Now David," said old Sol Zimmerman, sighing, catching the younger man by the sleeve. "You listen to me. We have been lucky. This wave of socialism that's sweeping over the rest of the Republic, it's barely made a ripple here. And we all started to take it for granted that we'd be spared the worst."

" '*Workers and Peasants of Mexico, Unite!*' That was Cárdenas's campaign slogan," said Brian. "I mean, we were definitely forewarned."

"Brian," said Don Enrique Acienega, "this whole conversation is pointless. Let's stop making excuses, and start making plans to take control of the situation again."

"Hear, hear!" said young Emilio Ballestero, jumping to his feet. "Let's get down to action."

"I move that we empower our chairman with authority to negotiate with the caudillo," said Floyd Calvin, an old English sea captain who'd married a local creole woman and was now employed as harbormaster, under the nominal leadership of the captain of the port, Ceferino Noriega, an incompetent relative of General Sánchez. "As high as fifteen thousand dollars American."

"Any seconds to that motion?"

"Seconded."

"You all heard the motion before the chair. All in favor say 'aye.' "

"Aye!"

There were no nays, and the next day Brian hastened with his man Gallo to Guadalajara to press for an audience with General Sánchez.

The general, a squat, swart, blustery old bowlegged bandido who for ceremonial occasions still affected the boots, spurs, charro pants, bolero jacket and wide black sombrero he had worn in the Revolution, received Brian in his suite at the comandancia militar with abrazos and wet, whiskery, mescal-scented kisses.

"Don Brian, Don Brian O'Hare!" he bellowed. "I am so enchanted to see you that I can barely believe my eyes. Is this a mirage? Such a fine-looking young caballero. And so simpático. What is it you need, my friend? My house, my horse, my car, my wife are at your orders. A gun? You want a gun? You should see the new Mausers I have just received from Germany. A personal gift from Herr Hitler. Ya? How about a woman, eh? There is a French lady in Guadalajara who got her training in the harem of the Bey of Algiers, they say. The most exquisite delights. You want her? She's yours. Just say the word."

"It seems a veritable dream, mi general, and I thank you from the bottom of my heart," Brian began. Yet, he was not foolish enough to take Saturnino Sánchez's effusions as anything but the most formal courtesy. And he proceeded to recite the supplicant's traditional flowery words of compliment and obeisance. "But I regret to say that I have come for other more mundane considerations. However, if on another occasion I might be permitted to avail myself of your unparalleled and justly celebrated hospitality, I should be overwhelmed with happiness. . . ."

A ritual out of darkest Araby. Brian did everything but prostrate himself before the fat little brown potentate. But it was all necessary if you wanted to survive and get on. Anyway, it was nearly second nature to him by now, as he had learned on his mother's knee how to deal with men of power and influence in Mexico: If you seek rights or privileges, then you must expect to pay, if not with abiding loyalty and obedience (for the world is treacherous and men are fickle by nature), then at least with respect and a tangible show of gratitude.

After Brian had bowed and scraped for the customary length of time, he finally came to the point. He outlined the current intolerable situation in Manzanillo and the state of Colima in some detail, and concluded with an impassioned plea that Colonel Mondragón be removed from his command forthwith on the grounds of "economic sabotage," or at the very least, gross incompetence.

But General Sánchez was a cunning old deceiver. And, as Brian expected, he did not reply immediately or directly. Instead, he began a long rambling monologue recalling his relationship with Colonel Mondragón.

"Raúl Mondragón is the son of a poor ranchero from Jalisco," the general said. "He joined the Revolution at the age of fifteen, and despite his years he distinguished himself in battle. He attracted my notice, and I saw that he rose up quickly through the ranks. By the time he was eighteen he was leading his own cavalry troop in the Battle of Celaya. For years he never left the saddle. He fought at my side from one end of Mexico to the other. But he was a sensitive boy, and he suffered bitter disappointment when he observed at first hand all the twists and turnings and cynical machinations that one had to pull off in order to survive in those chaotic times. After one such episode, when I was forced by political circumstances to suddenly switch allegiance three times in one month," the general said, laughing at the memory, "there were harsh words between us and he left my service to join General Cárdenas in Vera Cruz. But then years later, when I sent for Raúl during the Cristero Rebellion, he made no protest and he accomplished his task with honor. Likewise, when I sent for him only recently, he made no protest then either. And until this very moment I assumed he was performing his duties satisfactorily. But now from what you have just reported to me, Señor O'Hare, it seems that Raúl may have turned spiteful and ungrateful, and betrayed all the trust I have placed in him. Frankly, I'm afraid he's more under the thumb of General Cárdenas than I had supposed. Raúl's wife, Ana-María, you know, is a relative of Señora Cárdenas."

"No," said Brian, surprised and delighted to learn that Mondragón was married. "I didn't know."

"Oh yes," said General Sánchez, smiling, shrugging his shoulders. "So you see, it's a pity, Don Brian, but there is nothing to be done. General Cárdenas is President of the Republic, and I am only a mere regional military commander. . . ."

General Sánchez went on in the same vein for a few more minutes, protesting and complaining that there was nothing he could do, but Brian knew that the old fox was beholden to no man in this part of Mexico. President Cárdenas had not yet begun to consolidate his power over the states, and he was facing grave difficulties even in the capital. He had alienated the former president, General Calles, who had nominated him with the understanding that he would act as a mere figurehead for his own political machine. Calles had been unpleasantly surprised by his protégé's fierce independence, and now he was conspiring with an old guard faction of the army to topple him in a coup de'état. The conspiracy was no secret, indeed it was the talk of Mexico, and Cárdenas was desperately seeking allies wherever he could find them. Now that he had mollified the left wing of his own party, it was rumored that he was actually contemplating a secret alliance with the Catholics, who were still furious with him over his expropriation of their clerical schools and his commitment to "free, universal, socialist education." If the rumor was true, it only made General Sánchez more secure on his throne. Because, incredible as it might seem, he had enjoyed excellent relations with the archbishop of Guadalajara ever since the end of the Cristero Rebellion (when he permitted him to return from exile and serve Mass again in the cathedral), and the Church wholeheartedly supported his reign as caudillo in Jalisco and Colima States.

Nevertheless, and despite all of his suspicions, Brian took Saturnino's bad news in good grace. And in the baroque, euphemistical Spanish that one employed to communicate such things, he offered to double the general's monthly bribe.

His excellency pretended to misapprehend Brian's talk of money, however, and grumbled, "I'll do what I can." By which he meant: "I accept your puny bribe, only because I never refuse a bribe, but I won't guarantee anything." Then he signaled that the audience was at an end. By which Brian understood that he intended to make him sweat for a few more months, while he continued to play the Cárdenas regime for what he could get out of it, and then to extract even more money from the Company.

But Brian revealed none of this in his manner. He merely expressed his disappointment that there was nothing to be done at present, and ventured to hope that the situation might improve in the near future. He thanked the general kindly for his help, and made his departure from the comandancia with what he thought was a pretty clear idea of Saturnino's ultimate intentions. Eventually they would come to terms, he thought, and this gave him an optimistic view of his future in Mexico.

But on the train home to Manzanillo, with a bottle of tequila under his belt, he began to have his Irish doubts.

Apropos of nothing, he turned to Gallo and spoke his mind.

"You know," he said, gesturing out the window at the tiny, terraced fields of cane and corn, at the great smoking volcano beyond the yellow cliffs of the Sayula Grade, "I like to run this country down, but I don't know what I'd do if I ever had to leave."

"In the end," Gallo said, shaking his head insincerely, "there's only one way you're gonna beat 'em, chief."

"Are you pandering your sister-in-law again, Gallo? Because, if you are, this time I'm inclined to listen. The stakes have risen around here, all of a sudden."

"I couldn't be more in sympathy with you, chief," Gallo said. But he didn't sound very sympathetic at all.

After they had polished off the second bottle, Brian surprised himself by pounding the little dent-headed greaser on the back and hollering out in English, "I'm gonna do it, cuñado, I'm gonna ask her to marry me before she is utterly captivated by that ignorant idealistic sonofabitch!"

"Smart," Gallo lisped. "With a Mex for a wife the government will play hell getting ahold of your property."

But Brian in his ardor, and his cups, took offense at Gallo's cynical interpretation of his motives, and spoke sentimentally, as gringos in Mexico will do, of giving himself heart and soul to the "Cosmic Race," and even of "embracing the earth."

Gallo arranged a meeting as soon as they got home.

Ramona came to him in the empty after-hours dining room, still dressed in her barmaid's outfit. She wore a guarded expression which he was unaccustomed to seeing on a face so young. It gave him the faintest hope that she was trying to conceal some feeling of affection for him.

"I want you to be my wife," he said, before she could even reach his table.

"I think what you really want," Ramona said, standing across from him as if she were about to take his dinner order, "is to evade the law."

"What law?"

"The alien ownership law."

"Nobody wants to lose what he owns," he said. "But I would've asked you anyway."

"I could never be sure of that."

"You need time to consider. Maybe you'll change your mind."

"I don't think so."

"I'm sorry," he said, holding tenuously to his hope. He glanced around his mother's gleaming, candlelit dining room. "I marvel at your pride. I mean, to give up all of this . . ."

"Maybe I want to embrace the earth."

"Did Gallo tell you that?"

"He thought it was funny."

"I was a little drunk; I saw you as a symbol."

"I don't want to be a symbol."

"You have no choice in the matter," he said. "But I could make you happy."

"I'm not at all sure," Ramona said, turning to go up to her room, "that happiness is my fate."

"If you're thinking of Colonel Mondragón," he shouted after her, hating himself, "you might as well forget it! He's got a wife in Mexico City."

But Ramona did not deign to respond to his outburst, and went clicking up the marble stairs in her Cuban heels as if she had not heard.

CHAPTER 4

When the rainy season came—and it came a month early in 1935—the nights seemed to go on forever. Sleep was impossible. There was no rest from the heat and humidity of the day. The skin became feverish, even when exposed to the ceiling fan. The body trembled, yet it sweated like a mule, soaking through the sheet, attracting hordes of giant malaria-bearing mosquitoes that chewed through the netting to buzz excitedly around the feast. Even a moment's repose was difficult, under these extreme conditions, and peace of mind was unknown. In the Hotel O'Hare the walls between the rooms quit a foot short of the ceiling, and all the doors and windows were left permanently ajar, to allow for cross-ventilation. In such a place there were no secrets. You could hear a guest eating peanuts from across the courtyard. You could hear a fart from the fourth floor. If Don Brian or anyone else, anywhere in the building, started to snore, it sounded as if it were coming at you from every direction at once. A nightmare shriek from little Chris or Merle would awaken the entire hotel. And when a couple of honeymooners decided to make love, you were part of the act.

In rainy-season Manzanillo, night was the enemy, night was the little death. Yet, it was alive with sound. Thunder cracked over the coastal range, or far out to sea. And from deep within the Volcán de Colima the earth responded. In the town the church bells chimed every quarter of an hour. Dogs howled like coyotes at the moon. Cocks crowed around the clock. Cicadas sizzled like high-tension wires. And the long blue frogs by the riverbank never let up on their odd, roiling nightwhistle.

Then at six o'clock in the morning the great bell in the cathedral would ring so loudly you would think your skull was hollow and made out of brass. The little pardal birds that nested in the tacamo trees alongside the hotel would take flight in their thousands, flapping madly around the plaza. The ships in the harbor would start hooting back and forth at one another. And dawn like a scorpion would come creeping across the red-tile floor. Abruptly the town would awaken. The municipal band would come marching down the Avenida Mexico to assist the navy in the raising of the national flag outside the palacio municipal. Donkey trains from the outlying villages would come splashing and plopping through the muddy streets, followed by high-wheeled, ox-drawn carts and great herds of flea-bitten little goats with bells around their necks. Then vendors of newspapers, fruit juice, coconuts, tacos and pan dulce would appear, calling out their wares. And the entire population of Manzanillo, it seemed, would stand scratching and stretching and yawning by their front windows, shouting to the neighbors at the tops of their lungs.

A fertile breeding ground for insomniacs. And such was the night clerk Gallo Carrizo. Stark awake, he lay in his soiled boxer shorts on a cot behind the reception counter. It was the fifth morning of May, Cinco de Mayo, a national holiday in Mexico. And he was restlessly awaiting the arrival of his mother, the hotel cook, who would open the kitchen and set the coffee brewing.

But it was not only for coffee that Gallo yearned.

He had survived the night with catnaps and tantalizing dreams of El Dorado, interspersed with mental flashes of his beautiful sister-in-law Carmen's pubic area, from which he would awaken every few moments with a terrible start. It was the way he survived all his nights, and all his days too, for that matter. But it gave him a slightly demented, paranoid look that alarmed him when he saw it in the mirror, for he thought it made him seem shifty and unreliable, and he was convinced that he operated on trust.

Apart from an unsightly dent in his crown which he managed to hide quite successfully with his curly, luxuriant black hair, insomnia was the only lasting effect of the old head injury that Gallo had sustained at the hands of a renegade priest in the Cristero Rebellion. Unfortunately, however, Gallo's sleeplessness had become more acute since his return from Texas, and even his move from the squatters' camp last year had done nothing to remedy it. As a matter of fact, life at the Hotel O'Hare was not that much of an improvement over the squatters' camp, from Gallo's point of view. And the hours were much longer. Aside from his job as night clerk, for instance, Gallo was also a full-time employee of the Colima Pacific Railroad, assigned as a personal aide to the trainmaster, Don Brian O'Hare. In the evenings and on holidays he worked behind the hotel bar, and sometimes he even doubled as waiter. Likewise with Grandma Carrizo. She was not only chief cook and bottle washer at the hotel, she was laundress and chambermaid as well. And Carmen was not just a chambermaid, but a luncheon and dinner waitress and occasional body servant for Doña Maureen. Ramona was not merely a nanny to little Chris; she did all the shopping for the hotel, took care of her nephew Merle all day, and worked as a cocktail waitress after the children were put to bed.

Nor were living conditions at the Hotel O'Hare much of an improvement over the squatters' camp, as far as Gallo was concerned. The "servants' quarters," into which he had once been so anxious to move, were in reality nothing more than another one-room, thatch-roofed cane shack built on the flat roof of the hotel, handy to the laundry room and the clotheslines.

The truth was, Gallo and his family were better off at the hotel only perhaps in terms of plumbing and address. But address was important to Gallo. So important was it, in fact, that he had cut off all his friends and neighbors from the Fifth of May Encampment on the day he moved out, and forbade his womenfolk to recognize them if they ran into them in the street.

He saw himself as a man in a hurry, a man on his way up. He welcomed friendship only if it could be of use in the achievement of his aims. And his aims were extraordinary, for a man of his time and country and class. He wanted money. He wanted respect. He wanted power. He wanted to be a worthy patriarch of his family. And finally, he wanted Carmen, if he could afford to keep her. He resented servitude, and he would never forgive the O'Hares for treating him like a peón, though he had been so desperate when they hired him that even slavery looked like paradise to him. At the same time, he knew that there was no other way to the top except by riding on the O'Hares' coattails. Therefore, he could betray none of his true feelings. Not even his feelings for Carmen.

The problem was, her sister Ramona had laid waste to all of Gallo's most carefully laid plans. In her romantic determination to throw away her future—and the future of her family as well—she had declined Don Brian's honorable suit in favor of the tepid attentions of the espoused and encumbered comandante, attentions which consisted in any case of little more than a show of egalitarianism, a kiss on the hand when they chanced to meet in the hotel lobby, an occasional paseo in the plaza.

But Ramona had always been a disappointment to Gallo, ever since she was an early-ripe fourteen and willfully resisted his manful advances time and again while his wife was out at work . . . even ran and tattled on him, one time up in El Paso.

Carmen, on the other hand, had always been more open to reason. And her value in the sexual marketplace had increased inversely to her sister's recent decline. Gallo, marveling at his own selflessness, had even gone so far as to suggest as much to Don Brian.

"Hey, chief," he had whispered one day while he was shining his shoes, "why you mope around? You want Ramona? You got another one just like her, right up on the roof."

Regardless of current market conditions, however, Gallo could not resist sampling his own wares from time to time. He was looking forward to sampling them right now, in fact, if he could keep it quiet enough.

Fretting on his sweat-soaked bed, with an enormous erection throbbing in his boxer shorts, he could not wait for his mama to come down from the servants' quarters. He leaped from the bed, throwing on his white cotton pants, his white guayabera shirt and black gypsy hat, his shoulder holster with the 8mm Beretta that he never went without, and raced up the stairs two at a time. He had to hurry. The house was already starting to stir. On the second floor he could hear Ramona talking with little Chris.

"What're you doing up so early, Chris?"

"I can't *sleeeeeep* anymore."

"Why not?"

"Too excited, too excited!"

"What for?"

"It's the Cinco de Mayo, the Cinco de Mayo!"

"Leave me alone for another half hour, won't you, honey?"

"No, no, no, no, *noooooo*."

Up on the roof Gallo could see his mama, a black rebozo over her head, kneeling and praying before a tin-can shrine that she had dedicated to the Holy Infant of Atocha. She had covered the can with a colorful Indian blanket and pushed it up under the red-tile eaves of the laundry room, to keep it out of the rain. It was equipped with a grotto, a cross, a picture of the Holy Infant Himself, candles, offerings, ceramic cups, paper streamers, a manger, Xmas-tree ornaments, and several bunches of yellow cempasuchiles, the traditional flower of mourning hereabouts. Despite its small size and makeshift qualities, the shrine had about it the musty, well-used authenticity of certain old private chapels, and from Gallo's perspective it was a religious success. But he wasn't much for religion anyway.

He hid from his mother behind the long, damp lines of hotel laundry that she had hung on clotheslines across the roof, nursing his erection, waiting for her to disappear.

He shivered, though it was even hotter up here than down below. From between the hanging white sheets he could see the cathedral, the municipal palace, the customs house, the bank, all of them festooned with red-white-and-green flags and banners proclaiming revolutionary slogans—"Tierra y Libertad!" "Viva la Reforma Agraria!" "Obreros de Mexico, Unir!" "A Bajo el Sinarquismo!" The plaza was already crammed with peasants from the mountains and agrarian activists from the Fifth of May Encampment, squatting on the wet cobblestones in their rubber-tire sandals, smoking cornhusk cigarettes with their sombreros pulled down over their eyes, awaiting the beginning of the folk play that was performed in the plaza every year at this date. Farther away, over cranes and drydocks and sailboat rigging and swirling pelicans and the superstructures of tramp steamers from the United States, the lagoon and bay lay flat and dull as greenmold. Low, steamy white clouds clung to the steep jungle hills all around, and the air lay heavy on the roof of the Hotel O'Hare.

Gallo distrusted this roof.

One night he sneaked up for a quickie with Carmen and he saw a ghost. It was his dead wife. Grandma Carrizo had seen it too, a couple of times. And Carmen, once. Grandma consulted a bruja, to find out why María would want to haunt them so. "She died before her little one," the bruja said, "and the little one died unbaptized. They went to different places. Now the mama comes to find her."

But Gallo had his own ideas about why she came back.

He had loved his wife, in his own way, but he hated her ghost. He hated the past in all its forms. He lived only for the future, he told himself. And he planned out his life years in advance.

After Grandma Carrizo had finished her morning prayers and gone down the stairs to work, Gallo stepped gingerly across the white gravel of the roof to the servants' quarters and peeked through the ragged wet blanket that served for a door. Grandma's pallet was made up with a black-and-red Indian blanket. Carmen and little Merle lay sleeping on her straw petate by the opposite wall. Merle was naked and Carmen was wearing one of Don Brian's old cast-off shirts. The shirt had crept up over her hips and buttocks during the night. She was lying on her side, in the fetal position, a beautiful, half-naked young girl of twenty. And Merle had pressed his runny little nose into the exquisite archway of earth-colored flesh formed by her curving hip, her tiny waist, and her rib cage.

Gallo envied his son more than was decent. Merle had slept with her every night since María died. There had been a trauma when he crawled under the shroud to sleep with his mama after she'd already turned stiff and was laid out for the wake. Coming only a few days after the incident in the toolshed with the monstrous little Chris, María's death had thrown the boy into a state of shock. Ever since then Carmen had accepted him as her own. To the point where she had become fastidious of Gallo's attentions if the boy was nearby.

But now Gallo had an idea. There were pigeons that lived on the roof. And yesterday he had noticed that one of them had hurt its wing and couldn't fly.

He let the blanket drop. He went across the roof and found the pigeon right where he'd seen it yesterday, on the roof of the laundry house. It was a pretty, dun-colored bird, but it was in very bad shape. He grabbed it and held it and stroked its feathers and its neck while it trembled in his hand. Then he went inside the laundry house and found a saucer that his mother used to feed the hotel cat. He filled it with water and fed a little to the bird. It beaked it up as if dying of thirst. But Gallo only let it drink a little. He filled the saucer to the brim again and put it down on the floor. Then, stroking the pigeon, he went across to the servants' quarters again and awakened his son, shaking him softly by the shoulder. He had turned into a strong, brown, healthy-looking little bugger in the months since they'd come to the Hotel O'Hare, a match for Chris, though she was two years older. But he was afflicted with his mother's soft, sweet nature, which Gallo was convinced he must guard against if he didn't want the kid to grow into a pansy. Like the Mescaleros too he was a heavy sleeper, and it took a good shaking to bring him around. Yet, he awoke with a great big smile. "Hi, Daddy," he whispered in English, which was the language of the nursery where he spent all his days. And he seemed delighted when Gallo showed him the pigeon.

"Can I pet it, Dad?"

"Not in here. Come on outside and I'll let you feed him."

"Oh boy!"

"Shhhhhh, you'll wake your auntie."

Gallo helped him into a pair of cut-off pants and led him by the hand to the laundry room where he'd left the saucer of water.

"Now," he said, "I'll let you pet him if you promise you'll stay here with him till I get back."

"I promise, I promise," the boy said, eagerly accepting the bird into his hand, stroking it gently.

"Okay. Now, you feed him that water, and if he wants more, give it to him. I'll be back in about five or ten minutes."

Gallo was trembling when he got back to the hut. He unbuttoned his pants and crawled onto the pallet beside Carmen. She was still on her side, facing away from him in the fetal position. He smoothed up against her from the rear, pulled the collar of her shirt down, and started to kiss her on the neck and ears. Soon she was sighing and arching her back in her sleep. With one hand Gallo held her tight by the hipbone. With the other he touched her wet from behind, and guided himself inside. At some point he rode her over, and she began to fuck the sheets.

It was over too soon. But in no time he had another erection.

"Where's Merle?" she wanted to know.

"He's downstairs."

"Oh," she said, smiling at him drowsily. And permitted further indulgences. Then, just as he was getting his stroke, he heard her say, from very far away, it seemed, "Wait, wait, I can hear him. He's talking to someone in the laundry."

"He's talking to a bird."

"What?"

"A pigeon with a broken wing."

"Then you lied."

"What do you mean, I lied?" He laughed. "So what?"

"You know I don't like it."

"He's never seen us."

"He has too. And it scared him."

"He didn't see us. I got him out fast."

"You were too rough on him," Carmen said. "He's only a baby."

But Merle was no baby. At five years old, Gallo was already selling chewing gum at the railroad station.

"You're gonna make a sissy out of him," he said.

"Believe me, there's no danger of that. He's all male."

"Remember what the doctor said. . . . I'd rather be done with a boy of mine than see him end up like that."

"What do you mean? Don't talk like that."

"I'll talk any way I like. He's been cut, ain't he?"

"I think you just feel guilty, 'cause you left him off that time your mama said leave him at home."

"That's all over and done with now."

"Uh-huh. Well, let me tell you something. In case you don't recall, that little 'cut' you're so worried about . . . is what got us into this hotel."

"What's so great about this hotel?" Gallo parried, but he knew he was licked. What he wanted to do was smack her one for sassing him back and then make her do it again from the rear. But he didn't dare, because he couldn't afford the ruckus she would make.

And she knew it.

Cursing, he hauled himself up off her. As he was buttoning up, he happened to glance toward the shady end of the shack and made a discovery which he decided to keep to himself.

There, shining in the sunlight that filtered through the cracks in the cane thatch, the wide, slanted blue eye of his son blinked twice and was gone.

Later, he found the pigeon with its neck broken. But he said nothing to the boy. Hell, the whole thing, it'll make a man out of him, he thought.

At ten o'clock that morning Gallo drove the O'Hares to Mass. The cathedral was only across the plaza, but the señora insisted. It was the ritual of the upper classes. They arrived in their old Packards and La Salle touring cars, each outdoing the other in the sumptuousness of their summer frippery, the width and breadth of their straw sun hats, and in the number of servants and hangers-on who accompanied them. In the

O'Hares' case, however, only the nanny, Ramona, came along, apart from Gallo as the chauffeur. It was thought unnecessary to include Grandma Carrizo, Carmen and little Merle. Besides, who would watch over the hotel?

Then after Mass there was a serenata and paseo in the plaza, which continued till the annual Cinco de Mayo folk play began at eleven. The serenata and paseo were another ritual, in which the municipal band sat up in the ornate cast-iron gazebo playing martial music while the gentry strolled around in a tight circle, the bourgeoisie in a wider circle, and the peasants on the farthest edge of the plaza.

Gallo considered himself very fortunate today, because he could sit up in the front seat of the O'Hares' big old V-16 touring car and watch the procession from a neutral distance. "Neutral" was a word that loomed large in his vocabulary. He thought of himself as an observer of life, not an active participant. Even when he was making love to the voluptuous Carmen, a part of him was always sitting back watching. It was his technique of survival. His father had died when he was nine. He had supported his mother and family ever since. First by shining shoes. Then by selling dirty pictures. Then by playing the marimba at a waterfront cantina. Then by plunder and theft in the Revolution. Then by doing the things that nobody else wanted to do for the Colima Pacific, till that fucking gringo priest came along and busted his skull and cut short his promising career as a railroad dick. Then by driving a taxi up in El Paso, and coming home every night to his little wood shack in Mexican Town and working another eight to ten hours with María and Carmen and Grandma Carrizo—Ramona being privileged to attend night classes at the local high school—doing piecework sewing, stitching and dyeing for a pennypinching Lebanese clothing manufacturer. . . . A highly checkered career, but he had never given up hope, though the odds seemed stacked against him from birth. What he did was—he remained detached, awaiting the breaks. He needed the distance of objectivity. He could afford no mistakes. Yet even when he did get a break, he never pounced like a cat. He sat back and watched for a surrogate through whom he could act.

Another reason that Gallo liked to stay neutral during the paseo was on account of the class warfare that went on in the plaza. Every Sunday and holiday there was much jostling for position on the fringes of the three estates; duels had even been fought over one's rightful proximity to the bandstand. And this was only one of the more simple and traditional forms of class warfare in Manzanillo, in addition to which there existed fantastically complex and numerous crosscurrents of envy and hatred that one could never explain to foreigners, no matter how long they had lived in the town. Expressed in its most elementary, vertical form, the class structure looked something like this: The peones envied the mestizos and could not wait to put on shoes, mingle their blood with their betters, and become mestizos too. Yet at the same time they hated the mestizos for their class privileges and desired nothing more than to topple them from their high horses and bring them down to their level. For their part, the mestizos disdained the peones, but could not help fearing them for the righteous anger and resentment that they displayed just under their show of humility. Meanwhile, the mestizos romanticized the peasants and pretended to yearn for a return to the simple, clean lives of their bucolic ancestors. Their attitude toward the creoles was exactly like that of the peones toward them, with this exception: They could not aspire to become white because it took too great a leap of the imagination. This gave them a fatalistic outlook that rendered them effectively the most stable of local classes. As for the creoles, they abused the peones, exploited the mestizos, and loathed the gringos while at the same time envying them their Yanqui self-assurance. The gringos looked down on everyone, and ridiculed the entire nation as a land of clowns and buffoons.

As a general rule, however, class in Manzanillo was a matter of color rather than cash, and the poorest, most rum-ridden gringo could always count on admission to the gazebo's inner circle, while the richest mestizo could never hope to rise out of the second circle. Servants were the one exception to the rule. And Ramona, for example, was permitted by custom to stroll around the gazebo as tightly as she pleased, as long as she had little white-skinned Chris along with her.

Today she had the tall young comandante by her side as well, and the two of them were engaged in animated conversation. They made a handsome couple, a symbol of the new egalitarianism that was sweeping Mexico—at least other parts of Mexico—and Gallo's heart softened toward them.

To think that a relative of Gallo Carrizo the garbage man's son could hope to be the mistress of such an elegant officer!

Confronted with a *fait accompli,* Gallo always liked to put the best face on things. After all, the colonel represented the federal government. And the government would be here long after the gringos were gone.

Who could know what the future might bring? Sometimes you got fooled, despite all your scheming. Gallo liked to cover all his bets, even the most implausible. With this in mind he had spoken to Ramona after breakfast this morning.

"That comandante has been pussyfooting around long enough. It's been months since he started sniffing at your door, and somebody better open up, let him in, and bring him to heel before he loses the scent. Now, if he really likes you, and he's the socialist he claims to be, how come he's beating around the bush? If you're good enough for the gringo to marry, then you sure as shit oughta be good enough for the comandante to take as his mistress. Who does he think he is? Look at them slanty eyes of his. And that low forehead. They ain't an Aztec in his woodpile somewhere back down the line, I'll kiss his ass."

Across the circle from the courting couple now, Don Brian had his mama on his arm. And he did not seem any too happy about it. Just couldn't get used to the idea of Ramona with Mondragón. Gallo'd never seen anything like it. He was losing weight. His eyes were red. His cheeks were hollow. Every morning it was another hangover worse than the last. He'd even laid off the whores here lately.

Gallo was encouraged by Don Brian's present symptoms, for they left him open to sabotage and eventual defeat. Ultimately, Gallo wanted it all. He knew his oppressor's weakness now, and he exploited it to the hilt every time he got the chance. And these romantic paseos in the plaza never failed to twist the knife.

After the serenata and the paseo came the obligatory patriotic speeches. But today they were mercifully brief, and the folk play began on schedule with a parade around the plaza. The play was called *La Batalla de Cinco de Mayo*. It was performed every year in Manzanillo, and it commemorated the victory over the French at Puebla on May 5, 1862. It treated of real historical events, and its characters were the opposing generals and their armies, played by a hundred or more local peasants and mestizo shopkeepers. Generally, the peasants were the troops and the mestizos were the officers. The creoles kept themselves out of the affair entirely, as they considered themselves above it.

General Ignacio Zaragoza had been commander of the Mexican army at Puebla, and each year a respected member of the petty bourgoisie was chosen by the mayor to play the role. The part called for him to ride a beautiful white stallion and to wear a magnificent silver-studded charro suit, a golden sword, and an enormous sombrero from the back of which dangled a "suncloth" embroidered with VIVA MEXICO! GRAL I. ZARAGOZA. All of which he had to pay for out of his own pocket. But the honor was so great that shopkeepers' sons fought for the role, and hawked their souls to Don Brian and other gringo usurers to pay off the debt.

This year the mayor had chosen Ildefonso Gochi, the scion of a prosperous family of mestizo fishmongers, to play the general. But the squatters at the Fifth of May Encampment, in honor of their namesake, had chosen a rival General Zaragoza. He was a landless peasant named Narciso Nieves, and Gallo knew him well, for they had been neighbors at the squatters' camp, and Narciso's wife Encarnita had even assisted in the birth of his short-lived baby daughter. Narciso was riding barefooted and bareback on an ancient swayback mule. A tall, cadaverous mulatto with nappy auburn hair, Narciso was dressed in his usual tatters, and in place of the general's elegant black felt sombrero and golden sword he wore a filthy battered straw hat with a stained rag hanging down the back, and a wooden sword like a child's toy. But Narcisco Nieves was far more exceptional than you could tell by looking. He had spent ten years in the United States, working in the mines of Arizona and Colorado. He had been a card-carrying member of the Wobblies until his deportation for syndico-anarchist agitation in 1929, and he was leader of an extremely well-organized agrarian activist and anticlerical faction called Red Shirts that ran the Fifth of May Encampment as a commune. The Red Shirts were a highly disciplined national organization of armed leftist radicals with close ties to the Mexican Communist Party. The display of poverty was therefore intentional, meant to call attention to the squatters' desperate plight, and to the fact that they were fed up with waiting for land under the terms of the Agrarian Reform.

But Gallo found he had little sympathy for their cause, now that he had removed himself from their squalid digs beside the city dump, and he laughed and ridiculed them along with the rest of the shoe-wearing population of Manzanillo, as they straggled around the plaza drinking homemade pulque and singing revolutionary songs off-key.

During the parade the competing General Zaragozas ignored each other, but when the play was about to begin they met in the center of the plaza with large retinues of inebriated compañeros behind them.

"Impostor!" Ildefonso cried.

"Lackey of the ruling class!" Narciso hollered.

The music stopped. The shouting died down on both sides. The crowd went still. And there was only the heat, the tropical humidity, the great sodden thunderheads massing overhead for the daily electrical storm.

"Get down off that mule, chango, before I knock you off."

"I'd like to see you try, chingado."

Ildefonso, obviously relishing the real-life drama, reared his stallion, jerked it around, and galloped furiously across the plaza to the cathedral, where he reined up before the reviewing stand in a cloud of dust, and appealed to the officials seated there.

"You hear the insolence, your excellencies, the defiance . . ."

"Ay, blow it out the other end, you bastard!" Narciso shrieked from across the square.

"This dog who dares to insult the memory of General Ignacio Zaragoza . . ."

"I'll insult you again, you stuffed shirt, if you ever come close enough!"

"Calmate, Ildefonso," the comandante demanded. "Calmate!"

But Ildefonso was past calming now, and more than a little caught up in his role. He stood up in the saddle, raised his golden sword above his head, and spurred his charger madly toward Narciso and the mule, screaming, "Die, false general, die!"

But before he got halfway across the plaza he was struck on the side of the head with a bottle thrown by someone in the crowd. He lost his sombrero. He lost his seat on the white stallion. He landed indecorously in the center of the plaza, bottom first, and his horse ran away with his silver saddle, never to be found again.

Some said later that the squatters *ate* that horse, and sold the saddle to a wandering Jew. But it was never proved.

Ildefonso was led from the scene with tears of bitter deflation streaming down his face. The police and the military moved rapidly to separate the two sides, and they were left to hurl insults at each other from opposite ends of the square, while all the spectators laughed.

"Get on with the play!" somebody hollered.

"This *is* the play!" Gallo shouted from the car.

Then Colonel Mondragón stood up on the reviewing stand and raised his hands for silencio.

"You ought to be ashamed of yourselves," he began, "embarrassing us all like this on our national holiday."

"You are the one who should be ashamed, mi coronel," Narciso piped up, as he approached on his spavined mule. "We heard that you were one of us. But our lives have not been improved since your arrival."

"Compañero," said Mondragón, "though I cannot condone your present behavior, I understand your frustrations. I too am disillusioned when I see the Revolution betrayed by corrupt officials."

"They why have you joined the ranks of the oppressors?"

"I am no oppressor! I have been a revolutionary since I was a boy and stole away on my father's horse to join Saturnino Sánchez's cavalry in the state of Michoacán."

"Saturnino Sánchez is a fascist, in league with the Church, the landowners, and the Sinarquistas!"

"What can I say, compañeros? Yesterday's heroes are today's bureaucrats."

"Like you, comandante?"

"Do not insult me, señor. I am a socialist and an agrarian reformist like you."

"Then kick the foreigners out and give us their land."

"We must await the decisions of the Superior Court."

"The Superior Court is corrupt."

"Then its decisions will be overturned by the Supreme Court."

"We are desperate men, mi coronel. That is too long for us to wait."

"We must have patience, compañeros. The Revolution was not won in a day."

"Then give us arms in the meantime, to defend ourselves against the counterrevolution which is gathering all around us."

"We must adhere strictly to the rule of law," said Mondragón. "The alternative is anarchy, and chronic underdevelopment."

"The alternative is freedom," Narciso shouted, "and the dictatorship of the proletariat!"

"Allow me to conduct you to the Fifth of May Encampment," said the comandante, coming down from the reviewing stand, grabbing the bridle of Narciso's little mule, looking around nervously to assess the effect of the mulatto's inflammatory words upon the polarized crowd. "There we shall be able to discuss such issues at greater length."

Whereupon the colonel led Narciso and his followers from the plaza.

But after the disturbance the folk play wasn't much fun anymore. The mayor cut it short and everyone went early to lunch.

Beyond a doubt, the best luncheon food in the state of Colima was served at the Hotel O'Hare. Grandma Carrizo had learned to cook at the Hotel Continental in El Paso, and she was unsurpassed in the art of Texan and Mexican cuisine. Apart from that, the Hotel O'Hare boasted the most relaxed and civilized atmosphere, the coolest and breeziest dining room, and the finest music: a three-piece conjunto of Veracruzanos whose soulful tenor voices and flying fingers on the harp, guitar and guitarrón were the hit of Manzanillo. As a consequence, every Sunday and holiday afternoon the place was jam-packed, and Mrs. O'Hare was obliged to put her entire staff and family to work. Even little Chris and Merle worked; they went around in fanciful peasant costumes serving candies, mints and party favors to the children. Even Don Brian worked; he acted as a genial floating host, circulating around the room, patting people on the shoulder and cracking jokes while his mama covered the entrance, checked reservations, seated customers and coordinated the activities of the kitchen, the dining room and the bar.

Gallo worked the bar. His job consisted mainly of drawing off cold Bohemia and Carta Blanca beer from iced kegs, and loading it onto Ramona's tray in great frothy mugs. As the luncheon wore on, Don Brian could be counted on to spend more and more time in Gallo's proximity, imbibing immoderately, receiving customers like a lord, perched above them on a bar stool. He received everyone, including rivals like Emilio Ballestero, David Whitlaw and Pancho Cuevas, for the Hotel O'Hare functioned exactly as Maureen O'Hare had intended, as a kind of living room or local public house for the creole and foreign communities, and it was accepted by general consensus as neutral ground. Even Colonel Mondragón, who had alienated practically the entire upper class of the district, was welcome at the hotel.

On the Cinco de Mayo the colonel got to the hotel later than was his habit, fresh from a fracas at the squatters' camp. His uniform was dusty, his puttees were muddy, he'd lost his forage cap somewhere, and everyone in the dining room suddenly quit talking to stare at him as he clomped over the marble floors in his hobnailed military boots. Ignoring the commotion he had created, he went straight across the room to the bar, where he sat down beside Don Brian and polished off a liter of Bohemia before he said a word.

To Gallo it was interesting to see Don Brian and Colonel Mondragón together at the bar, for it would have been hard to find two men less alike in character or physical appearance. Where Don Brian was middle-sized, blond and stocky, with homely battered features. Mondragón was tall, dark and slender, with refined aquiline features. Where Don Brian was loud-mouthed, energetic and excitable, Mondragón was soft-spoken, slow-moving and serious-minded. Yet both of them conveyed an impression of unusual intelligence, strength of character and sincerity, and in another world, Gallo thought, they might have been the best of friends.

"Oof!" said Don Brian. "That is some thirst you got there, comandante."

"Whew!" said Mondragón. "It was all I could do out there to hold them in line."

"Hey, you better hold them in line," said Don Brian, in a jovial tone that still did not underplay his meaning, "or I know some people who will."

"Señor O'Hare, you know what they called me out at that camp?"

"Don't tell me. Let me guess. Did you patch things up? It was only a falling-out among friends. Did they call you amigo? Compañero? How about comrade?"

"They called me traidor," said Mondragón, "because I wouldn't let them run right out and liberate a banana plantation."

"Traidor," Don Brian repeated, savoring the Spanish word, which is not quite so strong as the English "traitor," yet much more complex in meaning, and much more open to personal interpretation. "Traidor, that's what they call me down at the Club de Leones. 'How come you're so palsy-walsy with that Bolshevik comandante?' they say."

"Those men at the Club de Leones," said Mondragón, "they're just greedy. The ones at the camp are hungry."

"They're lazy," said Don Brian. "They want something for nothing."

"They only want what's theirs by right."

"I had to work for my land . . ."

"Their communal lands were stolen from them, way back in the time of Porfirio Díaz."

". . . and you want to take it away from me."

"I don't 'want' to do anything of the kind," said Mondragón. "I merely apply the law."

"Then why don't you start proceedings against the Hotel O'Hare?"

"The Hotel O'Hare? Then where would I eat? Where would I drink? Where would I go to cross sabers with you?"

"Oh, there will always be a place where we can go for that."

"Actually, your hotel is a family-owned and -operated business, an asset to the community. Your other property is purely speculative and exploitive."

"No matter what you say, comandante, there will come a time when we have to draw the line."

"I don't like to think of that."

"I might forget the rest," said Don Brian, trying a jest, "but I'll never forgive you for stealing my girl."

"Your girl?" said Mondragón, smiling. "She told me you barely spoke."

"You don't believe everything you hear, do you?" said Don Brian. And that set the comandante back for a while. He brooded over his beer mug, one down on the gringo. Then he pulled the surprise out of his hat, the one he must have been saving for just such a moment as this.

"So, Don Brian," he said, out of the blue, "you know how I got those Red Shirts to shut up finally?"

Don Brian shook his head.

"Well," he said, "I'll tell you. You know those LQCs that you've got standing out there on that railspur, right near the camp?"

"Uh-huh."

"I told them they could move in."

"You what?"

"That's right," he said. "Those cars have been sitting out there for years, from what I understand. And in case you didn't know, we've got a law in Mexico; it's called the Law of Idle Machinery, and it states that any industrial property that has remained empty or unused for a period of three years or more is liable to confiscation by the federal government or occupation by the dispossessed."

"Oh?" said Don Brian. "When did that one go through?"

"Just last week," said Mondragón. "It was an executive decree, ordered by President Cárdenas, until such a time as it's approved by the legislative branch."

"But goddammit, Mondragón," Don Brian hollered, so loud he turned heads all over the dining room, "that's private property you're fucking around with now. The railroad has not been reimbursed for its assets!"

"Señor O'Hare," said the comandante, very calmly, "there's one thing I hope you learn during your stay in our country. And that is—there are some things more important than private property."

"Like what, for instance?"

"How about human life?"

"Human life?" Don Brian mocked. "I tell you what. Anybody comes in here and tries to occupy my property is gonna lose his human life real fast."

"If I were you, señor, I would watch my mouth."

"You push me too far."

"I want you to remember something; we have another law in Mexico."

"Don't tell me: I bet I can guess."

"Actually, it's Article 33 of our Constitution."

"I was right!"

"And it states that any foreigner deemed 'pernicious' or a threat to public order is subject to summary deportation."

"Would you really go that far, comandante," said Don Brian, grasping him hard by the forearm, "just to get rid of a rival?"

"Rival?" he said, as Ramona came waltzing up again with a tray full of empty beer mugs, favoring him personally with her most radiantly beautiful smile. "Over what could we possibly be rivals, señor?"

The next morning when Gallo went up to lay out Don Brian's things, he found his boss still in bed, brooding about last night.

"I'm tired of fucking with Mondragón," Brian said. "We've got to get rid of him. It's either that or challenge the sonofabitch to a duel."

"You don't wanna do that, boss. He's a hell of a shot, I hear."

"What I want to do is force Sánchez's hand; I want to do it that way."

"Hey, you know, the general may not wanna play it our way."

"He's got to," said Don Brian. "In the long run all our interests coincide."

"How do you mean, chief?"

"You know what I mean."

"What? We stir up the shit over here till he's gotta get up off his ass? Is that what you mean?"

"Pretty close."

"Kinda—we don't stop them Red Shirts now, they're just gonna want more and more."

"There you go."

"Just leave 'em to me, boss."

"Think you can handle it, huh?"

"It's a cinch."

"Well, you won't have to do it all by yourself. I've got it figured out.

While you hike over the hill and fall on them from the jungle side of the tracks, I come around with a light engine and tie onto their rear end."

"Hey, all this time they gonna be shooting at you, you know."

"Oh no they won't. You're going to pin them inside with rifle fire. And then once they get moving, there's no way out of those LQCs. All they are is converted boxcars. There's no access to the ladders or the roof."

"What about the curves, chief? They gonna get you on the curves."

"I have no intention of going anywhere near a curve, cuñado. I'm going to push them forty Ks down the coastline to this abandoned guano plant that I know. Just a great long stretch of railspur between these giant black sand dunes with no water or human habitation for miles around. And there I am going to cut them loose. By the time they stop rolling, I'll be halfway back to town. And it's only going to be another day or two, without water, under the sun, before they leave my LQCs behind."

"Boss, you got a mind like a steel trap."

"Right," he said, "but as you can see, Gallo, we are definitely going to be needing some help on this one. Discreet help. People we can rely on."

"Yeah, I was thinking. I could run down to Boca de Pascuales and do some recruiting on the docks."

"No riffraff. I want fifteen good men. Five with me on the engine, and ten with you on the ground."

"Okay, chief, but what you want me to tell them?"

"Tell them the truth."

"The truth?" said Gallo skeptically. "What is that?"

"They are going to help us evict some illegal squatters from railroad property."

"And what if they balk?"

"Why would they do that?"

"Look at the odds. There's probably over two hundred of them Red Shirts."

"Tell them it's going to be a surprise attack. They'll be hitting them in the heat of the day, at siesta time when they least expect it. Tell them that most of them are only women and children."

"That oughta do it," said Gallo. "When you want to go?"

"The sooner the better."

"All right, but I certainly am gonna be asking a favor or two in return."

"That goes unsaid."

"Yeah, I need training, boss. I want a real future for myself, and for my family too. I would like to be assistant trainmaster when C.J. is gone."

"C.J. is a sick man, the poor bastard."

"I'm a quick learner," said Gallo. "I already know a lot. And there ain't a lazy bone in my body."

"Fine," said Don Brian. "You help me empty out those LQCs, boy, and you got yourself a job."

So a week or two later Don Brian gave Gallo an engine and a caboose and he rode over to Boca de Pascuales on a recruiting drive. The first person he looked for was his old compañero from revolutionary days—and recent archenemy—the black pimp Herculano. Herculano was one of those big black pure-blooded niggers from the Costa Chica; they had run wild in the jungle after their slave ship broke up in the days of the Spics. His woman, Eulalia, was of the same race, and she was famous up and down the coast of Colima for her versatility on the dance floor, and in bed . . . as Don Brian had found out a few weeks back. Gallo caught Herculano having lunch at Eulalia's place, a cane shack built upon stilts above the river. Gallo could see him through the strung-shell curtain that hung in the open doorway. He was squatting on his huaraches like an Indian, with his sombrero tipped low on his forehead, bent over a wooden bowl of fishheads and rice. And times were so bad that Eulalia and her old nigger mama went scrambling for the gills that he spat on the floor.

Gallo swung his head around through the door, smiling widely, rattling the strung shells.

"Hold it!" he hollered, when Herculano went for his knife. "Hold it, cabrón. I'm here on business."

"If you come in peace," said Herculano, rising cautiously up off the floor, fingering the stiletto at his belt, "you can go the same way."

"Cuate, 'mano," Gallo wheedled. "I know we had words in the past. . . ."

"Words?" said Herculano. And the way he said it, Eulalia and her mama had to laugh. Even her kid laughed, crawling on the floor across the room, and he wasn't but a year old.

"As I remember it," Eulalia said, "on one occasion there was bullets flying."

"When was that?"

"The time you cheated at monte, the time you took our gold piece."

"We have had our ups and downs, I admit."

"Uh-huh. Your ups and our downs."

"But now I'm looking for help."

"Help?" said Herculano. "I could use some of that myself. The policía shut down my card game, and they won't let me sell liquor to the Indians anymore, unless I cough up with a heavy mordida."

"I'll get your mordida for you, brother. I got a gringo who needs some men."

"What kind of men?"

"Good men, bravos, men of arms."

"What's the pay?"

"A hundred a head and a hundred a day."

"My head too?"

"Of course."

"I'll see what I can do," he said, and within an hour he had thirty hungry-looking veterans, ex-revolutionaries, crammed into Eulalia's little shack and strung out along the catwalk, dangling their feet in the river to keep cool.

In appearance these men were a typical local mixture of Spanish, Indian, Negro, Spanish-Indian, Spanish-Negro, and Negro-Indian, and in coloration they ranged from malaria yellow to midnight blue. They were dressed like ordinary peasants in rough white cotton, huaraches and sombreros, but there was something about them that set them apart. In general the peasants of this district sharecropped the same little hectare of ill-drained land from generation to generation. But these men were hombres de muchas partes—men of many parts. They had traveled from one end of Mexico to the other in the Revolution. For ten years they had never stopped. They had fought in the mountains, the deserts, the jungles and the high Altiplano. They had known victory and defeat, loyalty and betrayal, rags and riches. They had gorged themselves in fancy French restaurants in Mexico City and eaten the leather from their huaraches in the wilderness of Chihuahua. And it showed in their eyes: They were not humble eyes. In this they were like the squatters whom they would oppose. They had opposed such men before, and fought alongside them as well.

Treachery was not unknown among them, and Gallo's standards were high—especially when his own life was on the line—so he chose carefully, and in the end he came away with only twelve. Four for Don Brian and eight for himself. But they were the cream of the crop. With such men as the hulking Indian Palenco, a tracker and nightfighter of great renown, or the cold-eyed mestizo sharpshooter Alvarado, or the little Catalan ex-sailor Montjuich, expert with stiletto and garrote, famous for his uncanny ability to remove enemy sentries without a sound, not to mention the giant Negro warriors Herculano, Mercurio and Pegaso, Gallo could have sacked a town, or seized and held an entire district.

He loaded them all into his caboose and hauled them over to Manzanillo, where he issued them Mausers from the railroad armory. Then they all crowded into Don Brian's little office in the yard tower, facing the bald spot on the back of his head. And while the chief continued to peruse the railroad yard in the performance of his official duties, swiveling to and fro on his high-legged draftsman's stool in a characteristically nervous manner, he gave them a little pep talk.

"Muchachos," he said, "it is absolutely vital to the success of our operation that we avoid casualties at all costs, especially among the women and children. If we don't, we're going to bring the military down on our backs. So remember: Shoot to scare, not to kill. And if there are any accidents, bury them deep."

Then he gave them each a cold liter of beer from the passenger stores and patted them on the back and sent them on their way. Gallo led them across the rails single-file to the steep jungle hill on the other side of the yard. At the edge of the tracks the low wall of vegetation rose up before them, green and tangled and choked with vines. They unsheathed their machetes and went right to work hacking out a narrow trail, sweating and crying in the heat, swatting at spiders, gnats and mosquitoes while snakes, centipedes and scorpions rattled the leaves underfoot. For an hour they battled upward through the underbrush, inch by inch, foot by foot, toting their heavy weapons and bandoliers of extra ammunition. Yet, when at last the point man broke out onto the grassy spine of the ridge, there was no rejoicing and barely a sigh of relief, for the jungle began again just a few meters down the other slope. They collapsed in the shade of a spreading soyate tree at the edge of the forest and pulled the caps off their bottles of beer. They chugged it down in great long gulps, rolled themselves some cornhusk cigarettes, lit up, and looked back the way they had come. They could see the green ocean, the blue bay, the brown lagoon, the sugarloaf hills across the way, the little wood and black-dirt and red-tile city curling intricately along the shore like a poor man's Rio de Janeiro. Down the other precipitous slope, across the low wall of jungle, they could see the railspur where the squatters' train was parked, and the tiny dots of humanity that surrounded it. It was an active numerous humanity, scurrying like a tribe of termites, in and out of the LQCs, up and down the track.

"Take a look at that," said one of the men, the Indian Palenco. "This was supposed to be siesta time."

"Maybe they ain't got a clock," said another, the mestizo point man, Alvarado.

The other men laughed and flicked their cigarettes into the brush and rose to their feet, belching and farting and smacking the dirt off their trousers. It was the attitude of soldiers who are used to being lied to by their officers. Without another word they formed up and descended into the jungle. They fought their way downward through the underbrush for half an hour, and then Gallo called a halt.

"Now we crawl," he said. "We're near the train, and they might have pickets out."

As it happened, there were no pickets. But the jungle was alive with people from the squatters' train. People coming up to move their bowels in privacy and wipe their asses with leaves. People roaming the woods in search of firewood or edible roots. People chasing birds or iguanas or hunting eggs for supper.

And it wasn't long before a young couple, out for a quick matinee in the bushes, came squeezing up toward them, whispering urgently to each other.

"Here?"

"No, there's too many stickers there."

"Here?"

"No, I'll get my dress dirty there."

Wriggling through the muddy undergrowth on his belly, with his Mauser cradled in his arms, Gallo felt like a venomous reptile, a gila monster ready to strike, for he was sure they would stumble on him and raise the alarm. But they chose a place a few meters off to the left and soon he could hear them grunting happily together.

Gallo and his men reached their objective at 4:25 P.M., only five minutes off schedule. Quickly and silently they slithered into their prearranged positions along the edge of the railroad cut, just inside the treeline. The squatters' train was parked just below them, so near they could actually smell it. It was the smell of many poor people living close together in great heat and humidity. It was the smell of the tropics: rotting fruit, bad meat, unwashed bodies, human waste. It was a smell that Gallo had washed off himself only a short time before. The scene reminded him of something out of the Mexican Revolution—a revolution that had been fought mostly from trains, with the families of the soldiers in close attendance. And the squatters seemed a good deal more alert than he had been led to expect. There was a guard posted atop each LQC, and the environs of the train were crawling with cats, dogs, chickens, goats, cows, donkeys, horses, tame doves, parrots, naked potbellied children playing in the sand, women doing the family washing in the drainage ditch and spreading it on hot volcanic rocks to dry, men playing cards in the shade of railroad cars.

Gallo found the scene so painfully reminiscent of his youth as a revolutionary that he hesitated to give the sign to fire. It was as if he were waylaying his own adolescence, ambushing his younger self. And he might have shilly-shallied around there even longer had not Don Brian grown tired of awaiting his signal flare and come puffing around the slope of the hill in his little red switch engine.

The guards on the LQCs got suspicious and called out a warning: "Hay viene un tren!"

Gallo's men got nervous, and one of them fired off his Mauser by mistake. BOOM! It sounded like a cannon in the stillness of the afternoon, echoing in the railroad cut, and from hill to jungle hill. For an instant everything and everyone seemed to freeze: the men on both sides, the women and children and animals, the very trees and the birds in the air. Then all hell broke loose. Gallo and his boys opened up. The guards on the LQCs returned fire. The livestock stampeded. The domesticated birds took flight. The cats scampered for the forest, and the dogs started to howl. The women and children went running around in circles, screaming at the tops of their lungs, then scattered into the trees on the other side of the tracks. The Red Shirts clambered inside the LQCs, hastily armed themselves, and started firing raggedly at the treeline with their old bird guns and blunderbusses. Most of their shots didn't even reach the ambushers, and those that did went whipping into the trees above their heads. Some of the birdshot even fell on them, soft as rain.

As for Gallo and his boys, they did just as Don Brian had ordered. They scared the living Jesus out of those squatters with hot flying lead. They peppered the top of the train, sending woodchips and sharp pieces of tar paper whistling through the air, chasing the guards down the ladders for cover. They shot through the open doorways and windows of the LQCs and right out the back, keeping the gunmen pinned up inside. The Red Shirts foolishly expended their meager stores of ammunition by firing wildly out the doors without aiming. And shortly before Don Brian arrived with his switch engine their guns fell silent. Even so, Gallo and his men kept up the pressure, blasting away at the sides of the LQCs so no one had the nerve to poke his nose out the doors. Don Brian rolled up behind the train with four big masked men riding his cow-catcher, firing their Mausers into the air. He tied onto the rear end and got up his steam. The little engine wheezed. Smoke billowed out the stack. And slowly, ever so slowly, with its wheels slipping around on the track, it picked up speed. In five minutes the squatter train had disappeared into the heat haze on the horizon, and all was silent. The only thing to remind you of the battle was the soft crying of a baby in the thorn trees on the other side of the track, and a mountain of spent Mauser cartridges and shotgun shells.

Gallo turned to ask if anyone was hurt, but his question was answered for him before he could even get it out of his mouth. Beside him, with his face in the mud, lay Herculano, the nappy black top of his head blown off with buckshot. One of the guards on the train must have got lucky. Gallo couldn't say he was exactly sorry to see Herculano go. Figured he would've had to do the same someday, if the negrito didn't get him first. Then as if on cue the clouds which had been piling up overhead all afternoon opened up and it began to pour. It was the daily rainy-season deluge, accompanied by thunder and lightning and a strong humid wind smelling of the sea. Gallo was soaked to the skin in an instant, his face streaming with water. He liked it. It felt good. He laughed. His men laughed back.

"It'll hide our tracks," Gallo said. "When the military come they won't even know where we came from."

"What about the police?" Alvarado demanded.

"The police are on our side," Gallo said. "Now, Palenco. I want you and Garcia to sharpen some bamboo and dig a grave for Herculano while the ground's still soft. Alvarado, I want you to take Montjuich, pull your handkerchiefs over your faces, and go look for wounded. I want everybody back here in five minutes."

"What do we do if we find them?" the white man, Montjuich, asked.

"Bring them up here to me."

"If they are wounded it could be awkward for us."

"Now you got the idea."

Incredible as it might seem, after all the gunplay, only one casualty could be found. He had got hit on top of an LQC and fallen into the drainage ditch. By some astonishing act of will he had managed to crawl into a drainage pipe and hide himself amid the debris. When they found him he was unconscious and barely alive. They dragged him up the embankment, and Gallo smothered him in his own blood-soaked shirt. They buried him alongside Herculano on the hill and swore each other to secrecy.

"We'll forget that this Red Shirt ever existed," Gallo said. "As for Herculano, we'll split his share of the money, and tell his old lady that he left town with another whore as soon as he got his pay."

"Who gives out the pay?" the Indian Palenco wanted to know. He was something of a troublemaker.

"I do."

"How much of ours do you hold back for yourself?"

"A certain percentage."

"What for?"

"For cutting you into some class action, you miserable stinking peón, some capitalist action. Now take off that fucking sombrero in the presence of your patrón, and convince me why I shouldn't have you taken out right now and shot for insubordination."

CHAPTER 5

In Manzanillo there was a civil or religious holiday, a pagan or Catholic feast day, a parade or procession or penitential crawl or public self-flagellation or Solemn High Mass on an average of once every fifteen days. At five o'clock in the afternoon on the Fiesta of Corpus Christi, not a fortnight after the Cinco de Mayo festivities, the entire staff and ownership of the Hotel O'Hare were standing out on the front steps overlooking the plaza, waiting for another parade to pass by. In descending order of importance they stood: Brian on the top step in a white linen suit and a Panama hat. Mrs. O'Hare in an ankle-length beige silk dress, a blue straw hat and veil. Ramona and Chris in china poblana, the fanciful peasant holiday dress of Mexico. Gallo in his gypsy hat and a guayabera shirt with his shoulder holster bulging. Merle in traditional Corpus Christi costume—like a tiny peddler with a little canvas sack on his back filled with miniature pots, pans, pottery and jewelry. Then Grandma Carrizo and Carmen at street level in their maids' uniforms and bare feet.

They were all expecting the same shabby little procession they got every year at this time: a few dirty bedraggled Mexican soldiers in cast-off U.S. army gear "escorting" a simulated pack train of baby donkeys and goats encumbered with miniature pack saddles and toy merchandise, heading for the plaza, where local craftsmen had set up a scaled-down marketplace in which they sold tiny reproductions of their life-size creations for make-believe money.

But Ramona knew that today they were all in for a big surprise.

Instead of the tinkling of little bells, the bleating of baby goats and the sound of tiny hoofbeats that usually signaled the beginning of the parade, this year they heard something like chanting or grunting: *"Ugh ugh, ugh ugh, ugh ugh . . ."* They could hear it coming from all the way across town at the army base.

"Hey, what's going *ooooon*?"

"Let's wait and see."

"I know what it is."

"What is it?"

"It's Raúl's idea."

"Raúl?" said Mrs. O'Hare. "Is that the comandante?"

"Yes," said Ramona. "He's been working on it with them for weeks."

"Oh, I see," she said. "And what else did he whisper to you in the plaza last night, my dear?"

"Well," Ramona said, in an even tone (she never forgot how much she owed Mrs. O'Hare: Mrs. O'Hare never let her forget it), "we spoke about some of the problems he's been having lately."

"Problems? What sort of problems could he have? He's sitting on top of the world."

"Oh, you'd be surprised, Doña Maureen. There's the squatters, the—"

"The squatters? They ought to be living in Hog Heaven by now."

"Didn't you hear all the shooting, señora? It sounded like a regular battle."

"I heard nothing," said Mrs. O'Hare. "Or if I did I thought it was some more of those infernal fireworks going off. Or another vendetta. An ambush in the jungle. It's always something."

"Actually, it looks like they've . . . disappeared."

"They've what?"

"It's true."

"But where could they have 'disappeared' to?"

"Raúl says that Don Brian knows."

"Ramona, will you please stop referring to the comandante as 'Raúl'? I know that we don't often agree with him, but there is such a thing as respect. Now, Brian, what is this all about?"

"Hell, I don't know, Mother. Someone got ahold of a switch engine, I guess, and shoved them off the spur."

"Off the spur? Where off the spur?"

"Search me. I got better things to do than go around chasing after a bunch of damn Red Shirts."

"But how can it be that you don't know?" Ramona demanded. She had friends on that train, people who'd taken her family in when they came back from Texas without a centavo. "Nothing rolls on that railroad unless you say so."

"Ramona, I'm telling you I don't know," Brian said. "But even if I did, I wouldn't tell you. I can't be sure whose side you're on anymore."

"Why do there always have to be sides?" she said. "And why do we let politics come between us?"

"Politics?" Brian scoffed. "What makes you think it's politics? It's a matter of life and death."

"Don't you see, my dear?" said Mrs. O'Hare.

"No, señora, I'm afraid I don't."

"Well," she said, "so much depends on your point of view. The Red Shirts think they're right. Mondragón thinks he's right. We think we're right. We can't all be right. It's like trying to define beauty. It's all in the eye of the beholder. In the end whoever wins is right. So, Ramona, what you do is, you look over all the various sides that you find attractive and then you latch on to the one you think is a winner and you trust in God and if you come out lucky you're on the right side. Right?"

It was not a question that was meant to be answered. And it was uttered in such an offensive tone that Ramona thought the señora must have given up on her altogether. It pained her to think so. But ever since Ramona had turned down Brian's proposal of marriage, the señora's attitude had changed. She had turned cold and sardonic and short-tempered. She had ridiculed her in front of her family, humiliated her before the clients and guests. It almost seemed as if she resented her for following her orders so precisely, as if she actually thought her impertinent for refusing her son's advances.

Now the chanting was getting closer. It seemed to be coming from just behind the hotel. Suddenly a hundred double-timing Mexican soldiers burst out onto the plaza from the Avenida Mexico. They wore only green gym shorts and huarache sandals, and their dark, squat, muscular bodies and thick, straight black hair glistened with sweat. They were formed up in a perfect square, ten by ten, and they ran and chanted in flawless unison, a hundred left feet smacking the cobblestones at once, then a hundred right feet. *"Ugh ugh, ugh ugh, ugh ugh . . ."* Immediately behind them came another group dressed all in red. Then blue, orange, black, yellow, gray, purple. A thousand strong, the half-naked young bronze men went jogging round the plaza, past the reviewing stand, past the horsemen dressed in charro gear lined up by the custom house, past the miniature marketplace where peasant children stood around in the costumes of quaint little elfin peddlers, past the crowds of cheering campesinos in the plaza, past the Hotel O'Hare. Then back for another round at a faster pace. And another even faster. *"Ugh ugh, ugh ugh, ugh ugh . . ."*

To Ramona there was something wonderfully stirring about the performance. Aside from the physical aspect, which thrilled her in a way she would never have admitted, there was a patriotic emotion as well. She was proud of her mixed Spanish-Aztec race, and of the achievements of the Mexican Revolution. Usually, in these Corpus Christi parades, the soldiers would come slouching along in their outsized American uniforms looking small and clumsy and dispirited. Yet almost naked, with their smooth chests heaving, their brown legs pumping, their feet stamping, their voices raised in a barbaric chant, they seemed an altogether more formidable military force. And she could imagine their ancestors—her ancestors—running around this same plaza a thousand years ago, with their skin shields and spiked war clubs and obsidian knives, past the priests and chiefs on the temple steps, past the warriors gathered in the square, past the women in their feathered finery, past the children dressed as Indian dolls, past the captives lined up in the street to be sacrificed to the ever-angry gods.

Even the gringos seemed impressed.

"Now there goes an army!" Brian exclaimed.

"This is the way they were meant to be," his mother said.

"This is the way he wanted them," Ramona confided. "He wanted to remind them of who they are."

"I don't like it!" Chris squealed. "I don't like it at all. Me and Merle, we want the baby donkeys, don't we, Merle?"

"Here they come, honey," Ramona said, smoothing the little girl's raven hair. She hated to see Chris unhappy, even if she was unhappy for the most frivolous reasons. She was probably spoiling her rotten. She was far more indulgent with her than she was with Merle. And Merle's life was not easy. But Chris had so much more to bear. The worst thing to bear: an indifferent mother. "Look! See, Chris? Here they come now!"

And indeed they were coming, trotting down the Avenida Mexico, bells jingling, tiny hooves pounding, with their devout and humble Indian masters driving them on.

"Raúl disapproves of superstition," Ramona said, unable to resist the impulse. "But I persuaded him to leave this part in for the children's sake."

"How very white of you, my dear," said Mrs. O'Hare.

"That'll be enough of that, Mother," Brian said, for which Ramona was grateful.

Even so, it hurt her deeply. She'd always looked up to Doña Maureen as a lady with uncommon class and erudition, and she had flattered herself with the notion that Doña Maureen had seen something of the same in herself: "My, my, such hunger for learning!" she had exclaimed, only half ironically, on finding Ramona in the hotel library at two o'clock one morning, absorbed in the METAMORPHIC–NEW JERSEY section of the *Encyclopedia Britannica,* when she knew that Ramona had begun a few months before with the AALTO–ARITHMETIC section. And she was always complimenting Ramona on her taste in clothing, and the skill with which she altered her hand-me-downs. . . .

After the parade Ramona was still feeling sorry for herself, and she looked for sympathy from her family. But little Merle was too young to understand, Grandma Carrizo, whose English had rapidly deteriorated in Mexico, had missed the exchange entirely, and Gallo and Carmen avoided her eyes, assuming an air of smug complicity.

As they were heading into the hotel with the others to start preparing for the evening meal, Ramona caught Gallo and Carmen by the lobby door and pulled them aside.

"All right," she said. "What is it this time?"

"If you have to ask," said Gallo, "there's no use bothering to answer."

"You're mad because I got Doña Maureen riled up."

"Hell, I don't mind getting people riled up," he said. "But you just ain't playing it right. Not with the señora. Not with Don Brian. And not with Mondragón."

"How would you like me to play it?"

"I've told you a hundred times."

"Tell me again."

"With the tart you play it sweet," he said. "With the sweet you play it tart."

"And with the indifferent?"

"You stir up the interest."

"How do you do that?"

"You show a little leg."

"And then what?"

"You show a little more."

"You think that'll do it, huh?"

"Try it, you'll see."

"Obviously, you don't know Mondragón," she said. "He would probably deliver me a lecture on woman's proper role in the Revolution, and show me photos of his wife and kids to cool my ardor."

"You wanted my advice," Gallo said, shrugging his shoulders, starting to go in. Then he turned and said: "I'm about to give up on you. You know that, don't you, girl?"

"I'm not sure I care anymore," she said, as he disappeared inside the door.

Carmen started to follow him, but Ramona caught her by the arm and made her stay.

"From Gallo I expect this kind of thing," she said. "But from you it's something new."

"What are you talking about?"

"Carmen, what is it? We used to be so close. When Mama died we walked all the way from Michoacán together . . . two little girls alone."

"Look at me," Carmen said. "I go around barefoot. And look at you."

"You want me to take my shoes off?"

"Spare me the saintly act."

"So he's finally got you, eh?"

"Why not? I don't have a Don Brian chasing after me, or a Colonel Mondragón."

"I never asked them to chase after me, did I?" Ramona said, but her voice sounded coy, even to herself.

"I hate you, Ramona," Carmen said, after she had stood there glaring at her for a few moments. "You think you're better than me."

And when Carmen had gone into the hotel, Ramona thought that perhaps there was some justice in what her sister had said. She had always considered herself superior to Carmen, and *responsible* for her, as an elder and wiser sister, and she had not always been successful at concealing it.

I am alone, Ramona thought, in the self-dramatizing way that she had. I can't even call these little children my own. Merle belongs to Carmen. And Chris belongs to . . . herself.

Then, as if to disprove her own morbid ruminations, she ran to where Chris and Merle awaited her on the steps and grabbed them by their little necks and drew them to her roughly and hugged them and smooched their plump little cheeks and made them laugh and then whispered to them passionately, "Now, my little ones, your old Aunt Ramona is going to take you off to a magic land where for a wish and a prayer and a bit of play money you can have everything you ever desired. . . ." And she ran skipping and capering with them toward the toy marketplace, extremely conscious of the picture they made—the slender, shapely, soulful young mestiza girl in her native dress, the healthy, happy-looking children in their holiday clothes—from the perspective of the reviewing stand where Colonel Mondragón sat with the bishop, the governor, the mayor, the chief magistrate and the captain of police.

The toy marketplace was circular, a perfect miniature of the grown-up marketplace on the other side of town. It was set up around the gazebo in the center of the plaza, with corresponding sections for dwarf fruit and vegetables, stunted trees, freakishly small or freshly born animals, miniature candies, cakes and tortillas, tiny blankets, pottery and machinery, model towns, bridges and railroads, toy soldiers, Indians, peasants, cowboys and famous personages from Mexican history. A whole naïve little world, one-to-a-hundred scale, all of it handmade by local craftsmen and offered for sale on this one day of the year for play money as an advertisement for the full-sized goods that were sold in the great marketplace on every other day of the year. On the bandstand in the gazebo a children's orchestra led by a midget with a mock conductor's baton played tiny imitations of flutes, trumpets, violins, guitars, marimbas and harps in a shrill cacophony.

By tradition no grown-ups were allowed in the toy marketplace. Even the vendors were children of craftsmen. Parents, nursemaids and nannies were relegated to the cobblestones on the outside of the circle, where they watched the proceedings over the low red-tile rooftops of the model stalls.

Ramona stood amid a group of mothers whom she had known at the Fifth of May Encampment and took the opportunity to ask her former neighbor, Encarnita Nieves, if she'd had any word from her husband yet. But Encarnita pretended she hadn't heard, and soon she moved off to the other side of the toy marketplace.

"Just because I work for a gringo," Ramona protested, "does that make me one too?"

But none of the other mothers would listen either, and soon she was left alone by the baby livestock pen.

It was then that she became aware of a commotion among the children, and saw Chris and Merle fighting over Encarnita's little daughter, Delia.

"She's *my* friend!" Chris shrieked, pulling at the little girl's arm. "Let her come with me."

"No, no, she wants to come with me!" Merle protested, jerking at her other arm.

"Lemme go, Chris," said Delia. "I wanna go with him!"

"See? She's my friend."

"Mine!"

They fought over her till it looked as if they were going to pull the frail, ragged, wooly-headed little thing in half. They fought till they made her cry.

"Now look what you done," said Merle, starting to sniffle. "Why don't you leave us alone?"

Then Chris began to look distressed.

"I'm sorry, Delia. Don't cry," she said. And yet she herself had begun to cry. "I didn't mean it, honest. You want to play with Merle instead of me? All right, go ahead."

Watching the scene, Ramona found herself moved nearly to tears, though it was something she'd seen often enough in the past. Chris really didn't mean to do the things she did. She had no idea what made her so obnoxious. It caused her real sorrow when she was excluded from the other children's games. And there was nothing she'd have liked better than to be just like all the other kids. But that was not to be. Chris was different, and she always would be. She was a creature driven almost totally by instinct. She even smelled different from everyone else: slightly, ever so slightly, of cat.

"Come on, kids," Ramona yelled, laughing to disguise her emotion. "Now that you've all made up, why not shop together? All right? Lovely. That's it, hold hands, with Delia in the middle. And you'd better hurry, or the toys are all going to be given away!"

And was embarrassed to find the comandante suddenly towering at her side. He was wearing his suntan military uniform, but he was hatless.

Freshly barbered, his dark wavy hair shone in the sun; and he smelled of expensive cologne.

"You have a voice of command," he said. And yet it was clearly he, with his deep, calm, authoritative voice, who was in command.

"Maybe you should make me one of your sergeants," she said.

"You need a job?"

"I may very soon," she said. "The O'Hares and I don't always see eye to eye."

"I've had that trouble with them myself," he said, sniffing dryly. Mondragón never smiled. The sniff was a way of conveying his ironic or humorous side.

"I don't think they're really so bad," Ramona said. "They've been good to me, and to my family."

"They only seem like reactionaries, perhaps," said Mondragón, sniffing again.

"They just don't know any other way to be, Raúl. It's a blind spot."

"Unfortunately," said the comandante, "a lot of innocent people fall into that 'blind spot.' An informant came to me with a story today. He knows what happened to the squatters, he says. They're sitting out in their boxcars in the middle of some sand dunes about forty kilometers from here. They have no food, no water, several of them are wounded, and if they aren't moved soon some of them will die. He says that Don Brian is to blame."

"Who is this informant?"

"Someone close to Don Brian, someone who would know."

"I don't believe it," Ramona said. "Don Brian can be hard, but he's not a cruel man."

"That remains to be seen," said Mondragón. "I've just sent him a written order. I'm giving him twelve hours to move that train back to town."

Whereupon he left her as unceremoniously as he had found her.

Ramona did not find his abrupt departure particularly surprising. She had few romantic illusions about the colonel, whatever Gallo and the O'Hares might think. The mild interest that Mondragón had shown in her since his arrival had never struck her as anything more than a kind of fraternal solidarity, a public display of his egalitarian impulses. He had a puritanical streak that was rare in Mexico, and apparently he was faithful to his wife, which was almost unheard-of. He rarely spoke to

Ramona of anything but political, economic or social issues. And their relationship was more like that of a liberal-minded teacher and his bright pupil than a pair of lovers. If the comandante had a passion, it was for the future, for socialism, for the land and people of Mexico. Yet his emotion was real. It was instantly communicable. And it was one of the things—besides his powerful animal magnetism—that she found most attractive about him.

After the children had loaded up with miniatures and said goodbye to little Delia, Ramona walked them back to the hotel. On the way she thought about Raúl, and what he had said. It seemed to her that Brian had no choice but to comply with his orders. And then everything would turn out all right.

She had no desire to see a clash between the two men in her life. She did not wish for a reputation as a *femme fatale*. She cared for them both, each in a very different way, and it would grieve her to see either of them hurt.

When Ramona reached the hotel she found the place in an uproar. No one was manning the reception desk. Don Brian and Doña Maureen were nowhere in sight, and the dining-room guests were clamoring for service.

In the kitchen she discovered that Don Brian had sent Colonel Mondragón a message refusing to do anything for the squatters, and he was already packing his bags in expectation of immediate arrest.

That night Chris crawled into Ramona's bed, as she did nearly every night, begging to be "cuddled" against her breast. But as soon as Ramona took her into her arms she began to cry.

"What's the matter, baby? What's the matter?"

"I love you so much, Ramona. I want you to marry my brother. But I dreamed you married the comandante instead. And the comandante put Brian in jail."

At six o'clock the next morning, Colonel Mondragón sent out a squad of soldiers to ascertain if the squatters' train had been returned. When it was established that the train was nowhere in Manzanillo, the comandante came in person to the hotel, in an army car with a three-man detachment of military police.

Brian had packed his bag and was awaiting him in the courtyard with his lawyer, while his mother, his friend C. J. Hollister, United States

Consul Robert Jeffers, the hotel staff and most of its guests, and virtually the entire executive board of the Company, including Don Cruz Herrera, Sol Zimmerman, Dr. Weber, Frank Kelly, Don Miguel Castañeda, Don Enrique Aciniega, and old Captain Floyd Calvin, had gathered on the upper-story arcades and were looking down upon the scene in grave anticipation.

Brian had taken leave of his mother and little Chris a few minutes before. Mrs. O'Hare was still dabbing at her eyes with her hanky, and Chris was disconsolate, crying her heart out in the nursery across the arcade.

The comandante left his military policemen in the car outside and came into the hotel alone. In cavalry uniform, with a wide flat-brimmed khaki hat and high black boots, he paused in the archway, spotted Brian and his lawyer across the courtyard, and approached them, his ceremonial spurs ringing on the tiles.

"Don Brian O'Hare," he said, in measured, formal tones, "have you returned the rail cars and their occupants to Manzanillo, as ordered by the Provincial Military Command?"

Then Brian's lawyer, Aquilino de Benito, a fat little creole, stepped forward and prepared to read from a legal text. But Brian held him back, and spoke for himself.

"With all due respect, Comandante," he said, in the same stiffly formal Spanish, "I have felt no compulsion to obey your command, on the grounds that it has no basis in law."

A rustle of voices came from the upper galleries, while little Chris continued to cry softly in the nursery.

"Don Brian, do you fully recognize the consequences of your refusal to comply with the direct order of the military commandant?"

"I understand, but I cannot and will not accept or acknowledge responsibility for the actions of these so-called 'squatters' or Red Shirts who have, with the collusion of the military authorities, stolen the property of the Colima Pacific Railroad."

"I will give you one last chance, señor."

"I want no chance with you," said Brian, turning red, glaring up at the tall, cool comandante. "Unless it's a chance on the field of honor."

"The field of honor, Don Brian, was plowed over in the Revolution. It has no place in Mexico anymore."

"Are you afraid then?"

"I repeat, Don Brian, will you or will you not—"

"I will do nothing you say, Comandante," said Brian, very low, "for I do not respect you as a man."

While in the galleries everyone held his breath, and Chris continued to weep, broken-hearted, in the background.

But Mondragón would not be provoked.

"Then it is my duty, as officer in charge, to place you under arrest," he said calmly, "and to remand you to the—"

"You'll do no such thing," Brian said, losing control of his temper, lunging forward, as if to attack the comandante.

But Mondragón deftly sidestepped and tripped him with his foot. Brian went down on his face on the tiles, and Mondragón had him in a hammerlock, with a knee in his back, before Licenciado de Benito could reach his side.

"Tranquilo," he said, gesturing the lawyer back across the courtyard.

Then he pulled out a pair of handcuffs from his military jacket and clamped them first on one wrist and then the other while Brian stayed uncharacteristically quiet. Apparently he'd had the air knocked out of him.

"It is my duty, Don Brian," Mondragón repeated, breathing heavily, with his knee still in the small of Brian's back, "to remand you to the custody of the city prison authorities until accommodations for your summary deportation can be arranged pursuant to Article 33 of the Mexican Constitution."

Then he jerked the fiery Irishman to his feet by the seat of his pants and—while the gallery gasped in amazement and Chris continued to cry and Ramona reflected on how neatly Mondragón had settled his debt of honor without compromising his principles—duckwalked him out of the hotel to the waiting military car.

It all happened so quickly that it was a moment before Doña Maureen realized how utterly her son had been routed and humiliated. But when she did, she fell into a rage and struck out at her servants.

"Gallo! What're you laughing at? And Carmen, what're you standing there gawking at? Both of you, get back to work! And Ramona, what's that secret little smile I see on your face? You'd better wipe it off, if you know what's good for you."

And then, addressing the hotel at large, she said, "Colonel Mondragón has abused our hospitality and insulted my son. He is no longer welcome at the Hotel O'Hare, nor is any friend of his. And by this," she said, rushing over again to loom red-eyed and glaring like a banshee above Ramona and to point a long, freckled, accusatory finger in her face, "I refer specifically to you, young lady."

Ramona lost her breath. The blood rushed to her face.

"Well, what've you got to say for yourself?"

But Ramona had no idea what to say or what to do.

"It's either Mondragón or us."

And everyone was watching.

"Well, make up your mind."

Without really planning it, Ramona stooped to kiss her little nephew goodbye. Gathering what was left of her dignity, she kissed her sister, who seemed to pity her for a moment, Grandma Carrizo, who cried out loud, and even Gallo, who seemed to gloat. Then she turned and walked out of the hotel.

She didn't even stop to say goodbye to little Chris: It would only have added to her unhappiness.

A dramatic exit, perhaps, but Mrs. O'Hare had the last word.

"I bet she goes straight to Mondragón," she said.

Which left Ramona alone on the empty, early-morning plaza with nowhere to go.

Still, her pride would not allow her to hesitate or even appear to reflect. She walked straight across the plaza to the Avenida Morelos, not looking back. Hurrying as if to some pressing engagement, she continued up the Avenida Morelos to the Malecón, then along the bay past the Muelle Fiscal, the railroad terminal, the palacio federal, the Colonia Burocrática, the public slaughterhouse, the hospital civil and the Puerto Interior.

On the Avenida de Niños Héroes a little brown girl who resembled herself as a ten-year-old was chasing a white rooster around in circles. On the corner of Chapultepec and Alcaraz a pregnant Chinese woman was playing with her two-year-old boy, throwing him up in the air, making him squeal with laughter. Near the Playa de San Pedrito four fat whores were sitting on the curb on their cheap suitcases, waiting for the bus to the military barracks. Three of them were slatternly local Zamba types, a degenerate mixture of Indian and black. But one of them was a magnificent purebred Negress from the Costa Chica, tall and barefoot and beautiful as an African queen.

"Hey, little one, where you headed?" she leered as Ramona passed by.

Ramona ignored the whore, but it suddenly occurred to her that Mrs. O'Hare might have been right about her.

At the El Tajo rail cut she turned off the Malecón and followed the Colima Pacific tracks between the hills and along the lagoon. At last she had a clear idea of her proper destination.

She approached the Fifth of May Encampment from across the railroad yard, skirting the mud flats, the thorn trees and the city dump. There was a strange sickly odor about the place, and an air of abandonment. No more did chickens, piglets, goats and children scamper underfoot. Most of the huts' thatched roofs had fallen in the heavy rains, and there were no men around to repair them. The gaunt, hollow-eyed women and listless, nauseous-looking children lay huddled together in the ruins, with only tattered blankets and scraps of cardboard for shelter.

The old Carrizo jacal no longer existed. It had been burned to the ground and its ashes scattered to the wind. Only a circle of charred sand marked the spot where it had stood.

She found Encarnita in her old thatched hut next door, minus her husband and all her possessions.

"What do you want?" she snarled, when Ramona appeared behind the bottlecaps that she had strung together in her doorway.

Ramona started to say, "I've come to help," but thought better of it. Instead she said, "I need your help, dear." And there was nothing Encarnita could do but take her in.

Ramona tried to make herself useful with little Delia, and around the hut, and soon she and Encarnita had made it up again. When Colonel Mondragón had the squatters' train dragged back to Manzanillo, a couple of days later, she moved in with the Nieves family in their LQC.

On the train she busied herself with the children, most of whom were suffering from dysentery, worms and chronic malnutrition. The women quickly grew used to her presence among them, and they appreciated her help with the kids, not to mention the laundry and cooking. But they resented her advice on personal hygiene, and they completely ignored her warning about the need to boil the drinking water and dig latrines. There was also a good deal of jealousy about her effect upon the men.

The men believed her to be the ex-mistress of Don Brian and Colonel Mondragón, or little more than a prostitute, and treated her accordingly. They whistled at her, made lewd pursing noises with their mouths, pinched her bottom, squeezed her breasts, and generally made her life miserable.

Then, after she had rejected a few of them, and hollered at them to keep their dirty hands off her, they reviled her as a stuck-up bitch who felt too good for poor campesinos such as themselves.

At that point they began to turn really ugly, and it took all the power of Narciso Nieves to keep them from laying violent hands on her.

As for Narciso, he had designs on her himself. But she managed to keep him at arm's distance by appealing to his conscience as an anarchist, and sticking close to his wife and child. The situation was complicated by the fact that she felt drawn to Narciso as well. He was so strong, so sure in his convictions. He seemed to be constructed all of sinew and bone. The very smell of his Negro sweat aroused her. She woke up one morning from a dream of making love to him and realized that she was in danger of becoming exactly what the squatters believed her to be.

The time had come for Ramona to have a man; and she knew she would have to find one soon or face the consequences.

Though she did not feel at all noble or tragic in the role in which she had cast herself, she kept dreaming that Mondragón would come galloping up on his white charger and carry her away. Such fantasies were not new to Ramona. She'd had them ever since she was a little girl living with Carmen and their mother, Asunción, on the hacienda of Don Rodrigo de Pórras in Tacámbaro, Michoacán, and she would imagine that her papa was not dead and he would come home from the Revolución in one piece and he would go back to work in the patroncito's corn mill again as foreman and buy them out of the cave-house where they lived in squalor with the Indios and peones on the side of the arroyo of cactus and he would bring them back up to the little adobe-and-red-tile house where they had lived before the war with the other managerial staff and Ramona would be clean and pretty and enchanting again wearing shoes and store-bought clothes and when she grew up the patroncito's son Mauricio would notice her and come riding up to her house on his polo pony and he would ask for her hand in matrimony and she would ride away with him sidesaddle to his great pink tezontle stone house on a white hill that stood like an island amid a green sea of canefields. . . . And then even later, as a teenager up in Texas, working for the Luther Dickson family on East 11th Street as a cleaning girl in the morning, baby-sitting for the Lytle Parker family on Houston Avenue in the afternoon, going to high school Monday, Wednesday and Friday nights, reading and studying in the public library every Tuesday, Thursday and Saturday night, working at home doing piecework for the Lebanese clothing manufacturer all day Sunday, she would find herself having the same childish daydreams. She would imagine a tall, red-haired, freckle-faced gringo cattleman who looked like Tom Mix and wore a ten-gallon hat like Johnny Mack Brown and he would come clattering down East 11th Street, or Houston Avenue, or up the steps of the public library, or right into El Paso High School on his great white stallion with his hooves pounding in her ears and he would twirl his rope and she would hear it humming and he would lasso her and hoist her up behind him all trussed up like a sow for the slaughter and gallop away with her into the Llano Estacado, never to return. And even when she got older and realized how infantile the whole thing was, and even now when she was beginning to feel that she had an ideological commitment against such silly bourgeois fantasies, she found that she could do nothing to dispel them, and they persisted still, undiminished in their seductive power, their decadence.

One afternoon Ramona was up on the slope above the train hunting mushrooms when she was caught in a cloudburst. She had just stooped to investigate an interesting but possibly poisonous specimen when suddenly the humidity mounted frighteningly, the sky split open, and the air turned to water. Tons of it fell upon her in an instant, crushing her to earth, clogging her eyes, ears, mouth and nose. Blindly she crawled for shelter, feeling her way with her fingers and bare toes. She found a Judas tree and lay cowering under its canopy for what seemed a lifetime, trying to breathe under the leaves. Lightning exploded all around her, digging up great troughs in the earth, crashing into the LQCs, felling trees. Thunder rolled down the railroad line, resounding like cannon fire between the steep jungle hills. Within minutes the entire slope above her had turned to muck and was oozing down upon her. She felt it seep around her bare arms and legs and neck. She struggled to raise her head, but it flowed more and more swiftly, overwhelming her, dragging her down. It closed over her head and she thought she was dead. The bank gave way beneath her and she felt herself tumbling head over heels. She reached out frantically and found what she thought was a human friend. A body in the dark. A lover. And then another. She clung to them both as she clung to life, as she rolled down the slope, across the drainage ditch, up the railroad embankment, and came to rest at the door to an LQC car.

Ramona raised a hand weakly out of the mud. Narciso Nieves took it and dragged her up into the car. Encarnita grabbed her by the hair and clawed the clay from her mouth. She breathed. Narciso bathed her face with warm rainwater. Still gasping for breath, she smiled up at him. "I'm alive," she meant to say. But instead she said, "I'm in love." A look of dread passed across his face. She followed his gaze out into the coagulating ooze. A half-decomposed Negro lay there beside the imprint of her own body, with maggots crawling out of his hollow eyes, long gray worms curling from his nostrils and his grinning mouth. And close by: another man. A mestizo. She could even recognize his features. He had been a neighbor at the Fifth of May Encampment. His name was Calmento Noriega. She was surprised at herself for not feeling particularly horrified at seeing him there. What she felt was something more like pity. She knew that Calmento's wife, Lupita, was on the train, and his children, and she felt he wouldn't want them to see him that way.

"Bury them," she said, and fainted dead away.

Yet in the morning she was left with only a headache and a bad cold. Narciso came to her pallet in the railroad car and explained his plan.

"We're going to carry them down to Mondragón," he said. "It's the only language he'll understand."

"You mean the corpses? But one of them isn't even ours."

"He won't know the difference, and two make a better impression than one. We've got to get us some action, Ramona. After all we've been through, we still have no land."

"Do you think Don Brian knew of this?"

"Of course he knew; he's the one who was behind it."

"I still can't believe he would do such a thing."

"I don't care what you think."

"Are you angry?"

"No," he said. "I only wish you'd listen. Let's present the evidence. If Don Brian is innocent, he has nothing to fear."

"All right," she said reluctantly. "But you'll understand if I don't come along."

"Of course. I would like you to talk to him, though."

"Talk to whom?"

"The comandante," he said. "With you I think we can win him over." And the way he said it, she knew that it was true. She watched him closely. She was still fascinated by his clever mulatto face, his red-webbed eyes and lantern jaw. But now it was more than merely physical.

She felt like part of the clan. In the mudslide she had embraced her fate.

"I don't mind," she said. "But leave the Negro here when you go to town. Don Brian had nothing to do with that."

"Now, wait a minute . . ."

"Take it or leave it," she said. And he took it.

Later that day, the Red Shirts formed up two abreast and paraded through the streets of Manzanillo, carrying the stinking corpse on a stretcher between them. They halted in front of the municipal palace, firing their bird guns and blunderbusses into the air, shouting for justice. When the little mestizo mayor, Tito Bejár, stepped out on the balcony, they pelted him with rotten fruit, shouting, "You are the oppressor, give us the comandante!"

Mondragón arrived a few minutes later, riding a horse.

"Compañeros," he said, "I am here to serve you."

But he made no move to get down from his horse.

Narciso Nieves stepped forward.

"This is what remains of one of our men," he said. "His name was Calmento Noriega. He has been missing since the fight with the railroad. We thought that you should have him."

"I see," said Mondragón. "Well, of course I will take possession of the corpse." He turned to his adjutant, who was seated beside him on another horse. "Corrales, I want you to transfer this cadaver to the city morgue, pending an investigation."

"Is that all you're going to do?" Narciso wondered.

"Why yes," said Mondragón. "At the moment I believe it's all I can do. When the investigation is completed, I'll advise you of its results."

"That's not enough."

"I beg your pardon?"

"We want justice!"

"Then you shall have it."

"Is that true?"

"Trust me."

"Then why is it that Don Brian O'Hare, the instigator of this crime, faces no punishment worse than deportation?"

"Compañero, until this moment I was not aware of the seriousness of the attack."

"Then come with us now, comandante. Talk to Ramona Mescalero, the girl who discovered the corpse. Let us show you where it was buried."

At last Mondragón agreed to visit the train.

He rode out alone on his horse, and Narciso brought him to see Ramona where she lay on her straw petate in the railroad car.

"What're *you* doing here?" he wanted to know. And it pleased her to hear the concern in his voice.

"I had nowhere else to go."

"Are you all right?" he asked, bending over to peer at her more closely, and to touch her fevered brow.

"I suppose I'll survive," she said, shivering with pleasure to see his long, dour, mustached face so near above her, and to smell his expensive cologne once again. "But I'm not so sure about them," she said, pointing to the ragged circle of squatters.

"Haven't they enough to eat?"

"Someone is conspiring against them," Ramona said. "The big shots in this state are trying to steal back everything we won in the Revolution."

"You were only a baby in the Revolution," said Mondragón. "Who put these ideas into your head?"

"You did," she said.

"I just polished them up a bit!" Narciso piped up from the rear of the crowd, causing everyone to laugh.

"Comrades," Mondragón said, rising to address the crowd. "We are at a delicate stage right now. In the capital President Cárdenas is still in a precarious position. And here the economy is on the verge of collapse. For the moment I'm afraid it's a choice between a little more tyranny or a lot more hunger and chaos."

"Comandante," said Ramona, softly, "we have already made our choice. And we would like you to join us."

"I'm sorry, Ramona . . ."

"Let me quote from President Cárdenas," said Narciso, emerging from the crowd. " 'If state governments do not satisfy the needs of the people, turning them over to domestic and foreign exploitation, then the great proletarian masses will put an end to those governments.' "

"Here it is premature for such an action," Mondragón said, glowering. "It can only lead to disaster."

"Then we'll have to go it alone."

"What do you mean, 'go it alone'? I told you the time is not ripe. If you won't see reason, I'll have to take steps to save you from yourselves."

"Please help us, Raúl," Ramona called after him as he took his leave. But he did not seem to hear her.

That night, however, he sent his troops to occupy the port, the railway station, the post and telegraph station, the radio station, the palacio municipal, and even the cathedral. Then, without consulting his superior in Guadalajara, and quoting President Cárdenas to justify his actions, he fired the governor, the mayor, the chief magistrate and the captain of police, and replaced them with loyal army officers.

In the morning he came riding up to the Red Shirts on his horse to tell them that he'd declared martial law.

"I have done so against my own better judgment," he said. "But I bow to the will of the masses."

"And you will not be disappointed in us," said Narciso.

"It's not you that I'm worried about," said Mondragón.

CHAPTER 6

"Oh, I just love you to do my hair, Mama," Chris purred, as Maureen, late for a visit at the city prison, sat with her in the backseat of the touring car, running a brush through her straight black bob.

"Not so long ago," she muttered, "you'd have screamed 'Ow, ow, ow, you're hurting me!' at the top of your lungs, and made your nanny's life unbearable."

"I like you much better than Ramona, Mama."

"Well, that's not the way I remember it."

"Uh . . ." said Chris, squirming in her seat. "That was before."

"Before what? You certainly have a short memory. She's only been gone for three months. If that's the kind of loyalty you've got, I'd hate to imagine what you'd think of me if I went away for a while."

"But you won't go away, will you, Mama?"

"Sit still, dammit," Maureen said. "Quit your fidgeting."

"I'll be good, Mama, I'll be good."

"So," said Maureen, "you like me better than Ramona, do you?"

"Oh yes I do, ever so much."

"Well, let me tell you something," Maureen said. She couldn't help it. She had meant to be nicer. She wanted to love her. But the child irked her so. "I don't much care for this meek little lamby-pie voice you've affected ever since Ramona went away."

"I won't do it anymore, Mama, I won't do it."

"Really, I'd find you much less obnoxious if you'd leave it off, dear."

"I promise, I promise, I promise to God."

"Well, good. But let's leave God out of it, shall we? Where are you getting all of this religious instruction lately?"

"Grandma Carrizo."

"What does she tell you?"

"All about the Virgin."

"Which Virgin?"

"The Virgin of Zapopán, the Virgin of Remedios, the Virgin of Guadalupe . . ."

"Chris, I would leave my religious instruction to the priests, if I were you," Maureen said, as Gallo's mean little eyes flitted across the rear-view mirror. "Señora Carrizo is just an ignorant, superstitious old woman."

"Yes, Mama."

"And don't agree with me so much. I find you much more sufferable as a little wench. Though I do wish we could strike a happy medium, somewhere along the line."

Gallo drove them out to the city prison the long way, ten kilometers around the Puerto Interior and the Laguna de San Pedrito, avoiding the ferry crossing at the mouth of the port, and the stinking slums of Las Brisas, where a gang of red-shirted agrarian activists and striking stevedores, armed by Mondragón and calling themselves "the popular militia," had set up a roadblock and were stopping traffic to collect "political taxes" while the purged local police looked the other way.

The jail was located in a massive old stone structure covered with moss. In colonial times it had been a tobacco factory, but it more closely resembled a medieval Spanish castle. It was somber and high-walled and romantic, built high out on a point overlooking the Bay of Manzanillo. And it had a reputation as a mankiller, because of the dankness of its dungeons. But Brian had his rooms in the Hidalgo Wing, a section reserved traditionally for the rich and noble, and they were light, pleasant and airy, even chic: two red-tiled and tastefully furnished floors in a stone tower above the walls, complete with terrace, a magnificent view of the sea, the city, the mountains. And with a weekly rent to match.

They arrived at the prison an hour late. It was nearly siesta time when

Gallo honked his horn outside the massive front gate. A sleepy-looking guard swung it open, and they drove into the courtyard. After a cursory shakedown by a couple of apologetic prison officials, they were conducted to Brian's digs in the tower, where he was just sitting down, along with Licenciado de Benito, Bishop LeFevre, Assistant Trainmaster Hollister, and United States Consul Jeffers, to an elegant repast of chicken mole, white California wine and fresh fruit salad. The meal was served by Carmen, who worked now as Brian's personal servant, trundling over every morning on the rickety prison bus with food, clean linen and news of the world.

The men all looked a bit grim as they rose to greet Maureen and her daughter, and to nod in Gallo's general direction. Indeed, poor C.J. looked even worse: He had gone all hollow and yellow in the face; and it was said he had not long to live.

But Carmen seemed unusually bright and commanding today. And if what Maureen had deduced from the unexpected appearance of all these important personages was correct, Carmen had every right to be. Watching her now as she bustled about with a secret smile, serving Brian's guests the meal she had cooked in his kitchen downstairs, Maureen saw that all of her hopes for Brian were soon to be dashed. And her spirits fell to their lowest ebb since Brian's arrest, his indictment for murder, since the flight of Father Dowd and the birth of her bastard daughter . . . fell so perilously low that she let out a small involuntary cry of pain and nearly caused a scene.

She understood that a marriage of convenience was imperative at this time, if the O'Hares weren't to lose everything they possessed. And she was not particularly surprised that Brian had failed to consult her beforehand; he had always been headstrong and he would have anticipated her veto. Even Carmen's close relationship with her sleazy little brother-in-law did not overly concern her. Maureen could always handle Gallo. He was susceptible to bribery.

What really devastated her was the cumulative effect. Here was still another defeat—just one in a long string of them—that she had allowed this wretched country to inflict upon her. It was as if the climate took something—some vital force—out of you, leaving you torpid and will-less. She'd even given up trying to write stories in recent years, and she found it more and more difficult to focus her attention on poetry and serious literature, and wasted much of her time reading trashy romantic novels.

"The reason I've gathered you all here today," Brian said, in the resigned, chastened tone that he had employed since his humiliation at the hands of Mondragón, "is to announce that I have proposed to Carmen, and she has been pleased to accept."

She blamed it all on Father Dowd. She saw that she had been waiting for him all these years. Yet now if he suddenly appeared she would run from him in terror. She had been waiting for nothing. . . .

"Come up here a moment, dear," Brian called down to Carmen in the kitchen. "I want you to hear this too."

If he had not died, if he had not disappeared . . .

And when Carmen had scurried up the circular iron staircase in her bare feet, she sat her by his side at the head of the table.

. . . she would have gone home while she still had some influence over Brian. He would have followed her to San Francisco. By now he would be a junior vice-president at the Southern Pacific or the Santa Fe . . . would be gladdening his mama's heart by marrying a beautiful, cultivated young lady of his own race and class. . . . Instead . . .

"You can count on me, Carmen. I'll never let you or your family down. And who knows? With time?"

. . . here he was in a Mexican prison, accused of murder, with a future you could count on only till the next twist of fate, marrying a silly little mestiza girl who should have remained his maid. . . .

"In return, dear, I must rely on you and trust you to accept all my property in your name, with the understanding that it will revert to me again when the rule of law returns to this state."

Her saucy little cupid's-bow mouth curled downward into a solemn look . . .

"Do you accept me under these conditions, Carmen?"

. . . she was actually crying now, tears of joy rolling down her plump brown cheeks . . .

"I do," she said.

"Then," he said, pulling a rolled parchment paper from his oak floor chest, "please sign this document to that effect, dear. Licenciado de Benito will notarize it in our presence; and Consul Jeffers, Mr. Hollister and Gallo will serve as witnesses."

"But I wanted him to marry Ramona!" Chris whined.

"Shhhhh, mind your manners," Maureen said. And then wondered why she had bothered.

The bishop performed the church service in the prison chapel. Brian sent Gallo down to the municipal palace to bribe the city clerk to come up and perform the civil ceremony, and before the afternoon was out they were man and wife in the eyes of both Church and State.

When it came time for the congratulations, Maureen slipped out with Chris and waited in the car, for she could not think of kissing the bride. Instead she thought of kissing her daughter, who seemed as in need of consolation as she. Maureen reached out tenuously to touch her little girl, but she could not. Unaccustomed to such displays of affection, she would have felt embarrassed before Chris.

Yet only a few days later Maureen had recovered sufficiently from her distress to assure her son in private of her intention to "make the best of a bad lot," and to accept an important commission on his behalf.

She left Chris in the reluctant care of Grandma Carrizo, the hotel in the capable but cupiditous hands of Gallo (she took it for granted that he would pilfer a certain percentage of the take, but as long as he didn't go too far—and he wouldn't—she figured it was worth it), and caught a rickety little open Model A Ford taxi to the Manzanillo station. She stopped at the rectory on the way to pick up Monsignor LeFevre. He was carrying an expensive leather suitcase and wearing a homburg hat and a gray pin-striped lounge suit; he looked like a prosperous banker on a business trip. They had a private first-class compartment on the new express train, and they were going to petition General Sánchez at the comandancia. The Company had decided that they would make the most effective lobbyists against Mondragón. General Sánchez had a weakness for redheads, it was said; and despite his cruel and despotic qualities and his "war" against the Cristeros in 1927 he was supposed to be a deeply religious Roman Catholic, with close ties to the archbishop of Guadalajara, as well as to the Church's hierarchy in Mexico City. Maureen was to appeal to him as a mother whose only son was wasting away in prison for a crime he hadn't committed. Bishop LeFevre would appeal to him on behalf of the Church, which had lost all of its parochial schools to the state, and was about to be shut down entirely. Together they would explain how Mondragón's policy of unreined socialist experimentation—including the seizure of land and property, union organizing, antibusiness agitation, anticlericism and vicious gringo-baiting—which he had pursued since his illegal declaration of martial law had had disastrous consequences on the local economy and morale. In order to ensure the general's cooperation, Mrs. O'Hare was carrying on her person (in her corset) an enormous bribe.

As the train was leaving town, it passed a long line of boxcars fitted out with living accommodations. It was pulled off onto a rail siding, near a large banana plantation, and it swarmed with ragged, barefoot women, dirty children, featherless chickens, and quick little black pigs. Armed peasants sat on the tops of the cars, shaded from the burning rays of the sun by their straw sombreros.

Maureen recognized no one on the train, and she was about to turn to Monsignor LeFevre to make some remark when her eye caught that of a pretty mestiza girl sitting under an agüilote tree, spoon-feeding a sick-looking little four-year-old. It was Ramona Mescalero. Maureen gaped in astonishment, and was about to pull down the window and shout something when she thought better of it.

The last thing she needed around the Hotel O'Hare was another Mescalero girl.

Still, she had underestimated Ramona. She had heard that she was working for Mondragón in some sort of "secretarial" capacity and she had assumed that meant a sleeping arrangement as well. Now she admired the girl for her pluck and her spirit, and made a mental note to send Gallo over with enough money to get her to Mexico City where she could make a fresh start.

"I don't suppose it can be much fun," Monsignor LeFevre was saying, "living on a train like that."

"Fun?" said Maureen, who was barely listening. "I should think it's fun. They've got everything they ever wanted. They even got that banana plantation, from what I've been told. You know, that's Davey Whitlaw's plantation. He inherited it from his father."

"That is so true," said the bishop, suddenly changing his tack. "I understand that Mondragón has even given them a deed."

"Well, Brian said that General Sánchez intended to make us really sweat. . . ."

"I think we've sweated enough, don't you, señora?"

"Enough for a lifetime."

"And I," he said. "I just go from Mass to Mass, hoping they'll let me serve the next. All these threats . . . yesterday I got one from the Red Shirts: 'Say your prayers, for tomorrow you die.' "

"And yet, Monsignor, here you are, still alive and kicking, aren't you?" she said, and immediately the atmosphere between them thickened.

"Actually," he said, swelling his chest, "I've never felt better."

"Why, you're a man in the prime of life," she said. "Still, it's probably a good thing to get out of town for a few days, don't you think?"

"Especially in such charming company," he said. "And who knows, eh? We might even do some good. No?"

"My son believes we shall."

"Your son is right."

"This time Sánchez will have to act."

"He has no choice."

"Mondragón has gone too far."

"Any farther and there won't be much left."

"Not even enough for a general to steal."

"Sánchez knows that, señora. In the next week or so, you'll see. Mondragón will receive a transfer to some remote outpost in the Huichol Indian country, and when he appeals to Cárdenas for help he'll get the runaround."

"Really?" she said. "You'd think Cárdenas would be perfectly delighted with him: He's put all of his most farfetched ideals into practice."

"Not so delighted as you might imagine, señora. I have it on the highest authority that President Cárdenas is actually contemplating a secret alliance with the Church."

"Oh come now, Monsignor."

"Look at it from Cárdenas's point of view. His most powerful enemy, General Calles, is planning an insurrection which has every chance of success. He's vulnerable on only one plane—the religious. As you know, Calles is a notorious atheist, Freemason and anticleric. What you didn't know, perhaps, is that he has made a secret alliance with the Red Shirts, whom he has encouraged to attack priests and destroy churches all over the Republic."

"Not in this part of the Republic he hasn't."

"The omission only proves the rule, señora. Listen to me. If Cárdenas could secure the support of the Church by disarming the Red Shirts and relaxing the anticlerical laws, he could undercut Calles and gain the most powerful ally in Mexico, all in one fell swoop. We Catholics still constitute a majority in the army and the Congress, after all, as well as in the population at large."

"A complicated strategy, Monsignor. And a cynical one as well."

"But a likely one, no?"

"Given your Mexican propensity for intrigue and double-dealing, I imagine so," she said. "And I have always felt that Mondragón takes all of this socialist rhetoric far too seriously. Haven't you?"

"It's only a passing phase, señora. An alien ideology. It has no roots in Mexico."

"Then what could Mondragón be thinking of?"

"Mondragón is one of our Mexican provincials. He spent some time in Europe as a military attaché. He came back with a lot of half-digested political ideas. He came into contact with a bunch of Red Shirts and peasant activists. . . . Here the peasant wouldn't know a Bolshevik from a New Deal Democrat, señora, a Ruski from a Yanqui—they're all a bunch of gringos to him. But he is disorderly and rebellious by nature. He's obsessed with a dream of his own little plot of corn, his own little bit of village common land for pasture. And every few years he rises up in armed revolt to obtain it. It's been going on for centuries. . . . So Mondragón came back from Paris and Moscow and he shot off his mouth. And all of a sudden he found himself riding a wave of popular sentiment over which he had no control. The wave is strong and fast, señora, but it is very shallow at the base. And now it's only a matter of time before Mondragón takes a fall."

"I must admit, I shall not be too much bereaved."

"He's a dangerous type," said the bishop. "Altruism has wreaked more havoc in Mexico than all the sinners combined."

"My son would agree, I think."

"Your son is a strange case himself . . . marrying that girl."

"We had little choice, given our financial and legal predicament. And Brian's . . ."

"Unfortunate predilection for the darker races?"

"Brian is a sensualist, I'm afraid. Like his mother."

"My dear Mrs. O'Hare, you will shock me if you continue. I am a man of God."

"A man of God is still a man," she said.

She was quite aware of the effect she had created on him. Besides, the bishop was fooling no one. He was a notorious lecher, and it was common knowledge that he had recently taken his mestiza housekeeper as his mistress.

The train stopped briefly in Colima and then headed up into the high country near the volcano. As they were crossing a suspension bridge over a deep barranca, Monsignor LeFevre pointed to a dirt road carved into the side of a cliff and said, "There is the place I spoke of once, at your reception—the place where Mondragón saved my life. And yet," he said, "now all I feel is—I owed him a debt and now we're even. I went to him, señora. I tried to make him see reason."

"Monsignor," she said. "I have a confession to make."

"This is hardly the time or place."

"Exactly where and when would that be?"

"Perhaps we can arrange something later?"

"Why, Monsignor LeFevre!"

"Well, what was it that you had in mind?"

"Your friend Father Dowd, whom you spoke of once."

"You knew him?"

"I kept him for a time in Colima when he was running from the law."

"Kept?"

"Yes, he was afraid for his life."

"His life?" said the Bishop, leering. "Or his soul?"

"Perhaps both," she admitted.

"Did you ever hear from him again?"

"Never."

"I'm afraid he died in a mangrove swamp," he said. "It appears that he went in, but he didn't come out. The swamp is inhabited by a tribe of Indians that worship a kind of bird that's supposed to live in an alamo tree."

"You think they murdered him," Maureen said, catching her breath.

"They are quite capable of it."

"Well then," she sighed. "Maybe I can finally let him go."

"I hope so," said the bishop. "Apparently the Indians could not."

It took Maureen and the monsignor only an hour the next day to convince old General Sánchez of where his best advantage lay. They left him with a certified check for thirty thousand dollars American, and an understanding that he would personally remove Mondragón from power, forthwith.

In case of resistance, he said, he intended to ship three companies of infantry by rail to back him up. He was not afraid of what Mondragón would do, he said. The colonel was a good soldier and he would obey orders. It was the Red Shirts that he was worried about. And with this in mind he advised that Maureen and the bishop stay away from Manzanillo "till the dust has settled."

They stayed with Dr. Bermúdez in Colima, in the hotel on the central plaza where Maureen had spent sixteen years of her widowhood.

Maureen sent a telegram to Gallo, arranging to have Chris and Merle sent up on the first available passenger train, with Grandma Carrizo as nanny.

They all arrived on a Friday evening, when the hotel was full of commercial travelers. Bishop LeFevre had to double up with Dr. Bermúdez. Chris, Merle and Grandma Carrizo slept in the servants' quarters. And Maureen was obliged to sleep just under the roof, in the little room where Father Dowd had lain hidden in 1927.

She approached the room timidly, with a candle in her hand, and opened the door hesitantly, as if it might be haunted by ghosts. Having ascertained to her satisfaction that she was alone in the room, she undressed and crawled into bed naked. It was the same little rough pine bed where she had slept so many nights with Father Dowd. It even smelled the same, she thought: slightly resinish. The room excited her, and stirred up all of her memories. She could see Father Dowd beside her in the moonlight, his pale, silky-haired chest slowly rising and falling. She could see his gaunt, martyr's face, his dark-rimmed eyes. Oh but Jesus and Mary he had been so young! He had made her young. The years fell away and she was sixteen again, standing on the steamer slip in San Diego, setting out for another adventure, the warm wind whipping up her petticoats. And then, years later, she could see young Father Dowd rising from her bed, making for the door. She could see herself leaping up, getting him around the knees, holding him back. She could see the look on his face. She withered at his look. And saw him setting out into the night, heading steadfastly toward the mangrove swamp that she had warned him specifically against. She wondered whatever had possessed him to do such a thing. And then she decided that she knew.

It was the way he had paid.

Chris was the way she paid.

She wondered if by some miracle Father Dowd might still be alive somewhere in the mangrove swamp. She thought of traveling there, of seeking the truth. She wondered what he would look like now, if he were still alive. He would still be quite young, of course, only thirty-five years old. But life would be hard in the swamp, and the Mexican sun is cruel to fair skin. She wondered what his life would be like, had he stayed among the Indians. She imagined that they would come to adore him, if they hadn't killed him. She thought that they would love him as she had done.

She tossed and turned, sweating and dreaming, and then in the wee hours she was awakened by a scratch at her door. At first she thought it might be the hotel cat. But when it persisted, she rose to see what it was.

"It is I," he said.

Her heart stopped. She staggered back toward the bed. And yet she found herself suddenly wet and aroused, as if she'd already done it once, and was in immediate expectancy of doing it again.

"Can it be?"

"I assure you, it can."

"Is it really you?"

"In the flesh," he said, and his cynicism snapped her clear.

"Monsignor," she said, "what can you want at this hour?"

"What he wanted."

"He is dead."

"Well, now it's my turn," he said, pushing at the door, "for the kiss of death."

"Why, what a sinful thought."

"You attend to the body," the bishop said, drawing her toward the dark bed, "and I will attend to the soul."

CHAPTER 7

Raúl saw himself as a boy again, an eighteen-year-old second lieutenant of cavalry, riding a stolen palomino, wearing the equipment of five dead men: a black sombrero, crossed bandoliers, Mexican riding boots with jangling silver spurs, a Colt .44 with a bone handle, a U.S. Cavalry saber. The year was 1915. His unit, the 4th Cavalry Regiment of General Álvaro Obregón's Constitutionalist Army, had participated the year before with General Pancho Villa's Northern Division in the destruction of the corrupt Federalist government of General Huerta. But the two armies had fallen out over the issue of social reform—the Villistas and their allies the Zapatistas wanting radical reforms, the Constitutionalists desiring only moderate reforms—and they had engaged in battle at Celaya in April of 1915. It was a long and bloody battle, the most vast and destructive in Mexico since Cortez's Siege of Tenochtitlán, over four hundred years before, and almost no one on either side escaped injury. Raúl himself sustained a flesh wound on his thigh, and even General Obregón lost an arm. But in the end the Constitutionalists emerged triumphant, and General Villa took to his heels. Raúl's unit pursued him all the long way up the Northern Railway line. But he gave them the slip in Chihuahua, in his native hills. And then suddenly he appeared outside their quarters at Nogales, on the Sonora-Arizona border, having traversed the snowy Sierra Madre without food or clothing in a storm of ice. Apparently he believed he could take them by surprise, since no mortal being could perform such a feat of arms. But by now they were used to the ways of their old Pancho, and they were ready for him with prepared fortifications—trenches, barbed-wire entanglements, high-tension wires, machine-gun concentrations, crossed fields of fire—all of which they had learned about by reading newspaper reports of trench warfare in Europe. They had even arranged with the U.S. army in Nogales, Arizona, to line the border with powerful searchlights, in case of night attack.

They first caught sight of him at dawn. Raúl would never forget it—six thousand wraithlike warriors and three thousand animals crossing the arid plain in a great billowing cloud of dust that blotted out the rising sun and, through some trick of the prism, cast a shadow on the desert as dark and red as blood.

General Villa had brought two batteries of field artillery with him, and thirty light Maxim guns. But his men were worn down by their ordeal in the mountains, and his opposition on the Constitutionalist side consisted of seven thousand fresh troops, ten railway cannon and a hundred heavy-caliber machine guns.

All that morning they dueled with artillery across the barren flatlands. The Villista fire was uncannily accurate. It was as if old Pancho had an observer with a mirror on top of the palacio municipal. Raúl took two direct hits on the adobe wool warehouse where he was quartered with his troop of horse soldiers, and suffered a number of serious casualties.

Then in the hazy light of early afternoon General Villa led his cavalry against the Constitutionalist lines in a wild charge across a dry lake. But he faltered almost immediately, and he crumbled to bits in the trenches and barbed wire, the enfilading machine-gun fire, the incessant bombardment of the five-inch railroad cannons.

Raúl and his men lay behind a low sandy ridge of juniper windbreak on the edge of town and aimed for Villa's horses with their Mausers, bringing them down by the dozen, picking off their riders as they tried to limp off into the cactus and mesquite. When the charge was done, a thousand Villistas lay dead with their animals on the floor of the desert, and hundreds more lay wounded and bleeding in the sun, or flapping like scarecrows on the wire, while great black-winged zopilotes wheeled overhead and dove shrieking to squabble over the spoils.

Yet General Villa had brought no provisions with him. He had to win the town in order to feed his starving army.

That night he resorted to a desperate mass attack across the open desert. But his foot soldiers activated a trip wire that had been strung across the alkali flats. Over the border the arc lights switched on automatically, and the Villistas were caught in their powerful beams. Their shadows grew suddenly long in the night. Their eyes flashed like rabbit eyes in the light, and they fell prey again to an intricate and terrible crossfire of mortar, massed howitzers, machine guns and Mausers. They screamed in panic. They ran for their lives. But the lights pursued them even into the hills.

Raúl and his men mounted up and gave chase. Howling like Yaquis, they rode the Villistas to earth, smiting them down with their sabers, trampling them into the dust.

They trapped a hundred of them in a waterless box canyon and drove them back to town like sheep. Raúl lined them up in front of the municipal palace and when his commanding officer appeared at dawn he asked:

"Qué hago con estos cabrones, mi comandante?"

Raúl was in awe of his grizzled little bowlegged Tarascan Indian commander, Major Saturnino Sánchez, whom he had followed across Mexico for two years through thick and thin, and he already knew the answer.

"Shoot them."

He herded them into a donkey corral on the outskirts of town. Some of them were crying. Some were groaning in pain. Some were begging for water. Others cursed their luck, or commended Obregón and his mother to the devil, or called him a gringo and a foreigner (the name Obregón was a Spanish corruption of the Irish O'Brian, but the general's family had resided in Mexico for nearly a hundred years). All of the prisoners were gaunt and ragged and hollow-eyed, and several had already lost control of their bowels.

Raúl set up a Maxim gun in the gateway and gave the order to fire.

"Wait, wait!" an anonymous Villista cried, causing the machine gunner to pause. "Why waste bullets on burros?"

Everyone laughed, even the most frightened and horribly wounded. Even the machine gunner. Even Raúl.

The Villistas drove four small donkeys from the pen, swatting their tails, kicking them in the withers, making wry and jealous comments as to their charmed fates.

Raúl raised his sword again.

There was not a sound in the corral but the dry wind blowing, the sand hitting the wood slats on the fence.

Just as he was about to let the sword fall a bearded Villista officer caught his eye. They knew each other well. They had fought together against the Federals in the state of Tlaxcala in July of 1914, and they had met in Mexico City after the collapse of the Huerta government a month later. His name was First Captain Hipolito de León. He approached timidly, though he was a much older man.

"Raulito," he whispered. "Without me how will my family live?"

Raúl's first impulse was compassionate. He had been introduced to de León's family once. A charming little creole wife, a boy of six and a pretty little girl of nine. They came for a weekend when they were stationed together at Chapultepec Palace and they all went for a stroll in Maximilian's garden, sniffing roses.

Yet, because he was very young and afraid of being viewed as weak or softhearted, and because he considered de León a disgraceful coward for begging for his life when his comrades were consigned to the grave, his sympathy turned instantly into a blind and homicidal rage.

"Let them eat crow!" he shrieked, and thrust at him viciously with his sword.

The death of Captain de León was like a signal to the machine gunner. He opened up and slaughtered the Villistas to a man. They lay in the dirt in their own evacuating feces, in piles of three and four, bleeding like pigs. The Constitutionalists attacked the corpses like scavenger birds, looting the bodies, prying out gold fillings, stealing boots, belts and bandoliers.

Though Raúl would repent of this and other crimes that he committed in the name of the Revolution, and though he would leave the service of his bloodthirsty comandante after his participation in the conspiracy to murder Zapata in 1917, this episode at Nogales would continue to haunt him as a recurrent dream over the years.

In the dream, which was always the same, he was no longer a Constitucionalista but a Villista. He was captured and about to be killed. He searched out the youngest of his enemies, an officer with a sensitive, intelligent face that resembled his own, and begged him for mercy in the name of his wife and children. He scanned his overexcited, boyish eyes, that were murky and hazel-colored like his own, hoping for some sign of compassion. But he saw only the purest bloodlust there, an unaccountable, hereditary rage to kill. *"Let them eat crow!"* the young officer shrieked. Raúl raised his hands to protect himself, but the boy thrust with his saber through his outstretched fingers and the palms of his hands. He was pierced by the sword several times in the chest. It was as if his skin were a cloak to keep him warm, and the holes let the cold come in. He was invaded by icy drafts of air from the snowy Sierra. The cold became more and more acute, till all the cold in the world seemed concentrated in his lungs. They imploded into a billion freezing particles and he was transformed into a block of ice. Yet when he awakened, he was invariably bathed in sweat.

The dream recurred about once or twice a year, and Raúl had found that it was nearly always an evil omen, a harbinger of ill tidings.

And so it was twenty years after the violence at Nogales, on September 15, 1935, when he awakened from his terrible dream to find his orderly standing over him with a tray of café con leche and panes dulces and a telegram from General Saturnino Sánchez:

COLONEL MONDRAGÓN RELIEVED
OF DUTIES COLIMA STATE
EFFECTIVE THIS DATE REPORT
MILITARY HQ GUADALAJARA
WITHOUT DELAY

Later, as he sat drafting a reply to General Sánchez's telegram, he went over in his mind their long years of association. He remembered a bright summer day in his native village—Jocotepec, on beautiful Lake Chapala—when Saturnino came clattering into the market plaza on a great black warhorse, leading a troop of irregular cavalry. It was June of 1913, two years after Francisco Madero, with the aid of such men as Pancho Villa in the north and Emiliano Zapata in the south, had brought down the tyrannical thirty-year regime of Don Porfirio Díaz, proclaiming a new era of democracy and social justice; and it was less than six months since Army Commander Victoriano Huerta had deposed and murdered President Madero in a coup d'état.

Saturnino reined up near the fountain, where the women sat gossiping as they filled their water jars, and gave a pugnacious little recruiting speech.

"Is there no one in this miserable hole who is man enough to join us in avenging the death of the President of the Republic, Francisco Madero?"

He sat astride his dark prancing charger in a tight-fitting charro outfit and a great black sombrero, and to Raúl—a mere village lad, a herdsman of goats and cows for his father—he seemed the soul of romance.

Raúl ran up to him in his bare feet, shouting, "Let me come, mi capitán, let me come!"

"How old are you, muchacho?"

"Seventeen," he lied.

"Have you got a horse?"

"I can get one."

"Andale pues!"

He stole a kilo of tortillas from his uncle's tortillería, saddled his papa's piebald mare, and he was off in a cloud of dust.

"Where are you going, my son?" his mama called after him.

"To the front!" he cried, though there was nothing so defined as a "front" in those early days. "I'll be back in a few weeks!" He would not see her again for over a decade, and he would not leave the saddle for thirteen years.

He remembered that long and bitter first year when Saturnino and his squadron of irregular horse fought alone against the Huerta forces in the mountains, the deserts, the jungles of Morelos and Michoacán while their Constitutionalist allies—General Obregón and General Pancho Villa—slowly battled their way down toward them from Sonora and Chihuahua. He remembered the weeks they spent trapped with the battered remnants of the squadron in a cave on the Volcano of Zacapu while the Huerta troops sat patiently encamped at the foot of the mountain, waiting for them to descend for provisions. He remembered eating insects, moss, shoe leather, and finally human flesh. He remembered their miraculous escape—only six of them, all that remained—in a violent rainstorm, creeping past the sheltering Huerta pickets on their bellies, like salamanders or water snakes. He recalled everything that Saturnino Sánchez had taught him of the art of war, and all that he had told him about the Revolution, which he described as "the Battle of Mexico, the fight that's been going on ever since Cortez landed in Vera Cruz on Good Friday, 1519, the war of the Haves and Have-Nots, the white and bronze, the landed and landless, the indigenous and the foreign, the Mexican and the Ultramontane." He remembered the stories that Saturnino told of his former life, especially the one in which his tribe of Tarascans was swindled of its communal lands on Lake Pátzcuaro and left to wander the cities as beggars and tinkerers, rattling their little tin cups from door to door. He remembered that Saturnino promoted him to sergeant when he was seventeen, and lieutenant at eighteen, and that he had saved his life more than once. He also recalled the fact that—compelled by some kind of irrational, almost filial loyalty—he entered his service twice more after his treachery of 1917. He even remembered a time in the twenties: Saturnino came to Europe on holiday with his wife. Raúl was attending the French Army War College at St. Cyr, after having completed a preliminary course of study at the École Militaire in Paris. "Can I come down and visit?" the general telegraphed. "Of course you can," Raúl wired back, with a sinking feeling. Saturnino left Señora Sánchez with Raúl's wife, Ana-María, in Paris, and caught a train to St. Cyr. That night in the officers' mess Saturnino created such a furor with his crude and vulgar antics—loudly discussing the merits and demerits of all the French whores, French perfumes and French frippery that he had known in Mexico—that Raúl was obliged to come to his defense, which resulted in an ungentlemanly fistfight and his instant expulsion from the War College just a week before matriculation. "Raulito," Saturnino said, with tears in his eyes, on their drunken train ride back to Paris, "I beg you to forgive me. I'm only a poor Indian. My father could neither read nor write. These Frenchmen eat like pussycats, and preen themselves like birds of paradise."

"My only regret," Raúl replied, only half in jest, "is that I have but one career to give up for you, mi general."

Nor had Raúl forgotten his mentor's cunning, his cruelty, cupidity and deceit. He remembered when Saturnino joined up with Obregón in 1914 and looted Guadalajara of gold. He remembered when Saturnino sacked Mexico City later that same year, and betrayed his friend Pancho Villa in 1915. He remembered the women he raped, the honest Chinese tradesmen he quartered for sport, the prisoners he tortured, the innocents he slaughtered in countless villages. He remembered exactly how he conspired with the Carranza government against Zapata and helped seduce him to his death. He remembered when he betrayed the archbetrayer, the unfaithful Constitutionalist President Venustiano Carranza, and hunted him to his death in the Sierra Madre Oriental. Nor did he forget his own culpability in many of these actions, especially in the early years when he was much under Saturnino's sway.

His reply to General Sánchez's telegram was brief:

REQUEST THREE-MONTH DEFERRAL OF
ORDERS TO FACILITATE ORDERLY
TRANSFER OF POWER

General Sánchez's response, which Raúl received within the hour, was even briefer:

OBEY

His duty as an officer was therefore quite clear. It was his conscience that bothered him. He decided to seek advice directly from President Cárdenas, with whom he enjoyed excellent relations.

In the long telegram that he composed for the president, he outlined his achievements in Colima State since his declaration of martial law. He spoke of the considerable strides he had made in his plans for local land reform, health care, education, organization of trade unions, co-operatives and collective farms, suppression of bureaucratic corruption, and curtailment of the reactionary influence of the Church. He emphasized the fact that he had barely gotten beyond the planning stage as yet, and that he would need at least another six to eight months to set the Revolution in Colima State safely on its way. He did not hesitate to appeal to the president on an emotional basis as well. He recalled the fond relations of their wives, who were first cousins and frequent correspondents. He reminded him of his long service as his aide-de-camp, and of the long cavalry campaigns that they had fought together. "For two years, mi presidente, from 1917 to 1919, we tracked the bandit General Manuel Palaez across the pestilential flatlands of tropical Huasteca, only to find that he was bankrolled by Yanqui oil barons with an interest in reversing the progress of the Revolution. And in 1923, when General de la Huerta, the gringos, the Church and the landowners conspired again to overturn our elected government in a counterrevolution, I was by your side from our first battle, at Jiquilpan, Jalisco, on 12 December 1923, when you were gravely wounded, until our final victory in March of 1924." Raúl also spoke of the many values of socialism that they shared, and of their long-held vision of a resurgent, prosperous, egalitarian Mexico free from foreign domination. He confided to the president his very strong suspicions that General Sánchez was in the pay of the archbishop of Guadalajara, and was conspiring with him and a local clique of rich foreign traders and native latifundists to defraud the peasants of Colima of all the fruits they had won in the Revolution. And finally he expressed his extreme views on the subject of regional caudillos in general, alluding to them as "bloodsuckers and parasites who must be eliminated if this nation is to survive the next decade."

He received President Cárdenas's response the next morning, and on the afternoon of the same day he called his troops and his peasant and worker auxiliaries together in the central plaza to convey to them his final determination.

"Compañeros," he said, standing on the steps of the cathedral, gazing out on a brown-skinned throng of Red Shirts and army—perhaps two thousand men, women and children—which packed the Jardín Obregón from end to end. "It is my sad task to inform you that General Sánchez has relieved me of my duties in Colima State, and ordered me to report to military headquarters in Guadalajara."

"Que no! Que no! Que no!" the crowd began to chant, but Raúl held up his hands for silence.

"I have been in touch with President Cárdenas, compañeros, and he has advised me to obey."

"Then he is no friend of the proletariat!" shouted Policarpo Reyes, the leader of the Stevedores' Union.

"Nor is he a friend of the campesino!" bellowed Narciso Nieves.

"Listen to me, comrades," Raúl said. "We are not strong enough to defy General Sánchez militarily. And the federal government, preoccupied as it is with its own survival, is in no position to come to our aid. I have decided to leave for Guadalajara tonight. My advice to the troops is to return to your barracks and await your new commander. My advice to the popular militia is to disband and disperse, at least temporarily, for General Sánchez is sure to move up several companies of his own troops to enforce his authority."

"But we have no place to disperse to!" cried Narciso Nieves, to the deafening cheers of his audience. "Unlike you, comandante, we are rooted to one spot!"

"I know it may cause you hardship," Raúl said, when the tumult had died down, "and I am sorry if I have encouraged your hopes too strongly. But the time has come to face reality, compañeros. It would behoove us all to make ourselves scarce for the time being, and await a more opportune moment."

"The moment is now!" shouted Narciso Nieves. "Cárdenas cannot allow us to be defeated. He will lose his reputation as the 'friend of the proletariat.' The moment is now!"

"Que sí! Que sí! Que sí!" the crowd thundered back.

"President Cárdenas simply hasn't got the means to help us. We must take the long view," Raúl protested, but he doubted if anyone heard him.

"Sin vergüenza, sin vergüenza," they hissed at him as he descended the steps of the cathedral. "Shameless one, shameless one!"

Soon they grew tired of that game, however, and they coalesced around Narciso Nieves, who stood in the gazebo in the center of the plaza, exhorting them to insurrection.

". . . We shall resist to the death. We shall fight to the last man, the last woman, the last child. We'll never give up. Our very bones will protest from the grave, and our ghosts will pursue the oppressor in his dreams. . . ."

On his way from the plaza, Mondragón met his secretary, Ramona Mescalero. She was waiting for him near the flower garden, in a group of five or six excited and angry young people, and apparently she had filched a red rose for her hair. She could do with the color, as her work for Raúl, the Red Shirts and the squatters' train had left her little time to recover from her ordeal in the mudslide, and the pneumonia that followed it. Pale, haggard and underfed, Ramona was still an extraordinary beauty, even in the drab military fatigue uniform that she and her friends wore, and Raúl could not fail to appreciate it, in the same way that he appreciated her other remarkable qualities. Ramona had almost single-handedly organized his "office of civil administration" in the first hectic days of martial law. Later, she had acted as his special assistant, in his capacity as chief civil administrator, and lately he had begun to trust her with virtually the entire day-to-day running of the city. At the same time, unfortunately, he had fallen a little in love with her. In deference to her innocence, however, and with rigorous application of the principles of socialist self-discipline, he had managed to keep himself at arm's distance from her. But now her life was at stake, and it was no time to mince words.

"Come with me to Guadalajara," he said, pulling her aside.

"What for?" she asked him bluntly. She was standing before her compañeros, who had just rejected him, and obviously her loyalties were torn.

"Narciso means what he says. He will lead you against Sánchez. And Sánchez will kill you."

"If *you* stay, Raúl, the troops will support us. And then we'll have a fighting chance."

"My dear, you never had a chance."

"Then what was the use?"

"The use? Well, you have organized yourselves. You have gained experience. Next time, perhaps . . ."

"But there won't be a next time," she said. "And you have left your job here undone."

"There's no use in dying," he said.

"Are you afraid?"

"I'm not particularly concerned about my own fate," he said. "My wife and children are in Mexico City, far from any fighting that might take place, and they are well provided for in my will. But if I spend my life cheaply now, who will get Sánchez in the end?"

"The *survivors* will get him," she said fiercely, waving toward Narciso on the bandstand. "You must seize the hour, comandante, whatever it may bring."

"If anyone could convince me, soldadera," he said, flashing her one of his rare grins, "it would be you. Are you sure you won't change your mind?"

"My place is here," she said. "But there is something I must tell you, Mondragón. I will never forgive you for this."

"If I were to resign my commission, Ramona," he said, choosing his words carefully, "and to join you in your struggle against the caudillo, as I admit you tempt me strongly to do . . ."

"It would be an act of faith," she said, "in all the things you profess to believe."

"It would be the worst kind of irresponsibility, because it would only serve to encourage you in your folly," he said. "Adiós, señorita, and good luck."

But she had already turned her back on him and rejoined her friends by the rose-garden wall.

CHAPTER 8

In the beginning, Carmen's marriage to Don Brian seemed little more than a formality, and it did nothing to change her life. She still had to cook and clean and sew for him in his tower. She still had to leave the prison every evening at dusk with the other servants and spouses. She still had to wait tables at the Hotel O'Hare every night. And she still had to ride the bus back every morning with food, fresh laundry and news of the world.

Then, after Colonel Mondragón went away, the prison was cut off from Manzanillo for several days, and Carmen was trapped inside. The Red Shirts had commandeered the Las Brisas ferry and set up a roadblock on the coastal road. Apparently they were going to resist General Sánchez when he arrived, Don Brian said, because they had occupied and fortified all the strategic positions that the army had abandoned when it returned to its barracks.

Locked in the prison tower with her new husband day after day, with nothing to do but fuss about his rooms, scrounge his food from the warden and cook his meals, Carmen grew restless and bored. She missed her boy Merle, and Grandma Carrizo, and Gallo. She even missed Ramona. And she began to feel herself tempted by the pleasures of the flesh.

There was an oddly righteous and fastidious side to Don Brian's Irish character that encouraged temptation. It was as if the business nature of their relationship precluded other more fragrant possibilities, as if dalliance were somehow illegal or unethical in his mind. Yet even Gallo had said that he had no objection to the consummation of their marriage. He had insisted on it, in fact. And her own inclinations toward the gringo, though never particularly fond or sympathetic, had always been strangely, perversely physical.

It was his pale, lightly freckled skin that did it, and the fine yellow hair of his foreign body, and the notion of it coming up against her dark and smooth opposition. It was the things that Gallo had told her about him. The way he danced on broken glass, and fucked niggers in shacks. It was what she and Gallo were going to do to him, when they got the chance.

She seduced him in the bathtub one morning after she had scrubbed his back. Ran her soapy brown hands down his white hairy chest and kissed him softly behind the ear. Watched him rise pinkly out of the water. Came around and went down on him without a sound. Drank him down. Then she made him laugh. Climbed into the bathtub with her sandals on. Hiked her skirt up over her hips and rode him like a pony in the bubbles, going giddyap, giddyap, giddyap, sending water swelling from one end of the tub to the other, splashing it out onto the floor that she would later have to mop. Then he turned the tables on her. Dragged her out of the tub, stripped off her things and flung her on his bed. Intent upon his labor, flexing his white muscles, astride her while the springs violently squeaked and bounced, he seemed cold and fearsome and delicious, a force of nature, a colossus of the north.

Later, when she tried to recall all the days that followed, she found that she could remember nothing they had said, only what they had done. Mostly what they did was just laugh and run around naked and make love. They made love for hours, for days on end. They made love in every position, and in every room of the tower. They made love till they fell asleep from exhaustion in the very act of love. They made love till they were sore and bleeding and then they made love some more. Yet in all that time Carmen learned nothing about the gringo beyond what she could see and feel. Not that it really bothered her that much. Actually, she thought she preferred things that way.

Only when they put on their clothes did she feel guilty, or dirty, or lonely for her own kind.

The truth was, even if she had wanted him, she could never have him. It was clear from the way he looked at her that he still loved Ramona, and considered Carmen something less. And though he went on and on about Ramona's "betrayal" of his family, and her joining up with the Red Shirts, he could not hide his jealousy over her role as Mondragón's private secretary, or his gloomy certainty that she'd followed the colonel to his new posting.

The prison was isolated for ten days, and then suddenly one morning the warden came with an order for Don Brian's immediate release, signed by General Sánchez himself. And an hour later, when Don Brian came walking out with Carmen, the general sat waiting for them in his touring car.

Small, plump and brown, he seemed lost in the backseat of his great long automobile. And to Carmen he looked perfectly harmless, almost cuddly, like a teddy bear dressed up as a soldier.

But false impressions such as this, she knew, had often proved fatal in the past.

"Get in," said the general happily. "Forgive me, señorita, if I am a little drunk. But I am celebrating."

The chauffeur took their bags. They joined Sánchez in his spacious backseat, and soon they were heading back into town by way of the Las Brisas road.

"How are you doing for money?" the general said. "Here, let me give you a couple of thousand. Lots more where that came from. No? How about a little shot of tequila then? Or maybe you'd prefer wine, señorita. Have a cigarette. They are imported from England. What do you say to a little California red? Eh? Champagne? Perhaps it's cooler in the heat. Have a cigar, Don Brian. . . ."

Carmen accepted an English cigarette and a glass of champagne, which she held with steady hands despite the fact that the car was bouncing violently, and General Sánchez had chosen to rest his horny old hand on her round little knee. Don Brian went for a fine Havana and some tequila, which he drank straight from the bottle, passing it back and forth with General Sánchez. But Don Brian was not nearly so steady as Carmen, and he spit up a mouthful of tequila when the car went over a large pothole.

"G-General," he stammered, "please forgive me."

"It is nothing," he said. "But why so nervous, Don Brian? It's not like you at all. And apparently you have achieved your every desire. No? You wanted Mondragón removed. Eh? Well, he is gone. You wanted order reestablished in Colima State. Bueno. I am here to execute your will. What more can you ask for?"

"Believe me, your excellency, I am not unmindful of your kindness and generosity," Don Brian said. "But my release from prison has come so suddenly."

"Prison?" said the general, as if it were the farthest thing from his mind.

". . . that it leaves me feeling rather . . ."

"Prison?" the general said again. He seemed to enjoy Don Brian's confusion.

". . . feeling a bit unreal."

"Prison?" Sánchez repeated, taking a great gulp of tequila, belching, thrusting it roughly into Don Brian's trembling hands. "Well, I hate to admit it, Señor Gringo, but you're probably right. Prison is just not a natural state, is it? The worst kind of torture for a man of free spirit. I'd rather be executed, I think, than spend a year behind bars. I remember one time back in the Revolution when old Pancho Villa captured me in Chihuahua. The jail was infested with lice. Three months I was in there. They nearly ate me alive. Until Pancho himself got thrown into prison in Mexico City. Then I got out, and I had a bath. You could have planted rice in the bathwater. But the nurse still had to shave off every hair on my body to get rid of the vermin. They were so big, so fat, so juicy and numerous, the doctor said, that they had sucked out liters of my blood. Another week and I'd have died of anemia, I think."

"Another week in city prison," Don Brian said, as they drove up onto the ferry, "and I'd have gone mad with curiosity. What's been going on, General? We heard that Colonel Mondragón was relieved of duty. But where is he now? And what happened to the Red Shirts?"

But General Sánchez chose not to reply directly, and merely continued his monologue as if he had not been interrupted.

"Now I've had lice before," he said, as the ferry started across the narrow channel of bright-blue water, heading toward Carmen's little pink-toned, palm-fringed adopted city. "I've had every kind of vermin, all over Mexico. And my usual remedy is—if you'll forgive me, señorita—I go out and I get me some gasoline and I pour it all over my hair. It burns like hell, especially if you're dealing with crab lice, down around the private parts, but it does the job. And then you know what? You are not going to believe this, but when I get rid of the little bastards I feel a tiny bit disappointed. I get used to passing the time by plucking them out and popping them between my fingernails and watching them squirm and wiggle their little claws. And I even miss telling the same tired old joke about them to the muchachos when they ask me how to get rid of them and I say, 'The only way you can do it is to throw gas on your hair, light it afire, and stab the little devils to death with an icepick when they come running out of the flames.'

"Well," said the general, laughing at his own cleverness, finishing off the bottle of tequila, "you know, Don Brian, to answer your question, I will feel just about the same kind of disappointment, for pretty close to the same reasons, when I exterminate the Red Shirts today."

"Where are the Red Shirts?"

"The Red Shirts have retreated in the face of overwhelming force."

"But where to?"

"Have patience, Don Brian. I've been saving them just for you," said Sánchez, laughing wickedly. And his laughter was infectious to Carmen. Something wild and anarchic within her responded to it instinctively. And she could imagine the general in the Revolution, spearing barnyard chickens with his bayonet, dragging rich creole ladies from their fine haciendas and raping them behind an adobe wall, riding his horse into cantinas, firing his pistols at the chandeliers, sitting at a long table full of spilled wine and broken crockery with other dirty, mustachioed bandidos like himself, pinching a pretty barmaid on her bottom as she passed by. . . . He reminded her of Gallo, and of stories that he had told of the Revolution. He reminded her of her own father, who had died in the Battle of Celaya.

His laughter was so infectious, in fact, and Carmen laughed so loud and long, that Don Brian was apparently reminded that he had not yet presented her as his wife.

"Your wife?" said the general, who was rumored to have at least three wives in various parts of Mexico, along with several concubines, and over fifty children. "Forgive me for not discovering it myself, señora, but you are far too young and pretty to be classified as a mere wife."

"Perhaps you have more important things on your mind, mi general."

"No," he said, squeezing her knee. "No, it's only that I'm carried away by your beauty, or I'm still lost in a delirium of success."

"If it is delirium, your excellency," said Don Brian, rising to the occasion at last, "then you have every right to it. Your victory over the Red Shirts is assured."

"The Red Shirts are nothing more than scum, canalla, godless barbarians in service to the heathen General Calles. Two days ago I received a telegram from President Cárdenas. 'DISARM RED SHIRTS,' it said. Well, soon they will be disarmed. It is nothing to get excited about."

"Then, if not the Red Shirts," said Don Brian, who had not yet fully realized the implications of this new intelligence, "perhaps Colonel Mondragón is the source of your good spirits. You have achieved his removal with remarkable dispatch."

"Mondragón? He did as he was told. I have sent him on a thirty-day leave. After that he'll join me in the capital."

"I beg your pardon."

"You heard correctly. He will serve as my chief aide there."

"Your what?" said Don Brian, unable to conceal his astonishment.

"There is no end to the marvels, eh? But seriously, what better man can you think of as liaison with President Cárdenas?"

"I'm afraid I just don't follow you, General."

"Haven't you heard?"

"We have heard nothing."

"Well, I've been invited to join the government in Mexico City. Imagine. Me, the son of a poor Indian from Pátzcuaro. You know, when I run into critics—gringos, foreigners—I point to this kind of thing. Before the Revolution . . ."

"General Sánchez, I am absolutely dumbfounded by this news. Were you not . . . ?"

"Don't act so surprised, meester. It is not flattering. I have been asked to serve as minister of transport. My old comrade-in-arms, President Cárdenas, requires it of me. I realize that he just wants me where he can keep an eye on me. But there you are. It is my duty, nevertheless."

"But . . . but the problem of trust, mi general."

"Trust? I trust no one."

"Yet Mondragón . . . is he not a dangerous man?"

"Mondragón will know only as much as I want him to know. Or rather, only what I want conveyed directly to the ears of the president. Anyway, Cárdenas and I are allies now with the Catholics, so we have nothing to hide, eh? It would almost be sacrilegious, no?"

"General, I just can't understand how so much could have happened in so short a time."

"Events move swiftly in the political arena, Don Brian."

"I must confess that your Mexican gift for the quick about-face can sometimes leave the foreigner gaping in wonder."

"We may do things strangely by your lights," said the general, his good mood suddenly turning sour, "but it is our way, and we do not appreciate comments on our behavior from north of the border."

"A sus ordenes, mi general," said Don Brian, as they pulled up at last in front of the Hotel O'Hare. "I will esteem what you have said, for it is a lesson to remember."

"Adiós," said Carmen, smiling brightly, as the chauffeur deposited their bags on the front steps, and Gallo descended from the lobby to pick them up.

"No, it is not adiós," said Sánchez irritably. "I have decided to come inside and join you for another drink."

The only time that Carmen was really interested in Don Brian was when she wanted him. But she found that she wanted him more and more all the time. She suspected that he felt the same about her. Already when they reached the hotel they desired each other again. And their interest had increased to the point of fascination over the picture they made together in the full-length, gold-plated mirror in the lobby.

Don Brian had taken a good deal of trouble over his appearance before he left the prison. And he had sent Carmen next door in the Hidalgo Wing with enough money to outfit herself from the wardrobe of a stylish young widow accused of murdering her wealthy aged husband.

Brian looked very ruddy and vital now in his Panama hat with the brim turned down at either end, his natural silk suit with a brown open-necked shirt and white-and-brown Palm Beach shoes. And Carmen looked lush and sexy in her white ankle-length cotton sundress with blue polka dots, her bare legs, her blue-and-white wingtip pumps, and the high white turban she had wound about her hair.

Carmen was so enthralled by the picture, in fact, that she bade Gallo seek out the hotel camera to preserve it for posterity.

In ten days her world had changed. She would never be a servant again. Yet she dared not believe what was already apparent until it was captured forever on celluloid.

After the photo session Don Brian invited General Sánchez to the bar for a drink on the house. The drink turned into five or six and the general started to get ugly.

"Why did you marry a gringo when there are so many good Mexicans around?" he wanted to know.

Carmen thought for a second, and replied, "I was carried away by passion."

Don Brian and Gallo laughed. But General Sánchez did not appear to be satisfied with her answer.

"What are you laughing at?" he demanded of Gallo.

"Pues nada, mi general."

"Come out from behind that bar."

"Para servirle, mi general."

"I am the best shot in Mexico."

"I believe you," said Gallo, who was beginning to sweat.

"You trust my word?"

"Implicitly."

"Then come with me," the general said. And dragged him cringing out to the patio, stood him up against the wall, stuck a cigarette in his mouth, and prepared to shoot it out with his service revolver from ten paces, blindfolded.

"But General," Carmen protested. "He is my brother-in-law."

"Don't worry," he said, tying a table napkin around his head. "I've only missed once before."

"You're not serious," said Don Brian. "Are you?"

"Serious?" said General Sánchez, affronted. "I'll show you how serious."

He raised his .38 and took aim. Gallo turned pale and fell to his knees.

"Stop!" Carmen cried, and ran forward instinctively to put herself between them.

"I'm afraid I'm going to have to ask you to give me the weapon," Don Brian said, stepping forward.

Sánchez staggered backward, blindly, drunkenly.

Above him, on the third- and fourth-floor arcades, hotel guests gathered to watch.

"You know what we used to do in the Revolution, Don Brian?" he said, fumbling with the napkin with one hand and waving his pistol around with the other.

"The gun, please, General."

"We used to make gringos dance the two-step."

"Be that as it may . . ." Don Brian said, reaching for the pistol. "Don't come any closer, or . . ."

The report of the shot was loud and metallic in the confines of the small courtyard. The bullet ricocheted off the tile floor, narrowly missed Don Brian, traveled into the dining room, and shattered the mirror behind the bar.

The accident appeared to sober the general. He looked around at Carmen and up at the hotel guests on the arcades as if to say, "Did I do that?"

"I beg your pardon, señor," he said, focusing again upon Don Brian, bowing contritely in his direction. "If I am sometimes uncouth, it is only a result of my rude birth."

"It is not for me to accept your apology, mi general," said Don Brian, who had stood his ground. "It is my barman who has perhaps been offended."

Gallo was still on his knees by the wall. General Sánchez tottered over to him with the smoking pistol still in his hand and patted him clumsily on the shoulder. Gallo winced every time he touched him, and regarded the swinging pistola with distrust.

"A thousand pardons, old man. But you knew it was a joke, didn't you?"

Gallo raised his eyes, nodded, and tried a grin. The result was ghastly.

General Sánchez weaved over to the bar and slapped ten thousand pesos on the counter.

"For the damages," he said.

"You are my guest," said Don Brian.

"Por favor."

"I cannot accept it."

"Then I will repay you," the general said, "with a show you will never forget. You wanted to know about the Red Shirts?"

"I wondered what happened to them."

"I will take you to them now."

"Vamonos."

They got into the general's touring car again and drove to the funicular railway station near the teeming central market. Sánchez had the chauffeur park outside, and beckoned Don Brian and Carmen to follow him out onto the tracks. He pointed up and down the line, which ran straight from the summit of a steep hill on the west side of town to another on the east. A slum called the Colonia Barbara, the Barbarian Colony, flooded haphazardly down the eastern hill from an old stone church, while an elegant modern neighborhood called the Barrio Chino—for a rich Chinese trader who had once lived there—neatly topped the other.

"The Red Shirts are there," the general giggled, waving tipsily up toward the Colonia Barbara. "They've got a machine gun and a hundred Mausers behind the sandbags at the edge of the incline. They've got their women and children in the church on top of the hill, and they've got a Maxim gun and a lookout post in the church tower."

"How long do you think they can hold out?"

"One of them deserted a couple of days ago," the general said. "Before we shot him, he admitted under interrogation that they were prepared for a month-long siege."

"But what can they hope to accomplish?"

"Mondragón gave them some land—a banana plantation—and they want it back. They figure they'll make it so rough on us, and so embarrassing for President Cárdenas, that we'll find it easier to negotiate than go on fighting with them."

"And what do you think their chances are?"

"They haven't got a prayer," said General Sánchez. "All over Mexico, the Red Shirts are a dead item."

Then he motioned them back into the car and drove them slowly toward the Colonia. A squad of his military police had set up a roadblock a couple of blocks from the foot of the hill. The middle-class neighborhood around the base was swarming with artillerymen.

They pulled up in front of another funicular railway station, and immediately Sánchez was accosted by a wispy, elderly mestizo colonel wearing a pince-nez.

"Mi general," he said, glancing nervously from Sánchez to Carmen to Don Brian and back again, "my men are anxiously awaiting your word of command."

"Momentito," General Sánchez said, and left the frail, goateed old officer to scurry along at his heels while he took Don Brian and Carmen on a tour of the "theater of operations."

"This is my artillery," he said, indicating five old wood-spoked, horse-drawn Montegrón field guns in the street outside the station. Then he led them out of the built-up portion of the neighborhood and a hundred meters up the hill to where some ill-dressed, poorly armed and badly fed troops lay lounging about the tamarind trees and under a rusty Gatling gun, smoking cornhusk cigarettes and playing monte. "These are my assault troops," he said. The troopers made no effort to rise or salute when the general walked by, and several of them grumbled openly about the incompetence of their officers, and the endless delays.

One brave little Yaqui corporal even approached the general to demand his back pay.

General Sánchez ignored the corporal and turned to Don Brian.

"Never mind the insubordination," he said. "It is the nature of the Mexican soldier."

"But will they take the hill?"

"They will. It may take time, but they will."

"How can you be so sure?"

"Señor, I did not gain my reputation in the Revolution for spit and polish, or iron discipline, or brilliant tactics," the general said. "Essentially, I rule by fear. These men will take the hill, or they will die. And they know it. All the rest is trimmings, military flimflam."

Then without further explication or consultation with the anxious little colonel who trailed behind them, General Sánchez escorted his guests back to the car. He drove them across town again, and up a steep switchback road to the wealthy precincts of the Barrio Chino. They passed another roadblock and pulled up in front of the funicular railway station on the summit of the hill. A pale, blue-eyed young lieutenant ran out of the ticket office, saluted breathlessly, gesturing toward a little open funicular car that sat on the track, and said, "When can we let her go, mi general?"

She was packed to her fringed blue sunshade with wooden crates marked DANGER—HIGH EXPLOSIVES. A three-man detachment of military policemen stood nearby, poised to push her off down the hill.

"Get back to your post," the general said, "and wait till I give the signal."

"What is the signal, mi general?"

"You will know it when I give it," he said, and showed Don Brian and Carmen into the station. They followed him up to the business office on the second floor. "Now Don Brian," he said, steadying himself on the edge of a cluttered desk, affecting a sober mien, "have you discovered my plan of attack?"

"I'm afraid I have."

"You have your doubts?"

"I can only hope that you have first-rate technicians, mi general, and excellent timed fuses."

"Technicians? Timed fuses?" the general laughed. "I have dynamite. I have a lieutenant with a match."

"Have . . . have you made no attempt to alert the people of the town?"

"The people of the town? I am not aiming at the people of the town. I am aiming at the people on the hill," said the general impatiently.

And gave the signal, which he invented on the spot: He made the motion of clanging an imaginary trolley bell and started singing Luigi Denza's Neapolitan air, "Funiculi Funiculà," which had enjoyed a great vogue in Mexico during the twenties, at the top of his lungs.

Lesti, lesti, via montiam su là—
lesti, lesti, via montiam su là—
funiculi, funiculà, funiculi, funiculà!
via montiam su là, funiculi funiculà. Là!

The lieutenant smiled and clanged back. The soldiers cheered, ran forward, and set their backs to the funicular car.

"Now wait a minute," Don Brian said, but it was already too late.

funiculi, funiculà, funiculi, funiculà!
via montiam su là, funiculi funiculà. Là!

The lieutenant released the brake, the men strained their backs, and slowly the car began to move. The lieutenant lit the fuse and jumped down on the track. The car went rattling and clanging downhill, rapidly picking up speed. The soldiers let it go. The lieutenant whooped for joy and lent his voice to the general's in a rousing last chorus of "Funiculi Funiculà."

"You are going to regret this," Don Brian said, when the song was done.

"I regret nothing," the general replied, and picked up the phone. "Proceed as ordered," he said.

Faster and faster the little red-and-blue trolley rolled down the hill, its fringed sunshade flapping gaily in the wind, its wheels clattering, while far below in the town, toy pedestrians, horsemen, vehicles, and beasts of burden crossed and recrossed the tracks, unaware.

A line of infantrymen in olive-drab uniforms and steel helmets appeared on the slopes of the opposite hill, on either side of the funicular railway tracks, climbing upward through the tamarind trees. Down in the town artillery boomed, and shells whistled through the air, erupting on the crown of the Colonia Barbara, near the old yellow stone church.

The funicular car hurtled through the center of Manzanillo, scattering people, machines and animals every which way. But from Carmen's perspective it was all soundless and remote, and she found it hard to imagine that anyone was actually getting hurt. Don Brian, on the other hand, apparently had little difficulty in imagining it, for he had begun to tremble and to sweat, and his eyes were wide with fear.

The trolley started up the opposite hill. It raced past the line of advancing infantrymen, causing them to stop and raise their fists in a victory sign.

General Sánchez stuck his head out the window, laughed exultantly, and bellowed out another chorus of "Funiculi Funiculà."

Down on the funicular tracks the lieutenant and his men smiled and gamely joined in, but the song soon died in their throats, and they all began to look uneasy.

The trolley had begun to lose its momentum.

Slower and slower and slower it went, while the whole world seemed to hold its breath in expectation. Even the artillery fell silent, and in the town all the traffic came to a stop.

For an instant it looked as if the car might make it to the top, and General Sánchez breathed a sigh of relief. But about twenty meters short of the sandbag fortifications of the Red Shirts it crept to a halt and started back down the track.

A faint cheer rose from the Colonia Barbara, and a ragged line of red-shirted skirmishers appeared on the crest of the hill and ran down toward the advancing infantry. The Sánchez troops broke ranks and scattered into the tamarind trees on both sides of the tracks, leaving the Gatling gun undefended.

The funicular car picked up speed again. It passed the Gatling gun, reached the bottom of the hill, and sped back through the center of town, sending pedestrians and domesticated animals fleeing before it.

The lieutenant and his men stood on the edge of the Barrio Chino incline, on the railway tracks, peering down upon the scene in horror. Don Brian turned his head away, as if unable to contemplate such destruction. But Carmen found the whole thing terrifically exciting, and

General Sánchez sat calmly on the windowsill, twirling the cylinder on his service revolver, replacing the cartridge he had fired off in the Hotel O'Hare. He was stone sober, his face an Indian mask.

The little trolley reached the marketplace, ran into a beer truck that had stalled on the tracks, and disappeared in a ball of fire. Debris floated into the sky in slow motion, and a dense boiling cloud of black smoke rose over the center of town. A shock wave struck the Barrio Chino station, rattling the windows, and the sound of a tremendous explosion rent the air.

"Oh my God," Don Brian kept saying. "Oh my God."

But Carmen, watching General Sánchez go down the stairs with his pistol drawn, experienced an unprecedented, uncontrollable sense of physical elation.

General Sánchez approached the young lieutenant stealthily, from the rear, taking aim for the back of his head.

Don Brian broke the window with his arm and screamed: "Nooooo!"

The lieutenant started to turn, but he never knew what hit him. The general fired into his temple from a meter away. The lieutenant jerked backward and rolled down the hill.

"What are you looking at?" Sánchez asked his gaping soldiers.

"Nada, mi general, nada," they hastened to assure him.

"You know the penalty for dereliction of duty."

"Claro, mi general, claro, claro."

"The lieutenant made me a promise. He was an engineer, he said. He would not misjudge. But it appears that he was mistaken. No? Now recover the body and bury it."

"Sí sí, mi general, sí sí," said the sergeant in charge. "But where?"

"Where?" the general said. "Anywhere. What do I care?"

Slowly the smoke and dust rolled back from the marketplace, revealing what had been hidden before. Every adobe house within a fifty-meter radius of the explosion had been leveled to the ground. The stone houses had lost all their windows, doors and roofs. The covered market had collapsed in upon itself. The market stalls in the plaza no longer existed; their colorful wares lay scattered across the singed cobblestones, and the square was strewn with rumpled bundles of gay clothing which might have been human bodies.

Farther away, across town, the Red Shirts had overrun the Sánchez infantry lines. They had captured the Gatling gun and were busy hauling it back up the hill to the Barbarian Colony.

Already the sky was filling with zopilotes.

"What have we done?" Don Brian kept gasping. "What have we done?"

"But you have done nothing," said Carmen sharply. She found that she had little patience for his gringo regrets.

"It is I who must bear the burden of responsibility," the general said, coming briskly up the stairs. "And believe me, those peones on the hill are going to pay dearly for it."

CHAPTER 9

October 1, 1935

"Why so dull, Ramona? Cheer up!" I keep telling myself. But it gets harder all the time. For five days the Sánchez artillery has been quiet, and the joyful mood of our first victory has worn thin in the daily grind of camp life. We women and children spend all of our days and nights in the church, while the men go out in shifts to defend the sandbag fortifications and to act as pickets in the tamarind trees down the hill. We are besieged on the crest of a steep, circular jungle hill that is completely surrounded by the city of Manzanillo, and for that reason an attack could come from any direction.

October 2, 1935

Still no sign of action. Meanwhile, life in the Barbarian Colony goes on. A baby is born, an old man dies, married and unmarried couples make love, children get sick and cranky and cry. Everyone is suffering from a mild form of gastroenteritis, because the one well in the Colonia has been contaminated with ordure, and our cooks, despite repeated warnings, rarely bother to boil our water long enough to purify it. Needless to say, there is never enough water for a decent bath. But at least we are brothers and sisters in our misery—we all smell so bad that no one can complain.

October 3, 1935

A single artillery shell flew over the Colonia today at noon. It whistled by inches above our lookout post in the church tower, missed the hill entirely and landed with a great roar on Sánchez's positions on the other side. The news cheered us like nothing in days, and we laughed and capered around the altar like imps.

October 4, 1935

Though we are besieged on all sides, and we can see the Sánchez forces creeping up the hill inch by inch every day, there are still some bright spots in our lives. And every day we count our blessings. We still have plenty to eat, as we have kept our store of rice and beans dry by burning a fire in the storeroom at the back of the church twenty-four hours a day. The laying hens which peck about our feet in the church are giving plenty of eggs. The nanny goats deliver enough milk each day for all the children under six. Our sow has just given birth to a litter of piglets. We have quarantined two little girls with measles and thereby avoided an epidemic. And our hopes are kept alive by Narciso's constant lectures on our objectives. "Why are we here?" he shouts every hour or so. "To inspire the peasants to revolt!" comes the refrain. "Why do we want to revolt?" "To bring down the caudillos and win back our land!" "Why must we hold out as long as we can?" "To embarrass Cárdenas, 'the Friend of the Proletariat!' " "Why do we want to embarrass the President of the Republic?" "To make him get off his culo and come to our aid!"

October 5, 1935

Things are so quiet that I would say that boredom is our major problem at the moment. Because we are bored—yet under constant threat of bombardment—our tempers grow short. We women get into petty squabbles. The men get into fistfights. The children are obnoxious. And everybody's faults are exaggerated. Last night Narciso sneaked over to my petate in the wee hours and insisted we make love.

"But you have a wife," I said.

"She doesn't mind."

"Fine," I said. "Tell her to come see me tomorrow and give her permission."

She never came, of course, but tonight I noticed that her attitude toward me has changed. She won't let Delia play with me, and when I look at her she avoids my eyes. Though I am as chaste as a nun, she is jealous of me. From her friend Lupita I heard that she has promised to stab me with a butcher knife if she ever catches me with Narciso.

October 7, 1935

Last night when I was helping to man the bucket brigade—a human chain by which we rid ourselves of our daily wastes, tossing them over the sandbags in the direction of Sánchez's lines—I looked down upon the brightly lit city and I could see the Hotel O'Hare illuminated by floodlight and decorated for a party, with colored streamers hanging from the balconies. Smartly dressed couples kept arriving at the door in chauffeured touring cars and disappearing inside. And I suddenly realized that it was the birthday of Mrs. O'Hare. I remembered last year when there had been a similar shindig, with all the gentry of Colima State invited. The incredible contrast of our situations was driven home to me as never before, and it gave me a renewed sense of struggle, and a will to fight on. Then, just as suddenly, I was overcome with a terrible loneliness. I found myself missing little Chris and Merle, and my clean small room in the nursery. I even missed my night job as a waitress, and the clean peasant frock I wore, the charming smile I aimed at my customers to prompt a generous tip, the rich chocolate and cream pastry that I used to steal from the kitchen and eat in the toilet. I found myself weakening, regretting the past, starting to miss the security of my life as a servant. Since Mondragón betrayed us, I have not been tempted by visions of knights on white horses. But now I caught myself thinking of Brian again, and it took all my will to leave off. I wondered if he is still imprisoned, like me. I know him so well. I still can't believe what everyone here takes for granted: that he is guilty of the crime of which he is accused. Sometimes I daydream about him. That I change him. That I make him see things from our point of view. That I marry him.

October 8, 1935

They attacked us this morning at dawn. They softened us up with a two-hour artillery barrage during which the church was struck twice by exploding shells but survived largely undamaged. Then they came at us through the tamarind trees. But our Gatling gun worked miracles, Narciso said, and we soon had them running down the hill. Our boys jumped over the sandbags and gave chase. They never caught up with them, but they managed to recover thirteen Mausers and a .30-caliber machine gun. Our losses were two killed and seven wounded, probably a tenth of what the enemy lost. But here on the hill all wounds are serious, as we have no doctor, no medicine, and extremely unhygienic conditions. The situation is made worse by the swarms of insects—maggots, flies, gnats, ticks, mosquitoes, cockroaches. And anything but the most minor flesh wound is invariably fatal. Our men know this, and they usually prefer to put themselves out of their misery. Tonight a boy named Juan Calaveras kissed his novia goodbye and put a bullet through his head. We heard it in the church, and everyone cried except the children. They are so used to firing by now that they laugh and play through all but the loudest and closest bombardment. Mostly what they play at is war. They throw dirt clods against the church and pretend they are bombs. They scream, clutch their tummies, double over, and pretend to be gut-shot. They pretend to be priests delivering the last rites, though there are no priests among us. We have tied a couple of long ropes to the rafters of the church and fixed up a swing, but they rarely use it. It hangs here in the center of the church, a symbol of their former innocence.

October 9, 1935

Today we heard firing on the outskirts of town and convinced ourselves that the Cárdenas forces had come to rescue us. We even convinced ourselves that Colonel Mondragón had had a change of heart and was leading them on. But it must have been target practice—or a firing squad—because nothing happened all day long.

October 10, 1935

I have just discovered a child with smallpox, and I've decided to keep it to myself. I put him with his mother in a separate quarantine and then found myself praying for his life. Though I no longer believe in God, I don't think, his illness seemed to me so unjust. In the United States children are routinely vaccinated against the disease, and I myself am immune, since I went to school in El Paso.

October 11, 1935

Tonight we were sitting around in the church eating our dinner of tortillas, rice and beans when Narciso burst through the front door, screaming, "Everybody down!" And at that instant the sky lit up and a shell exploded directly behind him. He stood there outlined against the flash, and I was sure he was dead. But when I got up from the floor he was standing there unscathed. Nor was anyone else in the church injured. This will give him much caste among our people, for they are very superstitious. Already it is whispered among them that he is invulnerable to bullets. Only I—and perhaps his wife—know how very human he is. Last night he came to me again and breathed into my ear.

"What if you die?" he said. "What if you die without ever having made love?"

"How can you think of sex at a time like this?"

"This is precisely the time for it."

"You must think of your wife."

"In the jaws of death one thinks only of oneself."

"And your child?"

"This has nothing to do with children."

"It has everything to do with children," I said, and that seemed to set him back on his feet, for the moment.

October 14, 1935

Last night our pickets heard sounds in the trees and gave the alarm. Immediately a star shell burst overhead, illuminating the Barbarian Colony like day. The Sánchez assault force, which had crept up to within a hundred meters of our fortifications, let loose with everything they had, and artillery shells started landing within our perimeter. Our pickets retreated under heavy fire, and were clambering over our wall of sandbags just as they were bracketed by several tremendous explosions. Sánchez had brought up a five-inch siege gun and set it on a flatcar on the funicular railway tracks. Our men were literally blown off the wall. By some miracle they landed unhurt in the tamarind trees, and scrambled to their feet, only to find themselves surrounded by the enemy. But the Sánchez forces were so astonished to see our muchachos materialize among them that they withheld their fire for an instant. It was long enough for our boys to collect themselves and run for the wall. They came over in a hail of bullets. No one was hurt, and we welcomed them into our lines like heroes.

Their miraculous good luck had inspired us. It seemed that fate was on our side. We fought like demons and drove them back with many losses, while suffering only three casualties and one fatality: Miguel Hernández, a child of thirteen who was blown to pieces by the siege gun while running to supply our fighters with water. After we had driven the enemy back down the hill and the artillery barrage let up, Narciso could not contain us. Everyone in the church ran outside to embrace the men on the wall and feed them with tortillas and beans. As we danced and laughed on the wall the siege gun boomed, and a last artillery shell whistled over our heads. It struck the roof of the church, exploded, and blew the lookout from the tower. We ran to help him, but he was already dead when he landed. We went inside the church to check the damage and found the rear portion of the roof stove in, and a fire raging in the storeroom. Our entire store of rice and beans was burned up in a few minutes. It was a terrible loss, but we did not forget to count our blessings: Thirty women and children (including myself) were in the habit of sleeping in that section of the nave, which now lay under tons of volcanic stone, heavy oaken beams, and tile from the roof.

This morning we were able to salvage some of the rice and beans that lay under the ashes, probably enough to last us another three days on half-rations. Meanwhile our chickens, pigs and goats have flourished and they should provide us with enough meat for another week after that. This afternoon the little boy with smallpox died, and two other children have come down with the symptoms. It is for the little ones that my heart bleeds, because it is they who will suffer most in the coming days of deprivation.

October 15, 1935

Today we were struck by a torrential rainstorm that was worse than anything Sánchez has thrown at us. The church filled with water, the children shivered with cold, and we were forced to move to the abandoned cane shacks in the Colonia Barbara. Within hours the two children with smallpox died, and three others came down with pneumonia, including Amalia Rodríguez, the baby who was born our first night here, and who had come to symbolize our whole struggle on the hill. It was the worst blow we have suffered, in a spiritual sense. As soon as the church dries out, we must move back in, for its heavy stone walls are our only real protection against the Sánchez bombardment. Also, Narciso has dispersed his stores of ammunition among the huts, and we are afraid that one near us will be hit by a shell.

October 18, 1935

I slept the past two nights in a cane shack with my two orphans, Angel and María, whose father died in the lookout tower and whose mother died while we were still on the squatters' train. They are very pale, thin and weak. Their skin is covered with open sores and boils from a lack of green vegetables, and they suffer like all of us from insect bites, which tend to become infected rapidly. But they are still quite happy and energetic, and they have adopted me as their mother. I have vowed that

I will keep them always, and raise them as my own. I made them as comfortable as I could in the jacal, the roof of which leaked like a sieve, and slept close to them to keep them dry. It rained without stop for forty-eight hours. At least it kept the Sánchez artillery quiet. Last night in the darkest and dampest hours I heard someone creeping through the mud in back of the hut and I was afraid it might be an infiltrator from the Sánchez side. But I should have known better. It was Narciso, who had acquired tequila from someplace and was quite drunk. He crouched over me, snorting like a bull, fumbling with his trousers. I pretended not to recognize him, and screamed at the top of my lungs: "Infiltrator! Infiltrator! Infiltrator!" Instantly the hut was surrounded by armed campesinos, and Narciso would have surely been shot dead had he not shouted, "Stop, stop, it's me, your leader!" The episode caused much laughing in the ranks, especially when Narciso came running out hitching up his pants, but I'm afraid of what he might do in the end, for he is a proud man, and hates more than anything to be seen as ridiculous.

After the noise had died down and everyone was gone, I lay on my petate with my angelitos and wondered why I bothered resisting him. He was right when he said to me once, "It's such a waste, a woman like you, made for love. . . ." And I do not deceive myself about my chances of survival here. It occurred to me that Narciso and I are much alike. My defense of my virginity has become a kind of end in itself. Just like Narciso's defense of this hill. Our causes are probably equally senseless, as well as doomed. But still we fight on.

I see other similarities between us too. Our stubborn resistance against impossible odds has made us both a little crazy. In the face of death, I have never felt more alive. Never closer to God. A little like Saint Teresa of Avila, of whom I used to read so much in the library of Doña Maureen. And I can see in Narciso's wild eyes that he feels much the same way. He seems possessed by some terrible vision. One night he told me, "I can see my own death; it is glorious." He is driven by the energy of many demons. He never sleeps. He is everywhere at once, in the church, on the wall, in the huts, scouting the enemy down the hill, up in the watchtower. He never lets go of us, not one of us. The women whisper about his lustfulness. He makes love to his wife several times a night, they say, and when she says, "Enough," he seeks out other men's wives. Most of them are afraid to resist him, and none dare reveal the truth to their husbands. Narciso and I are like two sides of the same coin.

October 19, 1935

Today we ate the last of the rice and beans. We still have some corn for grinding and making tortillas. And tomorrow we'll begin killing the animals. The smallpox seems to be contained, for the moment, but the pneumonia continues to plague us. A mother and daughter died today, and we burned them up in a jacal to avoid an epidemic.

October 20, 1935

Encarnita and three other women were killed today when a shell from the siege gun landed on the well as they were drawing water. Their end was quick and they did not suffer, but the wailing of their seven children was impossible to endure. The shell had the unintended result of tripling our water supply, for it somehow tapped an underground spring, which rose pure and clear and bubbling from the smoking, cordite-smelling crater.

October 21, 1935

Narciso goes around wearing a black armband, and he pretends to be suffering terrible grief over the death of his beloved wife, but his intentions toward me are unmistakable. How shall I resist him now that he has no wife to deceive? He has given little Delia over to my care. I could not refuse her, because I love her dearly and she suffers terribly from mosquito bites, which cover her little feet and have become so infected that she is unable to walk. But how can I continue to resist his advances, now that I am the "mother" of his child? And why, really, do I bother?

October 22, 1935

The rains have gone and we are back in the church, where we all feel much more comfortable. It is not so crowded now because death has cut deeply into our ranks. For the same reason our food is lasting a bit longer than we anticipated.

October 23, 1935

Today one of our pickets deserted to the enemy. He will undoubtedly tell them how very weak we are, and how very low on ammunition. Expecting an attack any hour, Narciso took a party of men down the hill and fired some of the cane shacks outside our sandbag perimeter, in order to deny them as refuge or hiding place for the enemy. He found a malingerer there. He had stolen a bottle of tequila from our medicinal stores and was sleeping off a hangover. Narciso brought him up to the Colonia and was about to shoot him against the church wall when I ran up and asked him what he thought he was doing.

"I am going to make him an example," he said.

"Well," I said, "while you're at it, you might as well put the pistol up against your own head, because I missed another bottle a week ago and that night you came sniffing around my hut like a drunken dog."

Everyone laughed, but Narciso looked as if he might turn the gun on me. He salvaged his dignity by kicking the culprit in the pants and sending him up on the wall to defend the most dangerous position. The man promptly deserted his post and ran down the hill toward the Sánchez lines. "Shoot him!" Narciso ordered. And everyone on the sandbags opened up on him. Whether by design or chance they all missed him, but the shooting alerted the Sánchez forces, and they cut him down with Maxim-gun fire. "Let this be a lesson to you," Narciso said when he saw me next. I pointed inside the church to where the man's wife and four children sat huddled together by the wall, sick, hungry and despondent. "Let that be a lesson to you," I said. Though when I think about it now I'm not sure what I meant.

October 25, 1935

The flies swarm over everything, getting into the children's eyes and mouths. Mice and great fat rats scamper around brazenly in the light of day, as if they suspect how weak we are. All of nature seems to suspect, and the zopilotes sit in a line atop the church, as if gathering for a feast.

October 26, 1935

Little Delia's feet are swollen to the size of cantaloupes. A brown spittle collects at the corners of her pale little mouth, and her fevered eyes are rolled far back in her head. She has caught gangrene, and the poison is working its way up her legs. Narciso came to me today and said, "Allot her one of the nanny goats. With enough milk we can save her."

"Nothing can save her now," I said. "Not even a doctor. And we need that milk for all the other children who still have a chance."

He broke down in tears then, crying, "Our children are so far gone that they die of mosquito bites."

And I comforted him. I allowed him to lay his head in my lap, which is no longer so fragrant as it once might have been. His is such a bony, cadaverous head. It's as if he were already dead.

"Of course you're right," he said. "Why should my kid have special privileges? It goes against everything I've been fighting for all along."

"But it's completely understandable," I said. "It's human nature."

"I am against nature!" he shouted, rising up off my lap. "I am for reason and pure will!"

He sounded utterly mad.

Tonight three of our fighters deserted to the enemy. Last night two.

October 27, 1935

Delia died this morning at four, but we couldn't bury her till late tonight, because Sánchez attacked from two sides at once. By the time we got to the poor little thing she had already begun to smell. I remember her playing on the beach near the squatters' camp with little Chris and Merle when she was three, a clever bowlegged little doll with bright eyes and a mischievous grin, running into the sea, kicking up spray, making sand castles on the strand. . . . And my heart turned to ice. I wanted to sneak down the hill through the trees and gain entrance to Sánchez's quarters through feminine wiles and murder him in his bed. Yet I found that I could not cry for my poor little Delia because I was simply too tired. After a terrific three-hour artillery bombardment, and an hour of vicious hand-to-hand fighting on the wall, the enemy breached our fortifications today for the first time. They came in from behind the church, and for a minute it looked as if they had us. But Narciso led a machete charge that closed the gap and cut off a party of twelve Sánchez infantrymen. When they saw that they were surrounded they threw down their arms and raised their hands. Narciso took the officer, a young mestizo captain, to one of the outlying cane shacks, where he tied him up and kept him under close guard. The others he put in the church. Meanwhile our muchachos had beaten back the enemy attack, inflicting heavy losses. Narciso took the youngest prisoner aside and gave him instructions to run down the hill with a message for Sánchez.

"But General Sánchez is not here," he said.

"Where is he?" Narciso demanded angrily, as if he resented the opposing commander for being remiss in his duty.

"He is in the capital," the boy said. "He has been made minister of transport in the cabinet of President Cárdenas."

"You lie!" Narciso screamed, and shot him dead.

"Jefe, you should not have killed that poor boy," said one of the other prisoners. "For he was telling the truth. General Sánchez has been gone for over a week. We are now under the command of Colonel Cienfuegos, of the Olimpia Battalion."

In the end the prisoners convinced him that they were indeed speaking the truth, and he sent the next youngest one down the hill with the following message:

> We have taken twelve hostages, including Captain Morales. We killed one today, we will kill one tomorrow, and we shall continue to kill one every day until the following conditions are met: We want food, legal amnesty, and free passage from the state of Colima.
>
> Sincerely,
> Comandante Numero Uno

October 28, 1935

The last of our food is gone. We lost seven fighters yesterday, and ten wounded. Three of the wounded have already shot themselves. Smallpox has broken out again. I have had to isolate five adults and three children. The prisoners have told us much that we didn't know about events great and small in the outside world. Brian has been released from prison and is married to my sister. Mondragón now works for Sánchez in the capital. Cárdenas has ordered that the Red Shirts be disarmed; he has formed an alliance with the Catholics, and he has exiled our national leader, General Calles, to Texas. We have been betrayed on every side, and there is no hope, not even for amnesty, for Colonel Cienfuegos sent up an officer with a megaphone today to tell us that he will not negotiate. "Surrender!" he shouted. "Surrender now and only your leaders will be punished!" In answer Narciso took one of the prisoners up on the wall, shot him, and threw him down the hill.

October 29, 1935

Our situation is one of extreme desperation. Even cowardice is no longer a possibility, as our prisoners have informed us that they've shot every deserter who has crossed over to their side. All day today the men argued about what to do. While they argued, three children died. One of them was my darling Angel, who departed after only two hours' illness. They are so weak now that a common cold takes them. In the end the men came to the conclusion that we must fight on, at all costs. After Angel died, I got very emotional. I ran to where the men were meeting and screamed: "What are you afraid of? Cienfuegos has offered us amnesty if we deliver up our leaders. Well, let's deliver them up and save our children!"

Narciso grabbed me by the arm. "Don't you see?" he said. "It's only a ploy. They will kill us all."

"They won't kill the children," I said. "And for that I'm willing to die."

But none of them would see it my way.

"Without us," they said, "our children will die anyway, for who will care for them?"

October 30, 1935

Early in our stay here in the Barbarian Colony a nanny goat named Bartola fell in love with a boy named Norberto. She followed him everywhere he went. She even slept with him. When we killed all the other animals we let her live because she gave so much milk that she was worth more on the hoof than in the fire. This morning Norberto died of fever, and Bartola would no longer give milk. We killed her and ate her tonight. After dinner we discussed the morality of cannibalism, and determined to start eating our remaining prisoners tomorrow. We shall begin with Captain Morales. He is young, so he should still be rather tender. Immediately after the discussion, the majority of those who had voiced disapproval of cannibalism, five in all, deserted over the wall. Perhaps they thought they could slip through the enemy's lines. But it is highly doubtful that any of them made it, as we heard firing down the hill shortly after they were reported missing.

October 31, 1935

Late this afternoon a young man shot himself in the head. He had not been wounded, and he seemed in at least as good health as anyone else in the Colonia. His wife, who had been left with two grievously ill babies, ran to where he lay dead behind the church, spat in his face, and kicked him repeatedly.

"How dare you do this to me?" she cried. "Have you no sense of responsibility?"

November 1, 1935

Narciso never bothers me at night anymore. It is I who bother him. I crawl onto his petate and press my filthy, breastless body and my scabby, pustulous face against him, wrap my bony arms around his neck, and whisper: "Do it, do it, do it to me now!"

"No, no, no," he protests, suspiciously, half deliriously. "I must save my strength. All you want to do is weaken me."

And he's right. I must convince him to surrender, on condition that our children be spared and cared for by the state. Slim as it is, it is their only chance. I care for nothing else.

November 2, 1935

Today is the Day of the Dead, a national holiday in Mexico, and for days He has been everywhere present. In town they are baking cakes with skeletal faces, and the children are dressing as ghosts and goblins. Here He is especially present, as yesterday our church took a direct hit. The entire roof caved in on us. And then the belltower came tumbling down on top of the rubble. It took them seven hours to dig me out. Yet I came out with only minor cuts and bruises, and all I desired was a drink of water. For twenty-four others of our loved ones, including our eleven remaining children, things were not so fortunate. At least four of the little ones were alive through the night, for we could hear them crying and pleading for water. Little María, my dear one, cried so long and so loud and so pitifully that I was moved to yell at her, "You'd better stop that whining, María," as if she were merely crying frivolously in the next room. I think it gave her some comfort. I know it did me. She never made another sound. And within an hour the last of them fell silent.

November 6, 1935

All day today it has rained, and all day we have stood here on this wall of sandbags waiting for an attack that never seems to materialize. Yet we can see them below us, gathering on two sides for the assault. It will be the final assault, because we have used up all of our ammunition, and we shall face them now with our machetes and bare hands. There are thirty of us left, ten of us women, and if we are not very well armed, at least we are well fed, for we have just slaughtered the last of the prisoners and cooked him up in spicy filets flavored with wild green chile. I suppose this is as good a time as any to confess, and indeed it seems pointless not to: Last night in mutual delirium Narciso and I coupled in the mud like a bag of rattling bones. I bit him and scratched him and beat him with my fists, and it felt as if he would pound me into clay with his body. When it was done he looked at me, wide-eyed with terror, and gasped: "You have won!" But now as I sit here on the wall, watching them roll their field guns into position for the final bombardment, I wonder what Narciso thought I might possibly have won.

CHAPTER 10

In white shoes, white knee socks, white short pants, white shirt, white belt, white boater hat, with a small bouquet of white margaritas in his hand, Merle stood in the dirt by the high black stone wall of the San Carlos Borromeo School, sweating in the noonday sun. He was standing in a long line of boys all dressed alike, beside another, equally long, of little girls in white Mary Janes, white stockings, white skirts and white blouses. An escort of four scrawny Spanish nuns and a large plump mother superior in white habits and white sandals went clucking and strutting busily among them, picking at their uniforms. The children had been placed in their queues according to height, so Merle's group of second-graders was far behind that of Chris's fourth-graders. Yet he could see her quite clearly up ahead. Every once in a while she would turn to look at him. Then he would stick out his tongue at her or make a funny face, and she would burst out laughing. "Silencio," the nuns would say. "Stop fooling around." But Merle just couldn't stop. Chris so rarely laughed. And she was so pretty, otherworldly all in white. Like an idealized Saint Joan as a nine-year-old with her pale skin, pale eyes, her thin straight nose and thick black hair that her mama kept cropped and fringed in a Dutch-boy style.

Merle was fascinated by Christopher, fixated on her, frightened of her. She was like no other person he knew, or ever would know. When you touched her you could feel how special she was. Her temperature was always way above normal, her body wound up tight. Sometimes it looked as if her eyes might pop right out of her head. And her voice was charged with this incredible, volcanic intensity, just barely under control.

Yet she was troubled by so many different things that Merle was convinced she couldn't function without him.

She had no other friends. Her mama ignored her. Her brother was always busy. Carmen only pretended to like her. At school she was ostracized, even by the nuns. Though she was capable of the most brilliant work, her performance was erratic, and what they valued most was obedience and steady growth.

In short, Merle was all she had in the world.

After Ramona ran off to the Red Shirts and disappeared (there had never been a positive confirmation of her death in the siege of the Barbarian Colony), Carmen had assumed the duties of hotel nanny. And, preoccupied with her new marriage, and her rivalry with Doña Maureen—who still insisted on treating her like a servant—Carmen had often left the children to their own devices. They played together in Chris's playhouse every day. They slept in Merle's bed in the nursery nearly every night. They even bathed together, occasionally, when there were no adults around. In fact they had grown so close in recent months that people were beginning to talk.

"What's the matter with you?" his teacher, Sister María Ignacio, had said. "Why don't you play with the boys?"

And Gallo had gone even further: "How come you spend so much time with that crazy little bitch?" he said. "You wanna turn into a pussy? I always been afraid of that, with you."

But how could he abandon her now?

What would she do without him?

She was riddled with fears and phobias of every kind. She couldn't walk down the stairs of the hotel without help, though her eyes were better than his. She wouldn't go near the ocean anymore, or any other body of water, yet she had a fetish about cleanliness, and took two or three showers a day. She was convinced that someone wanted to poison her, and she wouldn't eat until Carmen had tasted her food, but she had an appetite that would put a grown man to shame. At night she saw faces in the window and crept into Merle's bed, pressing herself against him, holding him tighter and tighter, till he was afraid she might smother him.

"Don't be afraid, Chris, don't be afraid," he would whisper, desperately. "There's nobody there."

But her powers of persuasion were remarkable.

"Oh yes there is, Merle," she would say, and proceed to invent a story so plausible in all of its terrible detail that at last she would succeed in convincing him that there really was some monstrous deity just outside the window, ready to gobble them up.

Christopher was mad, she was flawed, she was cracked in the head.

Like a vase that had been broken and then painstakingly put back together again, she could shatter at a touch.

Yet to Merle there was something . . . pure about her, something perfect and beautiful in her fragile imperfection, that put all other comparisons to shame.

He could not think of life without her.

Her madness was luminous, beguiling, ultimately suffocating.

He felt that she was leading him into a beautiful garden that he knew would eventually turn into a dark tunnel with no end. But he had this deep compulsion, altogether voluptuous in its intensity, to follow where she led, regardless of the outcome.

Mother Superior pulled out her police whistle and gave a sharp little toot, and the procession moved off down the Calle Independencia, with two stout, devout sixth-grade boys at the forefront, transporting a large candle-lit picture of the Blessed Virgin in a gilt frame.

At the corner of Independencia and Guerrero a large crowd of onlookers were jostling each other and craning for a better view.

"Hey, muchachos," one of them hollered insolently, "how come you're all dressed up that way?"

"You ought to *know* why!" Mother Superior retorted. "Tell the man why you're dressed in white today, children."

"Today is Mother's Day, El Dia de las Madres," they replied in unison, in the singsong voices of children who have learned by rote. "And we are dressed this way to honor Santa María Madre the Mother of God, for she is the Holy Mother, the Virgin Mother, stainless and white, the Mother of All Mothers."

But the heckler would not be put off. He followed along beside them, dragging a game leg.

"Where you taking them poor little lambs?"

He was a stranger, dressed for winter in the high Altiplano in a tattered woolen poncho. Tall and gaunt, with curly light-colored hair and slightly negroid features and great haunted yellow eyes, he reminded Merle of Narciso Nieves, who had caused such a big stir in Manzanillo a couple of years back. But he could not be Narciso, because Narciso was dead. Merle had seen him with his own eyes, dragged through the streets behind a mule, strung up by his heels and displayed like a prize fish in the portico of the municipio.

"Where you going with them innocent little ones?"

"They are going to the cathedral."

"What for?"

"What for?" said Mother Superior scornfully. "Why, to sing, and to praise the Blessed Virgin."

"Are you not aware that religious processions are against the law?"

"Not in this state they aren't."

"Since when?"

"Since General Sánchez and his men got rid of all the Red Shirts, anarchists and anti-Christs like you!"

The reaction to Mother Superior's outburst was curious to see. It was divided almost exactly according to footwear. Those in bare feet and huaraches hissed and booed, while those in shoes cheered and stamped their feet in approval.

Despite the support the stranger had won among the common folk, the commotion plainly frightened him. He slinked off down a side street and disappeared behind the public slaughterhouse.

"A suspicious character," said Mother Superior. "Probably a fugitive from justice."

And directed Sister Estéban el Mártir to lead the children in singing.

She decided on *Ave Maria,* which they had rehearsed for weeks. Loudly, fervently they sang it, their shrill little schoolish voices echoing from wall to adobe wall, all the way to the cathedral.

There on the front steps in a white biretta, white cassock and white sash, Bishop LeFevre stood waiting for them, flanked by a hundred mothers in white hats, white veils, white dresses, white stockings and white shoes.

"God bless you, my children, God bless you!" he cried, smiling upon them beneficently and raising his arms wide in welcome. "Have you anything for your mamacitas on this special day?"

"Sí, Monsignor, sí!" they shouted as one, and ran to deliver their small bouquets of margaritas into their mamas' hands.

In Merle's case, of course, there was no mama to run to. So he ran for Aunt Carmen, his honorary mama, who stood dark and pretty and beaming at him proudly on the steps, in discreet proximity to Doña Maureen.

The children presented their flowers with a traditional little bow or curtsy and a kiss and then joined their mothers and fell in behind the bishop, who led them into the cathedral for a special Mass in which he belauded at soporific length the virtues of mamas of every color and class and condition of servitude, and the Mother of Mothers above all.

After Mass, Merle and Chris strolled across the Jardín Obregón just behind Carmen, who lingered a few steps behind Doña Maureen and Bishop LeFevre, who went arm and arm, engrossed in deep conversation, sotto voce.

"I wonder what they're talking about, Chris."

"How should I know?"

"Can't you *guess*?"

"Just keep it up, Merle, you're gonna get it."

"Come look in the peephole sometime, if you don't believe it."

"It's not true."

"It is," said Merle, rolling his eyes. "I've seen 'em."

"It is not!"

"Behave now, children, behave yourselves," Carmen called out to them. But it was only a halfhearted attempt. She knew what Merle knew: The señora and the monsignor were amantes flagrantes; they wrestled and sweated and groaned together two afternoons a week in Doña Maureen's creaky old brass bed in the Hotel O'Hare.

The luncheon scene at the hotel had changed in the two years since Colonel Mondragón's departure. The local upper classes had prospered in the peaceful business climate of the Sánchez regime, to the extent that the dining room was no longer sufficient to contain them at their midday repast; they had invaded the patio and the ballroom as well.

As the gentry went, so went the Carrizos and the O'Hares.

No longer had Doña Maureen to act as hostess, or Carmen as waitress, or Gallo as bartender, or Don Brian as genial floating host, or Merle and Chris as purveyors of favors for the children. Only Grandma Carrizo had kept her old job in the kitchen, at her own request (and at Gallo's insistence: He didn't feel that his mother would "fit in," he said). The others sat at two semi-adjoining private tables in the patio, and their functions in the dining room were taken over by a solemn host of servants in fancy gold livery.

Gallo, Carmen, Merle and Chris sat at one of the private tables, while Don Brian and Doña Maureen sat at the other. Sometimes they were joined by Bishop LeFevre, Don Cruz Herrera, Sol Zimmerman, Consul Jeffers, Dr. Weber or some other important personage of the town.

Today being Mother's Day, a special occasion, the tables were pushed together, with Doña Maureen at one end and Don Brian at the other. Merle sat wedged in between Gallo and the bishop on Doña Maureen's right, while Chris sat with Carmen on her left.

"I propose a toast to my mother," Don Brian said, once they'd all been seated. "Happy Mother's Day, Mama!"

"Hear hear!" said Gallo.

"To mothers everywhere!" said the bishop.

"Hear hear!"

Then it came time for her offspring to offer their gifts. Don Brian presented her with a magnificent hand-crafted shawl from the Otomi Indian country, and Chris gave her something she'd spent weeks making in crafts class in school, a hammered copper plate inscribed with a pair of intertwined hearts and a message in English:

I LOVE YOU MOM DO YOU LOVE ME?

The señora seemed greatly moved by her son's gift, but when her daughter proffered hers she hesitated for a moment before taking possession of it.

"What is this, dear?"

Merle held his breath while Chris struggled to explain.

"Uh . . . uh," she said, cringing under her mother's steady gaze. It's, it's a . . ."

"Oh never mind," said Doña Maureen impatiently. "I'm sure we'll find somewhere to hang it."

Merle felt sorry for Chris and wished he hadn't been so cruel to her about the peephole (not that it wasn't true: He'd seen them in there often enough, a tide of overflowing pink flesh on the señora's pink bed, moaning like the wind, heaving like the sea, a spectacle of such grotesque violence that it had no more to do with his notions of love than similar couplings he had witnessed between Carmen and his father, or more recently—for he was still an instinctive voyeur—between Carmen and Don Brian). But Chris relied on him absolutely, he knew. In a sense he was her only conduit to the real world. And it was a breach of faith to tease her, he thought, even in fun.

He shot her an encouraging grin when she sat down to eat, but she pretended not to see it, and concentrated instead on cleaning her plate.

In an instant her plate was clean and she was leaping up, green in the face, choking out, "Pardon me!" And then it was off to the bathroom. A minute later and she was back at the table, looking as good as new. She heaped her plate full, wolfed it down and excused herself again.

"That'll be enough of that," Doña Maureen said, after Chris had returned from her third trip to the bathroom.

After the fourth trip she said: "Go to your room!"

"No!"

"Do as I say."

"I don't want to."

"Just keep it up, young lady, and I'm packing you off to Saint Anne's Academy. In *San Francisco!"*

"Oh well, I don't mind," said Chris, clicking up the marble staircase in her Mary Janes. "The food was horrible anyway."

Only after she had disappeared into the nursery on the third floor could Merle begin to concentrate on his own plate of food. But no sooner had he started to eat than he was put off it again by the sound of Chris's sobs floating down through the open courtyard.

And he wasn't the only one. The entire company just sat there staring at each other for the longest time, with their forks suspended halfway to their mouths.

"Don't let her bother you," Doña Maureen instructed. "That's just what she wants."

"Carmen," said Don Brian, "can you run up there and see if there's anything you can do?"

"Yes," she said. "As soon as I've had my main course, if you don't mind."

Doña Maureen glanced at her son, raising an eyebrow.

"I'd really appreciate it," said Don Brian significantly, "if you could do it for me now, dear."

Frowning, Carmen pushed her plate aside and rose to her feet.

"Excuse me," she said.

"Absolutely," said Doña Maureen.

"Wait," said Merle. "I'll go up, Aunt Carmen. I'm not too hungry anyway."

"Why, thank you, mijito."

"But don't get all tied up in that there playhouse for hours on end," Gallo scolded. "You spend too much time indoors. You oughta get outside and play with the fellas, sometime."

"Yes sir."

"What a nice little chap," said Doña Maureen, ruffling his hair as he went past her. And then she promptly changed the subject. "Monsignor," he heard her say as he went up the stairs, "is it true what we hear from Mexico City?"

"What do you hear, señora?"

"That General Sánchez has just resigned from the cabinet."

"Cárdenas has thrown him out," said the bishop. "Now that he's got things under control in the capital, he's showing his true colors."

"Poor old Saturnino," Don Brian said. "He was the last of the caudillos."

"Oh, I don't think he'll give up without a fight."

"Good Lord," said Doña Maureen. "Here we go again."

"Yes," said Don Brian. "It was short, but it was sweet."

"Ugly, ugly, ugly," Chris was saying into her mirror, when Merle came into the nursery.

"You're not ugly," he said, sitting down beside her at her vanity. "I think you're pretty."

"No, you don't."

"Yes I do," he said. "I can't figure out why she's so mean to you."

"She's not mean."

"What?"

"She only gets mad when I'm naughty."

"Then you must be naughty all the time."

"I am," she said, giggling. "Haven't you noticed?"

"Here, lemme wipe the tears out of your eyes," he said. He liked the picture they made together in the mirror. She was taller, thinner, smaller-boned, with wide hysterical eyes. He was dark, squat, almost a head shorter, but stolid and strong as a little bull, with slow blue slits for eyes. He could knock her block off if he wanted, but he let her lead him around by the nose.

"I like it when we're alone."

"I don't know why."

"Why not?"

"There's something wrong with me, Merle."

"Don't say that."

"It's true," she said. "That's why my mom doesn't like me."

"Come on," he said, pulling her off the chair. "Let's play."

"Naw."

"Please."

"What'll we play?"

"Whatever you like."

"Let's look in the peephole."

"I thought you didn't want to."

"I changed my mind."

"They won't go in there till siesta time," he said, holding her by the hands. Her hands were hard and sinewy, for a little girl's, and incredibly tense and strong. "Tell me a story, Chris, then after that I'll show you what they do."

He lived for her stories, though sometimes they scared the daylights out of him. She could weave them like nobody else, intricate and deep, abounding in twists and turns and pitfalls and cliffhangers of every kind. When he was older he would remember them all, as he would remember the smallest details of her physiognomy, her curious psychology, and incorporate them into the fabric of his work.

"What do they do?" Chris wanted to know.

"What big people do," he said.

"What's that?"

"You know," he snickered, pulling her close. "Like this! Like this! Like this!"

"Quit it, Merle," she said, playing the elder sister now. "Let's just sit down here on the bed and relax. What story would you like me to tell?"

"Not the Mean Queen."

"Why not?"

"Too scary."

"Well," she said, "make up your mind, boy, 'cause it's the only one you're gonna get."

"All right."

"Okay," she said, settling back on the bed, staring up at the cracks in the stucco ceiling, the shiny diamond-shaped glass pieces hanging down from the chandeliers. "Once upon a time there was a Mean Queen who lived alone in an enchanted castle in the middle of the forest. She was very beautiful and very cruel and very white, with white eyes and long white hair down to her waist. She lived on the blood of children, and she grew soft and fat and sleek until at last there came a time when there were no children left in all her kingdom. She went hungry for weeks and she was afraid she might starve to death until one day a handsome prince came riding by. He was dressed all in black, with a huge black horse, black saddle, black armor, black sword, black mask. She cast a spell on him and brought him into her lair. 'I need blood,' she said. 'Go back to your own domain and fetch me some plump, juicy little children.' Well, the Black Prince was not really an evil person, but he was captivated by her magic charm. He rode to his kingdom, where the children were still happy and healthy, and captured two of the finest. He tied them up with twine and slung them behind him on his saddle and rode to the castle of the Mean Queen. 'Ah,' she said, when she saw them, 'such fat, saucy little things! Come into my kitchen, darlings, and I will show you my knives. . . .' "

"Whoa," said Merle, putting a hand to her mouth.

"What's the matter?"

"Come on, I'll show you the peephole."

"Sure," she said, and they went into the nursery bathroom, where he showed her how to stand up on the sink and peek through the little hole where the pipe went through the wall.

"Can you see, Chris?"

"Yeah."

"What do you see?"

"I see the bed."

"Are they there yet?"

"Nope. Yeah. They just sat down."

"What're they doing?"

"They're arguing about something."

"About what?"

"She doesn't want to do it, she says."

"Do what?"

"I don't know. Listen," she said. And then, in an uncannily accurate reproduction of the adult conversation she heard through the wall, she whispered:

" '*I just can't live with it anymore.*'

" '*I told you, let me handle that part.*'

"*'I'm still not over the other . . . Father Dowd, the father of my child.'*

"*'Why do we always have to play this game, Maureen?'*

"*'And then there's my poor . . . You saw her today; you see what I've made of her.'*

"*'Don't let's get maudlin, dear. Here, look, I brought this.'*

"*'What is it?'*

"*'Something to spice things up.'* "

"What is it? What is it?" Merle demanded, jumping up and down on the bathroom tile.

"A book," Chris said. "Shhhhhh."

"What kind of book?"

"A little yellow book. He's showing it to her now."

"*'You are monstrous! You are obscene!'* "

"Huh?"

"That's what she said. Now she's getting up. She's mad. She threw it out the window."

"Where'd it go?"

"In the street. Go get it. I'll stay and watch."

Merle crept out onto the arcade. The courtyard was humid and somnolent. Even the banana trees seemed to droop in the afternoon heat, and the entire hotel had retired for siesta. He tiptoed down the stairs, through the lobby and out onto the hot, deserted Avenida Mexico. There, lying on the blazing sidewalk under Doña Maureen's window, was the little book. He could tell by the cheap, crudely drawn cover what it was. It was a Tijuana bible. They sold them in the newspaper kiosk in the Jardín Obregón, under the counter.

He thrust it into his pocket and sneaked back into the hotel, nearly running into Bishop LeFevre as the prelate came bustling down the stairs.

"Bless you, my son, bless you," he said, and disappeared out the front door.

Merle went up to the nursery and found Chris outside on the terrace, peeking over the wall. He approached her on his hands and knees and put his mouth to her ear.

"Is he down there?"

"Yeah," she giggled. "He can't figure out where it went. You got it?"

"Yep."

"What is it?"

"Tijuana bible."

"What?"

"Come 'ere," he said, pulling her inside.

"Wow, lookit what they're doing in this picture!"

"Yeah."

"Is that what they do?"

"Who?"

"Them," she said, pointing through the wall.

"Uh-huh."

"I don't believe it."

"I swear to God."

"All right," she said, sighing wistfully. Then suddenly she sat up on the bed and shook the little yellow book in Merle's face, grimacing and sticking her tongue out, as if it had been a dirty hanky, or a used Kotex. "So what're we gonna do with it?"

"I don't know."

"Why don't we take it to school?"

"What for?"

"Merle," she said confidentially, "this is something I want you to show the big guys. They are really gonna be impressed."

"Oh boy," he said. "Oh boy, oh boy, oh boy!"

"Now calm down," she said, "and I'll finish the story of the Mean Queen for you."

"No thanks."

"Why not?"

"Too creepy."

"This time it's gonna be different," she said. And she was right. This time the kids were not the victims—the kids won! They tricked the Mean Queen while she dallied with the Black Prince in her kitchen. They tripped her up in her long white skirts and she fell down on one of her own long knives. The spell was broken. The Black Prince turned good and led the children out of the Mean Queen's castle, out of the Enchanted Forest, and far away to his own land, where they all lived happily ever after in his great shining black castle by the Simmering Sea.

In the boys' bathroom next day, Merle had barely got the Tijuana bible out of his pocket before he was nearly trampled by big boys, fifth- and sixth-graders, fighting each other to get hold of it. They got him down behind the toilets and tore it out of his hands and ripped all the pages out and ran out to the play yard and passed them around to the others, hollering, "Guess who brought them to school. . . . Little Merle Carrizo!"

Never had he felt so proud.

Yet, at the same time, there was this nasty-dirty little feeling that he had, as if he'd forgotten to wash his hands after going to the bathroom, that kept getting stronger and stronger as the morning progressed, till it finally spoiled the good feeling entirely. He couldn't concentrate on his work in class. He couldn't even hear his teacher's voice, or see the paper before him on the desk.

And it did not particularly surprise him when Sister Estéban el Mártir, the prefect of discipline, appeared shortly before snack time, calling his name.

"I've got business with this one," she said.

And yanked him up by the ear and dragged him out of class and down the hall to Mother Superior's office.

Mother Superior had the pieces of the Tijuana bible assembled before her on the desk like a pile of old crumpled paper money.

"Where did you get this, Merle?" she asked, her voice deceptively sweet and calm.

"I found it in the street."

"Don't lie to me, now."

"It's true, Señora Madre, I swear."

"This is a very serious matter," she said. "I'm going to send for your father."

"Please don't."

"Why not?"

"He'll spank me."

"Maybe that's what you need," she said. "A good spanking. I'm shocked at you, Merle. You've never been in trouble before. Now, where does your father work?"

"At the railroad."

"What section?"

"He's assistant trainmaster."

"My, my," she said. "That little Gypsy has come up in the world. I remember when he was here as a charity case, before the Revolution."

She sent for Gallo, and locked Merle in her office until he came. A realization of the extreme gravity of his offense took effect, coming over him in great nauseous waves, each worse than the last. He began to whimper, and then to cry out loud. He cursed Christopher O'Hare for getting him into this, and fretted over what his father might do to him.

The truth was, his relations with his father at this time were not the best. The bone of contention between them was Carmen. Since her marriage to Don Brian, she had put her affair with Gallo on a back burner, while increasing her attentions to Merle. Since Dr. Weber had told her that there was only a very remote possibility that she could ever have a child, she had tried compensating by playing the doting mother: bringing Merle secret gifts of candy and toys whenever she had a free moment, swiping silver pesos from Don Brian for his piggy bank, letting him always have his way. And this had led to jealousy and dissension, for Gallo felt very strongly that a boy should be guided and disciplined solely by his father.

"You're turning him into a little fruitcake, a mama's boy," he said, and embarked upon a crash program to "toughen the kid up." He was alert to any sign of weakness, including tears. Deliberately he withheld his affection, and punished Merle severely for the slightest infraction.

Yet, when Gallo was fetched from the railroad yard, an hour or two after Merle had been locked in Mother Superior's office, he appeared astonishingly unconcerned about his son's transgression. In fact, he seemed to find the whole thing a marvelous joke, and just barely succeeded in hiding his delight at the reverend mother's obvious discomfiture.

"What's the matter, muchacho?"

"I'm in trouble, Papa."

"Who put you up to this?"

"No one."

"Come on, now. Was it Chris?"

"Sort of."

"I see," said Mother Superior grimly. She left the room and returned a minute later, dragging Chris by the ear.

"Are you the one who's behind this?" she said, gesturing without looking at the little pile of tattered pictures on her desk.

"Yes," Chris said, nodding, smiling oddly. "Yes, I'm to blame."

"I might have known," said Mother Superior. "Where did you get it?"

"I got it from my mother."

"I beg your pardon?"

"And she got it from Bishop LeFevre."

"Why, you vile little creature!"

"No," Merle said. "She's telling the truth."

"You lie!" she shouted, showering them all with spit. "You lie!"

"I wouldn't be too sure about that, Reverend Mother, if I was you," Gallo said. "But why don't you just have a talk with Doña Maureen, or Bishop LeFevre, and find out for yourself? Eh?"

"Buh, buh, buuuuuuh," she clucked, her great bosom rising and falling, her red wattles swinging back and forth on the white neckpiece of her habit while her huge hooded head jerked swiftly from side to side. "Buh, buh, buuuuuuh," she went. "I certainly shall, I certainly shall, the first chance I get."

"You wanna bet?" Gallo said, flinging it over his shoulder at her as he went out the door. "I bet you don't."

And he was right. There was never another word on the subject. But the rumor got around anyway—Gallo spread it—and it wasn't long before Doña Maureen was persona non grata in the creole community and the foreign colony again, just as she'd been in Colima. And Monsignor LeFevre, scorned by his flock, called to account before the Archbishop of Guadalajara, was reassigned to a missionary post among the Tzucacab Indians in the jungles of Quintana Roo.

Though the scandal was never mentioned at the Hotel O'Hare, everyone knew about the Tijuana bible, and how word of the affair had reached the ears of Mother Superior. And this knowledge—that each knew what the other knew—lay putrid and festering between mother and daughter until it burst open one morning at breakfast, when they received word that Ramona Mescalero was still alive.

For three years they had assumed her to be dead, killed in the final assault on the Colonia Barbara, as there were no reported survivors. They had never been sure, however, because the military—in order to hide its involvement in the summary execution of the survivors—had buried the corpses in a common grave immediately after the assault, and refused to answer any questions addressed to them by the families of the deceased. Now it appeared that Ramona had survived, and was in the penal colony in the Islas Tres Marías, sentenced to life imprisonment.

The letter with news of Ramona was written in an elegant swirling longhand by a fellow convict who took the liberty to contact them without Ramona's knowledge, he said, because she had too much pride to do it herself. Ramona was alive and as well as could be expected under the circumstances, he wrote, but if they could see their way clear to sending a few pesos every month or so, she could certainly put it to good use.

Stunned by the letter, they all began to argue.

"I think that one of us should go visit Ramona in person," Don Brian said, "and find out exactly what we can do to help her."

"I know it might seem cruel, chief," said Gallo. "But it's kind of hard to feel sorry for her. You know?"

"I can't believe she's alive," said Carmen. "Maybe it's some trick to get money out of us."

"You may be right," said Doña Maureen.

"Well," said little Chris, "you can all do what you like. But I'm gonna write her a letter."

"You'll do no such thing," said Doña Maureen. "I'll not have you writing to convicts, at your age."

"This is a free country," said Chris. "I'll write whom I like."

"You'll do no such thing, young lady."

"Who are you to preach to me, Mama?"

"One more word out of you, Chris, and you're going to regret it."

"How?" Chris said defiantly. "How will I regret it?"

"Remember what I said about packing you off to school in the States?"

"Anywhere," Chris said. "As long as it's away from you."

"So be it," said Doña Maureen.

And apparently this time she was serious, because it wasn't a month later that she had her on a United Fruit Company boat for San Francisco.

Merle would never forget the sight of her as she rode off to the docks in the touring car. So cool, so calm, so undaunted, it seemed, with her brother like a father on one side of her and her steamer trunk on the other. So jaunty in her white-and-blue pinafore with the white straw hat and blue ribbon. Smiling and waving to the assembled family and servants on the front steps of the hotel as if she hadn't a care in the world, as if she were just off on holiday and she'd soon be back.

It was September 13, 1938, and it would be thirteen years till he saw her again.

Nor would he soon forget sleeping in the nursery on the night that she departed. It was as if she had packed up all of his dreams when she sailed away, and left all of her own behind: It was not a fair exchange.

CHAPTER 11

Brian went with her part of the way, to catch a lighter off the Three Marías, as he was bound to see Ramona, whatever his mother or brother-in-law might say. For thirty-six hours they steamed up the stormy coast of Colima and Jalisco, worried by squalls and waterspouts (it being chubasco season), with the smooth blue folds of jungle mountains on their right and the turbulent green Pacific on their left. For once Brian was the talkative one, cornering her half the day in the first-class saloon, and the other half in their cabin, drinking mescal with Dos Equis chasers, repeating himself endlessly, hoping to break through her eerie calm. "Honey, it's all for the best, believe me. You were just tearing each other to pieces. You'll both be much better off, don't you think, if you can spend some time apart?"

Around Cabo Corrientes they struck out to sea, and by morning the weather had changed. Brian stuck his nose out the porthole and was surprised by the lack of humidity in the air, the pellucid sky, the glassiness of the sea, and its color: inky purple, the ship's wake whiter than white.

He dressed himself carefully in a tan tropical-weight suit, white shirt, brown dress boots and Panama hat. Strapped on his shoulder holster, stuck his Colt .45 inside and slid his snub-nosed Smith & Wesson .38 into the special compartment that he'd had built into his right boot. Packed his bag and set it by the bulkhead and went up on deck to watch the dawn. There was no mist, not a cloud from horizon to horizon. Stark, cone-shaped, primeval, the Three Marías emerged from the waves off the port bow and caught fire in the rising sun.

When he got back down to the cabin, Chris was still asleep. Jesus, he thought, watching her lie there in the bunk, her hands closed up in little fists, her small mouth pouting, her hair fanning over the pillow. She's only ten years old. And for a moment he was torn between love and duty: love for Ramona, who had never wanted or needed his love, and duty to Chris, whom he wanted to love but could not—precisely because she so desperately needed it.

Soothing his conscience, he thought of Miss Penelope Peabody, the gray-haired Protestant missionary lady from Nicaragua who sat across from them at the captain's table. Tall, raw-boned, farm-bred, calm and competent as a good trace mare, Miss Peabody had taken a shine to the newly subdued Chris, and promised to see her through to San Francisco. He thought of St. Anne's Academy on Gough Street, his mother's alma mater, now one of the most prestigious Catholic boarding schools in America, and of its headmistress, the Reverend Mother Clare, who had assured him by telegram that she would be waiting in person at the Embarcadero when Chris arrived. He thought of the British, who shipped their little ones off to public school at an even earlier age. But none of it did any good.

He pulled out his hip flask and had a nip of mescal, debating whether or not to wake her up before he left. He hated goodbyes. It was always much better to break away clean. And he could not endure the thought of seeing her alone at the railing, waving to him, dabbing at her eyes with her hanky, as his lighter drifted off and her small figure slowly receded and disappeared. Nor on the other hand was it pleasant to contemplate the notion of Chris starting awake, noticing his bed empty, his bag gone, and running up the gangway just in time to see his boat sail over the horizon.

Then he caught her left eye twitching, and it occurred to him that maybe she was only pretending to sleep. He listened to her breathing, and it seemed too shallow for truly deep sleep. And he reminded himself that she was usually up at the crack of dawn. And convinced himself that she dreaded the confrontation as much as he. Relieved, he took out his pen and wrote her a little note:

Dear Chris:
Please forgive me but I don't have the heart to wake you up. You look so pretty when you sleep. Be a good girl. Have a wonderful time at school. And write soon, especially if you need anything. I will deliver your letter to Ramona, as I promised. I will also give her your love, and tell her that you miss her, as you asked. I love you. And remember, you can always rely on me for help.

Buen viaje!
Brian

He propped it on the dresser, got his bag, bent over the sleeping child, and kissed her softly on the cheek, smoothing her dark hair with his hand. She never stirred. What a marvelous act! he thought. And he could not imagine what he had done to deserve such great good fortune, or such mature consideration from his little half sister—letting him go like this, with no tears, no remorse. At the same time, he was riven with guilt. He went out of the cabin and paused in the companionway with his ear to the door. He could hear nothing. He started to cry. He wanted so much to love her. Still, he was not tempted to go back inside. And once on deck he set his eyes to the wind and let his attention be taken by other things.

These waters off the Sea of Cortez, where the cold California Current collided with the warm Cocos Current, teemed with fish. He sighted the dorsal fins of sharks and killer whales. Swordfish and marlin leaped from the sea. Dolphins ran circles around the ship, and flying fish took to the air by the hundred. Giant prehistoric-looking pelicans swooped low across the water, scooping up prey in their shovel beaks, settling in the rigging to gulp it down. A strange breed of small streamlined waterfowl folded its wings and free-fell fifty feet to the sea, breaking the surface without a splash, never failing to come up with a catch.

A sail appeared from the direction of the biggest island, Santa María Madre. The captain cut his engines and the steamer coasted, while a number of inquisitive passengers came up on deck. The first-class passengers were mostly norteamericanos—traders and expatriate engineers going home on leave. None were from Manzanillo, and for this Brian thanked God. His mother's latest peccadillo had left him with a horror of encountering anyone he knew.

Long and low and slender at her beams, with a tall graceful lateen sail slanted sharply astern, the Tres Marías lighter came up fast, cleaving the waves like a torpedo, heading straight for the bridge. At the last possible instant the lighterman furled his sail, jammed his rudder into a full turn, and skidded across his own backwash to bounce gently against the side of the steamer.

Rope ladders were let down to the lighter from the promenade deck, and everyone hastened to the port side to watch the new passengers embark.

Furloughed guards and their families in khaki and calico, paroled prisoners and their families in sarapes, sombreros and homespun white, they crowded at the ladders on the heaving lighter, the men bellowing back and forth, the children crying, the women screeching excitedly, babies and bundles underarm, fighting for a place in line. A man fell overboard and the lighterman's boy had to fish him out. A woman lost her foothold on the ladder and dropped like a stone, her fall broken by the crowd below.

Once the Three Marías passengers were all safely aboard, the lighterman and his boy commenced loading cargo for the return voyage: canned goods, bags of sugar, cornmeal, rice and flour, bolts of cloth, crates of fresh produce. There wasn't much to load, and the lightermen were highly skilled, scrambling up and down the ladders barefoot and barechested with their burdens perched on their heads, and they were done in a minute. The steamer captain blew his whistle, and immediately a pair of armed guards appeared on the promenade deck, escorting four chained and manacled prisoners. Tall, slick-looking young creoles in rich city clothes—sport jackets, slacks and two-tone shoes—sporting gold crosses and dark glasses and long greasy hair combed straight back, they looked like Argentine movie idols. But it was clear that they were fascists or Sinarchists, part of a wave of political arrests that President Cárdenas had ordered since he consolidated power. The guards removed their manacles and escorted them over the side. As soon as they were aboard the lighter, the guards chained them together again and secured them to the anchor spool.

Brian was the only other passenger to board the lighter. He went down to the promenade deck and threw his bag over the side. The lighterman caught it neatly and signaled him to come aboard. As soon as he hit the deck, the lighterman's boy cast off. The lighter swung away, caught the wind and skimmed across the waves. Brian found a place in the stern, next to a great sleeping mongrel bulldog, and concentrated on the approaching island, trying very hard not to look back.

In the end, however, he found himself unable to resist, and regretted it, for there on the first-class promenade deck, very small against the railing, getting smaller and smaller as the steamer sailed off toward the horizon, stood his own worst nightmare in the white dressing gown of a little girl.

An hour later and the lighter was sailing past an anchored Mexican navy gunboat into a protected cove with aquamarine water so clear you could see the coral bottom fifty feet down. A wooden jetty extended from the palm-fringed crescent of beach. And behind that a whitewashed church, a two-story tile-roofed administration building and a multitude of rough thatch-roofed adobe huts climbed to the pinkish rim of a small extinct half-volcano.

The jetty was guarded by several armed sailors in white leggings and white web belts, but the beach was crowded with what looked like ordinary Mexican fishermen, casting their nets in the small surf.

"Who are they?" Brian wanted to know.

"They are prisoners, señor, just like me," said the lighterman, a gummy, gap-toothed grin creasing his brown weathered face. "We got the run of the island, but we got to feed ourselves."

"How do you do that? A diet of fish gets boring, no?"

"Well, chief, we do a lot besides fish. Guns aren't allowed on the island, of course, but we hunt birds with slings and we go after wild goats and pigs up in the mountains with wooden spears and dogs," he said, patting his great sleeping bulldog. "We grow our own beans, corn, greens, bananas, even sugar cane and cotton. We catch water in cisterns during the rainy season, and irrigate for the rest of the year."

"Not bad," Brian said. "But who's all the cargo for? The penal officers?"

"Them and the Sindicato."

"The who?"

"Figure it out, chief. The average chingazo who shows up here, what's he got? The shirt on his back. How's he gonna rent a garden plot? How's he gonna pay for water rights, let alone seed, fertilizer, tools and hunting dogs? He ain't. So what's he do? Well, he might cut himself a bamboo pole and go fishing. But like you say, it gets old. So sooner or later he finds himself working for somebody else. Usually that somebody is the Sindicato. Here you got the rich and the poor, just like anywhere else. The only difference being, nearly everyone is a convict."

"Ever have any escapes?"

"Very few."

"How come? It would seem easy enough to hire someone to sail over from the mainland and—"

"You see that gunboat, chief? She's fast. And she's got two double-barreled fifty-caliber machine guns, one in the bow and one in the stern."

"I see what you mean," Brian said. And then after a pause: "How many of you on the island?"

"Oh, about three thousand. But it's a small world. Everyone knows everyone else."

"Do you know a Señorita Ramona Mescalero?"

The lighterman leered. "Of course," he said. "She works on the other side, digging clams." In Spanish the phrase had a rhythmic sound—"excavando almejas"—which he turned to lewd effect.

"A little respect."

"Forgive me, please."

"She's family."

"I had no idea. . . ."

In the administration building, under a humorous quotation that some cognoscente among the prisoners had painted on the wall, ABANDONAD CADA ESPERANZA, VOSOTROS QUE ENTRÁN AQUÍ, Brian signed in with a fat, greedy-looking little federal captain of police, and checked his .45 with the duty sergeant. Ostentatiously, he folded a one-hundred-peso note in the visitors' book and slid a fifty-peso gold piece into his shoulder holster on the desk. He also took the trouble to bribe the two federal policemen standing guard at the door.

Brian ran into the lighterman's boy just outside the church. The lighterman had given him the rest of the day off, he said, so Brian hired him as a guide to the other side of the island. On their way the boy—a somber, muscular little chap of about seventeen—pointed out some of the sights. It turned out that the place was like any other Mexican town, with a dirt plaza, a marketplace, a couple of rutted streets lined with tamarind trees and shabby adobe shops. The only thing missing was a cantina, and a gun shop.

The sun was fierce, the path up the terraced hillside steep and circuitous, and by the time they reached the rim of the bowl in which the town was situated, Brian was dripping sweat. He signaled the boy to rest and squatted on his heels in the breeze, fanning his florid face with his straw hat, sipping mescal from his hip flask, getting his bearings. To his rear the pink volcanic amphitheater descended in steps (at each step a row of adobe huts, a garden with corn, beans, banana trees) to the town, the coconut grove, the white half-moon of beach, the clear cove, the blue horizon where the steamer had disappeared. To his right a razorback ridge ran six thousand feet straight up to the top of the volcano in the center of the island. To his left the ridge went steeply down to the sea, curling sharply at the end to form the outer wall of the cove. Ahead of him, broad and smooth and sandy, a plateau covered with thorn trees tipped gently toward a narrow green coastal plain, a mangrove flat, a muddy lagoon and a line of surf.

"There is the village of the clamdiggers," the boy said, pointing to a spiral of white smoke in the blue morning air, a clearing in the mangrove trees, and a circle of adobe huts with palm-frond roofs.

"Vamonos," Brian said, rising off his heels, feeling last night's goat-meat and green sauce—and this morning's mescal—suddenly in his throat.

The boy led the way barefoot across the plateau, nimbly avoiding thorns, cactus, prickly pear and scorpions, and a half hour later they reached the village, which consisted of twelve huts, a small circular plaza of hard-packed black clay, and a crude bamboo shrine dedicated to the Virgin. A pair of naked two-year-olds squatted in the center of the plaza beside a pair of skinny little pigs of about the same age. Chickens and goats were feeding at the edge of the trees. Somewhere back up the incline a donkey brayed.

"There is the jacal of Ramona Mescalero," the boy said solemnly, pointing to a one-room adobe hut on the opposite side of the clearing.

Brian tipped him five pesos and sent him on his way.

He approached the jacal hesitantly, drenched in perspiration, and rattled the strung shells which served for a door. A fly buzzed his ear, and a cloud of gnats swirled in his hair.

"Venga," said a male voice, weakly.

Brian bent and went through the doorway.

"What can I do for you, señor?"

The voice was soft and well modulated, yet slightly throaty, as if from a respiratory infection.

Brian stood in the center of the room, trying to adjust his eyes to the darkness. At last he made out a petate against the wall on his right, and an invalid lying there, propped up with a pillow made of straw and rags. He was a tall, consumptive-looking creole of about fifty, with thinning gray hair, deep dark circles under his eyes, and a patchy Vandyke beard. He was smiling—a fine, generous smile—though his lips were cracked and bloody, and his teeth rotten. A pair of thick broken spectacles was propped on his long pointed nose, and a stack of books and papers rested in his lap. He had the look of a former professor, severely down on his luck.

"You must be the one who wrote me about Ramona," Brian said.

"Januario de Falla, at your most esteemed orders, señor. And you can be none other than Don Brian O'Hare."

"I hope I'm not intruding."

"Not at all. Won't you sit down?" de Falla said, indicating a straw mat on the dirt floor.

"I came as soon as I could," Brian said, seating himself on the mat, leaning against the adobe wall. For the first time he noticed that there was another person in the jacal: a brown, thatch-haired child of about two sleeping in a bed made from an old tomato lug. "I'd like to help."

"Yes, I gathered as much."

"How is she now?"

"The same."

"And if I may ask," Brian said, glancing at the child, "what is your relationship to the señorita?"

"Ah," said de Falla, shifting his position slightly. He appeared to have trouble moving his legs. "That is not an easy question to answer, señor. . . . Friend, counselor, teacher, confidant, protector. . . . On Santa María Madre, you see, no woman can live without a protector. She caught my attention the moment she disembarked, and I offered her every assistance. I had no idea of her delicate condition at the time," he said, reaching out to soothe the child, who had begun to stir in sleep. "But I feared for her safety nonetheless. A young woman of her intelligence and sensitivity. . . . There are those here—El Sindicato, we call them—who would get hold of her if they could, and use her. In a house they have on the beach. It wouldn't matter to them that she had a child. They are ruthless. And they are a law unto themselves here, with a finger in everything. On the other hand, we do have one unwritten rule on the island, which has evolved over several centuries of our existence as a penal colony: No man may touch the woman of another. In short . . ."

"You struck a bargain."

"You could put it that way, though it is nothing so crude as you might imagine. For some years I have been indisposed. It's hereditary, I'm afraid. A result of my father's dissolute youth in Havana. Complicated by primitive conditions here on the island, and by injuries I received in the Cristero Rebellion—I escaped with a couple of friends from Huentitán by leaping from a second-story bathroom window into a river. In recent years I've found it more and more difficult to get around. The other girl with whom I had an arrangement got a parole, and Ramona arrived at about the same time."

"My apologies."

"Oh, not at all. To be frank, I wrote to you on her behalf because I'm worried about her. And the child. Rafael. My health has declined very rapidly in the past few months. I'm not long for this world, señor. Without me, they won't stand a chance. On the other hand, if Ramona had a bit of money, she could . . ."

"Pay off the Sindicato until she could find another gentleman with whom to make an 'arrangement'?"

"Something like that."

"I'll do everything I can for her," Brian said. "And for the child as well. But now I think I'd like to see her, if I could."

He found her down at the lagoon, up to her knees in thick viscous mud, her arms black to the elbow, in a group of five other bent-over women to whom, in her tattered black rebozo, filthy cotton dress and sun-darkened skin, she bore a touching resemblance. He approached her from the rear, splashing up to her through the mud. The other women caught sight of him, rose from their labors and froze like dark herons with their buckets and digging sticks in their hands. He halted just behind her and waited for her to recognize his presence. She turned, slowly, momentously, as if she had been expecting something like this today. But when she saw him she did not appear to recognize him at first. She stared up at him for the longest time, squinting, shading her eyes from the sun.

Small and spare and birdlike, cheekbones high and jutting, nose sharply prominent, Ramona had left all vestiges of her girlhood behind. Yet Brian found her even more beautiful with the harsh new lines of maturity showing around her mouth and eyes. At the same time, and quite incredibly, there was still an air of chastity about her, and she bore her suffering with a kind of nunlike serenity.

At last Brian understood the full implications of Ramona's choice. He wondered at her strength of character, and her vast conscience, while marveling at her naïveté. He pitied her for her self-sacrifice, but could not imagine what had inspired it. Her inscrutable Aztec countenance betrayed nothing. Yet she seemed so small and frail in her defeat, he wanted to take her into his arms and whisper that he loved her, that he would help her, save her, whatever the cost. But already the specter of her sister, his wife, hovered over them, between them, breaking the spell.

"Ramona, I wonder if I could talk to you."

She regarded him calmly for a moment, then her face contorted.

"Did I ask you to come?"

"No, but . . ."

She lunged at him without warning, striking him full on the face with her sharp digging stick, drawing blood, splattering him with mud.

It happened so quickly and it was so obviously unpremeditated that the other women assumed it must be some kind of joke, and giggled tentatively, glancing at each other for reassurance, their bare feet squishing and sucking nervously in the muck.

Unconsciously Brian reached for his handkerchief and wiped his face.

"Why?" he said, meaning to ask why she had wanted to do such a thing. But somewhere inside he knew that she had ample reason to strike him, and he felt that he probably deserved even worse.

On the other hand his surprise was genuine, and he could not be sure whether she had struck him for his role in the attack on the squatters' train, or the defeat of Mondragón, or the destruction of the Red Shirts, or the reestablishment of the Sánchez regime, or his cynical marriage to her sister.

"Why?" he asked again.

"Go away," she said, big-eyed, shrinking back from what she'd done. "Go away."

"Ramona, Ramona . . ."

"No."

"We've got to talk," he said, splashing after her, stopping her in the water.

"I don't want to talk," she said. But she made no move to break away. And her tone was almost plaintive, now that her anger, and her weak reserves of energy, had been expended.

"But I've come all this way."

"Go back, please."

"And your family is worried about you," he said, stretching the truth. "They had no idea where you were."

"My 'family' has known where I am for some time."

"What?"

"The people here," she said, waving back toward the town. "The authorities, they wrote Carmen two years ago. They notified her as next of kin."

"But she never said anything. She never even . . ."

"Gallo must have got hold of it, then."

"Would he?"

"Of course he would."

"I can't believe he'd go that far."

"You'd better believe it, or you'll live to regret it."

"Come for a walk with me," he said. "Maybe we could go somewhere along the beach."

"A walk?" she said, sighing wearily. "Why don't we just *sit* on the beach?"

The other women laughed and went back to work. He noticed for the first time that some of them had babies wrapped up in their rebozos.

"Where're all the men?" he wondered aloud.

"Digging salt," she said. "Working for the Sindicato."

Brian took Ramona's stick and bucket. She slipped on a pair of battered huaraches that she'd hidden in a bamboo thicket, and they made their way over a low ridge of black volcanic sand dunes to the ocean. They sat together on some driftwood near the tideline with their feet out of the sand, for it absorbed the full heat of the sun, and burned the skin even through leather soles.

Up the coast a few miles the plain suddenly came to an end, and a great gray flank of the central volcano shouldered roughly into the surf. Farther to the north, over the Gulf of California, a tropical storm was brewing. A chubasco or cyclone perhaps, with spectacular thunderheads mounting to the stratosphere. Southward across the lagoon and the mangrove flat the purple peaks of the other Marías, Santa María Magdalena and Santa María Cleofas, rose precipitously from the shining straits. And beyond that, the eternal Pacific lay smooth as marble, with no landfall at this longitude until Sala y Gomez Island, two thousand miles off the coast of Chile.

"You must feel close to God out here," he said.

"I don't look for God in nature, Brian."

"But surely, alone out here . . ."

"I think I feel closest to God when I'm in a great throng of people," she said. "I see Him as the sum of us all, the whole human race."

"You must've been doing a lot of thinking," he said.

"A bit."

"And a lot of talking with de Falla, I bet."

"We've had time on our hands."

"Who is de Falla?"

"A fallen angel."

"Why is he here?"

"He killed a soldier."

"When?"

"Years ago, in the Cristero Rebellion."

"Do you know how it happened?"

"He told me," she said. "He was up against a wall. He had made his peace with God. But the soldier's rifle jammed and instinct took over."

"What does de Falla teach you?"

"Everything he knows," she said. "Anything I ask."

"Did it ever occur to you that he might be wrong, or badly informed?"

"That's the chance you take with any teacher," she said. "The main thing is to get the brain cells functioning, multiplying. It's the exercise that counts."

Brian turned away from her, defeated for the moment, to gaze out at the waves. The surf on this windward side of the island was extraordinarily high, churning up gray matter from the bottom, cresting in shallow water, breaking thunderously on the shore, sending up great clouds of green spray that cooled the air.

"La Ola Verde," he said. "The Green Wave."

"Yes," she said. "It comes with the chubasco season. But it's much bigger here than in Manzanillo. Sometimes you can see the swells lining up all the way to the horizon. Sometimes it even washes away the salt-diggers' village around the point. Sometimes I wish it would wash me away."

"And I thought you looked so serene."

"Sometimes I dream that I'm already dead," she said, "that I died in the siege and this is what it's like on the other side."

"But your child . . ."

"If it wasn't for him."

"I'm gonna get you out of here."

"That'll be some trick," she said bitterly.

"Maybe easier than you think," he said. "I've written to Mondragón."

"You had no right to do that."

"I figured it was an exceptional case."

"You might have saved the ink."

"Well, he's a very powerful man now."

"Yes, I heard," she said, with scathing sarcasm. "He's with Sánchez in the capital, isn't he?"

"No, dear. Cárdenas kicked Sánchez out of his cabinet over two months ago."

"You're not serious," she said. "On what grounds?"

"Corruption."

"What a laugh.'

"Cárdenas sort of lured him in, I guess, with the Catholics as bait."

"But I can't imagine General Saturnino Sánchez giving up without a fight."

"He didn't," Brian said. "And he took half the Guadalajara garrison along with him. But it was no contest. They sent Mondragón in after him with a cavalry regiment and it was over in an hour. Then there was some talk of putting him up in front of a firing squad. But Cárdenas took pity on the old bandit, 'out of consideration for his services in the Revolution,' and exiled him to Texas."

"Where he'll live like a king on the money he stole from the Mexican people."

"He was a relic of the past," Brian said. "I knew it was too good to last."

"Myself," Ramona said, "I was beginning to wonder. Who got his job in the cabinet?"

"Mondragón. Who else? I told you he was a powerful man now. And don't I know it? His first act in office was to nationalize the Colima Pacific, and terminate all foreign employees without compensation."

"An admirable decision," she said. "But I still won't accept any favors from him."

"Why not?" he said. "Looks to me like he and Cárdenas got everything you Red Shirts were shooting for."

"They're nothing but opportunists," she said. "We wanted Sánchez's head."

"All right then, *orgullosa,*" Brian said. "How about accepting a favor or two from me?"

"From you?" she said. "I'd have to think about that."

"I've got plenty of time on my hands now, you know."

"And who got *your* job?"

Brian laughed. "Talk about opportunists."

"My brother-in-law is coming up in the world."

"And he's joined the ruling party, you know. The Partido Revolucionario Mexicano. He's running for office as undersecretary of their Manzanillo chapter. Oh, I have no doubt that Gallo will do great things. After all, he learned from the best."

"At least you never made any bones about whose side you were on."

"Now we're talking about Mondragón again."

"I'm sorry," she said, and then suddenly she was crying. "It's so hard sometimes to admit that you were wrong about someone. And I've just never been able to get him out of my mind."

It was not the first time that she had broken Brian's heart.

"For the sake of your child," he said, "let me help you."

"For his sake," she said. "But I could never leave my friend."

"De Falla?"

"He's ill," she said. "Maybe he told you."

"Yes."

"When he's gone," she said, nodding, wiping away her tears.

"Then it's settled."

"But what's in it for you?" she asked. And then when she saw the look in his eye she broke into a smile; and the smile, so unexpectedly brilliant and white in the sunlight, lit her dark careworn face in an altogether new way. "I can't imagine what you see in me," she said, flicking the edge of her ragged black rebozo with the slender tips of her long fingers. "And you a married man."

"How did you know about that?"

"It was the talk of Manzanillo."

"Even up in the Barbarian Colony?"

"You'd be surprised at the rumors that reached us."

"How did you ever get out of there, Ramona?"

"I was one of three," she said. "All women. The soldiers had use of us."

"I'm sorry. . . ."

"Don't be," she said. "It probably saved my life. The other survivors were shot against the wall of the church, while 'trying to escape.' "

"Ramona . . ."

"Forget it," she said. "I have."

"How?"

"An hour, a day, a year at a time," she said. And then, sardonically: "Now this year it has been a very good year for the clams. By nightfall every day most of our buckets are full. We take them into town, where the man we work for—a great fat man at the market—gives us three pesos a bucket. We buy beans and loose corn and we come home and we cook up the beans and grind the corn for tortillas. Then we eat and fall asleep by the fire. In the morning we get up and go out to the lagoon again. I guess you could say that I've sort of lost my sense of drama.

"But you know," she said, "I used to have this really terrible sense of drama. When your mother insulted me, I went out and joined the Red Shirts out of spite. I said to myself, 'Well, she's thrown you out, and you've nowhere else to go, so why not throw in with the outcasts, the enemies of society?' Then I began to see myself as some kind of martyr or nun, and started to identify with the campesinos. When Mondragón betrayed us, and asked me to come with him to Guadalajara, I publicly turned my back on him in the plaza. The campesinos applauded because they took it for loyalty to their cause. Actually I probably would have gone with him if he hadn't a wife and kids in Mexico City. I cried all night when he left. In the morning, though, I came to the conclusion that maybe it was a form of loyalty after all."

"Why?" he said. "Why did you do it, Ramona?"

"It was a good cause."

"A misguided one, to say the least."

"It turned into mass hysteria," she said. "After you've been starved and bombed and shot at long enough, it tends to happen."

"Come with me now," he said. "Take the day off and we'll go to town."

"I've got to get back."

"What for?"

"We work as a collective. Every hand counts."

"You haven't changed a bit, have you?"

"Maybe not, but they rely on me."

"Can I see you tonight?"

"I don't mind."

"I'll buy you all a few things that you might need," he said. "If you won't turn them down."

"Oh," she said, standing on tiptoe to kiss him. "We won't turn them down."

He kissed her back, and she had to push him away to make him stop.

"I've got to know," he said. "If you had it all to do over again, would you . . ."

"This is pointless," she said. "You belong to my sister now."

"It's strictly a marriage of convenience."

"Does she know that?"

"Of course," he said. "We signed a contract."

"How is Carmen now?"

"I thought you'd never ask."

"I don't feel very close to my sister anymore," she said. "I got used to the idea that she didn't care about me, I guess. And now, I don't know. . . ."

"I wouldn't worry about her too much," he said. "She doesn't spend much time worrying about you."

"But she's all right?"

"She's thriving."

"Is she?" Ramona said, cocking her eye. "Any muchachos yet?"

"There's no question of that."

"You have no sexual relations?"

"Well, of course, but that's all there is between us."

"That's a lot."

"Ramona, I haven't given her a thought since I left Manzanillo," he said. "Please, it's very important to me. If you had it all to do over again, would you marry me?"

"Absolutely not," she said. "Frankly, Brian, you're a sonofabitch."

On his way back to town, Brian encountered a party of five villainish-looking young pig hunters, carrying crude wooden spears, leading a pack of ferocious dogs. Red-skinned, ragged, barefoot, with long lank black hair and sparse beards, they looked like prehistoric Indians, Stone Age men. Later it occurred to him that he might have been in danger, alone with them on that vast plateau of thorn trees. But at the time he was so preoccupied with Ramona that he barely noticed them.

For the entire hour's walk he racked his brain, trying to figure out what his options were. It seemed to him that the first thing he had to do was just get Ramona off the island. Then when she was free they would have plenty of time to figure out what to do with each other. Brian had persuaded himself that Ramona's rebuff was merely a matter of misguided loyalty to her sister. And the more he thought about it, the more he came to believe that a simple divorce might be the best solution, especially if he settled a large sum on Carmen, and bribed Gallo to use his influence on her to accept his terms. For now, Brian decided that the best and safest course was simply to lie to Ramona. He would leave her with some money and return to the mainland. There he would pursue his suit with Mondragón, hoping to obtain his help in winning a presidential pardon. Whatever Mondragón thought of Brian, he had clearly been very fond of Ramona. Once the pardon was signed, Ramona would have no choice but to comply with it, for she would no longer have a legal right to reside in the penal colony. If de Falla was still alive at that time, Brian would assuage Ramona's guilt by sending him sufficient funds for medical attention and nursing care.

Satisfied that he'd figured it all out, he hired himself a couple of donkeys and a driver in town and bought up a whole passel of goods in the open market. He bought candles, canned goods, flour and sugar. He bought coffee, chocolate, ground corn, a hundred kilos of beans, a hundred kilos of rice. He bought a live nanny goat, a piglet, a rooster and three laying hens. He bought rubber boots, kitchen utensils, clothing material, blankets, even a small Singer sewing machine. He bought so much that he had to add another three donkeys to the train.

Long before he reached the village of the clamdiggers again, late that afternoon, Brian could hear the grieving of women. It rose off the clearing like the cry of alarmed birds, its volume increasing as the pack train trotted into the plaza. And he already knew what the women would say, in their shrill peasant voices, when they came flying to him from Ramona's jacal with their mouths open.

"They took her! They took her! They took her away!"

He rattled through the strung shells in the doorway and found de Falla as he'd left him in the morning, his face lit by a tallow candle that he'd stuck into the dirt beside the bed.

"There were five of them," he said. "With dogs. They got her down at the lagoon."

"I thought you said there was an unwritten law?"

"There is," said de Falla. "They don't want her for that. They want money."

"Where's the child?"

"They took him as well."

"How much do they want?"

"Everything you've got with you."

"But why didn't they just take it from me?" Brian cried out, in agony. "They saw me on the way."

"That would be messy," de Falla said. "You look like an important man. Word of your largess has already traveled around the island. You might have powerful friends. This way it might be made to seem like a simple mordida, a matter of business."

"And what if I pay them? What'll happen when I'm gone?"

"They'll probably leave her in peace until I'm dead, señor. Then they'll take her again, unless she finds another protector. She's a valuable asset, you know."

"I'm gonna put a stop to this right now," Brian said. "I'm going to the police."

"The police?" de Falla scoffed. "The police are in their pay."

"All right then, goddammit, I'll go over there and get her and the kid myself."

"Careful, señor. These are not people to trifle with."

"I have no intention of trifling with them," Brian said, pulling the snub-nosed .38 from his boot, twirling the cylinder, counting the cartridges.

"Bueno," de Falla said, impressed. "Let's say you get her out of there. Then what?"

"Hell, I don't know—bribe the lighterman, I guess."

"What makes you think he's open to bribery? If so, he'd already have a thriving business ferrying people to the mainland. The Sindicato has grown rich on captive consumers, señor, and it is very strict about attempted escape. The penalty is death. So let me give you some advice," de Falla said, rising up on his pillow, warming to his subject. "After you get them out of the house, then by all means go to the police. But not just any police. Go directly to the captain of federal police. He's open to bribery, but he's afraid of his superiors, and of the Sindicato even more. So bribe him, by all means, but give him the moral satisfaction—and the alibi—of pointing your gun at him. He will get you past the naval guard on the jetty, and he will overcome the objections of the lighterman. Then you'll have to hope the sentry on the gunboat is asleep, or that the captain can convince him you're out for a moonlight sail. But let me warn you, you're not going to get anywhere unless you talk with Ramona first. She will not leave this island until I am dead." De Falla laughed. "So tell her I'm dead. And you may not be far off the mark. The Sindicato does not take kindly to defeat. But better to go quickly, and for a good cause, than a little at a time. No?"

"You're a good man, de Falla."

"Not that it matters much now."

"It matters."

"To whom?"

"I take it you're not a religious man."

"Let's put it this way," de Falla said. "I doubt if there's anyone at home up there. Or else He's a very young God. Who else but a random boy would construct such a perfect model, and then abandon it out of perversity?"

"Adiós, padre."

"Vaya con Dios," he said, laughing, coughing, wincing because it caused him pain. "But how did you know?"

"It's written all over you."

"Ah, and this is the land of wayward priests," de Falla said, reaching inside the makeshift cradle that sat beside the bed. "Here," he said, handing Brian a small, tattered, schoolchild's notebook. "It's the diary that Ramona kept in the siege. She wouldn't leave without it. And give her this as well," he said, pulling something from around his neck. It was a gold cross on a chain. "It'll bring her luck. And tell her . . . tell her . . . Oh well, you'll know what to say."

"Oye, padre," Brian said, as he was going through the door. "What do you want me to do with all the provisions I brought?"

"Scatter them among the poor, my son," he said, delighting in his own satiric wit. "I'll not be needing them where I'm going."

Night fell as Brian was crossing the plateau. Yet from the rim of the bowl he could see the house quite clearly. Festooned with colored lanterns, paper streamers and flags of the Republic, it stood just beyond the coconut grove, on the far northern end of the beach. Elevated high above the tideline on three-foot stilts, and constructed entirely of bamboo, with a palm thatch roof and an open-air bar on the front veranda, it looked more like a seaside restaurant than a house of pleasure.

Brian approached the house obliquely, skirting the town, picking his way down the terraced hillside, coming on it from the rear, through the coconut grove. At the edge of the grove he halted, listening. He could hear victrola music, laughter and conversation from the bar, but not a sound from the rear of the house, which was completely dark. He was surprised that there were no dogs barking.

He drew his pistol, held it cocked and ready in the pocket of his jacket, and padded across the sand, making for the back door.

"Quíen vive?" somebody said. It was a frightened young voice, and quite familiar.

"I've come to see the boss," Brian said.

"Right this way, señor," said the voice, and the lighterman's boy emerged from the shadows, smiling and carrying a long spear.

"So you work for the Sindicato too."

"We all do, señor," he said gravely. "At one time or another."

"Where are the dogs?" Brian said. "I expected dogs."

"We don't let them out at night."

"Why not?"

"They are precious, señor. They're our hunting dogs."

And he started around the house, beckoning Brian to follow.

Brian could not believe that the kid would be so stupid, or so trusting, as to turn his back on him. At first he suspected a trick. But then he felt almost sorry. He pulled out his weapon and struck the boy on the crown. His legs collapsed and he dropped to the sand without a sound.

Brian dragged the boy and his spear under the house. There he waited, listening, with the young man cradled in his arms. On the victrola now in the bar Lolita López was singing "Siboney."

When Brian had determined to his satisfaction that all was well, he whispered, "Sorry, kid," and hit him another one. Then he laid him down quietly on a bed of cobwebs, broken glass and strewn condoms and crawled out the back way, emerging just to the right of the rear steps. He rose to his feet, went up the steps silently and tried the latch. It was locked, but the door was made of bamboo, and flimsy. He was tempted to lean on it till it gave, but he thought better of it. There was a window to the left of the door, about eight feet above the ground. And it was open. Brian put the gun in his pocket, leaned out as far to the left as he could, got a grip on the windowsill, and swung over. He pulled himself up and peeked inside. The room was dark, but when he nuzzled through the dusty, gauzy curtains a faint white light came in from over his shoulder. A quarter moon had risen above the rim of the volcano. The room was empty, save for a straw rug, a petate, a washbasin, a pin-up girl on the wall. He hoisted himself up and came in through the window, landing a little harder on the wood floor than he would have liked.

And heard footsteps approaching.

He pulled out his piece and crept to the side of the door. It opened inward, onto Brian, and one of this morning's villainish-looking young pig hunters came in, with a spear in his hand. Brian stepped out from behind the door. The man turned to find the cold muzzle of Brian's equalizer pressed to his throat.

"On your belly."

Brian held him down with a boot to the neck, and swung. He struck him just above the ear, cracking his skull. The sound—"Dhunk!"—was very loud in the small space, so he decided not to hit him again.

He went through his pockets, got his keys, and slipped out into the corridor. As his eyes adjusted to the darkness, it seemed to him that it was rather long, with three doors on either side. From somewhere down the hall he could hear a woman moaning.

He tried the door facing him. It opened, creaking. There was no one inside. He closed it and tried the next one. Empty. But from inside the door across the hallway he could hear a couple making love, the man grunting, the woman loudly simulating the sounds of ecstasy.

The last room on the right was empty. The one across the hall was locked. He pulled out the keys. From inside the room a child began to cry. The door swung open on his first try.

"Quíen es?" Ramona said, in a small frightened voice.

"It's me," he said, and closed the door softly behind him.

Mother and son lay cowered against the wall, in pale moonlight, under a barred window.

"Shhhhhh," Ramona whispered, but the kid kept right on crying anyway.

Just then a door slammed and a light went on in the corridor.

"Qué pasa?" someone said. It was the same husky female voice that had been moaning a moment before.

"It's the baby," a male voice said.

"Where's Melchior?"

"Melchior!"

Ramona shuddered as the footsteps approached, and shrank with her kicking, shrieking child into the corner.

"Señorita?"

"Sí."

"You all right?"

"Sí."

"You haven't seen Melchior, have you?"

"No."

"He's not in there bothering you again, is he?"

"No."

"He's probably out front," the man said.

"You can bet it's somewhere he don't belong," the woman said. And they went out the door at the end of the hall.

Brian put a finger to his lips and pulled Ramona up by the hand. She clamped her palm over the baby's mouth, held it tightly to keep it from kicking, and followed him down the corridor to the back of the house. Brian listened at the door, and pushed it open. Between the house and the coconut grove there was no one he could see. Out on the veranda Lolita López was singing "Donkey Serenade," and voices were raised in excitement.

"Melchior, cabrón, donde fuiste?"

Brian took the child and clamped a hand over its mouth, hard. It was rigid with primal fear now, its little heart palpitating wildly, its eyes rolled back in its head. He ran with it down the steps and across the beach. Ramona hastened along behind him. At the edge of the coconut grove they stopped to catch their breath and calm the child, but by then it had hyperventilated and passed out from fright. Ramona took it and rocked it gently, and soon its breathing returned to normal.

"Melchior, Melchior, qué te pasa?"

"Let's go," Brian said, taking the child from her again. "They found the guard."

"What'd you do to him?"

"I knocked him over the head," he said. "Knocked the other one over the head too."

"Where are we going?" she demanded, panting to keep up. "They'll go straight to de Falla's, you know."

"We're not going to de Falla's," Brian said. "We're leaving the island."

"I told you, I won't leave my friend."

"I'm sorry to tell you this, Ramona, but your friend is dead."

"What?"

"They killed him."

"I don't believe you."

"When I got there, he was on his way out. Here, he gave this stuff to me," Brian said, handing her the diary and the cross. "He said you'd want to have them."

She cried all the way across town. He had to slap her and beat her to keep her moving. To make things worse, the kid woke up and started screeching at the top of its lungs. By the time Brian got them to the administration building, he was in no mood to fool around. He dragged them past the pop-eyed guards at the door and up to the sergeant's desk and demanded to see the captain of federal police at once.

"But he's at home, señor, he's having his dinner."

Brian slammed a thousand-peso note on the desk.

"Emergency," he said.

"By all means," the sergeant said.

The captain lived in a spacious garden apartment just across the courtyard from his office. He was seated at table with his wife, his mother and his three teenage daughters when they burst in with the sergeant.

"Qué significa esta intrusión?"

"Un caso de urgencia, mi capitán."

"If I could have a word with you in private, comandante," Brian said, pulling out his wallet as if searching for some important document there.

"A sus ordenes, señor," the captain said, rising from his chair, patting his greasy face with a napkin.

Then he dismissed the sergeant, excused himself from the dinner table and escorted his unexpected guests into the anteroom at the rear.

"I have a request of the utmost urgency," Brian said, talking fast, laying ten thousand pesos in crisp new bills on the lamp table between them. "Señorita Mescalero is a close personal friend of General Raúl Mondragón, minister of transport in the cabinet of President Lázaro Cárdenas."

"But wait . . ." Ramona protested.

"Shut up," Brian said. "Perhaps the señorita doesn't appreciate it, but her life is in danger here, and the general has charged me with removing her from the island at all costs. A letter of explanation, and a formal presidential pardon, will follow. As for now," Brian said, reaching for his .38 and pointing it in the captain's fat sweating face, "we require your assistance in securing immediate transportation to the mainland. . . .

"Thank you, comandante, thank you," Brian said, as the captain hastily scooped up the money and moved for the rear door.

They got past the naval guard by claiming they had an invitation for dinner with the commander of the gunboat. But the lighterman was not so gullible.

"I can't leave the jetty after dark, mi capitán," he said. "You know that. It's against the rules."

Brian showed his gun. The lighterman's dog growled. Brian put five thousand pesos in the lighterman's torn shirt pocket. The dog quit growling and went back to sleep.

"Set a course for the mainland."

"But there's a chubasco brewing, chief."

Brian looked around and sniffed the wind. The sea was stirring, the humidity rising, the wind picking up. A cloudbank was sweeping in off the channel.

"So much the better."

"We're gonna get wet," the captain said. "We're gonna get sick."

"We'll be all right," Ramona put in, settling in the stern with the child.

"If you say so, señorita," the lighterman said, going forward to unfurl the sail.

"Ditch that gunboat," Brian said, "and I'll double your money."

"Bueno. You take the tiller, señor. This is gonna be a fast trip, or it's gonna be our last. . . ."

The captain jumped overboard as soon as the gunboat started after them, and Brian let him go. The gunboat stopped to fish him out, giving them the minute they needed. They beat her to the cloudbank and lost her in the squall.

For two days and two nights they ran before the wind. They ran so fast the chubasco couldn't catch them. Ran so fast they blew right by Manzanillo. Ran so fast they probably wouldn't have stopped till Guatemala—had the lighter not hit a reef off the mouth of the Río Coayuayana, and stove in her bottom, with the tide going out.

It all seemed so unreal. They were only a hundred yards off a beach where people were walking around—Indians in white pajamas and long dresses. They were having a fiesta. A fish fry. And one of them had a canoe pulled up on the sand.

Brian jumped up and down and shouted and waved, but the Indians were not inclined to respond. Indeed, they barely seemed to notice him, and went about their business of cooking and eating and singing and pulque-drinking as if the foundering lighter just offshore were only a source of mild, skeptical amusement.

"Why don't you holler at them?"

"Ain't worth the trouble, chief."

"Why not?" Brian said. "Come on. Get them to paddle out here with that canoe."

"They won't do it."

"How do you know?"

"Hell, I was born not far from here," he said. "These are my people."

"Then why not give it a try? Tell them I'll pay."

"It don't matter what you pay," the lighterman said. "They know it ain't worth it. Once they got out, they'd never get back in."

"They could wait for low tide."

"They ain't gonna wait for nothing. In a few minutes, you'll see. They're gonna break camp and drag that canoe over the dune to the lagoon side and paddle for high ground as fast as they can go."

"Why would they want to do that?"

"That tide is chubasco tide. It's gonna go all the way out. And then it's gonna come right back in again . . . with a bang."

"What in God's name are those crazy fucking Indians doing out here at a time like this?"

"It's some kind of a religious service, I think."

"A what?"

"That chubasco is powerful medicine."

"You're joking."

"I wouldn't lie to you, chief."

"So what are we gonna do?"

"We wait."

"Then what?"

"When the tide is out, we run like hell for the first tree we can find."

"How far is that?"

"About three kilometers, I'd say. It's across the lagoon. But it ain't deep. You can wade."

"What happens if the tide catches us?"

"Oh, it'll catch us."

"What do we do then?"

"We swim."

"I can't swim," Brian said.

"Then you're just gonna have to stay with the boat, chief," the lighterman said. "And hope it floats."

Ramona elected to stay aboard with Brian, in spite of the fact that she could swim. She felt the boat would be safer for the child. The lighterman and his dog went over the side as soon as the ebb tide began to slow. Brian gave him another five thousand pesos, in consideration of his boat, and begged him to notify Mrs. Maureen O'Hare in Manzanillo, in case of death. The lighterman and his dog made it to shore, and disappeared over the black sand dunes in the direction of the lagoon.

After they were gone, Brian, Ramona and the child had an hour alone. They sat together in the stern, facing out to sea. Ramona fed the baby at her breast, and sang it a lullaby in English. Brian watched, with his arms around both of them, and selfishly considered that he would never be happier, no matter how long he lived. And ran through all of his possible lives and lived this last impossible one as if it would never end.

It was astonishing how much got said, once the kid went to sleep. They had ample time, it seemed, to lay the past to rest, and to make their peace with one another at last. They thought of all the years they had lived, and might have lived, and of all things they had done, and might have done, together and apart, and they understood finally that it never could have been. As Ramona put it: "I never could think of life without you, Brian, but I never could have lived with you either." And he dared not imagine what he had done to deserve such an ending, for he had gained in death what he could not have obtained in life.

Their only concern was Rafael. They put Padre de Falla's good-luck cross around his little neck and tied him into a watertight reed basket and crammed an entire lifetime for him into the hour between the tides. Brian became the father he never would have been, and Ramona became the wife she never could have been, and they all lived happily ever after in an imaginary resort hotel by a beautiful tropical sea. The child grew into a man and fell in love and got married and had children of his own and grew old and died—as his parents had done before him.

It all seemed so simple. A family of seagulls settled in the bow, squabbling over sardines. A kingfisher sat lopsided on the lateen-rigged crosscast, swallowing his catch. It all seemed so unreal. They listened to the wind, and the sail flapping. They watched the sun go down into the sea. They prayed for the soul of the innocent child. They said goodbye. Brian even remembered to give her the letter from little Chris: *Dear Ramona I hope you will forgive me I don't always remember to pray for you at night. . . .*

Then the Green Wave came along and carried them all away.

The Indians found Brian and Ramona in the morning. When the waters receded they dressed the corpses according to their rites and carried them to the cemetery island in a procession of black-painted canoes. They saw the lighterman on the shore, and were about to dispatch him with their machetes for desecration of the dead when they noticed a small child—apparently the same one they had seen yesterday on the foundering lighter—sleeping in the shade of the great spreading alamo tree.

In faltering Nahuatl, the lighterman told of how he'd found safety with his dog in the alamo tree, and of how, late that night, in the moonlight, he'd seen the child come floating by in a reed basket. He had untied it from the basket, and brought it into the tree. He had held it up by the heels and shaken the water out of it. He had kissed its little mouth and blown the breath of life back into it. The child's name was Rafael, he said. After Saint Rafael the Archangel.

As it happened, San Rafael was the patron saint of the Indians' village. This, taken with the child's miraculous survival, and the divine intervention of their sacred alamo tree, they perceived as a marvelous convergence of auspicious omens, and they offered the lighterman safe passage to the mainland.

He traveled to Manzanillo to inform Mrs. O'Hare of the death of her son, but Gallo intercepted him at the reception desk of the hotel and paid him off.

"But what about the kid?" he wanted to know.

"Just leave him with the Indians," Gallo said, and went to find Carmen in the hotel room she had shared with Brian.

"They're both dead," he said. "We've got to move fast."

A few minutes later they walked into the vital-records section of the palacio municipal, where Carmen filed death certificates for Brian and Ramona, with the lighterman as witness. Afterward they went across the hall to the federal police station, where the lighterman turned himself in to the authorities and filed a deposition describing his kidnapping from the penal colony, and the deaths of Brian, Ramona and her child. The captain of federal police wired the Islas Tres Marías, confirmed the lighterman's story, and took him back into custody, with the understanding that he be held as material witness in a coming court case. The next day, Carmen filed suit in Superior Court to have herself declared the sole legal administrator of her late husband's estate.

At the trial—delayed by Maureen's nervous collapse which followed news of her son's death—Licenciado Aquilino de Benito, who was representing the mother of the deceased, produced a marriage contract, signed by Carmen and witnessed by several prominent citizens of the town, including Trainmaster Gallo Carrizo, which stipulated that Carmen had no claim to any O'Hare property whatsoever. But the magistrate—a new man, an appointee of the revivified Cárdenas administration—ruled the marriage contract a moot point, because the Mexican Constitution specifically forbade alien land ownership within fifty kilometers of the sea.

Carmen was awarded the estate of her late husband, as well as the property of his mother. Mrs. O'Hare appealed the case, but her scandalous liaison with the former bishop of Manzanillo had undercut her standing with the traditional power brokers of the town, just as their standing had been undercut by the exile of General Sánchez. Her appeal was denied.

Distraught over the death of her son, and her sudden reversal of fortune, Maureen lost control of herself as she was being evicted from the Hotel O'Hare by the municipal authorities, and railed at Carmen—who stood at the top of the front steps with Gallo, Grandma Carrizo, little Merle and her new servants—for her "monstrous duplicity and ingratitude." Later that same day she boarded a train for Colima, where she was met at the station by her old friend, the homosexual Dr. Bermúdez.

She caught sight of him on the station platform even before the train had stopped. A thin, goateed, red-faced little man with pinched white lips and kindly, watery gray eyes, he wore an impeccable gray pinstriped suit and vest, a gold watch chain and an anachronistic derby hat, and looked more like a Central European gymnasium professor of the previous century than a contemporary Mexican physician of modern methods.

"Doctor!" she called to him through the window, and he hastened to follow after her car with a handsome young Indian mozo tagging along behind him. She descended the stairs and embraced him, while the mozo squeezed around them and went for her bags.

"I've come to throw myself on your mercy," she said, crying softly onto the doctor's frail little shoulder.

"I would never have expected anything else," he said gallantly, patting her on the arm.

"I have nothing to bring but myself."

"That is more than enough."

"And you're sure I won't be in your way?" she asked, glancing at the Indian boy, who came clattering down the stairs with two of her suitcases balanced precariously on his head.

Dr. Bermúdez laughed.

"A mere form of prostatic nostalgia," he said. "I assure you, my dear, he has served a purely decorative function these past few months."

Shortly after Maureen's departure from Manzanillo, Carmen married Gallo, and suddenly Gallo found himself in possession of everything he'd ever wanted. He bought his wife a new chauffeur-driven touring car, and sent Merle off to one of the most exclusive private schools in the United States. He retired his mother on a full pension, bought her a home in the Barrio Chino and maintained her in a style to which she was manifestly unaccustomed until her death later that year of overeating, after which he built her a gaudy family mausoleum in the San Juan de la Cruz cemetery in the state capital—as a symbol of his statewide political and financial aspirations—where he entombed her in glory.

Then he set about consolidating his position and making plans for future expansion. As trainmaster of the Colima Pacific Railroad, with absolute veto power over the shipment of perishable crops, he was in an ideal position to exert pressure on local planters to relinquish in his favor a certain percentage of their yearly profits. As undersecretary of the Manzanillo branch of the Partido Revolucionario Mexicano organization, he was able to exert similar pressure on merchants and landowners of the district, who feared the excesses of the Cárdenas regime. And finally, as heir to the O'Hare fortune, which consisted not only of the

Hotel O'Hare but of properties and investments all over Manzanillo and the state of Colima, he had gained the respect of the new power brokers of the town, who were nowadays more and more often people like himself, mestizo upstarts and entrepreneurs on their way to the top.

Gallo's first major move was in the political arena. Shortly before the election campaign of 1939, he scrutinized all the PRM presidential contenders and picked a long shot, a moderate, a virtually unknown cabinet minister named Manuel Ávila Camacho. Gallo had arrived at this decision by a shrewd analysis of the current national political situation. All over Mexico—and especially in Colima State—the ruling party was polarized by extremist factions of the left and right. The left passionately supported all of President Cárdenas's policies, and wished to see them continued through his picked successor, Francisco Mugica. The right violently opposed those same policies, and wanted to see them destroyed by their own candidate, a retired army officer with decided Sinarchist or fascist leanings. As Gallo saw it, these polarized factions would cancel each other out, leaving the field free for his own man. Accordingly, he made bold to contact Señor Ávila Camacho in person, volunteering to do some groundwork for him in Colima State. Ávila Camacho gratefully accepted the offer, and for the next couple of months Gallo barnstormed every PRM chapter in the state, making speeches in favor of the pragmatic, probusiness policies of Ávila Camacho, and against the extremism and disorderliness of the other candidates. Many of Gallo's fellow party members laughed at him, because Francisco Mugica especially seemed a much stronger candidate. But Gallo's choice proved uncannily accurate. And in January 1940, Manuel Ávila Camacho, a devout Catholic and successful bureaucrat, a compromise candidate selected by the ruling party precisely for his lack of factional support, was inaugurated as President of the Republic in Chapultepec Palace, with Gallo Carrizo in close attendance. Immediately afterward, President Ávila Camacho set about purging all the extremist officials who had been appointed by the previous administration. In the shuffle, Gallo was promoted to general director of the Colima Pacific Railroad, and elected PRM secretary for Colima State.

Meanwhile, Mrs. O'Hare continued to live with Dr. Bermúdez in Colima, and in a few years she prevailed upon him to marry her, for the sake of form. In this way she acquired Mexican citizenship of her own. Dr. Bermúdez fell ill soon after their marriage, and when he died a few months later Maureen inherited his small hotel. She sold it and took his insurance money and bought herself a much larger place in a dirty little fishing village on a beautiful bay, betting that one day it might attract wealthy American tourists. Her daughter, Chris, came to stay on school holidays. At first she came by boat, and then with the expansion of air travel to Mexico, she came by plane. The name of the village was Acapulco.

PART II

CHAPTER 1

The Indians carried the child to Xochitlán, their island village among the lily pads. Word of his miraculous reprieve from death preceded his arrival, and he was met on the banks of the circular canal by a delegation of important men, including the padre, the presidente, the síndico, the régido, the secretary of the cuatequitl or fishing cooperative, and the huehuechique or witch doctor. The huehuechique, who knew the ancient Nahuatl words and rituals, and the green-eyed foreigner Padre Dowd (pronounced "Dau" hereabouts), who was conversant with more modern methods of sorcery, agreed that the child's recovery from the Green Wave was an important event in the history of the pueblo. The huehuechique recalled the old legend of the Child from the Sea, who would come from the north to lead the people of the mangrove swamp in battle against the mainlanders.

The elders consulted among themselves to determine who should have the honor of raising this special child—known hereafter as El Niño—and at the padre's suggestion it was decided to award the prize to a poor fisherman from the barrio of Mexcaltitán named Pedro Martínez. Pedro stepped forward, and the padre presented him with the soggy little cloth-bound diary which had been found on the body of the child's mother. He recounted a parable from the days of the Cristero Rebellion, when he had encountered a poor, starving little girl of this same name—Ramona Mescalero, he would never forget it, he said—and rejected her pleas for charity, and then, in a fit of guilt, showered her and her little sister with coins and mea culpas. Pedro promised to keep the diary among his most sacred possessions, for it was obviously very powerful medicine.

Two years later, however, when an emissary of the bishop of Manzanillo was sent around on one of his brief and infrequent tours of the swamp, nothing was said of the legend, as nothing was said of the padre—the town's true and unofficial priest—who darkened his face and hair with dye and disguised himself as a poor fisherman. The child was represented as an orphan from another village, baptized according to the rites of Rome, and inscribed in the church's official registry book as Rafael Martínez. Meanwhile the entire village continued to call him El Niño; and in any case, he had already been baptized by Padre Dau and the huehuechique long before, according to their own evolving traditions.

Though Pedro Martínez had won a glittering prize, and was the envy of all his neighbors, and was even being talked of as the next secretary of the cuatequitl, he was still just as poor as ever. Moreover he was no longer a young man, and not so handy with his fishing nets as he once was. He had buried his first family in a famine and plague that swept the village in the year 1927. And he lived with his wife, Marta, his four young children, six chickens, two goats and his canoe in a one-room, dirt-floored adobe house and tiny, muddy courtyard on the narrow, refuse-laden Mexcal Canal.

The courtyard of the little house, with its mangrove stump, palm thatch and bamboo outbuilding and open sewage pit, functioned as kitchen, bathroom, launching ramp and work space, while the room inside served as sleeping chamber, dining area, and rainy-season parlor. Daytimes the quarters were not so crowded, as nearly everyone—and everything—was out and about in the village and the swamp scrounging for food. But at night, when the evil spirits and the "bad air" held sway over Xochitlán, the entire family was packed together in the house—a space about twice the size of a prison cell—making life exceedingly uncomfortable in the tropical heat and humidity.

Rafael was the youngest of the children, and by custom he slept between his parents till he was six years old. His first memories were of the sounds of love, followed by a grunt of pain as his arthritic father rolled over him, and a sweatbath that continued until his parents' overheated bodies cooled down.

In accordance with native customs, Pedro Martínez raised his youngsters harshly. From their earliest years he tolerated no play, no tears, no backtalk, and he punished them severely for the slightest disobedience. At five they were carrying heavy clay jugs of water from the well. At six the boys were being sent out to guard the animals on the pig island. At eight they were spending ten-hour days hoeing weeds on the corn island. From the age of ten on, they were joining their father at work on a daily basis, learning his trade of fisherman.

In his relations with his youngest son, however, Pedro went against all tribal lore and tradition. He treated him as if he were a thoroughbred colt, or a prize pony, pampering him with lumps of sugar, honeycombs, cactus and tamarind candies, coconut milk, and special, separately prepared high-protein dinners based on dried shrimp and fish meal. He never raised a hand to him. Never even raised his voice. Though Pedro took great care to teach El Niño the noble trade of fisherman, he never required him to work with his brothers, or help around the house with his sister. Indeed, he devoted months to fashioning him beautiful personal toys—intricately carved canoes and donkey carts, Indian dolls stuffed with straw—and allowed him to linger at play as long as he liked. In this way he displayed El Niño to family, friends and neighbors. In this way he maintained his value in the town. The boy was immensely precious to him. More precious than his canoe dug out of one great conacaste tree and passed down from father to son. More precious than his shrimp traps laboriously constructed of heart-shaped palm-leaf ribs and miniature lanterns with candle-sized flames. More precious than his reed dip nets, his hemp fish nets, his plot of ground on the communal corn island or his share of pastureland on the pig island. And certainly more precious than his two loutish elder sons, gnarled and stunted from malnutrition and overwork, nearly bald from an attack of scarlet fever. For he—wondrous child—had succeeded in doing for his family what no other Martínez since the Aztec Empire had done: He had enhanced its status in the village, and pointed the way to an illustrious future.

When El Niño grew old enough to speak, and to make his wishes known, his father redoubled his efforts to curry his favor. He jumped at his merest suggestion, deferred to his slightest whim, and required his wife to do the same. Marta waited on him hand and foot, fed him goatmilk curds and honey from a wooden spoon till he was six, wiped his ass with palm leaf and rose water till he was seven. The kid wore hand-stitched tunics and calzones when his siblings wore rags, leather huaraches when everyone else in the family went around barefoot. He had his hair cut by a barber when his father lopped his own off with a fish knife, and he bathed in the river twice a day when his mother was lucky to find time once a week. As a consequence of all this care and attention, he soon fulfilled all his father's fondest expectations. He grew tall, well formed and comely, a masculine image of his heavenly departed mamá. With ample time to develop his native gifts of imagination and intelligence, he quickly surpassed his elder siblings in language and learning skills, and by the age of eight he seemed to know even more than Pedro and Marta. The neighbors, observing the rearing of this special child from a vantage point across the canal or over the courtyard wall, waited in gleeful anticipation to see El Niño grow into a spoiled, insufferable brat. And at first it seemed that they would not be disappointed, for it was clear that he held himself above everyone else in the barrio, and required of his family instant obedience to his will. But he was never heard to be loud, obnoxious or demanding, and very early in his childhood he became known throughout the village for his dignified, introspective air, and a rare serenity. In short, he quickly mastered the role assigned to him: El Niño, the Chosen One. Besides, he had no need of tears or tantrums. A simple look of impatience was enough to send his father, his mother, his sister, even his aunts and uncles and cousins scurrying to fulfill his least desire. . . . With his brothers, however, Rafael's relations were somewhat more complicated. They had conceived a murderous jealousy of him on the first day of his arrival, and tormented him in secret until he was old enough to report their actions to Pedro. After that, just the mere possibility that he might tattle was enough to hold them at bay, for they knew that Pedro would whip them mercilessly, and banish them to the courtyard to sleep with the evil spirits and the "bad air" all night, if he ever found out.

Eventually Rafael became so secure in his exalted position that he could even indulge himself in the luxuries of charity and compassion. With a full belly, he could turn down a steaming bowl of tortillas and beans so that his starving sister might eat. Having never felt the sting of his father's hard hemp rope, he could rebuke him publicly when he cracked it over his poor brothers. So El Niño won the hearts and minds of even his most envious and rebellious inferiors, and soon he counted some of his worst former enemies among his greatest devotees. In the same way, he was so remote from the everyday squabbles and jealousies of the Martínez household that, while still a boy, he could become the arbiter of all family quarrels, the measurer of each meager share, the judge of every minor transgression. Thus, effortlessly, did he bring justice to his rude family, and for this they would always revere him.

But reverence is not love, and though Rafael would not dream of relinquishing his favored status, he would sometimes catch himself feeling a bit lonely, and he would long to have his sister make tearful confessions to him, as he'd heard her do to Marta, or he would wish that he might experience a passionate, rough-and-tumble, adversary relationship (called "cuate" or "twining" in the native dialect) such as his brothers enjoyed. Yet he knew that this was never to be, and from his earliest years he felt that he was alone, like Padre Dau, not really part of the village, not even really part of his own family, but high over it, looking down on it: as if his family, his village, his people, were somehow part of *him*. It was a notion that was communicated to him every day of his life by the pueblo's unspoken attitude toward him and Padre Dau, which consisted of an almost worshipful deference combined with an unmistakable wariness. And there was never a moment when he was not made aware that he and the padre were responsible for them, in some unknown way, or that he would someday be made to pay very dearly for the privileges that were accorded to him in their name. Indeed, he could see clear indications of the nature of his debt in the example of Padre Dau, who was said to be merely middle-aged but looked as old as time, who grew smaller and smaller, grayer and grayer, more and more stooped and halting and wizened every year, as if his strength, his heart, his juices, his vital forces were being slowly devoured by parasites, as if he were in some way *food* for the village. For this reason El Niño feared the padre, and avoided him as others avoided the evil eye.

When Rafael was nine the government sent an eager young graduate of Colima University to found a school and teach the children of the village. There had been another school, another brave and idealistic young teacher, a decade or so before. But Padre Dau, who had an almost pathological fear of the outside world, convinced the villagers that they would be corrupted by alien influences, and goaded them into burning down the school and sending the teacher packing. But this time things were different. First, this new teacher had been sent with a personal letter from the President of the Republic, and the villagers revered the president as a half-mythical Higher Authority. Second, this young man, unlike the other, was pure raza, and spoke Nahuatl like a native. And third, the padre no longer seemed capable of opposing their collective will. Or rather, his individual will had over the years merged with that of the pueblo, and he no longer possessed a separate vantage point.

When the maestro landed with his canoeload of books on the banks of the circular canal, the whole village was there to meet him, including the padre. Later, Rafael accompanied the maestro to the central plaza, where he watched with the others as he tacked onto the weathered oaken door of their oddly used church the letter he had from the President of the Republic. The maestro explained and described this letter in great detail, but it remained completely incomprehensible to them even after he—and later the padre—had taken the trouble of going over it a dozen times or more.

"It doesn't surprise me," the maestro said, after a few more days of trying. "I can't make you understand its meaning because it just doesn't translate. You're going to have to learn to read, write and speak Spanish before you'll be able to make any sense of it."

The letter was so mysterious that it piqued the Indians' interest in the occult. Virtually overnight they built a new adobe school for the maestro on the ruins of the other. And soon they were sending their children to him in droves. Even so, the letter remained there on the door of the church, inexplicable, indescribable, for twelve full months before any of the natives of Xochitlán could make head or tail of it.

As everyone expected, El Niño was the star pupil of the new school, and he quickly emerged as the teacher's favorite. Yet his success was not such a foregone conclusion as they might have imagined, inasmuch as it was based on a couple of false assumptions. The first was that Rafael was the smartest kid in the village. In fact there were several young people who, despite all his advantages, were his equal in native acuity. The second misapprehension was on the part of the maestro himself. He observed the respect with which Rafael was treated in the village, and assumed that it was on account of his superior intellect. Accordingly, he devoted a much larger proportion of his time and energy to Rafael; and the other pupils fell rapidly behind. Thereafter, in a kind of self-fulfilling prophecy, Rafael's education progressed by leaps and bounds. Before long he was worlds above his peers in real, measurable terms, as well as in a symbolic sense.

And it was he—to no one's particular surprise—who was the first of the village children to decipher the mysterious presidential letter on the door of the church:

Minister of Education
Office of Indigenous Affairs
Anti-Illiteracy Branch
New Schools Division

Citizens of ________

The law establishing the National Campaign Against Illiteracy, signed by myself, your president, Manuel Ávila Camacho, in August of this year 1944, specifies that each citizen who is literate in the Castilian language must teach at least one illiterate citizen to read and write. It further stipulates that, in municipalities where no literate person exists, new schools shall be established, with the purpose of teaching the population their letters. It is the duty of each citizen to cooperate with the graduate teacher who shall be assigned to his area. The said teacher shall be considered the legal representative of the Ministry of Education and entitled to all the courtesy and respect pertaining thereto. The slogans of our campaign are "EACH ONE TEACH ONE," and "ILLITERACY IS TREASON." Citizens are conjoined to learn them and teach them to their non-Spanish-speaking neighbors. And please remember, compatriots, that an education is the greatest gift that God can bestow, for it opens the gate to the treasure house of knowledge.

Sincerely,
Manuel Ávila Camacho

After Rafael had conveyed to his people the meaning of the writing on the door, nobody understood it any better than before. But as long as the arcane knowledge was in the possession of the padre and their beloved Niño, they figured it was in good enough hands.

When he told them some of the stories in his mother's diary, however, they understood them perfectly well, as they resembled their myths of epic battles in ancient times.

Rafael himself read her words as if they were some sacred manuscript, telegraphed to him by magic from beyond the grave. For years he pored over the text, trying to discover the secret meaning behind her allegory of the Barbarian Colony. He never came to any satisfactory conclusion.

But in his struggle to understand, he unconsciously absorbed many of her most cherished values. Consequently, Ramona had a more profound influence on her son's life than she might ever have imagined.

In the months following El Niño's explication of the letter, interest in the new schoolhouse waned. Parents kept their children home for the most frivolous reasons. The size of classes grew smaller and smaller. And Rafael shone brighter and brighter by comparison. Even so, he still kept pushing himself to learn more. He did it not so much for the sake of abstract knowledge as for a practical means of escape from the island, should such a drastic choice ever become necessary. Already at the age of ten, therefore, Rafael found himself on the horns of a monumental dilemma. On the one hand he was far too habituated to his life of privilege to ever give it up. On the other hand he was certainly not prepared to accept the debt to which his privilege obliged him. He had been eerily aware for some time that his tribal name and the name of the sacred alamo tree—Cenzontle, for a brightly colored bird that was purported to nest there—were rarely mentioned aloud by the padre or the huehuechique; but when they were, it was always in the same breath. Cenzontle, he knew, presided in some way over the souls of the dead. And he wished for no such connection.

An additional reason for Rafael's remarkable achievements in school was that his teacher—whose name was Jose-María Cassales del Río but was never known as anything but el maestro—was dreadfully bored. In Xochitlán there were no genteel or middle-class families with leisure to invite him to an occasional meal or an evening of music or conversation. The padre kept to himself, and in any case he seemed much more comfortable in the company of peasants than with educated folk. The local Indian maidens, though sometimes attractive in an unkempt kind of way, and free with their favors during the licentious fiesta of San Martín, were standoffish with strangers. There wasn't even anyone to visit the cantina with, as the bravos of the town were known for their quick tempers when under the influence of pulque, and their handiness with the Collins machete. There was nothing else to do but devote himself heart and soul to his brightest and most willing pupil, and hope that one day he might repay his efforts with some grand success, such as a national scholarship, which would be a real feather in his cap, and a possible steppingstone to a regional directorship.

When Rafael was eleven and his sister, Conchita, had just turned a luscious fifteen, he made a decision to compensate his teacher for all his kindness, while at the same time ensuring the maestro's continuing interest in his academic career. He browbeat his father into allowing Conchita to receive private tutoring at night, after her household chores were done, though such a thing was unheard of in the village. "I'll be the chaperon," he said, when in fact it was his intention to leave the young couple to their own devices in the maestro's second-story living quarters, while he did his homework downstairs in the school. Conchita, a gay and lively girl, was quite bowled over by this slender, handsome, sophisticated young man from the fabled city of Colima; the maestro was lonely, unhappy and amazingly ardent after these three years of deprivation, and nature quickly took its course. Conchita turned up pregnant, left her parents' home with her few belongings and moved in with the maestro. In Xochitlán this was considered a legal and binding state of matrimony, in that Western-style church or civil weddings were quite unknown. At first there was some talk, and even scandal, over the arrangement, because no swamp girl had ever taken up with a mainlander before. The talk stopped, however, when it was learned that El Niño had given the couple his blessing, and the padre had declared himself neutral—or, more specifically: "What's done is done, and cannot be undone."

Part of the maestro's commission from the Mexican government related to the "establishment of civilization" in Xochitlán. Shortly after his marriage to Conchita, he embarked upon a campaign to rename all the town's walkways and canals for national heroes and for European places that, he hoped, would encourage the Indians to absorb a certain amount of Western culture. The Mexcal Canal he renamed the Hidalgo Canal. The Tenex Canal he renamed the Juárez Canal. The circular canal he renamed the Círculo Venecia, for a city in Italy that no one had ever heard of. None of these foreign terms meant anything to the people, so they ignored them and continued to call their walkways and canals by the names that had been in currency among them since the twelfth century, when the village was founded. In frustration at the recalcitrance of the natives, the maestro enlisted the support of his young brother-in-law and star pupil, whose powers, he now realized, went far beyond and could not be explained by his superior mental capabilities. El Niño let it be known that he would be pleased with compliance to the maestro's wishes, and from then on only Spanish nomenclature was heard.

Even in the frivolous matter of flowers, the maestro's campaign to civilize the village had an impact. Having been raised in his father's florist shop in Colima, he had a tremendous green thumb, and he'd carried several packets of seeds with him from the mainland. He planted them in the courtyard of the schoolhouse and watered and fertilized them faithfully, picking the aphids off by hand. He put them in his windows, his kitchen and his bathroom, he hung them from the rafters and eaves, and soon the scent of roses, azaleas, cempasuchiles, passion flower, honeysuckle, tiger flower and even jasmine was wafting about the central plaza. Rafael learned to love the smell of the flowers, and he put it out that it might be nice if everyone in the village planted a few to sweeten the air, which was often foul with rotting fish and shrimp. An enterprising local potter ordered seeds from the mainland and started throwing red clay pots by the dozen. In a short time the whole town smelled of flowers, and neighbors were competing over how many potted plants they had hanging outside from their eaves. In his letters to Colima the maestro—who yearned for the company of his own kind even after his marriage to the beauteous Conchita—extolled the wonders of Xochitlán, referring to it as "the city of flowers, the Venice of Mexico, the quaint and charming repository of ancient Aztec language and culture." And within a few years of his arrival the town was receiving a few tourists every year, especially during the Fiesta of San Martín, when the natives came out in all their barbaric finery.

Obviously the visitors needed accommodations. There was no hotel in the village, so the maestro rented the house next door, and let out rooms there for five pesos a night. Since five pesos was more than an able-bodied man could make in a month of heavy labor, it wasn't long before some of the better-off villagers were cleaning out unused rooms and renting them to strangers. Presently the competition became so fierce among them that they were sending their children out to accost the tourists at the boat landing. Next they were sending their sons out in canoes to meet them in the swamp. In the end they were posting themselves on the mainland side and pestering them all the way across to Xochitlán.

Another of the maestro's commissions was to organize a local post office and train some literate person to run it. As soon as he had taught his wife to read, he made her postmistress. He allocated a front room to her in the rented house next door, and had constructed there a post office over which she proudly presided—first with one little brown baby at her feet, and then with two and three—every day from nine to one, and from four to eight. In the beginning no one could imagine what earthly good a post office might serve, since nobody in the village ever sent or received mail. But there is a law of nature: If a thing exists, it will be used. The maestro's efforts increased the literacy rate in Xochitlán tenfold in his first two years of teaching. That is to say, with enormous difficulty he taught ten little Indians to read and write. Each of those ten was obliged by law, and on pain of the President of the Republic's extreme displeasure, to teach another little Indian to do what he could do. And each of those another. Within five years Conchita's post office was doing a booming business sending and receiving letters to and from relatives on the mainland or the other side of the swamp, cashing money order remittances from local braceros working in the United States, and accepting greetings from the minister of defense for young men who had never even heard of compulsory military service before the advent of civilization. And this is not even to mention the mail traffic of the tourists, who, attracted by the colorful traditions of the natives, and the renowned fragrance of the village, came in greater and greater numbers all the time. Tourism begat photography. Photography begat the postcard industry. The maestro taught Rafael to use his camera and to develop his own film. It was beneath his dignity to go hawking tourist photos in the plaza, but he had no trouble hiring a couple of appealing street urchins to do it for him, and soon he too had a thriving business.

So it went with the science of home lighting. No one in Xochitlán had ever possessed even a single lantern. Generally the entire village went to sleep with the sun. On rainy-season nights they lit their tiny lamps and set them out upon the waters of the delta, but that was only for the shrimp. Then when the maestro came he brought two Coleman lanterns with him. Every night he would stay up late, reading esoteric directives from the Ministry of Education in his second-story study. The schoolhouse was the tallest building in the village, besides the church. Both were visible for a great distance across the swamp. It wasn't long before the fishermen started using him as a beacon in their navigation of the delta. Likewise, pedestrians who found themselves abroad in the town on a moonless night used the maestro's cheery light as a direction finder, and to dispel their fears of the fantasmas and mal aire. When Conchita opened her post office, she brought one of the Coleman lanterns over and set it up on her desk. One day the village presidente came in and asked where he might find a light such as this. "I'll get you one," she said. With the aid of her husband, she sent away to the United States, charging the presidente for postage, C.O.D. charges and a small profit for herself. Soon everyone in the village with money to spare, or something to barter, was asking the same favor of her. She invested her profits in other hard-to-get items, such as white flour, salt, sugar, coffee, chocolate, cornmeal, and canned goods. Suddenly, almost without realizing it, she was running Xochitlán's first general store. The influx of goods necessitated a reliable means of transport so she hired her two elder brothers, Juan and Eusebio, to paddle to the mainland for her. At first they went once a month, for a peso each way. Then once a week. Then they were going every day. In their first year of operation their profits were over two hundred pesos, a princely sum in the village. With their sister's backing, they invested the money in several new canoes, hiring compadres to paddle them back and forth to the mainland. Now the products of the village—fish, shrimp, squid, clams, fishnets, reed baskets, clay pots, straw toys, handmade dug-out canoes—had a steady market. Juan and Eusebio bought more canoes, and hired more men to handle the increasing trade. In shrimp season they rented their unused canoes out to fishermen too young or too poor to have their own. The yearly catch doubled and then tripled with all the new hands. The fish merchants on the mainland no longer dared to cheat them, as they had done for generations, for many of the Indians could now read, write and count as well as themselves.

And so the village prospered. Before long a majority of the population had flower pots, lanterns, a red-tile roof. But the prosperity was uneven. Those with more luck, or more initiative, or a relative in the know, progressed more rapidly than the others, especially the traditional types who resisted innovation. Some barrios had one hundred percent home lighting and red-tile roofs, while others had none. The richer Indians tended to associate with each other, even to the exclusion of their own relations, while the poor did the same. In a short while the society of Xochitlán, which had remained basically communal, egalitarian and democratic for eight hundred years, possessed the rudiments of social classes, and the distance between them increased in direct proportion to the gross municipal product.

Of all the success stories in Xochitlán, the greatest was that of the Martínez family. They blessed the day when the padre recommended Pedro on the banks of the circular canal, and their status rose toward the sun, despite the grumbling of the neighbors. Pedro, who had just completed his first term as régido, was elected síndico, one short step from the village presidente.

As for El Niño himself, he was still in awe of his maestro, who was paid by the federal government, one hundred pesos a month, which made him by far the wealthiest man in the village. Not only that, he read books for pleasure, ate with a knife and fork, used a flush toilet, slept in a bed, and had traveled to the city of Mexico, which made him the most worldly, cultured and civilized man in the village, with the possible exception of the padre. But no one really knew anything about the padre. Like El Niño, he had simply *arrived*.

When Rafael was twelve he realized that if he was ever to get on in the world outside the mangrove swamp, there was a lot more he had to learn than just reading, writing and arithmetic. And shortly thereafter he prevailed upon his parents to let him go live with his sister and brother-in-law in the schoolhouse.

The maestro was not an inspired natural teacher, and he tended toward pomposity and long-windedness. But he made up in kindness, patience, objectivity and erudition what he lacked in imagination, and Rafael thrived under his tutelage. By the time he was thirteen the maestro was ordering special books for him from the capital, books on algebra, geometry, physics, Latin, grammar, civics, Spanish language and literature, philosophy, history, religion, economics, political science, natural science, psychology and even art appreciation. By the time he was fifteen the maestro had declared him his equal in learning. And by the time he was seventeen the maestro had realized his long-held dream of seeing him win a full scholarship to the Autonomous University of Colima.

On April 2, 1950, a week after Rafael had received official notification of his bursary, an official of the Ministry of Education arrived in the village by special naval motor launch, direct from the port of Manzanillo. With him he brought a brass band and several state politicians, including the secretary of the ruling Partido Revolucionario Institucional (which recently, in deference to the moderate policies of President Ávila Camacho, had changed its name from Partido Revolucionario Mexicano). They conferred the prestigious award upon Xochitlán's brightest young pupil in the central plaza while the band played, firecrackers exploded, churchbells rang, the flag of the Republic waved proudly from the post office, and the entire population of the mangrove swamp looked on. The official from the Ministry of Education extolled Rafael as "a fitting representative of our vibrant young nation which, in the years since 1942, has enjoyed the highest growth rate of industrial production in the entire world, and has been transformed from a backward land on the edge of barbarity into a modern country of a kind with the Western model." The PRI secretary, a wealthy National Railway official and real estate operator named Gallo Carrizo, took the opportunity to announce that in accordance with the Rural Electrification Program of the federal government, and in conjunction with the Public Works Department of the State of Colima, an electrical power line would soon be constructed from the mainland, "marching across the benighted swamp from island to island, conquering darkness, abolishing ignorance."

After the officials and the brass band had sailed away, there were several months before Rafael had to leave for Colima, and it was at this time that he began to backslide in his resolve to leave the island. Now that he was older, surer of himself, he found that his previously overweening ambition and self-interest had diminished, as had his fear of the unknown, of Padre Dau, of the alamo tree and of what lay in store for him there. And with the strange fatalism of postpubescence he began to contemplate his destiny in the village with a certain amount of satisfaction, contentment, even resignation, a kind of religious feeling.

And he began to attend Mass again on Sunday, after years of absence, despite the objections of his agnostic maestro, and his cruel jokes about "native mumbo jumbo."

In Xochitlán, Mass was served in both Latin and Nahuatl, and it combined elements of both Catholic and native liturgy. The huehuechique, for example, functioned as a kind of subpriest, reciting ancient prayers to Cenzontle, the spirit of the alamo tree, and whirling about drunkenly, quaffing sacred pulque from a silver chalice, while Padre Dau read from the scriptures, or burned incense, or fooled around at the altar. Of the two rituals, the villagers found Padre Dau's far more exotic. And they liked things that way. They had a reverence—and a deep-seated spiritual craving—for visible manifestations of the mysterious and unknown. Accordingly they demanded and received longer and longer recitations, more and more generous servings of the blood and body of the Lord of Miracles, till now the service went on from noon till four in the afternoon, including performances of native music, singing and dance, heavy consumption of pulque, peyotl buds and magic mushrooms, and seemed to leave the poor padre more and more drained each week. Though he was only a man in his early fifties, he was stooped with age, his step was hesitant, and he looked fifteen or twenty years older. But the draining was physical, rather than spiritual. As Padre Dau's body shriveled and cracked and browned and folded in upon itself, his emerald eyes shone brighter and brighter, his preaching grew more inspired, his expression more thanscendent, and his voice—as if invested in some way with the soul of the tribe—resounded in the little abode church like a choir of angels:

"The Lord is my rock and my fortress and my deliverer; my God, my strength, in whom I will trust; my buckler, and the horn of my salvation, and my high tower. I will call upon the Lord, who is worthy to be praised: so shall I be saved from mine enemies. The sorrows of death compassed me, and the floods of ungodly men made me afraid. The sorrows of hell compassed me about: the snares of death prevented me. In my distress I called upon the Lord, and cried unto my God: he heard my voice out of his temple, and my cry came before him, even into his ears. Then the earth shook and trembled; the foundations also of the hills moved and were shaken, because he was wroth. There went up a smoke out of his nostrils, and fire out of his mouth devoured: coals were kindled by it. He bowed the heavens also, and came down: and darkness was under his feet. And he rode upon a cherub, and did fly: yea, he did fly upon the wings of the wind. He made darkness his secret place; his pavilion round about him were dark waters and thick clouds of the skies. At the brightness that was before him his thick clouds passed, hail stones and coals of fire. The Lord also thundered in the heavens, and the Highest gave his voice: hail stones and coals of fire. Yea, he sent out his arrows, and scattered them; and he shot out lightnings, and discomfited them. Then the channels of waters were seen, and the foundations of the world were discovered at thy rebuke, O Lord, at the blast of the breath of thy nostrils. He sent from above, he took me, he drew me out of many waters. . . ."

It was this, echoing from wall to village wall, that drew Rafael to Mass again, and it was this that drove him at last to seek the padre's advice on the restless state of his soul. He found him in his tiny rose-covered cottage behind the church. He approached him like any other Indian, averting his eyes, bowing to kiss his hand. "Look up, look up, my child," the padre said, and his voice was marvelously compelling, though it had lost all its Sunday resonance, and quavered and cracked as if with the weight of centuries. Rafael raised his eyes and beheld the padre smiling upon him as he had smiled upon him when he was a small child, with a wise and peaceful expression on his pinched, thin-lipped Irish face, his eyes filled with humor and irony and . . . distance. "Now let me tell you what's troubling you, my son," he said. "Your soul is unquiet. You want this, you want that. You want to go, you want to stay. You want to learn new ways, yet you see the wisdom of the old ways. And there is also perhaps a girl you're interested in. No?"

The padre was right on all counts. The girl was fifteen. She had smiled and stared at him in the marketplace where she was selling fresh huachinanga. Her name was Benicta Herńandez. She was the daughter of the presidente, Don Pablo Herńandez, and a direct descendant of the ancient chiefs. She had the brown voluptuous body of Xochitl, the goddess of pulque, and a profile right out of the Aztec codices. She was the most beautiful girl in the entire delta of the Río Coayuayana, and she had enflamed his heart and his loins.

Rafael nodded his head.

"The elders and I have been aware of your quandary for some time, my son," said the padre. "We have been observing your activities a good deal more closely than you might have realized. After the ceremony in the plaza we conferred in secret and decided that your government scholarship, while apparently reflecting much honor upon our village, is in fact a trap, a devious plot of the mainlanders to seduce you from us. The man who spoke in the plaza, Gallo Carrizo, he is an evil man. I have known him for many years, and no good can come of anything he touches, as all he touches turns instantly to dung. After much reflection we concluded that you must stay with us. If you go away, you might never come back to us. Or, if you come back, you may be changed, corrupted by the mainlanders, and bring disaster upon us. On the other hand, we decided not to actively oppose your departure, for we were sure that you would rebel against us as a matter of course, in the way of all young men testing their first wings. For this reason I am happy that you have come at this time to seek my advice. And now listen please to what I have to say. You are immensely dear to us. We want you to stay. If you go, a part of us will die. But we ask only this: Defer your decision until after the Fiesta of San Martín, and the Battle of the Saints."

"I will do as you ask," said Rafael, and took his leave, understanding that in some way as yet unexplained, the saints would make his decision for him.

The Battle of the Saints, to which Padre Dau had referred, was the result of a religious feud between the barrios of Mexcaltitán and Tenextepec. Tenextepec was the richest barrio, the quarter of the presidente and the ancient chiefs. Nearly all of its houses possessed red-tile roofs, and it even boasted a couple of whitewashed walls. Both barrios maintained shrines to their patron saints, but the people of Tenextepec had become so wealthy and self-confident in recent years that they had no need to ask favors of the saints. Hence, they no longer paid much care to their shrine to the Virgin Mary. She was called the Virgin of the Candelaria. She was nearly life-sized, and she wore a long, rather moth-eaten white sackcloth dress, a tattered pink veil, a battered crown inlaid with colored glass beads, a fishy-smelling seashell necklace and tarnished silver earrings of a kind worn by the most ordinary village women. In one hand she carried a naked infant Jesus, in the other a faded bouquet of pink paper flowers. She was very old, dating back to the time of the first Spanish missionary, who was buried on the cemetery island, under the alamo tree, along with a lot of other old secrets.

On the far side of town, halfway round the Círculo Venecia, was the barrio of Mexcaltitán. There most of the people were still very poor. Yet, because of the example of their neighbors the Martínezes, they were quite ambitious. They took enormous pride in their shrine to San Martín and invested many of their more outrageous fantasies in him. His shrine was spacious, and it boasted whitewashed walls, a gleaming red-tile roof, an oaken door with shiny brass fixtures, and windows hung with the finest native cloth. The image of the saint was about half-size, but elegantly fitted out in a black chamois charro suit, a pistol and cartridge belt, silver spurs, a red poncho, and a splendidly embroidered black felt sombrero. His horse was painted black, carved of one solid block of beautiful conacaste wood, and amazingly lifelike, with fierce snorting nostrils, prancing hooves and waving tail. As islanders, swamp dwellers, the people of Mexcaltitán had rarely had the occasion to see a handsome caballero on a mount such as this, and they cherished him accordingly. Every year they endowed him with a lovely new hat and charro suit. They loved him so much that they almost believed he was actually *alive,* and it was said among them that on moonless nights he would ride over the rooftops to the barrio of Tenextepec, where he would visit with the Virgin of the Candelaria while San Jacinto held his horse outside, in readiness for a rapid getaway, should the Lord of Miracles get wind of his indiscretion.

Though the people of Tenextepec took little care of their Virgin, they affected a deep resentment of these aspersions against her reputation. Indignantly they insisted that she would never dream of receiving a gentleman at night, though he be a saint.

On Tuesday, on the Octavo of San Martín, a ritual battle was staged every year between the young men of the two barrios. The Fiesta of San

Martín came in April, just after the corn harvest, shortly before the first major shrimp run of the season, and it was the grandest and longest fiesta of Xochitlán. For seven days the young bravos of the town imbibed vast quantities of a special high-powered pulque called Ometochtli, or Two Rabbit, which was brewed for the occasion. And by the time the Octavo rolled around, the blood was up on both sides.

In the year 1950, Rafael was informed by the elders of the town that he had been chosen to lead the young men of Mexcaltitán in battle. Though he was not surprised by the decision he felt very deeply honored nonetheless, and prepared himself accordingly. For twenty-four hours prior to the engagement he permitted himself no food or drink save pulque. He shaved his head and pubic hair and painted his face according to a ritual prescribed by the huehuechique. And finally, he put on a special yellow-and-black-striped, hornetlike costume and headdress that had been passed down for generations, and took up a ritual sword and shield of woven reeds and alamo wood. Thus dressed, he appeared before the cheering people of his barrio, and was led first to the church, where he was blessed by the padre, and thence toward the shrine of San Martín, where the other young men of the barrio were assembled.

From this point on he was supposed to perform his role in the pageant extemporaneously, and be judged as a future leader by the powers of invention that he displayed. As El Niño, naturally, the Chosen One, he felt himself under tremendous pressure to perform exceptionally well, to shine like no other leader in memory. But it was suffocatingly hot in his heavy costume, and he was intoxicated and nauseous from all the liters of pulque he had drunk. His head was whirling. His legs were unsteady. He could remember nothing of his role, and he could not get a clear fix on what he should do next. He staggered forward, nearly weeping in frustration.

Now I will shame myself, he thought. And everyone will laugh.

The clay pathway, the grinning crowd, the lily-clogged canal, the mud walls, the coconut palm above his head, the shrine shining white in the vertical light, the sky, the sun, the clouds, the entire world spun about him, and he dropped to his knees in the dust. He tried to get up, to move forward, but it seemed he was rooted to the island.

He could hear the crowd hooting with laughter now, shouting derisively, "Get up, Niño! What's the matter? Get up!"

He vomited and fell on his face, tasting dirt, salt, blood, acrid half-digested pulque. The crowd suddenly went silent, and all he could hear was a gourd rattle being shaken above his head.

"What's the matter, Niño?" the huehuechique sang, in a high trilling female voice.

"What's the matter, my son?" said the padre, in his ancient quavering voice.

El Niño raised his head and saw the padre on one side of him, swinging a stick of incense in the air, and the short, muscular huehuechique on the other, shaking his rattle in an intricate syncopated rhythm, doing a slow, hip-swiveling, effeminate dance, rolling his great bleary eyes in a parody of seduction.

"Querido, whatever can the matter be?" he mocked. And suddenly squatted down beside him, spreading imaginary skirts like a woman about to take a pee in a corn patch. Then, grinning impudently, he leaped up and struck him with the gourd, very hard, on the head.

"Get up, cuckold," said the huehuechique, hitting him again.

"And go with God," said the padre, swinging the incense by his nose.

Instantly El Niño's head cleared, and as if by magic all his symptoms of discomfort disappeared. He felt that he was out of himself now, guiding himself from afar, and he could do no wrong. To wild applause he rose from the dust, wiped his face with the back of his hand, and strode off self-confidently toward the shrine.

"Have you prepared yourselves?" he asked the young men, about thirty in number, who waited outside in the costumes of Montezuman warriors.

"We have, Niño, we have!" they cried as one, brandishing their baskets full of sticks, stones, firecrackers, rotten tomatoes and eggs.

"Now lift up San Martín and his horse," he said, "and follow me to victory!"

Seven bravos ran inside and brought the image out on their shoulders. Then, while a joyous throng of villagers pelted them all with flowers, El Niño led them down to the canal, where they loaded the saint into a specially decorated black canoe that was tied up beside half a dozen others of the same color. At the stroke of noon, when the churchbell rang, El Niño uttered an ear-splitting war cry and ran to the canoe where San Martín was waiting. Whooping like savages, his men followed and took their places with black paddles poised. El Niño threw off his line and, while the entire barrio shouted approval of his performance, dipped his paddle proudly into the lily pads and struck out for the barrio of Tenextepec, leading his men in Aztec battle formation, chanting, "*Amoato-rili-rili-rón, amoato-rili-rili-rón, amoato-rili-rili-rón*"—words that had sprung to his head as if by witchcraft, the meaning of which was lost in the mists of antiquity. He disembarked not far from the shrine of the Candelaria, and entrusted San Martín to an honor guard of three. He brought his men together, and led them in a phalanx toward a thirty-foot bamboo and palm-thatch fence, which had been constructed by the natives of the barrio to prevent access to their Virgin. By now the whole population of the town, as well as a number of foreign tourists, had gathered around, and they were all anxiously awaiting the outcome. El Niño halted his men before the wall and called out, tauntingly, "Show them what their Virgin looks like!" His little baldheaded brother Eusebio and another man brought forward a half-sized, straw-stuffed image of the Candelaria, done up as a painted harlot, dancing lewdly on a tall bamboo pole. "Now show them what's going to happen to her!" he commanded, and she exploded in a burst of firecrackers and fluttered in little pieces to the ground. The opposing leader, a tall, well-built fellow named Blaz Puente who had been watching through a crack in the wall, called for an effigy of his own. Presently a ragged little black doll and papier-mâché donkey could be seen dancing on a stick above the wall. "Here's your San Martín," said Blaz Puente. "See how stupid he looks!" And the image burst amid a spectacular explosion of cherry bombs. In retaliation, El Niño ordered his men to hurl missiles over the wall. The other side responded with a barrage of its own, and seconds later the air was full of flying tomatoes and eggs, and then sticks and stones and lit firecrackers. The warriors of Mexcaltitán tried their best to fend off the missiles, but their shields were flimsy, and several of the muchachos were struck by stones and fell bleeding in the dirt. El Niño ordered one of his canoes to be brought forward and used as a battering ram. "Wham! Wham! Wham!" And a few moments later a large hole opened in the wall. "Aaaiiieee!" El Niño screamed, and leaped through the breach, attacking Blaz Puente with his sword, putting him to prearranged flight with a series of ritual coups about the shoulders and neck. "Demoralized" by the defeat of their chief, the other side retired from the field, leaving the Shrine of the Virgin undefended. El Niño formed up his men and proceeded with them in solemn step toward the shrine. Just outside the shrine they encountered a circle of twenty weeping maidens, the Virgins of the Virgin. Slowly, sadly, the girls danced and swayed to the shrill, bittersweet notes of the chirimía, played by an old man in Aztec costume, standing on the flat roof of the shrine. Inside the circle, Doña Blanca, the White Lady, danced alone. She was barefoot, wearing a long white skirt, a low-cut white blouse, with a wreath of white lilies round her smooth brown neck. This year the role of Doña Blanca was played by Benicta Hernández, the daughter of the presidente, and her beauty stopped El Niño in his tracks. Doña Blanca quickened her step when she saw him. She threw off her bereaved air and began to smile and sway provocatively, while singing in a high, sweet, tremulous voice:

"I am the little one
From Tenextepec
I want to marry
But cannot find a man

The servant of the priest
Sent to me a note
And to him I sent another
From Tenextepec

My mama found out
What a beating she gave me
An evil eye on the man
Who made love to me

To his house I went
And found him in tears
With the end of his sleeve
He dried his eyes

I like coffee
Chocolate too
But I like better
The eyes of the hornet"

Benicta finished the song and bowed her head. Her maidens set up a wail as if their hearts would break, and tightened the circle around her. The crowd was hushed now in anticipation. El Niño's heart was immobilized in his chest. It was only the two of them now, in all the world. She was looking at him now, smiling, swaying her hips. He threw down his sword and shield and started to buzz like a hornet. "Bzzzzzz, bzzzzzz, bzzzzzz," he went, doing the samba swiftly around the circle, bumping into her maidens on purpose, snatching at their breasts and loins, careening from one to another. Then he stopped, and turned to address his men in a strange, tiny, insect voice that came from he knew not where.

"The White Lady is covered
With pillars of gold
I will break down the pillar
The White Lady to see"

The circle of maidens weaved now to the right, now to the left, their arms raised as if in protection of their mistress, while Doña Blanca sang tauntingly, seductively, her ritual response:

"Who is this hornet
Buzzing around my house?"

The hornet answered in his insect voice, while dancing furiously around the circle of maidens, trying to batter his way inside.

"I am the one
I am the one
I am the one
Who's after Doña Blanca"

He broke the pillars down and pierced the circle. The circle closed behind him. Doña Blanca ran around and around, half frightened, half inviting. The hornet buzzed after her. Angrily he bit her on the neck, the shoulder, the breast. She screamed and fainted. The hornet fell upon her and continued to feast, to feast, to feast on her tender skin. The drunken presidente stepped forward from the crowd and poured pulque around them in the dust. Then all of Xochitlán erupted in laughter and applause, and chased the young couple from the barrio. He dragged her, half resisting, half conspiring, to the first canoe that he could find. He shoved her aboard and paddled swiftly from the village, while his mocking brothers and their friends paddled after them, calling out lewd suggestions. He hid from them in a flooded canebrake on the far side of the corn island, and waited, panting, till they disappeared in the distance. Then he lay rough hands upon the trembling White Lady. He hoisted her white costume over her head. He threw her out into the mud and pulled her up into the corn stubble by the hair. And there, on the brown body of mother earth, El Niño implanted his immortal seed.

CHAPTER 2

On Christmas Eve, 1953, at about the same time that Benicta was having her second little Martínez down in Xochitlán, Merle Carrizo pawned his winter coat in San Francisco. A week later and he was on the street. That night, at the very nadir of his fortunes, he stood out in the freezing Mission District fog asking himself, Why go on? Then on Townsend Street, near the Southern Pacific Railroad yard, he found a cable-car stop with a tin roof and a shrubbery windbreak. He lay down on the icy pavement beside another derelict, an old bearded Mexican tramp who seemed to be having trouble breathing. He covered himself with newspapers and fell asleep. When he awakened at dawn, hungry and trembling with cold, he was surprised and a little disappointed to find himself still alive. But the tramp was dead. Merle got up and dusted his pants off. Look at it this way, he told himself. From here there is only up. And caught a freight train for warm weather, five hundred miles to the south.

All the way down that cold and fogbound coast of California he lay huddled under a pile of stinking straw, reflecting on his past life, and on the many errors that he had made. His major failing, he decided, was the sin of pride. But Merle was too hard on himself. His fall from grace had come so suddenly, and with such astonishing and unprecedented totality, that never, not in his wildest dreams, could he have imagined it.

Just two years ago he had been a senior at Berkeley, supported by his wealthy father in Mexico. He owned a foreign sports car and an expensive wardrobe. He was an honor student, a class officer, a soccer letterman and a member of one of the most prestigious social fraternities on campus. A notorious Don Juan, he was pinned to a pretty Theta at Berkeley, a Delta Gamma at Stanford and a Pi Phi at Mills College. Then came the events of Homecoming Day, 1951: a rowdy drinking party at the Delt House, a hazing incident, and the accidental drowning of a fraternity brother, for which Merle, in a fit of grief, remorse and macho pride, accepted full responsibility despite the fact that a dozen of the others were at least as guilty as he.

Merle felt brave and noble in his self-sacrifice, and he looked forward to being welcomed back from jail with a rousing great cheer. But the Delts lost their charter over the incident, and a lot of them lost their campus identities along with it. Merle made his own bail and he went to trial alone. He was found guilty of involuntary manslaughter, received a six-month suspended sentence and a stiff fine. A week later he was expelled from the university. When he came to collect his things at the Delt House, the maid handed them out to him through the back door. When he called at the Theta House to say goodbye to his girl, her sorority sisters said she wasn't feeling well. The same thing happened at Stanford and Mills College. Then his student visa was revoked and he was given two weeks to leave the country.

Trouble was, he had long thought of it as his own country. He was born in Texas, after all. He was perfectly bilingual. He had been educated at a high-priced Jesuit school in Arizona, and at one of the finest public universities in the United States. When he added it all up he felt more American than Mexican, despite what his passport said. He had planned to get an advanced degree at Berkeley, and to go on to teaching comparative literature at the college level. Eventually he wanted to try his hand at writing fiction. He was a modern, sophisticated, city person, he told himself. He had no intention of returning to rough, provincial Manzanillo, Mexico, especially now that he would have to appear before his ever-critical father as a failure, a beggar, with his head hanging low.

He phoned the Bureau of Records in El Paso, asking if they had a copy of his birth certificate, but he was told that no such document existed.

Evidently his parents had not taken the trouble to register him at birth. Or else, as illegal aliens, they avoided dealings with the government.

So Merle just slipped out of sight. Got a room in a North Beach flophouse and lost himself in the bustle of the city. A dark, wiry, good-looking kid of middle height, with curly black hair, a ready grin, and bright-blue eyes, he could have been Jewish or Italian-American. San Francisco was full of immigrants anyway, many of them as illegal as he, and none of them more assimilated. When he ran out of cash he sold his car and lived off the profit. Didn't even write his Aunt Carmen to say what had happened to him, though he knew she'd be frantic with worry. Figured he'd just let the whole thing blow over and then resurface at some other university, perhaps under another name. Didn't even write his father, but that was nothing new, as their relations had been impossible for years.

The bone of contention between Merle and Gallo was no longer what it used to be, as Carmen's fundamental loyalty had been established ever since she signed over the entire O'Hare fortune to her husband as marriage dowry. Actually, the estrangement of father and son went far deeper than that. According to Carmen, it related back to something old Dr. Weber had said to Gallo, when Merle was only two or three years old: "Mentally the child may have some trouble later in life." Why Doc Weber gave this opinion, Carmen never would say. But for some reason Gallo became fixated on it. And eventually, when it began to appear that Merle was not going to turn out an athlete, an outdoorsman, or a street-fighter, that in fact he had a dreamy, literary bent like old Mrs. O'Hare, Gallo got it into his head that the "trouble" Merle might have in later life was homosexuality. By what process of muddled reasoning Gallo had arrived at this conclusion, Merle could not say. Surely there was no evidence to support it, as Merle's sexual predilections obviously ran in the opposite direction. Yet Gallo's nasty suspicion did not recede when it became apparent that his boy displayed no signs of budding pederasty. On the contrary it kept growing, feeding upon itself, till at last it became a kind of obsession. In order to prevent Merle's "latency" from becoming active, Gallo embarked upon a program that might have been specifically calculated to achieve the opposite result. He called him a sissy, a cry baby, a sob sister, a fruitcake, a fairy, and beat him with his razor strap whenever he whined or cried or complained. To further toughen him up, he purposely withheld his love, and affected a total unconcern as to his fate.

At about this time, Gallo sent Merle off to a private school in Arizona. It was a military school run by the Jesuits, and the regimen was just what Gallo called for: tough, strict and cruel. Yet Merle responded surprisingly well to its rigors, and excelled as a student despite his dreamy side. He coped by learning to dream in motion, while marching across the parade ground, playing soccer or doing chin-ups. He learned to compartmentalize his consciousness, so that he could diligently attend to his mountainous piles of dreary homework while concocting the wildest imaginary adventures.

When Merle came home to Manzanillo after his first year at school, he decided that he was no longer going to take his father's punishments lying down. He was going to fight back. That first summer he fought back by simply ignoring his father, by refusing to acknowledge his presence at the head of the dinner table, by neglecting to laugh at his humorous tales of life on the railroad or in the cutthroat world of politics and finance, by closing his ears to the advice he dispensed to Carmen and the servants as to the smooth operation of the Hotel Carrizo (formerly the Hotel O'Hare).

The next summer Merle took things a step further and affected to not hear his father's direct commands. This led to immediate and very serious repercussions, in the form of a series of razor strappings that Merle would never forget, as Gallo was never one to accept insubordination from an inferior.

The following summer Merle tried an altogether new tactic: He affected to be deathly afraid of his father, and treated him as if he were some kind of evil spirit, a dark shadow, a bad dream. He pretended to start in fright whenever his father walked into the room, and to shrink from him in horror. Gallo whipped him out of that little drama right away, but the next summer Merle came back with another strategy even more diabolical than the last. He began telling everyone that Gallo was not his real father, that they were not even related. He even went so far as to claim that Gallo was only a guest at the hotel, and was about to depart for places unknown.

In the summer of Merle's thirteenth year, Gallo evidently decided that he'd had enough. He gave up on the whippings and tried a more psychological approach. He began hinting darkly about some deep family secret, something really nasty and squalid and horrid that he knew about Merle, of which Merle himself hadn't a clue. Merle racked his brains, trying to discover what Gallo was talking about. Young as he was, it didn't take him long to realize that his old man was playing dirty with him, playing termite, getting right down to the fragile foundations of reality.

In the summer of his fourteenth year, Merle asked and was granted permission to attend a Catholic summer camp at a dude ranch in Wyoming, and after that he saw very little of his father. Secretly, he had written him off. He no longer considered himself a part of Gallo's family. As his own blood relatives receded in his memory, the O'Hares emerged more vividly than ever before. In his fantasies, Maureen, Brian and Chris became his kin, and the Carrizos and Mescaleros a mere part of the landscape surrounding those three and himself . . . though he did continue to accept Gallo's very generous monthly allowance.

The money from the sale of his sports car lasted Merle nearly a year, during which he did nothing to further his own cause, except for a desultory attempt to write an autobiographical novel. He was a Mexican gentleman to this extent: He had a horror of sullying his hands, and he let his fingernails grow as long as a flamenco guitarist's. In summer he went to Aquatic Park and sat on the beach. In winter he read in his room. Sometimes he mooned over Chris, who'd been packed off to this city for prep school and who'd presumably long since moved on. He even wrote her mother, at her last address in Colima, asking for news of Chris, but he received no response. In his loneliest moments he mourned Chris as if she were a departed relative, just as he had once mourned Ramona but now rarely did.

Merle made no friends out of fear that they would betray him to La Migra, the Immigration Service. He indulged himself in only the most furtive and fugitive fucks with cheap Mexican-American shopgirls and waitresses whom he picked up on the street, though at Berkeley he'd been renowned for his conquest of bluebloods, and his preference for blondes. He never gave his real name.

Then the money ran out. So he started pawning his clothes. He had an enormous wardrobe, and it kept him going for months. To save money he ate only once a day. To conserve strength he rarely went out. He grew thin and pale and drawn, and he began to shuffle when he walked. His landlord, a kindly Scot, was concerned for his health and begged him to go to a free clinic. But Merle refused to accept charity. When at last he had nothing further to pawn, the Scot said he could work as the building janitor for his keep. But Merle refused again. He was no wetback; he would not demean himself with manual labor.

On the morning of February 11, 1954, Merle awakened in a side-tracked cattle car near Calipatria, in the Imperial Valley of California. The sun came out from behind Picacho Peak and the Chocolate Mountains and shone through the wood slats and hit him in the eye. He crawled out of the railcar and staggered into a field of winter tomatoes and laid his clothes out on the bank to dry in the sun. Just as he had finished dressing, a labor bus pulled up and disgorged a gang of Mexican fruit-pickers who, with their lugs and buckets in their hands, quickly fanned out across the field. The straw boss, a plump mestizo with clever dancing eyes, came sidling up to where Merle sat on the track. "Oye, compañero," he said, proffering a bucket and a lug, "I'm a man short. You looking for work?" Barely able to believe he was doing it, half imagining he was somebody else, Merle took the lug and bucket and worked a day in the sun. At quitting time he climbed back up into the cattle car and went to sleep under the straw. In the morning the straw boss offered him another day of work.

Merle labored a week in the tomato field, and when it was done all he had to show for his time—after being docked for his midday tortillas and beans—was a pair of blisters, a case of diarrhea, and a twenty-dollar bill. He rode the labor bus into Calipatria, got himself a shave, a haircut, a hot meal, a denim jacket, a pair of blue jeans and a room at the local transient hotel. In the morning after coffee and a roll he was broke. Well, he thought, there's got to be a lesson here somewhere. And stepped out onto Route 111 and started hitchhiking for the Mexican border, twenty-six miles away.

His first ride was a mile down the road in a battered green Cheeby driven by an eighty-year-old Mexican irrigator with a white Pancho Villa mustache. His second ride was into the town of Brawley with a family of Okie date pickers. But his third ride was solid glamour: a brand-new Cadillac Coupe de Ville with a palomino gold paint job, a "Hollywood—City of the Stars" license-plate frame, and a California State Bar Association decal on the rear bumper.

He sprinted through a billowing cloud of white dust to catch it. But by the time he reached it, the cloud had blown away, leaving the Caddy miraculously undusted and lustrous in the sunshine.

He opened the door, smiling courteously. The couple inside smiled back. The woman's smile was perfunctory, professional, but the man's was enormous, shark-toothed, dazzling. She was a tall, suntanned blonde in a poodle cut: a knockout in white high heels, black capris, a white low-necked cashmere sweater. The guy wore a gray one-button-roll suit with a drape shape, a black fedora hat, a black shirt with a white knit tie, and pointy black shoes. He was tall and thin and very dark—darker than Merle—with an eagle beak, a Clark Gable mustache, and extraordinarily heavy-lidded eyes. The pair of them looked a bit bigger than life. But somehow they were just what you would expect, riding out here in the desert, in a car like that. They had a Los Angeles R&B station on the radio, "The Johnny Otis Show."

"Johnny Ot-is, bop bop bop . . .
Johnny Ot-is, bop bop bop . . ."

"Where ya headed, honcho?" the driver stage-whispered, in a raspy New York accent.

Merle thought a moment. He did not want these people to take him for a wetback. Yet his instincts told him not to reveal his true situation to strangers.

"Short-term, or long-term?" he said.

"Why don't you just lay it out for me, man?"

"Well, my immediate goal is the border, but eventually I'd like to wind up in Guadalajara."

The guy looked him up and down.

"You're traveling light."

"The way I always travel."

"Hop in," he said. His girlfriend scooted over, and Merle settled in beside her.

Instantly his pulse jumped. His heart skipped a beat. He tried not to stare, but he could not prevent himself from gaping in wonder. Her face was an adolescent fantasy, her body instant cheesecake. He could not place her scent, but it smelled wonderful. Smelled . . . warm. She was warm. He could feel her body heat right through his Levi jacket. And her forehead was beaded with perspiration.

Merle was left with the impression that she was angry about something, probably something her boyfriend had just said or done.

Fats Domino was on the radio now, singing "Goin' to the River."

"I'm goin' to the river
Goin' overboard and drown
'Cause the gal I love
Gone and done me wrong . . ."

"Tell me," the driver said, easing back out into traffic, "what's the best way to Guaymas and points south?"

"Well," Merle said, "you could cross the border at Mexicali and take Mexican National 2 to Santa Ana. Or you could take U.S. 80 to Tucson, 89 to Nogales, and Mexican National 15 straight down."

"Don't be coy, man, just tell me the way."

"As a general rule," Merle said, "you stay on the U.S. side as long as you can. In this case, you lose nearly half a day by taking the Mexican route."

"Why didn't you say so in the first place?"

"But you already knew all about it, Bo," the woman put in. "You swore last year you'd never take that Route 2 again." Her voice was soft and melodious, slightly breathless, her accent cultivated, Mid-Atlantic. She was an actress, of course.

"I did?"

"You know you did."

"Just testing," he said.

"You're always testing."

"That'll be enough of that."

"Bit of a bore, actually."

"I don't wanna hear no more shit from you, Chicken," he said, jabbing a long finger into her face.

The gesture seemed so overblown and uncalled-for that Merle wasn't sure whether to take it seriously or not. He took his cue from the woman: She ignored it.

"And you, honcho, what's so funny?"

"Nothing," he said, smothering a grin.

"You speak the lingo?"

"Like a native."

"Are you a native?"

"Well, I was born in the States, but I spent most of my childhood in Mexico."

"Been this way before?"

"Sure, every Christmas and summer vacation for the last ten years."

"You go to school in the States?"

"Went," Merle said. "I just graduated at midterm."

"How ya fixed for bread?"

"Just spent my last on breakfast."

"I pride myself on my ability to read character," Bo said, *charactah,* reaching into the glove compartment, pulling out a marijuana cigarette, lighting up. "Consider yourself on a retainer until further notice."

"Are you serious?"

"Never say anything I don't mean."

"Well, thanks a lot," Merle said. "Glad to be of service."

"Don't mention it," Bo said. "You smoke gage?"

"In Mexico we smoke sometimes," Merle said. "We call it 'mota.' But in the fraternity house it was considered déclassé."

"You a frat rat?"

"Was."

"Try it, man, you'll like it."

"Nice," Merle said, after a puff or two.

"One of my clients gave it to me," Bo said. "In lieu of payment."

"Here," Merle said, handing it to the woman.

"The name is Val," she said, dragging deeply, her breasts swelling spectacularly under the cashmere. "Val Raymond." Without vanity, she said it. Though it was clear she expected him to recognize it. He didn't. But he remembered the face: those great smoldering dark eyes, so unusual in a blonde, and those jutting cheekbones, the puffy bruised-looking mouth and flaring nostrils. He'd seen her in a couple of MGM musicals a few years back. He couldn't recall which, exactly. But one of them was with Desi Arnaz, and all of her roles had been minor.

"Mine's Merle Carrizo," he said, but he wasn't sure she caught it.

"I'm exhausted," she said, yawning, stretching provocatively. "We left a party in Malibu at four this morning. Been on the road ever since."

A few minutes later her head fell on Merle's shoulder and she went to sleep.

"Don't get your bowels in an uproar, man," Bo said, when he caught his anxious look. "I ain't the jealous type."

But Merle was not convinced.

It was all a bit too sudden. He did not know what to make of these people, as yet. All sorts of paranoid fantasies crossed his mind.

"*If you see Rosamary*," sang Fats, "*tell 'er I'm comin' home to stay. . . .*"

In El Centro they turned left on Highway 80 and headed east. Just past Meloland and Date City the vivid green fields of winter fruit and vegetables came abruptly to an end and the ribbon of blacktop, running alongside the bright-blue waters of the American Canal, sliced clean through a region of giant white sand dunes toward Midway Wells, Winterhaven and the Colorado River.

"This is where they make all the Foreign Legion flicks," Merle said, but Bo did not seem particularly interested. What he was interested in, apparently, was hearing his own voice. What he needed was a sounding board, and the hitchhiker was it. For hours the big fucker wheeled his great long Cadillac across the desert, smoking one mota cigarette after another, telling tales. In a hoarse, confidential tone he told them, as if the telling itself were somehow illegal or unethical. His accent, like the rest of him, was so exaggerated and Runyonesque that it seemed an affectation. Yet there was such an authentic ring to it, and such an air of unconscious menace that Merle was not foolish enough to let his guard down for an instant.

All his life people had come to Merle to bend his ear. They made confessions to him they wouldn't tell their best friends. There was something about him that encouraged them to open up. Maybe it was simply the fact that he was a good listener. Maybe they'd heard he wanted to be a writer. Whatever the case, and despite the fact that it was a vital part of his intended craft, Merle did not enjoy hearing these confessions. They made him feel uneasy, as if he had been entrusted with some precious and very fragile possession. And he instinctively mistrusted anyone who would open himself up to strangers. It was a natural reflex of the Mexican in him: "*Never turn your back on a man who talks too much*," his father had said.

But this fucking gringo sure could spin a yarn; you could not deny him that. A brilliant natural raconteur, he dared to begin his stories in the middle or the end and flesh them out later with intricately woven flashbacks. Or he would cut them off just before the climax and then suddenly take them up again in the middle of another story, merely to increase suspense. He told them in no apparent order, chronological or otherwise, but eventually a pattern emerged: It was the story of his life.

". . . So Sam the Man finds himself rounding the corner of Sixth and Bleecker, the fastest corner in Lower Manhattan," one of them began. "And the city is basking in the last golden rays of Indian summer. But Sam, he cannot say the same for his wallet, see. The morning itself is holding him up. All of a sudden a big Pierce-Arrow pulls up to the curb. Behind the wheel sits a well-heeled Italian friend, a relative of his old lady's. As it happens, Sam is standing out in front of the guy's club. The Monte Carlo. So the guinea gets out. He cracks a grin. 'Sam,' he says. 'What you doing up so early? Come on in. Gotta count up last night's receipts. We got so busy, I think we broke all records.' Now, dig it. This guy and Sam the Man, they go way back. When business goes down Sam is sometimes around. End of story. It's all a game. The morning is full of surprises. Through his fingers will flash thousands while in his pocket he has not a dime. So, inside, the joint smells of the morning after: stale smoke, spilled booze, wasted words. *Da moanin' aftah.* And the ginzo pours out a couple of Sambucas and opens his safe. Shoves a fistful of dollars at Sam the Man and they start counting the loot. A grand or more pass through their fingers before a word is spoken. 'Whasamatta, Sam?' says the wop. 'You are not yourself.' 'Listen, Joey,' says Sam. 'I am in a jam. The better half is about to pop the bimbo. There's no dough for the doc. And to cap it the Chase Manhattan got away with my car this morning. I went out there on Thompson Street and she was gone. And I know better than blame it on thieves in the night. Not in that part of town.' 'Hey, that's mob country,' says Joey. 'You're telling me?' says Sam. So old Joe he stops counting and he lifts his shaggy gray head. For a minute he says not a word. Then: 'I'll give you a jingle tonight.' And he lays two thousand smackeroonies in Sam the Man's hand. So Sam, he puts it together, you dig. Joey is giving him a way to go. And Sam is committing himself to what must be done. Things are picking up. But his life is again in hawk. A hell of a way to go, for a nice Yiddisher boy from Orchard Street. So, he bops on home to the pad, arriving upon the scene just as his old lady's water breaks. But he's gotta squat by the phone, see. So he hits her with a grand and sticks her in a cab and packs her off to St. Vincent's and at nine o'clock that night he gets his call. 'Sam,' says Joey, 'do me a favor.' 'Sure thing, pal,' says Sam. 'This contractor over in Hoboken,' says Joey, 'he is cramping my style.' 'What's the name?' Sam wants to know. 'De Sapio,' says Joey, 'but not to worry, he's no relation.' And that night, just about the time that Mr. De Sapio met his maker on the Jersey mudflats, yours truly, Joseph Samuel, alias Bo Brodsky, came into the world. . . ."

A few miles outside of Yuma, Bo suddenly yawned and quit talking, right in the middle of one of his stories, and guided the Caddy to a slow smooth stop by the side of the road.

"Hows about a spell at the wheel, honcho?"

"Why not?"

Bo rousted Val out of the back, and they all stepped out on the shoulder of the highway to stretch their legs. Then Bo and Val traded seats. Apparently they were no longer speaking.

Merle slipped behind the wheel and they started off.

"Wake me up in Tucson," Bo said, and went right to sleep. You could tell when he was asleep because he snored. His snoring was like everything else about him: loud and vulgar and unabashed, with a music of its own.

Merle had a kind of natural reserve, and he felt a bit shy alone in the front seat with a movie star, and Val seemed lost in her own thoughts. So they drove all the way across the Yuma Desert and the Painted Rock Mountains before they said a word.

Val said it.

"Cigarette?"

"Sure," he said, and she rolled them a fat one.

They smoked silently, passing it back and forth. When it was done they turned and smiled at each other.

"Yeah," she said, shaking her head.

"Yeah," he said, nodding.

After that he figured they had established a kind of rapport, though they spoke not another word for the rest of the journey, and she slept most of the way.

At five o'clock that afternoon they crossed over the Mexican border.

A warm, pleasant winter evening with the sun hovering just over the bleached brick buildings, the windburned willows and jagged desert foothills of Nogales. The Avenida Juárez crowded with commercial traffic: pushcart vendors hawking their colorful wares, battered old pickup trucks and ranch wagons revving their engines, huge international semitrailers spewing diesel smoke, great long Greyhound-style Mexican buses with their company insignia painted enormously along their outside panels—*Norte de Sonora, Tres Estrellas de Oro, La Flecha Roja.* Sidewalks spilling over with an amazingly motley and varied humanity: Indians in bare feet and long Apache hair, braceros in huaraches and straw sombreros, red-faced Arizonians in baseball caps and flower-print dresses, vaqueros in cowboy boots and black Stetson hats, whores in feathered finery from another era, dark, fat, corrupt-looking cops in dirty suntan military uniforms, railroad men in bibbed overalls and striped caps, local pachucos in grease-stained zoot suits.

It was good to be home again. His pulse jumped to catch the Latin beat. Yet, as always, he could have died of humiliation to see his people so, in dark and squalid contradiction to that scrubbed and white behemoth just to the north.

Bo parked the Caddy on a sidestreet.

"Watch the wagon for me, will ya, honcho?" he said. "While me and the little missus rustle us up a hotel for the night."

Val did not take kindly to his humor. And apparently he resented her lack of appreciation. They ignored each other as they went off down the street. But they managed to create a sensation anyway. Bo had a way of swaggering, loose-limbed, cocksure, with his fedora pulled down over his eyes, that caught the attention of passersby. "Who is this bandido?" Merle heard one of them say. Val on the other hand was so slinky and smooth that she appeared to glide down the street. Her movements, like her Mid-Atlantic accent, were highly stylized. Yet, the more Merle was around her, the more he came to believe that *she was really like that*. The style had originated in her training as an actress and dancer, perhaps, but by now it was second nature. Merle was no longer an objective observer, however, for already he was a little in love.

Shortly after the couple had disappeared into the crowd, Merle noticed a twenty-dollar bill that had slipped out of Bo's pocket onto the backseat. He thought about it for a moment, and decided that under certain conditions twenty dollars could mean the difference between life and death. He was about to reach for it when it occurred to him that the gringo might have planted it there on purpose as some kind of test.

The Hotel Paraiso, where they found accommodations for the night, was a newish, three-story adobe brick building located on the extreme southeastern edge of Nogales, across the street from an abandoned wool warehouse. Out in back there was a surprisingly well-tended little cactus garden with a fishpond, a bed of colorful desert flowers and a couple of "honeymoon cottages." The rear of the property looked out onto the open desert, and it was protected on three sides by a thickly planted windbreak of juniper and tall old cottonwood trees with silvery leaves. A plaque on one of the trees stated that one of the decisive battles of the Mexican Revolution had been fought on this spot, but Merle had never heard of it before.

Bo rented the honeymoon cottages for the night. They all had a siesta and a shower, and about eight o'clock he came around to Merle's cottage and let himself in. He was dressed for dinner in a tan lightweight suit, an open-neck black silk shirt and a Panama hat, and he looked like a million bucks.

"Lemme explain the deal," he said. "Like, someone has got to be with them bags at all times, man. Whether it's in the hotel or when we're out on the road. I got cameras. I got travelers' checks. I got some cash. No offense, but my experience down here is that you people will steal. So I want you to stay put in our cottage with the bags till we're done eating. Then you can run in and grab a bite. All right?"

"No problem," Merle said. He was too proud to mention his own ravenous hunger, or the fact that room service could send out a meal in a jiffy. "*Let me tell you how to handle gringos,*" his father had said. "*Bow, scrape, stoop, beg from the bastards, but never let them get close to where you live. Hold your pride inside, son. That way they can never hurt you.*"

So Merle sat out in their cottage till late that night. He tried to keep his mind off food by drinking lots of water, and by going through their things. But by ten o'clock he was reduced to pilfering Val's barbiturates, just to kill the hunger pangs.

There were other items of interest that he found among their things.

Two of the bags were open, and full of personal effects like maps and clothing and cameras and toilet articles. But another bag—by far the largest and heaviest—was kept double-locked. Merle deduced that the loot was in this bag, and there was much more of it than Bo had admitted.

It came to him that the guy might not even be a lawyer. There was a possibility that he was some kind of fugitive. The Caddy might be stolen.

It even occurred to him that he might steal the bags and disappear with them into the desert. Then he wouldn't have to show up in Manzanillo as a pauper, shamed before his stern father, with his hat in his hand.

Toward midnight Bo came in alone, fuming.

"Fucking cunts. They're like spooks, man. Give 'em an inch and they'll take a mile."

Again the queasy, uneasy feeling: Why is this guy confiding in me? What has he got up his sleeve?

Bo threw himself down on the bed and reached for his dope. And there was something about the way he moved on the bed that increased Merle's queasiness a hundredfold.

He found Val in the hotel bar, seated alone, sipping a margarita through a straw, listening to Andy Russell sing "In My Adobe Hacienda" on the jukebox.

He sat beside her and asked the bartender if the kitchen was closed yet. It was, he said, but there was a taco stand down the road that stayed open till two in the morning.

"Care to come along?" he asked.

"Why not?" she said, stepping down off the bar stool. She was barelegged, wearing a peasant blouse and a red skirt, and she staggered slightly when she hit the floor, rustling her petticoats. But her recovery was so smooth and nonchalant it might have been taken for a graceful little parody of tipsiness, rather than the thing itself. "Oh, you haven't got any money, have you?"

"Afraid not."

"I've got some."

"Thank you, but I'd like some company too."

"Any company?"

"Yours in particular."

"Must stay out till Bo's asleep," she said. "Had a bit of a row."

"Nothing serious, I hope," he said, guiding her out of the hotel.

"Oh, it'll blow over in a day or two. Actually, I'm not even cross at him anymore. It's Bo now. He's cross because I was cross. If you see what I mean."

"Sort of."

"Rather enjoys his little fits of anger, you see. Part of his act."

"What act?"

"You know, the tough-guy act."

"Could've fooled me," Merle said. "But he sure can tell a story."

"Bit tiresome, after you've heard them a few times," she said. "I've never understood Bo's romance with the criminal world. Sometimes I think he's suffering from a case of arrested emotional development, like some of his clients. And I tend to get onto him about it, from time to time. . . ."

"So that's what it was all about."

"What?"

"Today."

"Oh, no. It was over you, actually."

"Over me?"

"To be perfectly frank with you, Merle, I didn't want him to pick you up."

"Why not?"

"It was just once too often."

"You mean he does this a lot?"

"Oh God yes," she said. "Must have his entourage, you see. Likes a good, thick plot. A *pagaille,* as the French say. The more confusion the better. Collects people the way you might collect potted plants. Some of the most unsavory types. And he just loves having them on."

"Pardon me?"

"You know, always trying to find the weak point, always trying to keep one off balance. Tries it on me all the time. But you won't let him intimidate you, will you, Merle?"

"Well," he said, laughing as if it were the remotest possibility in the world, "I'll try not to."

"His bark is far worse than his bite," she said, and she was serious. There was something about Val that seemed absolutely valid and guileless, in spite of everything. "I can assure you of that. And anyway, you don't fit the mold."

"What mold?"

"You know, the types he picks up."

"Oh, well, thank you very much," he said. But she didn't catch his irony.

"No," she said. "You're not like all the rest, are you?"

"I don't think so.'

"You're cute," she said, leaning on his arm. "Nice."

For a guy who woke up in a cattle car two days ago, Merle was doing all right. But he had not by any means dropped his guard. What do these people want from me? What are their true intentions?

They marched down the dusty road through the desert for a kilometer or so till they found an open-air restaurant on the main highway. It catered to truck drivers and busloads of long-distance braceros, and everyone made a big fuss over Val. But the food was good, the beer was cold, and Merle was able to fend off the more importunate of curious onlookers with occasional blasts of fluent foul-mouthed Spanish.

"Some appetite you've got there," she said, when he'd come to an end of his mountainous serving of carne asado, rice and beans.

"Been a while since I last ate."

"Gathered as much."

"Yeah."

"You're not quite what you say you are," she said. "Are you, Merle?"

"Not quite," he said. "But then again, I guess none of us are."

"Suppose not," she said. "But you know, I sometimes wonder if my entire history isn't just written smack across my face."

"It's a beautiful face."

"Well, that's the point, isn't it?"

"I saw you a couple of times, Val. You were great."

"Was I?" she said. "Yes, I suppose I was. I started at sixteen, you know. Did nothing else for over a decade. Never seemed to get anywhere, though. Now here I am pushing thirty."

"I see what you mean," he said. But he didn't at all.

They strolled back to the hotel arm in arm, under a million twinkling desert stars. Val insisted that they sing "It Happened in Monterey" together, at the tops of their lungs.

"No one'll hear but the coyotes," she said.

"Awoooooo!" he howled. "Nobody here but us coyotes."

". . . *It happened in Monterey, in old Mexico,*" they sang. "*Stars and steel guitars and luscious lips as red as wine, broke somebody's heart and I'm afraid that it was mine. . . .*"

At her cottage gate she kissed him good night on the mouth.

"You're a good sport," she said.

He went to bed with the taste on his lips and dreamed that he was a young Desi Arnaz, dancing with her across a magical MGM sound studio with ceilings strung with electric lights to look like stars.

In the morning Bo and Val were still barely speaking. The only real contact they had was to pass a marijuana cigarette back and forth. Val lay in the backseat of the Cadillac, sometimes sleeping, sometimes smoking, sometimes reading an Agatha Christie mystery. Bo took the wheel and all the way across the Sonora Desert the rap continued, just as seamless and beguiling as ever.

". . . So after the friends of Mr. De Sapio catch up with Sam the Man and strap a couple of cement shoes on his feet and dump him in the East River his old lady she goes bananas, see. They haul her off to Bellevue in a straitjacket, and old Joey has to pull every string he can to get her out. So he gets her out and he says, 'Betty, clean up your act.' And she does, and pretty soon he gives her a spot as a hostess at his nightclub. But she starts to tippling in the lady's room and she spills drinks on important customers and eventually he has to show her the door. She takes up with one loser after another, anyone to keep her in the gin, and by the time her kid is five or six she is tied in with this Irishman named Jimmy Judge. Jimmy is an itinerant blacksmith, man. One of the last. He's got this little brown-and-yellow tinker's wagon that he's mounted on the flatbed of a Model A, and every spring he goes out on the road. Travels all over rural Long Island, from one potato farm to another, right through the summer and fall, shoeing horses and mules. For ten years they go out on the road with old Jimmy, from Nissequogue to Mattituck, from Wantagh to Amagansett, and the only time the Kid sees the inside of a schoolhouse is when the snow starts to fly. Well, this one year it flies early, see. They can't make it back to the Apple so they winter it out in Sag Harbor. The Kid goes to school every day on *snowshoes,* man. To a *little red schoolhouse.* But the winter is long and hard, the quarters are tight, and Jimmy and Betty, they do love their hooch. One thing leads to another and to make a long story short, Jimmy and Betty have words. More than words. He kicks the living shit out of her. 'Your fucking kid is driving me insane,' he says. 'I'm telling you, bitch, there's gunna come a time when you'll have to choose between us.' Now, Jimmy and the Kid have never gotten on, you dig, so the Kid he thinks nothing of it. Toddles off to school the next morning on his snowshoes, with his dog tagging along behind him. But when he gets back in the evening the dog, like, he goes nuts. Runs out in front and the Kid can hear him barking like mad on the other side of the trees. So he makes it over the rise and down by the iced-over inlet where the truck is supposed to be there is nothing. Nothing, man, except blowing snow. The Kid cannot figure out how the fucker got that Model A out of there. Must've had to tow it out on a sled. So the Kid starts looking with his dog. And they look all over Sag Harbor, North Haven, Noyack and Pine Neck for that truck. End of story. It's all a game. They will never find it. It's like a nightmare. To this day the Kid still cannot believe it. Did he really never find that fucking tinker's wagon? No, he never found it. . . ."

The higher Bo got, and the more deeply involved in his interwoven stories, the wider and sharkier his grin got. It was an absolutely devastating grin, at once cynical, mocking and exultant, and it had the continual effect of making Merle feel nervous and ill-at-ease. Also, Bo leaned too close when he wanted to pursue a point, and he touched Merle on the knee too often.

After a couple of mota cigarettes he developed further paranoid thoughts: The macho talk was only a front; the guy was a closet queen and Val was his shill. Yet even the paranoia could do nothing to diminish the fascination he felt for Bo. He had never met anyone remotely like him. He was so big, so loud, so brash, so aggressive and overwhelming as a personality that Merle became aware of a kind of shrinking within himself, a retreat of his manhood, an act of cowardice of the hormones. He realized that the marijuana was coloring his perceptions, but there seemed little he could do to prevent it. And it did no good trying to laugh at the gringo for foolishly running off at the mouth, for revealing his most intimate secrets to a perfect stranger, because he could not deny that the rendition itself was marvelously exciting. Merle began to sweat. He got the shakes. The woman Val receded into the background. It was just Merle and Bo in the saddle of that great palomino, galloping across the Mexican desert. . . . He gazed longingly out the window, daydreaming of escape into the Sierra de Batuc or the Desierto de Altar.

"Hey, what's happenin', honcho?"

"Nothing much."

"You know what, my man? You got a handsome face. But you're too *sensitivo*. You look a little green around the gills."

"I'll be all right," Merle said. But in his weakness he felt compelled to check himself, to reconfirm his own masculinity, much as he had done at college with his sexual conquests.

By the time they got to Hermosillo, the sweltering capital of Sonora State, Merle had just about decided he was going to have Bo's old lady somewhere along the line, just to prove that he could do it, just to cut this big loudmouthed gringo down to size.

Across a wide white plain as flat and featureless as anything on earth they sighted the blue Sea of Cortez, and at four o'clock that afternoon they pulled into the dusty, nondescript town of Guaymas, Sonora. Actually, Guaymas was two towns: a smelly little shrimp-fishing port on fetid Bocochibampo Bay, and a rundown winter beach resort on beautiful San Carlos Bay. The sectors were divided by an arid peninsula, and a steep range of bleak, lunar hills. Bo drove across to the beach side—called Miramar. Merle stayed in the car while Bo and Val got out to look for a hotel. They were still not speaking, and ignored each other as they had done yesterday. They found a modernistico little place at the far end of the beach, and signaled Merle to drive down to meet them. He was tempted to drive right past them and straight down the road to

Mazatlán, but he did as he was bid. Bo got them adjoining rooms on the third floor of the hotel, overlooking the sea, and they all had a siesta and a shower. At dinnertime Merle was left alone with the bags. Bo came in about midnight and immediately threw off his clothes and fell on the bed. It was as if the patter that he laid down every day sapped all of his energy, and he hadn't much left over at night.

"So what're you waiting for, man?"

"Yeah, guess I'll go in and get something to eat."

"Unless you got something else on your mind."

"What?"

"Go ahead," Bo said, waving him out of the room. "I'm gunna smoke me some gage and crash. Got a long day ahead of us tomorrow."

Merle found Val at the bar, slightly tipsy, and delighted to see him. The hotel kitchen was closed, so they took a stroll down the beach to an open-air seafood restaurant where Merle gorged himself on tortillas, guacamole, beer and Huachinanga a la Veracruzana. Val was barelegged again, barefoot, with her espadrilles dangling from her pinky finger, and by now Merle had convinced himself that he was far more than a little in love.

On the way back to the hotel they sat down on a pile of fresh sawdust, near the whalelike skeleton of a half-constructed tuna boat, to smoke some weed. They sat quietly, watching the white little curls of the waves, the phosphorescence in the water, and the moon as it rose over the Estero del Río Muerto.

It was Merle who broke the silence. Suddenly and apropos of nothing he confessed to her that he had lied about his college career, and he told her the story of the hazing incident. At the same time, he tried to maintain a heavily ironical, blackly humorous air, as if he felt completely objective about himself. Actually, he revealed nothing of himself. The story was for the most part a fabrication. In this way he separated himself from her imprudent lover, Bo, and avoided the pitfall of opening himself up to strangers. For even the most beautiful and beloved strangers might use one badly in the end.

"Used to love my nickname," he began. "Made it up when I first got to Berkeley. Called myself Mad Merle and created a character to go along with it. I was the original ratfucker. The first to say 'fuck' in front of girls. The first to 'hang a moon' at the Cal-Stanford game. The first to piss in a beer mug, chill it in the fridge, and serve it up to a fraternity pledge in a chugalug contest. But the trouble with ratfucking, it relies on shock for all its effects. Shock wears off. Your audience requires greater and greater shocks. Came to the point where I was running out of surprising and amazing things to do. Ended up as tragicomedy. About a dozen of us got hold of a fraternity brother who'd just pinned a little Pi Phi and as custom demanded we dragged him out to the end of Berkeley Pier and heaved him into the bay. The only thing was, he couldn't swim. 'I can't swim,' he kept hollering. 'I can't swim!' 'Get serious!' I said. 'Who ever heard of a Cal man who couldn't swim?' He dropped like a stone. 'He's only trying to scare us,' I said. 'He's hiding out under the pilings.' But my heart wasn't in it. A fisherman hooked him in the Yacht Basin a couple of days later."

"Poor Merle," Val said, in a mournful tone, as if it had been he who had drowned in the bay. "You poor kid," she said, and ran the soft back of her hand down the stubble on his cheek.

The truth was, there had never been any such person as Mad Merle. Merle Carrizo himself had been known at college for his studious habits, his editorship of the campus literary magazine, his dignified Latin aristocrat's air and his quiet way with the ladies. Mad Merle was an invention based upon the character of the young man who had drowned in the hazing incident, Crazy Eddie Watts. Crazy Eddie was the most infamous ratfucker at Berkeley, an antagonist of the staid and traditional-minded Merle Carrizo ever since they met at a rushing function at the Delt House in the fall of '49. Merle was merely one of a dozen or more fraternity members who tossed him into the bay despite his loud and repeated protestations that he couldn't swim. No one took his cries seriously because no one took *him* seriously: Crazy Eddie was the campus clown.

But it was Merle who found him under the pier after they had dived for him for half an hour, and it was Merle who insisted on performing artificial respiration. What he felt when he rode the dead boy he would never forget. Desperately he wanted to save him. Also, he wanted him to die. Never had he felt closer to anyone. Never more alone. On that blue young face he saw his own face. He saw his own death. It was like meeting a very old friend. He had known Him all his life. He had even eaten of Him, on the Day of the Dead. Never had he felt colder, crueler. Never more intensely alive. The confession to the police and the public flagellation later were merely part of the ritual, a ritual as old as the Aztecs.

"Do you think of it often?" Val asked, when he was done with his story.

"I never think of anything else," he said. "It has ruined my life."

"You're so intense," she said. "I like intensity."

Then suddenly she laughed and jumped to her feet, dragging Merle along with her. "Come on," she said. "How about a moonlight swim? That ought to cheer you up."

They stripped to their underwear and hung their clothes on the spars of the fishing boat. They raced across the beach and plunged into the waves, which they found amazingly warm and sticky with brine.

"Let's go," she hollered. "Let's go way, way out!"

They swam all the way around Point Kino and back. They swam until they were exhausted, and had to roll over and float, blowing water like whales.

Then, not fifty yards off the beach, Merle spotted an enormous shadow under the waves, gliding swiftly toward them. He could not be sure that it wasn't just a trick of his imagination. He hesitated to cry out, for he didn't want Val to think him an alarmist, or a sissy. But in the end he could not contain his own panic, and he turned from her suddenly and struck out for the beach, swimming as fast as he could.

Val barely seemed to notice that he was gone, and she splashed around in the bay for another ten minutes before she came in. He met her in the small surf, just as she rose from the sea.

"What happened to you?" she said, splashing water at him. "That was probably the most delicious experience of my life."

"Got a cramp."

"Okay now?"

"Fine," he said, and caught his breath. In the flesh her body was more than cheesecake: It was the act itself.

They came together in the water and kissed. She was slippery in his arms, and tasted of salt. He ran his hand down the curve of her hips and buttocks. He started to slip her panties down.

"No," she said, moaning, pressing herself wetly to him. "No."

And it was like the drowned boy, Crazy Eddie. Did she mean what she said? Or did she not?

She broke away and ran for the beach. He sprinted after her, kicking spray, and caught her in the shallows. They tripped and fell in a heap, kissing again, thrusting at each other instinctively, rolling in the sand.

"No," she said again. "No."

Was the show of resistance meant to be overcome, or not?

She escaped his arms, crawled out of the water, and raced for her clothes, her body sleek and undulant in the moonlight.

Merle let her go.

Figured there was plenty of time. And why make his move so early, when the stakes were so high?

They dressed and smoked some more mota by the fishing boat while their clothes dried. A couple of times Merle was tempted to throw her down in the sawdust, but in fact all they did was engage in small talk. Neither mentioned what had happened in the water. Val pretended it hadn't happened at all.

"Suppose you wonder why he leaves us so much alone," she said, on the way back to the hotel.

"It had occurred to me."

"Part of the pattern," she said. "He does it with everyone, even his law partner. Expects the worst of people. Throws temptation at them all the time, hoping they'll confirm all his nasty suspicions."

"Couldn't figure out why he'd want to trust a stranger with his bags."

"That's not the least of it. You don't know what's in those bags."

"What do you think he'd do if he ever actually caught someone taking advantage of him?"

"You know, I swear I think he'd die of pleasure."

"You make the guy sound so perverse."

"Oh, he is," she said. "He's absolutely demented."

"Then how come you stay with him?"

"Often wonder about that myself."

"How long have you been together?"

"Not long. Caught me at a weak moment, actually. Hadn't a clue what I was getting into. Then I suppose it was simply that no one else came along. I have no one to rely on, you see."

"You could rely on me."

"Oh Merle, you're sweet. But you're too young."

"I'm old enough."

"Are you?" she said. "I'll bet you are. But you haven't got any money, have you?"

"I will have."

"I'm sure you will. What do you want to do with yourself?"

"I want to be a writer."

"A *writer*? Good grief, you'll never support a woman on a writer's salary. God preserve us from the arts! I ought to know. And besides," she said, "I'm sick of stories. Got them coming out of my ears."

"Are they true, do you think?"

"Never been able to find out one way or the other," she said.

"Haven't you got any idea?"

"I can only judge from the way he acts."

"How does he act?"

"He has fantasies, Merle. Action, drama, mystery . . . part of the hoodlum act. I'll give you an example of what I mean. He's got a very fine law practice, but probably half his clients refuse to pay him in anything but cash. Since most of it is untraceable, Bo pockets it without declaring it to the IRS. Every year or so, when his wall safe overflows, he packs a suitcase full of money and carries it out of the country. Deposits it in this secret numbered account he's got down in Acapulco. He doesn't really need to do all this, you see. He makes more than enough money above the board. And it's rather stupid as well, because eventually I suppose the IRS is going to catch up with him. But he loves his caper, his 'baby' as he calls it, and he wouldn't give it up for the world. I think in his daydreams he sees himself as some kind of international wheeler-dealer, or Mafia don, or something."

"Well, why don't we do him a favor, then?" Merle said. It just popped out. He'd had no intention of saying any such thing.

"What?"

"Why don't we take it?"

"You're kidding."

"What do you think?"

"Still," she said, "wouldn't it be something? Serve him right, too. Oh Lord, what I wouldn't give to see his face. And I wouldn't feel a qualm, you know. He bloody well owes it to me. For sitting there listening to him for all these months."

Later, after she had gone into their room, Merle could hear them whispering through the wall.

"You get it on with the Bean?"

"None of your business."

"I make it my business."

"You're a nasty business."

"That's right," he said. "I'd like to watch. And then I'd like to fuck you both."

Merle was treated to his next installment of the seemingly endless Bo Brodsky Story in the morning, on the desolate Llanura Costera between Guaymas and Navajoa, while Val slept in back.

". . . So the Kid joins up right out of reform school, see. Two years in the South Pacific and all of a sudden they're pinning this Ruptured Duck on him down in Long Beach. Figures he'll just stick it out on the Coast. In the Apple he's a dime a dozen. Right? But here he's unique. So he bops down to a jewelry store on Pico Boulevard, orders himself a gold chain and a gold dollar sign, and dedicates himself to a life of success. Gets his GI Bill and goes to college, supplementing his income by dealing a little weed on the side. Carries on through law school the same way. Never had a problem with it morally, man. Considered it a public service. Anyway, to make a long story short, he hangs out his shingle on Sunset Boulevard, catering to the tinsel trade. Acquires a rep as 'the dopers' friend' when the doper has few, and bingo he's got himself a thriving practice. Takes in a partner. Opens another office in Beverly Hills. By now he's starting to get a few non-dope cases, one of which turns out to be Val Raymond. She comes flouncing into the office, looking sensational, with a tale to touch the heart of the meanest shyster in town. She's like *naïve,* man. A sucker for a sad story. Her one big mistake was making it with the head of production at MGM—this scumbag named Servo, sleaziest sonofabitch you ever wanna meet—because he had dark soulful eyes and a sincere way of speaking. The minute he sniffs fresh puss, of course, he drops her contract like it was something the dog laid in his hand. 'Never shit where you eat,' I tell her now, but she didn't know that then. . . . So she walks into the office, man, and right away the Kid can dig that she's been beat for the entire yolk. He tries to figure some way he can get the sleazo on breach of contract, but as it happens there is nothing he can do. The stupid cunt gave him power of attorney when they were shacking up, and he covered his butt on the sly. As a financial proposition, the Chicken is a total loss. As a movie starlet, she's all washed up. End of story. It's all a game. The Kid takes her in outa the goodness of his heart and . . ."

"I thought the lawyer-client relationship was supposed to be confidential," said Val, waking from her nap.

"Glad you reminded me of that, Chicken."

"Must've slipped your mind."

"Won't let it happen again . . . if you don't."

"What's that supposed to mean?"

"Like I was just telling the honcho, here, you're a sucker for a sad story."

"Have you been sneaking around again, Bo, sticking your nose where you hadn't ought?"

"Any more shit from you, bitch, and you go out."

"Right, you're the captain of the ship."

"Believe it."

"Just keep talking," she said. "That's what you're good at."

"It's when the talk stops," he said. "That's when you gotta look out."

"Never known it to stop yet."

A few seconds later, at a sign that said SELVA DE CACTUS, Bo turned off the main highway and headed up a dirt road toward a forest of giant saguaro cactus trees spread across the lower slopes of a high flat mesa. He drove into the middle of the forest and parked the car.

"Get out," he said to Val.

"What?"

"You heard me."

"What for?"

"I'm gunna *murder* you," he said. "Never mind what for. Get out."

Reluctantly, she climbed out of the backseat. Bo pulled a blanket from the trunk and joined her by the side of the car.

"Come with me."

"Wait a minute."

"Come on," he said, pulling her roughly by the arm.

"Where we going?" she said, digging her high heels into the dirt.

"I'm gunna fuck you in the ass."

"Oh no you're not."

"Wanna bet?"

"Yeah," she said, and kicked him on the shin.

He dropped the blanket and slapped her face, hard.

Val started to cry.

If she had called out, or even looked Merle's way, he would have gone to her aid. But as it was, he figured it was something between the two of them. Also, there was something ritualistic in their exchange, which led him to believe that other such dramas had occurred in the past.

Bo picked up the blanket.

"Let's go."

"No, I don't want to."

"You don't know what you want," he said, dragging her off into the cactus. "I gotta show you what you want."

"I don't want this."

"You do."

"I don't."

"Then I'll *take* it. . . ."

She fought him all the way until he got her pants down. The silence of the desert was so profound that he could hear everything.

Her surrender was magnificent.

As soon as it was over, though, Merle could hear her shrieking at him again.

"You don't love people, Bo, you fuck them!"

But it didn't stop him from doing it again.

Halfway through the second session, Merle couldn't take it anymore. Figured it was either drop the Caddy in low and disappear with the loot, or pound his pud. The thing that tipped the scales was he thought he heard air escaping. Would've looked pretty ridiculous trying to run off with a flat tire.

Unzipped his hard scarred self and whipped it off, spotting the windshield. Wiped up the mess with the sleeve of his Levi jacket.

Later, after he'd smoked some more dope, he noticed that another twenty-dollar bill had dropped to the floor on the driver's side. He thought about it for a while and finally decided to take it. Figured it was part of his retainer.

Then all of a sudden he felt very, very high. As high as the sky. He entered the heart of the zopilote, flying a thousand feet above the desert. He watched the gringos fighting and fucking in the saguaro forest, and the Cadillac parked on the white dirt road, and the faithful but furtive little Mexican retainer inside, groping on the floor for the twenty-dollar chingadera that the boss had dropped.

"Bullshit," he said, and got out of the car. He checked the left rear tire and found that it had indeed gone flat. He opened the trunk, got out the jack and the spare, and set about methodically changing the tire. It seemed as if it took him a hundred years to change that tire. As he was finishing up, he could hear the lovers coming back through the cactus.

"I hate you, Bo."

"All I do is show you what you are, Chicken."

"You make me less than I am," she said. "You have a talent for that kind of thing. . . ."

Merle put away the flat tire and the jack and climbed in behind the wheel.

"Where you going, honcho?"

"Mind if I drive?"

"Nah. Thanks for changing the flat."

"Nothing to it. We'll have to stop in Navajoa to get it fixed, though. These roads are murder on tires."

Bo got in back and went to sleep. Val sat in front, shamefaced, pretending to look out the window.

Merle bided his time. About an hour out of Navajoa, Bo woke up and said he had to take a piss. Got out of the car and went down the embankment, unbuttoning his pants. Merle waited till he got them open, then he stepped on the gas.

"Hey!" Bo hollered, with his cock in his hand. "Where you going?"

"He's got a good question there," Val said, laughing, watching her boyfriend recede into the dust.

"Haven't given it much thought."

"Mind if I come along for the ride?"

"That was the whole idea."

CHAPTER 3

". . . End of story. It's all a game. The Kid takes him in out of the goodness of his heart and how does he repay his kindness?"

"How much did they get away with, Bo?" the woman asked.

"A lot," he said.

"How much?" she insisted.

"A small fortune."

"What were you doing with that kind of money in cash?"

"That's what the fuzz wanted to know. Told 'em it was to buy a yacht in Acapulco."

"What was the real reason?"

"Trade secret. What's with all the questions?"

"I'm the inquisitive type," she said. "And this kind of thing has always fascinated me."

"Stick around, doll, 'cause you ain't heard nothin' yet."

"Why would she want to run off with a college boy like that?"

"Hey, like I say," he said. "It's all a game."

"What kind of game?"

"Like, even the Kid can relate to the fantasy of it all."

"Now let's just backtrack for a second, Bo," she said. "How did you ever get out of that saguaro forest?"

"I was just coming to that. The Kid has still got his wallet, see, and a wad of travelers' checks. So he hikes down through the desert to the highway and he sits himself down on this big, flat, hot rock and he waits there in the sun and wind and the swirling white dust for a few hours with the buzzards circling overhead and the heat and the glare off the blacktop driving him mad and finally this third-class Mexican bus comes putzing along, headed north, loaded to the roof. He flags it down, the peones make room for their better, and all the way back to Guaymas while the pigs are squealing and the goats are bleating and the passengers are hawking uplungers onto the floor and hen feathers are fluttering down his sweaty neck he is thinking, What to do? What to do?"

"But you're a lawyer, aren't you, Bo?" she said. "You would *know* what to do."

"Right. By the time the bus crawls back into Guaymas, late in the afternoon, the Kid has got it locked. Bops straight down to the policía and reports the robbery and the abduction of his wife. Phones the hotel, and has the desk clerk come down and make a notarized statement to the effect that Mr. and Mrs. Brodsky and Señor Carrizo were all registered together at the same time, Mr. Brodsky was paying the bills, and they were all seen leaving the hotel that morning in the palomino gold Cadillac which is now missing. He hits the chief with a C note to ensure that he pursues the case with unusual vigor and keeps the file open for at least a year. Then he hires himself an English-spicking shyster and they schlep down to the beach with a law clerk in tow and right away they strike pay dirt. Take a statement from this little fisher fella who was crashing in a half-built tuna boat and witnessed the amorous pair cavorting naked in the waves and disporting themselves on the public beach. Now, at this point the Kid gets a brainwave. He will put on a show that the Latin mind can latch on to and remember. He screams and raves and pulls his hair. He stomps up and down the beach, ranting and raving, 'I'll kill 'em, I'll kill 'em!' Drags everyone down to the policía again, submits this new evidence, and changes the abduction charge to 'alienation of affections.' All of which the chief duly files away in his dossier marked 'Carrizo/Brodsky.' "

"Why would you want to go to all this trouble, Bo? Why all the melodrama?"

"Glad you asked me that, doll. The truth of the matter—and this is strictly between you and me—at this time the Kid is toying with the idea of a *crime passionelle.*"

"A what?"

"Dig it. In Mexico it would be considered an 'affair of honor.' He would probably never do a day in the juzgado. And anyway, even if it came to nothing, see, he could at least savor the romance of it all. The classic triangle. The thrill of the chase. . . ."

"Uh-huh."

"What else you gunna do, when you been shit on to that extent?"

"I see."

"Frankly, the scene with the Chicken has gone a little flat," he said. "And this adds a certain zest."

"I like this, Bo," she said. "I like it a lot."

"So the Caddy turns up the next day in a dry riverbed outside Navajoa. The Kid cruises out with his fat little licenciado in his Hudson Terraplane and they find a witness who spotted this young, good-looking stud matching the Bean's description and this gorgeous blond gringa of the Chicken's description leaving the vicinity of the arroyo with two suitcases, an hour after the robbery. The licenciado launches his Terraplane again and freewheels it back up the highway for Guaymas, where he files yet another police deposition. The Kid saddles the big palomino, mounts up, and gives chase."

"But the trail must be getting a bit chilly by now, no?"

"*Aller sans dire,* doll. But the Kid ain't a member of the California State Bar Association for nothing. He thumbs through every telephone directory from Mazatlán to Mexico City, Mexico City to Acapulco. Rings every Carrizo in the book. Checks every motel, every guest house, every hotel . . ."

"Till you came to this one."

"Bingo."

"What'd you say his name was?"

"Merle Carrizo."

"Mmmmmm," Chris said, and ordered another drink from her barman, playing for time. "Taste this for me, will you, Bo? And tell me what you think. Sometimes he makes them too sweet."

This Brodsky character had intrigued her ever since he pulled into the Tropicana carport this morning, to the extent that she had dismissed her clerk at the reception counter and checked him in herself. He looked rich. He looked dangerous. He looked like some kind of gangster, or a dope dealer after Acapulco Gold. Yet, at the same time, his style was so excessive and overblown that he seemed quite absurd.

All her life Chris had dreamed of a rich and dangerous and larcenous yet highly mutable and mortal man—a man like her brother Brian, who had captured her imagination, won her love, then callowly abandoned her and suddenly died, as if the curse she sent after him from the deck of the United Fruit Company steamer had taken immediate effect. . . . And Bo's absurdity she felt she could deal with, given the immoderate tug that he appeared to have exerted upon her organs. Besides, all men were a little ridiculous, and full of themselves. It's what made them tolerable, and manageable. If Bo was an extreme case, then so could the results be extreme, for a woman with such a mind.

"You got a Merle Carrizo or a Val Raymond registered here?" he had asked, just as the mozo was about to lead him off to his suite of rooms.

"Let me see," she said, running her finger down the list of guests, trying to hide her astonishment and growing excitement. "No, I'm afraid not."

"Either name ring a bell?"

"The name Carrizo sounds familiar," she said calmly, when in fact she felt an indefinable yearning in her heart at the thought of Merle, whom she'd not seen in thirteen years, and the blood was pounding in her ears.

"Think on it, doll. It's important."

"I'll do that."

Then at lunch on the terrace, in his Panama hat, his Palm Beach shirt, his white suede shoes and his white pegged pants, puffing at a long Havana, reeling off one implausible adventure after another, Bo had positively reeked of crooked lawyer. And this had intrigued her even more. She felt that here at last was a kindred spirit, another outrageous oddball in a world of conformity. This one is larcenous by instinct, she thought, eyeing the golden dollar sign around his neck. In Bo she saw her Black Prince.

And all afternoon in her office while she did her accounts, signed payroll checks, talked to deliverymen, produce jobbers and liquor salesmen, dispensed Kaopectate and Intero-Viaform to gringos doing the Aztec Two-Step, and responded by rote to the familiar complaints of the guests—"It's too hot in my room . . ." "I'll send up the air-conditioning man . . ." "There's no water pressure in my shower . . . ." "I'll send up the plumber . . ." "I found a cockroach under my bed . . ." "I'll see that the maid is reprimanded . . ."—Chris was thinking of Bo Brodsky: What was his connection to Merle Carrizo? And how could she turn it to her advantage?

Apart from this, and excluding his very strong first impression of animal magnetism, the sheer expansiveness of Bo's personality had struck a chord in her repressed side.

Chris had held herself aloof, tightly reined emotionally, ever since she went away to school. It was the only way to keep her demons at bay. At St. Anne's Academy in San Francisco, and at Dominican College in San Rafael, she had single-mindedly devoted herself to the achievement of academic success. She felt that she must triumph at any cost. She must show her mother that she was wrong about her, that she oughtn't to have thrown her out, that she was worthy of her love and affection. Yet, under everything, she was convinced that Maureen was right about her, that she was not worthy, that she had earned Maureen's disdain with her own selfish and willful behavior, that she was stupid and crazy and incapable of excelling at school. So, she lied, she cheated, she copied, she stole notes. Cunningly she covered her tracks. She was never caught. Indeed, she was highly regarded by her teachers (if not by her classmates, who called her Pretty Poison) for her competitive drive. And in some sense she felt that she merited the good marks they gave her, for she labored so long at cribbing, plagiarizing and burglarizing offices that her efforts far exceeded those of her honest schoolmates. Even so, it was important to Chris to cheat, to beat the system, to have her secret little triumphs, to laugh up her sleeve, or into her mirror when she was alone.

Later she attended a year-long course in hotel management at the University of Lausanne, where she graduated at the head of her class. And afterward she told herself that maybe some of it rubbed off after all, for she returned from Switzerland with detailed plans to turn her mother's small, sedate hotel on La Caleta Beach into one of the showpieces of Acapulco.

Yet all the way across the storm-tossed Atlantic, in that chilly, perverse June of 1950, Chris kept asking herself, Why am I going back? What am I looking for in Mexico, in my mother's hotel? She had turned down several fine offers at luxury hotels in Europe and the United States. She had even turned down a proposal of marriage from one of her classmates, a sweet, ruddy, altogether presentable young Scot who reminded her a bit of her brother, Brian, and who was all set to take over his father's exclusive hunting lodge in the Highlands.

What for? she kept asking herself bitterly. What for? To go home and take more of Mama's abuse?

But the truth was that she missed her mother dreadfully, and thought of her almost constantly. Maureen was still the central figure in her life, beside whom no one could stand in comparison. In college she'd even had daydreams about her, and she'd felt chills of ecstasy running down her spine imagining Maureen growing old and decrepit, helpless and bedridden, with only her daughter to take care of her. Even her senile nagging and complaining and raving laments for her long-dead son would be music to Chris's ears, even her nitpicking and her obstinacy and her sarcasm and her total disapproval would be a form of caring.

When Maureen met her at the airport in Acapulco, with the hotel minibus, Chris realized with a sinking sensation that her mother would never be senile and decrepit. It was two years since they'd seen each other, and in that time Chris felt that she'd changed from a girl into a woman. But her mother had stayed relatively the same. She was sixty-seven years old, but her red hair was scarcely muted by gray, her complexion remained smooth, her waist was only slightly thicker than it had been years ago. And the Mexican peasant outfit that she had always worn—long red skirt, low-cut white blouse, long gold earrings and leather sandals—no longer seemed so eccentric or bohemian, as the style of dress had come into fashion that year.

"Mama!" Chris said, and ran across the tarmac to fling herself into her arms.

"I don't know why you've turned up in Acapulco, dear," Maureen said, holding her at arm's length. "You'll be bored to death here."

"Oh, I've got some great plans, Mama!" Chris said, feeling a little shiver of delight at her mother's cranky retort. "Just wait till I tell you."

"Well, it's just going to have to wait for now, Chris," Maureen said, hustling her through the airport waiting-room for the minibus. "We've got a double disaster on our hands at the hotel. . . ."

Apparently the Tropicana was in the middle of a garbage strike, and it was on the verge of being closed down by the municipal authorities for "harboring criminals." The strike was a result of Maureen's absent-minded failure to pay the Sanitation Workers' Union president his monthly bribe. Now the garbage was stacked up outside the hotel six feet high, and the guests were complaining about the smell, threatening to check out and asking for their money back. Yet the union president would no longer accept his usual exorbitant bribe of a thousand pesos. It was too late for that, he said. His pride was offended, and he was demanding a four-thousand-peso increase, which was outright extortion. To make things worse, one of Maureen's beach boys had seduced the wife of a powerful Mexican general—the current minister of national defense—stolen her jewels, locked her in her bathroom and disappeared in the direction of Mexico City. The general was outraged, and had given Maureen twenty-four hours to come up with the jewels, on pain of closure, and a civil suit. Things were so bad, Maureen said, that she had actually begun phoning her friends in the local hotel industry, looking for a quick buyer.

"You don't want to sell out now, Mama," Chris said. "This town is going to experience a tourist boom like you've never seen before."

"I don't know what else to do, dear. I'm at my wit's end."

"You ought to be more careful who you hire."

"My God, Chris, I've been at this for a number of years, you know. And I've learned a thing or two. I put every one of my employees through a virtual CIA check. I do everything but wire them up to a polygraph machine. But with all the jewels and money that people leave lying around, even a saint would be tempted."

"If I settle this thing for you in twenty-four hours, Mama, will you listen to the plans I've got for improving the Tropicana?"

"Chris, if you settle this, I'll be willing to listen to anything you say."

Chris went right to work as soon as she got back to the hotel. She looked up the addresses of the union president and the beach boy, caught a taxi to the union headquarters building on Costera Alemán, and confronted the boss just as he was going out for lunch.

"I'll buy you lunch, Señor Acevedo," she said, and took him to the most stylish restaurant in Acapulco, high atop the Princess Hotel. He was a fat little elderly mestizo, but he had an eye for the young gringas, so Chris plied him with liquor and come-hither smiles, and by siesta time she had him down to two thousand pesos, with the unspoken understanding that she would be receptive to his attentions at some unspecified date in the future. Chris left with a firm promise that the garbage would be removed in the morning, and caught another taxi to the Ejido Santa Cruz, a squalid slum on the hills above the town, where the wayward beach boy lived. The beach boy was long gone, of course, but his mama was at a neighbor's house, sick with fear, as the police had just come by making threats on behalf of the general.

"The police now know where your son is hiding," Chris said. "And they're about to arrest him, after which they will turn him over to the general. The general is a big shot in the government, and he has assured me that your son will not live through an army interrogation. Here are two thousand pesos, señora. If the jewels are here tomorrow at this time, I will make sure that you have three thousand more, and that your son is smuggled safely into the United States."

The jewels turned up the next day. Chris gave the mother three thousand pesos, and arranged to meet her son later that day at the Playa Dominguillo, in order to help smuggle him to the United States. Immediately thereafter she called the police. The police picked the beach boy up and put him in jail. Later the general arranged to have him sent up to the Islas Tres Marías, and saw to it that he spent the next six years of his life digging salt.

"All right, Mama," Chris said, after she had apprised Maureen of her success. "I'm going to hold you to your bargain now."

Maureen didn't respond to that. She just said, "You sweet-talk people, and then you stab them in the back. You're going to get yourself a terrible reputation that way."

"I'll worry about that when it happens."

"The problem is, Chris, I can't count on you. I can't trust you."

"If you can't, Mama, then I feel sorry for you, because I'm the only one who cares about you."

"And I certainly care about *you,*" said Maureen, indignant, as if an accusation to the contrary had been flung in her face.

Whether Maureen meant that or not, Chris wanted to throw her arms around her. Instead she produced her plans for the expansion and updating of the Tropicana Hotel.

"Look, Mama, we'll have two big new wings of rooms, a new nightclub, a penthouse, two swimming pools, expanded service, water-skiing and scuba-diving facilities, a much larger kitchen and dining room, and a wonderful terraced garden descending to a private beach."

"Lovely," Maureen said. "But how do you propose to finance all of this?"

"Mama, you own this place free and clear. It's a proven moneywinner. You owe nobody. You're a citizen of Mexico. You've been established in Acapulco since before the war, and you've been with the same bank for fifteen years. If you're not mortgage-loan material, then I don't know who is."

"All right, dear, you win. But I'm telling you right now I don't like it. I don't like it a bit. And I'm only going along with it to please you."

"You won't regret it, Mama," Chris said. "I swear it!"

Chris got Maureen the loan, supervised the building expansion and volunteered to take over the day-to-day management of the hotel as well, leaving her mother free to indulge herself in her neglected literary pursuits. And from then on, every morning between seven and twelve, Maureen would sit on her shaded terrace above the tropical garden, breathing exotic scents of tulipan, vanilla, mimosa, arrayan, cinnamon and papaya, picking away at her little antique typewriter, while every afternoon between siesta and tapa time she could be found curled up in her air-conditioned rooms on the third floor, happily reading the latest novels and poetry from the United States and England . . . "catching up on myself," as she said. Every evening at about seven, Chris would come in from work and they would have a sundowner on her terrace, chatting about the events of the day, and scanning the western horizon for evidence of a curious tropical atmospheric phenomenon called the Green Fire, which sometimes flashed spectacularly a few minutes after sunset.

Over the months their evening chats evolved into a kind of ritual, in which Maureen would ask what had been accomplished by the workmen that day and Chris would reply with a detailed account of their progress, after which Maureen would vehemently criticize their actions—"That foreman is an idiot . . ." "They're leaning on their shovels all day long . . ." "Their workmanship is terribly shoddy . . ." "This place is turning into an absolute wreck . . ."—intimating that it was all Chris's fault. As time went on, Chris found herself exaggerating the workmen's shortcomings, and her own, trying to elicit her mother's disapproval. And in the end the understanding between them was nearly total: Each got exactly what she wanted from the other.

Yet in all the time they spent together on the terrace, Brian's name came up only once.

"You don't know what I've been through, Chris," Maureen said. "I've never been the same since your brother died."

"Oh, but I do know, Mama," Chris said. "I can't separate your pain from mine."

Then the sun, which had been hovering just above the sea, suddenly dropped and splashed and submerged and the full moon which had been lurking behind the Sierra Madre del Sur shot into the sky and the black shadows of pelicans started coming in low across the water and a fat gringa woman in a long flowing purple muumuu that flapped madly in the breeze went strolling out onto the white beach and the single light of a night fisherman went bobbing by and the inky blue waves sounded hollowly on the sand and the jungle hills behind the hotel turned red as blood and the Green Fire streaked straight and clean across the clouds.

"Mmmmmm," Chris said again, sipping her rum and Coke, which Bo had tasted and tested and confirmed by his continued existence, and which now seemed somehow less delicious than her first cold sweet sip. In this it was like a lot of other things in her life. Like the sexual encounter that went from "divine" in bed to "great" in the shower to "all right" at the door to "not too bad" in the taxi on the way home to "disgusting" in her room alone that night. Like the vintage Pouilly Montrachet she had the other evening, the first sip of which was "heaven," the second merely "bliss," the third "fine," the fourth "slightly tart," the fifth "bitter," the sixth "absolute swill."

In her mother's hotel Chris was known as a perfectionist, an iron mistress, bane to the existence of every chef, wine steward, gardener, beach boy and maid. She took pride in her reputation, for it was an immeasurable aid in running the "tight ship" that she required. Actually, she enjoyed her work as hotel manager, as long as she was constantly faced with new challenges. And she felt that perhaps it was just the kind of job for someone with her "peculiar problems." She was thus aware of the pathological aspects of her character, including her tendency to rapidly convert all of her pleasures into pain, all of her joys into sorrow, all of her triumphs into dust. There was no cure for her ailment, she knew, and only one possible response: She must seek ever new rewards, ever greater victories, ever more bitter disappointments. . . .

"Mmmmmm," she said. "You know, Bo, I think I might know that Carrizo guy after all."

"Hey!"

"Yes," she said. "I believe I do."

"Lemme at 'em!" he said, making a great show of it, tipping his hat back on his head, giving his shoulders a graceful little mambo dancer's shake, displaying his barracuda grin.

"Not so fast," she said, laughing, patting his hairy hand on the bar. "In Mexico everything has its price."

"What's yours?"

"Cheap," she said. "Given the circumstances."

"Name it."

"I need a silent partner, an infusion of cash."

"How much?"

"Now hold on a second, Bo," she said. "Hear me out. I've got an option to buy a place across the cove. It's a huge old beast of a pseudo-Moorish place, but I can get it at a pretty reasonable price, and it's in an ideal location, overlooking La Caletilla Beach. There," she said, pointing out across the patio, the garden and the cove. "You can see it, right through those big gujamachi trees. It was built in the twenties—prematurely—and then abandoned. I want to rebuild it from scratch, to my specifications."

"What's wrong with the place you got?"

"It's my mom's place, and we don't always get along. Now, don't take me wrong," she said, eyeing her mother at the bridge table across the lounge. "She's a grand old lady, and I owe her everything. But you know, I've doubled her profits here and she's never even thanked me for it. Just sort of takes it for granted. Actually, I could quadruple her profits, but she won't let me do what I want with the place."

"What would you do with it?"

"I'd put in a revolving nightclub on the roof, with glass walls and a panoramic view of the bay. I'd get rid of the upstairs piano bar and bring in a couple of big, brassy mambo bands. But she won't hear of it. Thinks it'd be too noisy, attract the wrong class of people. . . . Look, Bo," she said, sliding smoothly into the sales pitch that she aimed at every likely-looking investor who passed through, "this town has had a phenomenal growth rate since the war. But we haven't seen anything yet. When they finish the superhighway to Mexico City next year, and complete the lengthening of our airfield to accommodate the biggest four-engine planes, Acapulco is just going to take off. It can't help it. The Ruiz Cortines administration is very keen on foreign investment just now, and it's relaxing the laws against the alien ownership of property. It's investing a fortune in the expansion of tourism, with a special emphasis on Acapulco, which they see as their greatest potential source of foreign exchange. Besides that you've got cheap land, cheap labor, a devalued peso, a quaint and colorful Mexican ambiance, miles and miles of unspoiled white sand beaches, and three hundred and forty-five days a year of sunshine."

"You don't look like you get too much sunshine."

"Too busy."

"You got skin like porcelain."

"Don't admire me, please," she said, shuddering. "Admiration throws me into a panic. But, you know, getting back to the subject, Bo. What

I've got in mind for the hotel is kind of making a virtue of the Moorish look, giving it the atmosphere of a seraglio: intimate, enclosed, protected, richly furnished, exclusive, expansive, yet completely informal. I want a dugout bar by the side of the smaller swimming pool, with underwater bar stools. I want a mambo bar built around the largest pool, with a tile floor for dancing in bare feet and bikinis. I want people wandering around all night half-nude, with drinks in their hands, doing the cha-cha-cha with perfect strangers. I want a place where anything can happen, and if it does, it's okay, because all the riffraff has been weeded out by exorbitant prices."

"Wow," said Bo.

"Yeah," said Chris. "It's never been done before. But I'm telling you, the people we've been getting here lately are a new breed."

"What kind of breed?"

"They're the kind of people who're going to make this town, Bo, once we've got our transportation problems ironed out. I'm talking about the rich swinging set," she said, her voice rising in excitement, yet slightly ironic, as if she held herself apart from such individuals, and considered them merely an important ingredient in the commercial success of her hotel. "I'm talking about the high-lifers, the high rollers, Hollywood people, film people, fashion people, European aristocracy, New York money. . . . These folks are starting to rebel against our strict Spanish-style dress codes. They come down here to unwind, to let go, and what happens? They get some snotty maître d' telling them they can't eat because they aren't 'dressed' for dinner. I want to be the first to relax the rules. I want midnight skinny dips off the rocks. I want nymphs and satyrs wandering my gardens at dawn. I want afternoon surprises on the pathway down to my private beach. I want room parties that end up as twenty-four-hour orgies. That's the mood I'm after, and it's the thing that's going to make my place the hot spot of Acapulco within its first year of operation."

"Sounds good," Bo said. "But how much is all of this gunna cost?"

"That's the best part."

"Tell me about it."

"It's not going to cost a dime."

"Get outa here."

"Bo, I've already made a deal with the contractor," she said. "He's willing to rebuild the entire place, furnishing all labor and materials free of charge, in exchange for twenty percent of the profits, in perpetuity."

"Groovy," he said. "But how about the down payment? And the operating costs?"

"Brace yourself."

"I'm braced," he said, gulping down his drink, grabbing hold of his bar stool as if it were about to launch itself into space.

"Merle Carrizo is going to finance it for us."

"Now you're reaching, doll. How you gunna pull that one off?"

"We'll get to him through his dad."

"Who's his dad?"

"One of the richest men in Colima State."

"Say," he said, his lazy bloodshot eyes igniting at last, and then locking, bewitched, upon the heavy opaque lenses of her dark prescription glasses. "This conversation is getting more interesting all the time."

"This conversation isn't going on for another second," she said, "unless you give me your word that you're in with me all the way on this thing."

"Am I in?" he said, doing his mambo number again, rolling his eyes, showing his teeth. "I'm in!"

"I think this is something we should discuss in private," Chris said, after they shook hands. "Would you care to join me in my office?"

"You know what, doll? Let's go down to my pad," he said, spinning smoothly off the bar stool. "We'll be more comfortable there."

"Fine," she said, and barked an order to the barman. "Carlos, mande dos Cuba Libres a la caseta!"

Towering above her, Bo escorted her through the tables of chattering sunburned guests, past the bridge table where her mother pointedly ignored them (she didn't approve of Bo), around the bandstand where the three-piece combo was harmonizing, ". . . *Solamente tu cha-cha, y tu cha-cha, y tu, y nadie más que tu* . . . ," across the patio under the colored lights, and around the shimmering green swimming pool.

Chris faltered on the uneven flagstone steps of the terraced garden path and leaned heavily on his arm. She hated this winding, dimly lit pathway that others found so romantic. Its descent was so steep it made her feel giddy. It seemed to fall away directly into the sea, which she could hear churning on the rocks below.

"You know, doll," Bo said, as if sensing her sudden frailty, and unable to resist the temptation to rub it in, "you oughta get rid of them glasses of yours. I bet you'd be a knockout without 'em."

"Without them I can't see," she said, though this was not strictly true.

Chris had given Bo the finest suite on the property, a magnificent, self-contained stone cottage built high on the rocky point separating La Caleta Beach from its neighboring La Caletilla Beach, affording an extraordinary view of the Boca Chica Channel, the Islas Roqueta and Guadalupe, and far away across the wide mouth of Acapulco Bay, the lighthouse at Punta Los Monitos and the dark spires of the Sierra Madre del Sur.

But Chris and Bo sat inside under the air conditioner, sipping rum and Coke, ignoring the view completely.

"Do you mind tasting this? Tell me what you think, Bo. Sometimes they vary from drink to drink."

"Do you mind if I smoke?" he said, a few minutes later.

"Not in the least," she said, and he proceeded to pull out a small cellophane tobacco pouch and some cigarette paper and roll himself a long torpedolike thing which, when he lit it, smelled strongly of narcotics.

"You want some?"

"Never touch the stuff," she said. "Though I know a man—one of our regulars at the bar—who grows it by the acre on a farm in the mountains."

"Does he smoke?"

"Won't have it in the house."

Bo laughed and ran his tongue carefully along the fold of his cigarette. And then, holding it between his fingers, hitting it on the surface of the oak dressing table, packing it tight, he said, "Hey, this could be a sketch. You know a guy with acres of weed. I know the guys in L.A. who deal it."

"Yes," she said, in command of the situation again, now that she was inside, under the lights. "But first things first. Listen to me carefully now, please. Merle's father, Gallo Carrizo, is a mestizo, a parvenu. He used to work for my brother as a manservant. Now he owns three hotels, a couple of banana plantations, a coffee finca, a cement factory and a whole lot of real estate. But his most important asset is his government post as head of the railroad in Colima State."

"Why's that?" he asked, lighting up, inhaling, holding it deeply in his lungs, speaking in a small constricted voice. "Why's that?"

"Because," she said, echoing something her brother had said years ago, "the railroad means power. And in Mexico only the people with power have any rights. The rest of us have no rights whatever, except the ones we beg, bribe or demand *as a favor* from those in power. Now, in recent years Gallo's gone up very high in the PRI, the ruling party from which all favors flow. But like a lot of Mexican bureaucrats and party hacks of the nouveau riche class, he's become very protective of his reputation, and extremely careful in maintaining all the outward proprieties."

"Now lemme get this straight, doll," Bo said, leaning forward suddenly. "Are you suggesting that we blackmail this guy?"

"Absolutely not," she said. "I'm suggesting that we operate strictly according to the law. I suggest you go to Colima, and hire a lawyer of my acquaintance there. . . ."

"Sounds fabulous, doll," Bo said, after she'd finished running it down for him. "But let's say that things don't work out according to plan."

"We've lost nothing, and we've had ourselves one hell of an adventure," she said. "If things do work out, however, we'll take what we've earned and invest it in our new hotel. Or, if you prefer, we can first invest in a quick-money scheme I have in mind—one that turns on the fact that I know the Mexican producer and you know the Los Angeles distributors of a highly valuable cash crop, thereby eliminating the twenty percent we would owe our contractor."

"You're a genius, doll."

"Not at all."

"There's just one thing."

"What's that?"

"Where you gunna be, all this time that I'm putting my ass on the line up in Manzanillo?"

"Right here waiting for you, Bo," she said, removing her glasses suddenly, regarding herself in the mirror behind the massive Spanish dressing table. What she saw in the mirror was not the small, neatly dressed, delicate young woman—pale as a ghost in her shiny black pageboy haircut—whom she'd seen in her office mirror an hour or two before. What she saw was an arch and wicked little five-year-old with an expression too cunning for her years. "I can't go along with you to Manzanillo because I'm known there, you see, as the daughter of the woman Gallo swindled and turned out into the street."

"Hey," he said. "So we both got a grudge."

"That's the perfection of the thing."

"And you knew who the Bean was all along."

"But I didn't know who *you* were."

"Smart," he said, reaching out to fumble with one of the buttons on her blouse.

"Just common sense," she said, removing his hand, obeying an instinct that superseded her physical attraction entirely. "And let's not try mixing business with pleasure, Bo."

"Listen, don't worry about it," he said, blinking twice, waving his hands in the air to suggest a voluptuous female form. "You ain't my type."

"It's better that way," she said. "Don't you think?"

"You know it, doll," he said.

But he wasn't fooling anyone, and he knew it.

"The reason I say that, Bo," she said, "I had this investor a few months ago. Good-looking young oilman from Texas. Rich as Croesus. After we shook hands on the deal he took me up to his room to sort of . . . put his seal on the thing. 'All right,' I said. 'But there's only one thing. Don't touch my clavicle!' I have a horror of anyone touching my clavicle bone, you see. A kind of phobia. Sends me right up the wall. He wouldn't listen, though, and the whole thing was an unmitigated disaster. In the morning he said he wanted out."

"Count it as a lesson, doll," said Bo, regaining a measure of his old self-confidence. "Like I used to tell the Chicken: 'Never shit where you eat.' It's the golden rule."

CHAPTER 4

After they had ditched the car they took a train to Mazatlán. On the way Merle didn't have too much to say. Actually, he was shocked at what he had done. Val, on the other hand, stayed pretty high, and it was hard to tell how she felt, one way or the other. They checked their bags at the station and caught a taxi to the central plaza. As it happened, it was carnival time in Mazatlán, and the town was jumping. That is to say, the rich and the middle class of the locality had hired some mariachi bands, outfitted themselves in fantastic costumes and masks, gotten themselves tanked up on tequila, and were dancing in the streets with one another's spouses, while the poor—the vast majority of the population—looked on in solemn disbelief, or attempted to sell them trinkets.

Merle and Val got adopted by a young German-Mexican brewer and his wife almost immediately, and were swept about the wealthier sections of the town in a whirlwind of partygoing. Though the gaiety was frantic, the dancing and drinking wild and abandoned, neither Val nor Merle felt much like partaking. They allowed themselves to be led around by the nose, introduced, displayed, chatted to, danced with, without really feeling much. In fact they were overcome by a kind of fatal inertia, as if they were merely waiting for Bo, or the law, to catch up with them.

Dawn found them strolling along the public beach at Olas Altas, barefoot, and a bit dazed. They decided to walk out to the end of the breakwater to catch a little breeze and to watch the sun come up out of the Sierra Madre. On the way, they ran into an Indian couple from the mountains. They were sitting on a rock, cross-legged, in their native costumes. They had a huge pile of marijuana in front of them, and they were sorting the stems from the leaves. The man smiled at Val, and at Merle, and asked if they would like to sample his wares. Merle said they would be delighted, but they had no cash on them at the moment. The man said, "No importa," and proceeded to roll them all a cornhusk cigarette stuffed with his best sinsemilla.

Val and Merle joined the Indians on the rock and sat there smoking with them for most of the morning, chatting about this and that: the weather, the boats on the water, the fish they could see bubbling in the channel. By noon they were wasted. They could barely stand. But the Indian couple had not once shifted their position on the rock or ceased their skillful culling of the stems from the leaves.

"Bye," Val said.

"For the road," the Indian said, and gave her a kilo of mota in a cornmeal sack.

"Gracias," Merle said, and guided her slowly, unsteadily back to the city.

They caught a taxi to the railway station, retrieved their bags, and—on a lark—agreed to take the first train that came along, no matter which way it was going. As it happened, it was bound for Guadalajara. They found a couple of seats in first class and curled up, and they didn't wake up till the train reached Guadalajara Central, at eight o'clock that night.

They got out, rolled themselves a fat one in the parking lot, and started again where they'd left off that morning. This time the first train that came along was the Colima Express. It was packed, but they found a space in a third-class car full of Mexican army soldiers. They were going out to evict a band of militant squatters from a rich landowner's property and were weighted down with combat gear, including loaded M-1 rifles and twelve-inch bayonets.

As the train rolled out of Guadalajara and wound its way into the mountains, the soldiers began sniffing and exchanging glances.

"Qué es esto?"

"La mota?"

"Que sí!"

"Quién tiene la mota?" they shouted. "Who's got the mota? Give us some now or we'll call the conductor!"

"What's going on?" Val wanted to know.

"It's our bag," Merle said. "They smell it."

"So what do we do now?"

"We offer them some," Merle said, "if we're smart."

And sent her over to pour a half-kilo into the corporal's kit bag.

"Muchas gracias, señorita."

"Don't mention it," she said in English, flashing her most photogenic smile.

And for a while everything was copacetic. The soldiers smoked and laughed and joked among themselves and broke into their K rations and gorged themselves on Hershey chocolate. Someone brought out a bottle of mescal, and soon they were singing military songs. They sang "La Valentina," "La Cucaracha," "Adelita" and others of less renown. The songs got louder and louder, lewder and lewder, and presently the soldiers were ogling Val, inviting her to come over and ride on their laps.

"Maybe we ought to display a more neighborly spirit," said Merle.

"You think that'll do it, huh?" said Val. "All right, let's roll a couple of numbers and join the party."

"Señores, may I have the honor of presenting my wife?"

"Encantado, señora, encantado. . . ."

The gesture defused some of the sexual tension, but it did nothing to diminish the noise level. In fact, Val's proximity tended to make them even rowdier, and soon they were competing for her attentions by firing their weapons out the windows, and screaming "Muerte a los oficiales!—Death to the officers!" at the top of their lungs.

And then, to uproarious laughter—"Matalos! Matalos!—Kill them! Kill them!"—the conductor came forward and tried to make them see reason. "Por favor, señores, por favor . . ." But when he encountered resistance—"Matalo! Matalo!"—he withdrew discreetly to wire ahead for reinforcements.

When the train pulled into Tuxpan a whole platoon of Azules, the dreaded head-cracking national police of Mexico, was drawn up on the station platform.

Val and Merle exited out the other side of the car while the train was still in motion and made their way swiftly out of town. Soon they found themselves walking down a long, straight, white-sand road in the light of a full moon.

"Where we going?"

"Damned if I know."

"These bags are going to get heavy."

"Do you mind?"

"I doubt it."

"I have never been higher in my life, Val."

"I've never felt closer to . . ."

"God?"

"Death."

"Same thing."

"Of course," she said, and they laughed together in the silence.

And then the cacti around them melted down and oozed into the cracks in the stone walls beside the road, and suddenly there were a million moons in the sky. The white road stretched away in the white moonlight to infinity. At the end of infinity was a tiny speck that grew larger and larger and became a rural policeman riding a mule, with an old Springfield rifle resting on the pommel of his saddle.

Val and Merle walked straight past him, not even sure he was real.

Apparently he wasn't sure that they were real, either. He blinked his eyes, passed his hand over his face, and sniffed the air. He waited till they were fifty meters down the road before he could clear his throat to speak.

"Alto," he said.

Val and Merle kept right on going. The white road stretched out in front of them again between the cacti and the stone walls, into infinity.

"Alto! Alto! Alto!"

The voice kept getting smaller and smaller behind them. Finally it became almost pathetic, almost begging them to stop.

"Alto?"

Then they heard the report of a rifle shot. The air cracked between them, and whistled away into the distance. The cacti quivered in fright and hid among the rocks.

But Val and Merle kept right on walking, one foot ahead of the other: They were too high to die.

They walked for another hour or so and then a ghostly apparition rose in the moonlight before them—a pair of tall conical mountains, one crowned with snow, the other spouting fire.

Without saying a word, they both knew simultaneously that this was their destination.

"There's a refuge up there," Merle said. "A stone house and a spring with fresh water. You can rent it from the Forest Service for ten pesos a night."

"He'll never find us there."

"Not in a million years."

At the base of the volcano there was a sawmill, a lumberyard and a small village, Atenquique. They awakened the proprietor of the company store and rented a room for the night. In the morning they bought firewood and provisions, took the refuge for fifteen days, left their bags in the care of the Forest Service, hired themselves a guide and a couple of donkeys and set out for the mountain. And they didn't stop till they had reached the stone house, on a saddle of black rock at twelve thousand feet, between the fire and the snow.

They sent the guide and the donkeys back to town. They watched the sun go down. They smoked some more dope. They ate. They drank. They pissed. They shit. They fucked. They slept.

The next day they looked at the view. They could see a hundred miles to the north and south. They could see Guadalajara, Cocula, Ciudad Guzmán, the lakes of Chapala and Zapotlán, the Sayula Grade, the gorge at Diablo Canyon. They could see the entire state of Colima, including the coffee plantations on the slopes of the volcano, the capital city, the coastal banana plain, the delta of the Río Coayuayana, the Lagoon of Cuyutlán, the harbor of Manzanillo and the black Pacific littoral. In the afternoon they fucked again, hungrily, and slept the dreamless sleep of the drugged. They sat up all night, smoking dope, not talking, only touching. There was not a sound in the world but their own breathing—sometimes slow, sometimes fast. No people. No machines. No animals. No insects. No plants. No wind. No rain. It was dry season, and the air was amazingly warm and balmy for this altitude.

They stayed on the mountain for fifteen days, and when they came down Merle knew very little more about Val than when they went up. Yet he was convinced he knew all there was to know.

Her real name was not Val Raymond. "No one is named Val Raymond," she said. Her real name was Maya Kovaks. She was one-quarter

Huron Indian, and three-quarters Slovak, and hailed from Toronto, Canada. She had a basically very sunny disposition, a great sense of humor, and a special feeling for children, animals, poor folks, Mexicans and Negroes. Her education was sketchy, her mental powers unremarkable. She had very little curiosity, and rarely came up with an idea of her own. What she did was—she reacted. But she reacted beautifully, instinctively, playing your sounds right back at you, with maybe an inspired little riff of her own at the end. Yet, all appearances to the contrary, Val was not a shallow person. In fact, Merle found her very deep. As deep and empty as the Sea of Cortez. She was so empty that she was . . . *profound*. She was like space. She was everywhere and she was nowhere. She was anything and everything. She was whatever Merle wanted her to be, and he knew she'd been the same for Bo. You wanted her sweet, she would coo like a dove. You wanted her salty, she would claw your eyes out. You wanted it soft, she would lie there with a smile on her face and you'd never know when she came. You wanted it hot, she'd work you over like the best at the Mustang Ranch. She was a nature girl, a goddess of love. Why else would they want to make her a movie star? In the end he grew to fear her: Without meaning to, with all the best intentions in the world, she might swallow him up without a trace.

"It was great," he said, when they caught the train for Manzanillo. "But it couldn't last."

"No," she said, "I suppose not."

"Where you headed now, Val?"

"Home, I should think."

"Back to Bo?"

"For a while, perhaps."

At the top of the Barrio Chino hill, in a modernistico mansion that overlooked the entire city and bay of Manzanillo, in a long white room with a rollaway glass sunroof, a swimming pool of near Olympic dimensions, and potted palms, flowering tropical plants, glass furniture, handmade Indian rugs and signed originals of Orozco, Siquieros, Rivera, sat Merle's little father, Gallo, presiding over his bountiful luncheon table while a bevy of pretty servant girls in native costume stood behind him, anxiously awaiting his next word of command.

Gallo was in his mid-fifties now, like the century. Manzanillo had changed enormously since he began his journey on a hill across the town, in the slums of the Barbarian Colony. A low, raw, muddy frontier town constructed mostly of rough unpainted timber had been transformed into a bright modern city of paved avenues, streetlights, parks, and two- and three-story stucco buildings painted white, pink, terracotta, sky-blue, green and gold. Indeed, the entire nation had changed since those violent, chaotic days of Gallo's youth. Now there was a visible order in the land, and nearly thirty-five years of relative peace. Now superhighways soared across the mountains that Gallo had so painfully traversed on foot or muleback in the Revolution. The world outside Mexico had changed too. But Gallo, even in his new toupee, and despite the fact that he'd given up his gypsy look for conservative suits and ties, looked exactly as he had always looked, ageless, beyond time.

It was Gallo, in fact, and people like him, who had achieved this miracle of order, this unprecedented peace, this prosperity for the lucky few.

To the right of the patriarch, in the place of honor, sat Val Raymond, the guest of the house, the *pièce de résistance,* big and beautiful and indisputably blond, but looking sullen and uncomfortable in the heat, and splotched all over her face, neck and arms with hard, red, measlelike little insect bites.

To his left sat Merle, the prodigal son. And though Gallo was especially angry at him today, he was also immensely proud, as he had confided last night in the privacy of his book-lined study: "You know, son, for years I could've swore you was gonna turn out a fairy. Taking up 'literature' and all of that shit, like that old cunt Maureen. Then goddam if you don't come walking in with a Hollywood starlet on your arm. Caramba, it was almost worth all the worry you put your aunt and me through for the last two years, and all the money we had to pay out. . . ."

At the other end of the long glass table sat his wife, Carmen, no longer so slim as she once was, but still just as pretty as ever, in the fleshy, overpainted way that Mexican men found attractive. And wealth had done wonders for her temperament: She never pouted or put on saucy faces anymore, and she often went about with a mysterious, self-contented smile, like a fat little brown tabby who'd just made quick work of the mistress's yellow canary.

Carmen was speaking:

"How you like our country, Miss Raymond?"

"I hate it," she said. It was the strongest opinion that Merle had ever heard her express. "I can't wait to get back home."

"We were attacked by mosquitoes on our last night at the refuge," he said. "And I'm afraid that Montezuma's had his little revenge as well."

"The Mexican secret weapon," said Gallo, chortling. "Us chilebeans, we got cast-iron stomachs, no?"

"When you gonna catch your plane, honey?" Carmen wanted to know.

"Tomorrow," Val said wearily. "Unless it breaks down again."

"Say," chirped Gallo. "Is this guy Brodsky really your husband?"

"I beg your pardon?"

"Yeah," he said, smiling insincerely. "He come around the other day with a lawyer from Colima, and Captain Ochoa of the state police. Served me with a denuncio."

"What's a denuncio?" asked Val nervously, turning to Merle for a translation.

"A denuncio," he said, "is a legal document denouncing somebody who's injured you in some way."

"Denounced you kids," said Gallo energetically. "Said you stole his money and ran off in his car and left him out in the desert. Had all kinds of notarized testimony and police depositions to prove it."

"But we haven't touched that money!" Merle protested.

"Where is it, then?"

"Why, it's still in the bag," said Val. "Right where he left it."

"I want you to tell me something, son."

"Sure, Dad."

"How did this guy find us?"

"I don't know."

"And how did he know to file that denuncio in Colima, where I ain't got the clout that I got here? And how did he know to go to Captain Ochoa, who's been a political enemy of mine for the last ten years?"

"Well, I didn't tell him, I can assure you of that."

"Nobody said you did, boy."

"What did he want from you, Mr. Carrizo?" Val inquired.

"Wanted money."

"Did you give it to him, Dad?"

Gallo dropped his fork onto his plate with a clatter. He raised his eyes to the glass ceiling, shrugged his little shoulders and raised his tiny yellow hands, palms upward. "What else could I do?" he said.

"Your dad is going public now, Merle, as a sociedad anónima," Carmen put in, rather proudly. "And we just could not afford a newspaper scandal at this time."

"Like I told the guy," Gallo said, lowering his voice, looking quickly over each shoulder, "'If you was a Mex I'd have you killed. Being as you're a gringo, and just at this moment we in the PRI are courting your President Eisenhower . . .'"

"So what did you do, Dad?"

"I only had one choice, son."

"What was that?"

"Settle out of court."

"How much did he want?"

"Fifteen thousand dollars."

"Whew!"

"Just a moment, Mr. Carrizo," Val interjected. "There is only ten thousand dollars in that bag."

"The compensation, Miss Raymond, was not only for the money. He had a whole list of things that his lawyer had drawn up: theft of property, abandonment, nervous distress, alienation of affections . . ."

"Alienation of affections?" said Val, baffled. "We're not even legally married."

"In Mexico, dear," said Aunt Carmen, "any couple living together in the same house is considered legally married."

"And a judge," Gallo hastened to add, "he might not have too much sympathy for a gringo who lost a bunch of money he shouldn't have been carrying in the first place, but running off with a man's wife is a serious offense."

"Dad," said Merle, "somebody down here must've taken that guy by the hand and led him every step of the way."

"Your daddy's got enemies, Merle, honey."

Merle struggled to suppress a smile. He said, "So what're we gonna do about it?"

"Why don't you tell me, son? I mean, I hate to mention it, and your Aunt Carmen and me are glad to have you back after all this time, but you're the one who got us into this."

"Well, Dad, I don't . . ."

"The way I figure it, boy, we only got two ways to go. Either Miss Raymond gives us the money in the bag, and we call it even, or . . ."

"Now, wait a minute, Dad. That bag is not hers to give. I can't ask her to do that. It's a question of honor."

"Don't gimme that creole shit. We put that to rest in the Revolution."

"I'm sorry, Dad, but it's not up to Val to give us that money."

"Oh, no?" said Gallo, menacing.

"No," said Merle firmly. "But tell me this, Dad. Do you know where Bo is now? Is he still in town?"

"I had a man follow him," Gallo said. "Last time he seen him, he was heading south out of town in a gold-colored Cadillac."

"Do you know any way we could contact him, Val?"

"Sure," she said. "Just phone his law office in L.A. His partner always knows where he is."

"All right," Gallo sighed, gesturing to the youngest and prettiest of his maids. "Traeme el teléfono, por favor."

When she had brought the phone to him, he smiled at Val and said, "Do you mind, Miss Raymond?"

A few moments later she had Los Angeles on the line. "Hello, Morris? Hi, this is Val. Listen, I'm down here in Mexico and Bo and I had a little spat. Got separated, I'm afraid, and now I want to make it up, but I haven't a clue where he's got to. Where? The Tropicana? In Acapulco? Thanks. Bye, love. . . ."

"Now we're getting somewhere," said Gallo, beaming.

"Old Mrs. O'Hare's hotel!" said Aunt Carmen, with real satisfaction.

"You're kidding!" said Merle, growing almost giddy, hurtling backward through time, into his childhood, restraining himself from reaching out for something with his hand in order to regain his balance. Reaching out for Chris's little hand, he thought, in a half-conscious way.

His aunt's voice brought him back to himself. She said, "Nope. Your daddy and me was down there at a railroad convention last year. And some of our friends were staying there. They say Chris is running the place for her, but the old bird is as spry as ever."

"What makes you think she'd put him up to it?"

"She got a grudge, ain't she?" said Gallo, smiling at the memory. "I mean, we sure didn't give her much time to pack her bags when we took over the Hotel O'Hare."

"Not that she didn't deserve it," said Carmen. "Treating us like a buncha peones."

"Val," Merle said, with sudden decision. "You know what I think we ought to do? I think we ought to fly down to Acapulco today."

Val shrugged. It was all the same to her.

"You got it, boy. You go down there and you give him his wife and his bag," said Gallo. "Then I'll have my money back."

"What if he won't give it up?"

Gallo looked at his son with withering scorn, not deigning to answer such a question. He said, "You ladies get to know each other better," and motioned for Merle to follow him into his office next door.

In private he turned on Merle and said, "What kinda asshole question was that? I want that money or I want his balls. I'll give you a week. . . . Here, take this." He reached into his desk, pulling out a slender 7mm Beretta with a chrome finish. "Pussy gun, but it oughta do for you."

CHAPTER 5

". . . So the Kid's dog gets hit by a truck and all of a sudden he's on his own," Bo was saying, when a camarero came across the terrace carrying a phone, calling, "Llamada para Señor Brodsky, Señor Brodsky, por favor."

"Excuse me, doll," he said, patting his mouth with his linen serviette, waving his arm at the waiter. But then it seemed as if it was all just too much to hold back, and the story continued to burble forth anyway, as if it had a life of its own.

". . . And he goes to live with his aunt and uncle, Tony and Bunny Boggiano, down in Little Italy," he said, while the camerero stood sweating in the sunlight, holding the phone. "Now, Tony and Bunny, they are not married, you dig? They are brother and sister. Tony is a widower and Bunny is a maiden aunt. . . ."

"Bo, just a moment," Chris said, smiling up at her incredulous waiter. "Manuel, puedes dejar el teléfono. Gracias."

The camarero put the phone down on the table and went to take the order of a party of sullen French Canadians across the terrace. The phone, with the receiver still off, lay quietly on the white tablecloth, beside an enormous pitcher of Ramos Fizz, as if it too were now mesmerized by Brodsky's incredible patter.

". . . So Bunny is an invalid, see. Never gets up in the morning till everyone is outa the apartment. Hits the sack again as soon as the Kid and his little cousin Jimmy get home from school. Stays in her bedroom behind locked doors for the rest of the evening, scoffing peanut brittle on the sly, listening to the radio with her earphones on. . . ."

"Bo, listen," said Chris. "Listen." But he would not listen. She doubted if he could even *hear* her. Never in her life had she met anyone so driven, so excited by himself, so utterly bound up in the plots and characters of his own imagination. Though the origin of his compulsion was still just as mysterious as ever, it was not nearly so intriguing to her as when he first arrived. The reality of his life, she thought, was bound to be a disappointment after all his fabulous tales. And this notion had the effect of diminishing their impact. Now she often let her mind wander when he talked, and already she found it hard to imagine what she'd ever seen in him. Never had she experienced such a strong physical reaction, followed by such a disappointing letdown of her emotions. On the one hand she was vexed at Bo for failing her, for not living up to her expectations, while on the other she thrilled at the vistas of financial fortune and unfettered freedom of action opening up before her. "Listen, Bo, listen, please," she said, reaching across the table to grab hold of his wrist. "I really think you should take this call. It may be important."

"What? What? Oh sure, doll," he said, reaching out to pick up the receiver.

"Hello! Who? Val! How the fuck you find out where I'm at? Oh yeah? He oughta know better than that. Where you at? Where's the Bean? Uh huh. Figured as much. Nah, that's cool. End of story. It's all a game. Stay right where you are, Chicken, we'll be right there. . . ."

Then he hung up the phone, forgot about what he'd been saying before the interruption, and attacked his cold steak and eggs with a vengeance, with all the energy and concentration that he had devoted to his story. Watching him, amazed as ever by the extremism of his character, it occurred to Chris that he might not have long to live. His talk was too fast, too furious. It would soon burn him out. Not to mention the drugs that he took. And his pulse was too quick, his heartbeat too uneven. His face went an unhealthy red with his exertions. And there were those telltale bags and black circles under his droopy, heavy-lidded eyes. She wondered if Bo knew this about himself, on some level, and if this wasn't the answer to his burning, inexplicable need to dramatize his existence. She hoped that she was wrong about him, and God forbid that she should ever wish it on anybody, but secretly she was glad there were two names on the numbered account they had opened together at the Bank of Acapulco, and that the president was a steady customer at her mother's bar. . . .

"Wanna come for a ride, doll?" he said, after he'd sopped his plate clean with several tortillas and chugalugged the entire pitcher of Ramos Fizz. "Gotta go pick up my old lady and her boyfriend."

"I was about to phone our man in the mountains," she said. "There's still a couple of things I'd like to go over with him."

"Can't it wait?"

"How long?"

"Long enough to drive out to the airport and back?"

"I don't see the point, Bo. I mean, won't it just make things more complicated?"

"I'll tell you a secret, doll. This is how the Kid operates: The more the merrier. Throw everything in the pot, mix it up, apply heat, and see how it all comes out."

"What if it doesn't come out the way you want?"

"I have varied tastes," Bo said. "And I love surprises."

"I see," she said, refolding her napkin carefully on the table. She also had varied tastes. But she hated surprises.

"Or better still," he said. "Why don't we just drive straight up to the mountains?"

"With them and their bags and all?"

"Sure," he said, taking her arm, escorting her across the terrace and into the lobby. "They still got the money, you know. I imagine old Merle's gunna eventually be asking for his daddy's fifteen large. But for the moment they ain't spent a dime."

"Oh," she said. "Well, that's pleasant news. Now let me see. With a discount for volume, it should buy us twice as much merchandise, which should net us four hundred percent at the border, which means that we may not have to take out a mortgage loan on the hotel at all, because with cash in U.S. dollars the owner is bound to come way down on the price."

"And you know," Bo said, as they went down the stairs and across the parking lot, "we may have some use for the Bean on this deal. We still ain't got a driver, you dig."

"Why would Merle want to get involved in a thing like this?"

"We'll tell him he don't get Papa's bread back," Bo said, getting into the Cadillac, "unless he does what we say."

"Will he get it back?"

"No," he said, switching on the air conditioning. "But he don't know that."

"I see."

A resistance was building inside her. Though she'd been willing to use Merle, she had no desire to see him hurt. The truth was that her motives in this caper were vague and conflicting, and had been from the very beginning. On one hand, she had wanted to seduce Bo into some kind of partnership. On the other hand, she had wanted to get back at Gallo on behalf of her mother, and win a measure of her respect, if not affection. And on some level the whole thing had been a mere ploy, she thought, to reestablish contact with Merle and find out what sort of man he had become.

"How do you know he won't just run off with the goods again, Bo?" she asked.

"He can't do that."

"Why not?"

"You can't take that much dope and just, like, sell it on the street, doll," Bo said, as they drove down her mother's jacaranda-lined driveway to the Costera Alemán. "You gotta have a whole distribution network set up. And also, those cats he's gunna be dealing with, they are bad. They'd have his ass, no matter how far they had to chase him."

I'll have yours first, Bo, she was thinking, as they tooled along by the sparkling blue waters of Acapulco Bay, past the yacht club, the central plaza, the Mercado de Curiosidades, the custom house, Fort San Diego, on their way to meet the only friend Chris could recall ever having.

They were standing out front, under the carport, beside a pile of expensive, battered luggage. A leggy, vacant-eyed blonde in a sweat-stained blouse and wrinkled capris, and a good-looking Mexican, several years her junior, in a tan, new-looking Ivy League suit and loafers. They had attracted a circle of curious onlookers, several of whom appeared to have recognized her. There was something illicit in the couple's aspect—a suggestion of sexual misconduct common enough during the film festival season but rarer at this time of year—that pandered to the crowd's basest instincts.

Bo pulled up on the right and sprang out to open the trunk for the porter, leaving Chris to welcome his rather sheepish guests. Chris got out tentatively, said nothing at all to the blonde—who made her feel suddenly tiny, anemic and prim—and hurried past her to Merle.

"Would you recognize me anywhere?" she laughed, in a shy, girlish way, quite genuine, for she had never been less sure of herself than she was at this moment.

"Sure, you still look like a kid," he said, smiling uncertainly, clearly disarmed. He was as he had been as a boy, dark and solid, with an incongruously sensitive mouth and an indefinable aura of future promise.

"I didn't want you to forget me!" she said, and threw herself into his arms.

"I gathered that," he said, "from recent events."

"I've had very little to do with recent events," she whispered, contriving to sound as if she were in some way Bo's captive. "Don't judge me."

"I won't," he said, holding her at a distance, searching her face, "if I get my father's money back."

"You'll have to take that up with Bo," she said helplessly, and turned to include Val in the conversation.

And they all stood there awkwardly under the carport for another minute or two, making small talk, waiting for Bo to finish with the porter. Yet, as soon as he'd seen to the luggage and locked the trunk, he inexplicably ran around the other side, jumped in behind the wheel again, and honked the horn, shouting, "Come on, let's get a move on!" as if they were all in some kind of dreadful hurry.

Chris opened the door on the passenger side, and Merle climbed into the backseat. Val squeezed past her and sat in front with Bo. Chris climbed in back with Merle, and they were off.

It was Val who spoke first.

"When we start assigning blame, Bo," she said, as they were rounding the Diana Fountain, "I want you to know that the whole thing was my fault."

"Nah."

"Really."

"Hey, you know what?"

"What?"

"The Kid had it coming," he said, and pulled her roughly to his side.

"I'd like to offer my apologies too, Bo."

"Put 'er there, pard."

"Now that all that's settled," Merle said, with an unduly humorous air, "how's about letting me have my old man's bread back? Otherwise he's gonna disinherit me."

"Say, that'd be a shame, wouldn't it?" Bo said. And then, catching sight of Merle's face in the rearview mirror: "Hey, a joke! A joke! Seriously, honcho, I don't have it in liquid, at the moment. Chris and me, we are floating this deal."

"How long before you have it in cash?"

"Depends."

"On what?"

"You."

"Me?"

"Yeah."

"How?"

"I'll let you know."

"When?"

"When the time is right, man," he said. Then he lit up a marijuana cigarette, passed it around, and suddenly resumed his brunchtime story, right where he'd left it off.

"So, where was I, Chris? Oh yeah. So my Aunt Bunny, she is like a fat lady in the circus, man. She's the most monstrously fat human being you have ever seen. Says she's got 'female trouble' but nobody outside the immediate family believes her. Never leaves the apartment, even for Mass. Has the priest come to *her*. She's got everyone bamboozled. Lives like a fucking queen. End of story. It's all a game. She's got her nephew Jimmy eating out of her hand. Her brother is selflessly devoted. The bitch will outlive them all. . . ."

"Say, just a second," Merle said. He had noticed that Bo had passed by the hotel strip on the La Caleta Peninsula and was heading out of town on the Calzada de la Cuesta. "Where we going?"

"To Aguas Blancas."

"Where's that?"

"In the mountains."

"What're we gonna do up there?"

"We got business."

"What kind of business?"

"You'll find out when we get there, honcho. Now lemme finish the story," Bo said. ". . . So Aunt Bunny, she weighs in at four hundred and fifty pounds and she's got a head like a bowling pin but everybody loves her. She's even got a *boyfriend.* Little guy named Harry. Comes calling every Sunday, just before the priest. Bald-headed, bulbous-eyed cat with bad breath. Lives with his eighty-year-old father over on Elizabeth Street. Looks like an ax murderer. Works for the Sanitation Department. . . ."

As Bo's voice droned on, and the car droned on, and Val nodded off in the front seat, Chris let her mind wander into the past. She saw herself and Merle as kids, playing on the black-sand beach with little Delia, kicking up spray and letting the wind blow it back into their mouths. She saw Ramona, looking impossibly young, impossibly beautiful, in her brown cotton dress and French heels, standing on a sand dune in the wind, calling them back. In her daydreams she often thought of Ramona with Brian, though she'd rarely seen them together in life. . . . She saw Brian come walking up behind Ramona on the sand hill, in his straw hat turned down at either end, his white linen suit and two-toned, wing-tip shoes. And the two of them just stood there smiling, waving, calling out, "Come back, kids, come back now!"

But the drive seemed to have the opposite effect on Merle, the effect that Bo obviously intended: He sweated, he fidgeted in his seat, his breath came in short anxious gasps.

"Chris," he whispered in Spanish, leaning close. "I feel like I've just taken up right where I left off with these people. It's like nothing has changed."

"Oh," she murmured, glimpsing the outline of a small pistol in his back pocket, "things have changed all right."

"What?" he said, perhaps noting the shift from the helpless tone she'd used before.

"Shhhhhh," she said, patting him gently on the thigh, shivering at the feel of his breath on her ear. "Estoy a tu lado, mi amor. No tengas miedo—I'm on your side, my love. You have nothing to fear."

And allowed her mind to meander pleasantly again, into the happier byways of their mutual past—certainly not challenging her own subconscious motivation, or the mystery of her allegiance—watching the scenery whiz by outside her window.

They were riding north on a narrow coastal plain, through groves of bananas, papayas, guavas, chirimoyas and coconut palms, with the bright-blue Pacific on their left and the brown, dry-season foothills of the Sierra Madre del Sur on their right. A BAJO EL IMPERIALISMO YANQUI! said a sign painted on a boulder in red. And another, in black, on the wall of an adobe schoolhouse: LIMPIEZA ES CULTURA—Cleanliness is culture. And yet another, on a billboard, showing a buxom peroxide blonde tilting a bottle of light-colored beer: LA RUBIA QUE TODOS QUIEREN—The blonde that everyone wants. The plain was rich and tropical green, thickly cultivated, but the people were miserably poor, and their villages consisted of little more than clusters of jacales made of bamboo and scrap tin and palm thatch. Every five or ten miles a shallow river made its way to the sea. There the women washed their pathetic bundles of rags, potbellied children played, and gaunt, hollow-eyed men watered their dusty mounts. Once or twice a decade these peasants of the hinterlands of Guerrero, the poorest and most backward state in Mexico, rose up in armed revolt, demanding LAND TO THE TILLER, and the army had to come along and put them down. The last uprising had been only a few months ago, when Chris and her mother, to their utter dismay, learned that the officer in charge of putting down the insurrection was none other than their former fire-eating adversary on the left, General Raúl Mondragón. Chris and Maureen had been brought up to date on the general's career by Señora Limantour Ortega, the wife of the minister of defense, shortly before her unfortunate adventure with Mrs. O'Hare's beachboy. Apparently Mondragón had made a lot of enemies in the late thirties, when he was minister of transport in the cabinet of President Cárdenas. In a misguided attempt to democratize the National Railway, he had given over its administration to elected committees of workers and union officials, with the predictable results. Having no executive experience, they spent all their time arguing, and never could agree among themselves long enough to formulate an effective plan of action. Incompetence, waste, pilferage and corruption prevailed. Railroad lines and rolling stock fell into disrepair. And by the time the Ávila Camacho administration came to power in 1940, the railway had virtually ground to a halt. The plight of the National Railway seemed even more serious when viewed in contrast to the Colima Pacific Railway, which had been left under its previous administration, and was still running at a profit. In the inevitable reaction to the excesses of the Cárdenas regime, Mondragón's head was among the first to roll. He was demoted to major and exiled to a remote post in the Revillagigedo Islands. After four years in the islands, however, in the arid doldrums five hundred miles off the coast of Colima, Mondragón saw the error of his ways. And for the next decade or so he slowly worked his way back up the ranks through loyal service to the ruling party, and unquestioned obedience to his commanding officers. Over the years, he attended several staff colleges abroad, as well as the United States Army Jungle Warfare School in Panama, and he established a reputation as an expert in antiguerrilla warfare. Therefore, Señora Limantour Ortega had said, it was only natural that he had been selected by the high command to lead the operation against the insurrectionists in Guerrero State.

Mexico, Mexico, Chris was thinking, trying to imagine Mondragón's transformation from radical revolutionary to loyal supporter of a sclerotic status quo. And then she thought, as she often did, of something her brother, Brian, had once said: "Mexico, Mexico, the more you change, the more you stay the same!"

Meanwhile, Val had begun to lightly, daintily snore in the front seat, and Merle in his agitation—despite Chris's assurances—seemed about to scream, and Bo's voice carried on without a pause, without a thought, with nary a breath.

That mouth simply cannot be left to go on indefinitely, Chris thought.

". . . So old Harry, he takes the Kid out for a walk this one time, see. Over to Washington Market, in the produce district. There's this vacant lot on the banks of the Hudson where he's got an old junked Model T jacked up on blocks. A kind of clubhouse, with curtains, a bed, a little table, the works. He's even got a little front yard, with grass and flowers and rocks piled up in queer shapes. The only thing is . . . the Kid checks it out and it's all littered with bone chips and little pieces of rotting meat. 'You gotta dog, Harry?' the Kid asks. 'Nope,' says Harry. And the Kid gets a little nervous, then, you dig. And he looks around some more and he finds this sort of tower that Harry has built out of scrap lumber and driftwood, with a crow's nest—sort of like a tree house—that he's built up on top. The Kid climbs up the ladder and has a peek inside. There's more meat and bones and a funny smell and grafitti all over the wall. GODHELPME GODHELPMEGODHELPMEGODHELPME, it says, scrawled over and over in what looks like blood. Well, the Kid makes it down that ladder like a bat outa hell and splits for home. But by the time he's halfway there, he's already starting to think that he must've imagined the whole thing. Like, this is his aunt's *fiancé,* for Christ's sake. . . ."

Just beyond the Río Tepextixtla Bridge, Bo turned off the main highway and followed a dirt road that wound along the river into the mountains. AGUAS BLANCAS—10 KILOMETROS, said a rusty, bullet-perforated road sign. The origin of the name was no mystery, as everything in these parts—the road, the sun, the sky, the rocks, the walls of the canyon, the riverbanks, the water, even the dusty tamarind trees, and the goats that grazed on their lower branches, and the village itself, when it came into sight—was a blinding, overexposed white.

Bo drove into the central plaza, trailing a great cloud of dust, sending pigs and chickens scurrying for cover. Unlike the villages of the coast, this was a permanent, substantial kind of place, with a church, a municipal palace, a police station, and tile-roofed houses instead of flimsy jacales. There was even a branch of the Bank of Acapulco, reflecting the prosperity of the local economy, which depended entirely upon the illicit crops that were grown on tiny plots of terraced land in virtually inaccessible parts of the nearby Sierra.

It was siesta time in Aguas Blancas, and the plaza was deserted, save for a couple of scrawny chickens that remained on the steps of the church. Bo pulled up in front of an ancient two-story adobe house next door to the shuttered bank. On the whitewashed facade of the house an old-fashioned horse-drawn hearse and a coffin were crudely, hugely represented in black, under which, in vivid red, a sign was painted:

FUNERALES ALTAMIRANO
Capillas Confortables—Translados Internacionales
ALEJO ALTAMIRANO, PROP.

ALTAMIRANO FUNERAL PARLOR
Comfortable Chapels—International Shipments
ALEJO ALTAMIRANO, PROP.

On the low, tile-roofed veranda that ran the length of the front facade, a manila hammock was hanging between two of the supporting pillars. In the hammock, swinging slowly, lay a bald, paunchy, yellow-faced man of about forty-five, with a three-day growth of beard on his face. A mangy, dun-colored, Egyptian-looking dog reclined beneath him, next to a radio turned up to top volume and tuned to a popular music station. The white dust settled. Flies swirled about the veranda. Cicadas buzzed in the dusty alamo tree in the center of the plaza. The man continued to sway, the dog continued to sleep. On the radio a Danzón number concluded and a Huaracha began, very hot and catchy and danceable: But who would want to dance, at such a time, in such a place?

Bo let his engine die. The air conditioning stopped. The temperature in the Cadillac soared. Val awakened from her nap, wiped her brow. Merle looked as if he might melt right down into his own anxiety, into his sopping Ivy League suit. But Bo made no move to open his door, or to lower the electric windows. And nobody said a word. And the white dust lay like a pall upon the golden car. And the story went on.

". . . So this one Sunday, old Harry, he comes to call as usual, see. And he's got this big canvas bag with him. Says he's got a present for Bunny. She lets him in her room and she locks the door and gives him his weekly kiss and he sits down on the edge of the bed. 'I brought this for you, honey,' he says, and pulls out a human head. It's the head of an old woman, with long gray hair. Bunny starts screaming and gets him scared and he pulls out a collapsible Boy Scout hatchet with a blood-stained blade and starts fitting it together while Bunny just sits on the bed squealing like a stuck pig, too fat to move, and the Kid and Tony and the priest, Father Falco, are outside the door pounding on it and Harry raises the hatchet and just as old Bunny is about to be *beheaded,* Tony breaks down the door. 'Now you stop that, Harry,' says Father Falco. 'You put that hatchet down this instant!' And Harry, like, he is a devout Catholic, you dig, and he *listens.* Uncle Tony calls the cops and they haul him down to the First Precinct and grill him for twenty-four hours and . . . end of story. It's all a game. Turns out the cat's just what he looks like, an ax murderer. Admits to seven unsolved crimes. All women, all overweight."

"Never heard that one before," Val said, reaching for the door handle.

"I tell my stories to illustrate a point."

"What was the point of that one?" Merle wanted to know.

"If you don't know that yet, honcho," Bo said, getting out of the car, "you ain't playing with a full deck."

Señor Altamirano was not happy to be bothered at siesta time, even on a matter of business. He was slow to respond to Chris's greeting, slow to swing out of his hammock, slow to offer his hand, and even slower to welcome them all into his house, which doubled as a funeral home and mortuary. The place was dark, tile-floored, sparsely furnished and spacious, with long cool corridors and mysteriously locked doors and gaudy little side chapels decorated with Christmas lights. He led them through to the inner courtyard and motioned them to make themselves comfortable at a table set out on the tiles. Then, quite unceremoniously, he left them. It was not so hot in the courtyard, but the cicadas in the shade tree made such a racket you could barely hear yourself think.

"Can someone tell me what's going on here?" Merle pleaded, looking from one of them to the other.

"No te preocupes, querido," Chris said, but he did not seem reassured.

Altamirano came back out to the patio a few minutes later, trailing a little Indian maid with a tray of ice-cold beer. She popped the tops neatly with an old-fashioned church key and passed them around with lime and salt. And nobody said another word until they had all downed their first bottle and were working on their second.

"Señor Altamirano," Chris said. "My friend has an offer to make."

"Tell it," he said, expressionless, folding his hands in his lap.

"If you double the shipment, he will give you an additional ten thousand dollars in cash."

"Only ten?"

"That's all he's got."

"Well, all right," he said, unfolding his hands, reaching for another beer. His hands were as yellow as his face. It was as if he had jaundice. And his fingernails were extraordinarily long and dirty. "But it will take some time to get it ready. Would you care to accept my hospitality for the night?"

Chris said they would be pleased to accept, and he showed them to their rooms on the ground floor.

"There are only two rooms for guests," he said gravely. Altamirano was incapable of humor. "How shall we arrange it?"

Chris looked at Bo. Bo looked at Val. Merle stared at the wall.

"If no one has any objections," Chris said, "I think it might be best if we separated according to sex."

"Fine by me," said Bo. And, grinning malevolently, he threw an arm around Merle and pulled him off down the corridor. "You don't mind sleeping with the Kid, do you, honcho?"

"It's the last room on the left," said Altamirano, and opened the door to the ladies' bedroom.

It was a surprisingly comfortable room, Chris found, with running water, cool tile floors, smooth whitewashed walls five feet thick, enormously high ceilings, a single dangling light bulb, and narrow, tightly shuttered windows to keep out the heat and light from the courtyard.

After Altamirano had disappeared, Chris rang for the maid and sent her out for a bucket of ice and some more beer. Then she and Val took off their clothes—which were covered with white dust and saturated with perspiration—washed them out in the bathroom sink, and hung them up to dry on the shutters, the door handles, the hat pegs, and the bedstead. Then they each had a nice, long, cold shower and came back out to sit naked and cross-legged on the old Spanish bed, with the counterpane turned back and the sheets coolly exposed. Their hanging panties and bras, the empty beer bottles that collected on the floor, the curling smoke of Val's marijuana cigarettes (which she insisted on smoking despite Chris's warning that Altamirano didn't like it) and their nude young bodies gave to the room an intimate, festive air that belied the awkwardness of the situation and the utter alienation that each of them felt from the other.

Naked, in fact, Chris felt like a mere wisp, a token before the altar of Val's flesh, and it was several minutes before she could bring herself to say a word. "What a glamorous existence you must've led, Val," she finally said, just to break the ice.

"What? In Hollywood? You must be joking!"

"Was it that bad?"

"Oh," she said, laughing carelessly. "Maybe not so bad as all that, while it lasted."

"What're you going to do now?"

"Dunno."

"You're not going to stay with Bo?"

"Well," she said. "That's what I thought I might do. But you know, as soon as I got into his car and he started up on those bloody stories again, I thought, oh dear God, here we go again. And I wondered if I wasn't going to have to play this role forever."

"What role is that, Val?"

"You know," she said, pursing her lips, fluffing her poodle cut and cocking her ear in an expert mime of a doting little wife, hanging on to her husband's every word.

"Then don't play it."

"What else is there to do?" she said.

She was one of the most hopeless cases that Chris had ever come across. And you come across a lot, running a hotel in Acapulco. The idea of such will-lessness, coupled with such exquisite beauty, was immensely exciting to her, and aroused all her most manipulative and acquisitive instincts.

"Val, I'm going to need a hostess in my new hotel," she said. "Someone very chic and worldly and pleasant to look at. The pay is great. I'm even willing to discuss a commission deal, or a share of the profits."

"Will Bo be investing in the hotel as well?"

"Yes," she said, wondering what was going on in the room down the hall. "But I have a feeling he won't last long."

"No?" Val said. "No, I suppose not. Well, I'll give it some thought."

But it was apparent that she wouldn't. She'd have to be roped into it. She was incapable of making a decision on her own.

"What's he like in bed?" Chris asked, a while later.

"Who? Bo? You mean you don't *know?*"

"Oh, it's strictly business between us, Val."

"Well, to be frank," she said, "it's not very nice. I don't think he likes it, in any normal sense. I've always had the feeling he was just sort of . . . using me. To attract people. You know."

"What kind of people?"

"All kinds, really. But more often young than old, men more than women. He has a style that appeals more to the masculine mind, I think. At home in Beverly Hills we've always got these houseguests. Out-of-work actors, drifters, free-loaders. His stories, you see, they're exhausting. They're voracious. He has to keep finding new fodder all the time."

"Are they true, do you think?"

"His stories? I don't know, really. I don't think he knows, anymore."

About midnight, Bo knocked at the door and asked if they felt like a bite to eat.

"You bet!" Chris hollered back. "We're starving!"

She and Val wrapped themselves in sheets, and a few minutes later he came swaggering in, wearing only a pair of white skivvies, his golden dollar sign and a Panama hat. He was bearing an enormous steaming platter of Mexican food. Merle tagged rather sullenly behind in jockey shorts, carrying a tray of beer.

Merle sat down with Chris and Val on the bed to have his dinner, but Bo paced up and down the room, stuffing whole tamales in his mouth, drinking beer from a liter bottle, telling tales. At first his stories were just sort of run-of-the-mill Bo: loneliness, alienation, violence, betrayal, death. Then after the meal, and a couple of mota cigarettes, they began to take a sexual turn.

". . . So, the Kid comes up early, you dig. By the time he gets outa I.S. 70 he's already got a five-o'clock shadow, and eighteen-year-old Rican chickens are fighting for his action under the stoop. So he fast-talks his way into an Arthur Murray gig in Times Square, dancin' and romancin' older ladies for what he can get. And, hey, he gets a lot: cash, jewels, dinner at the Waldorf, stocks and bonds, new cars, threads, expensive presents. . . . End of story. It's all a game. And don't knock that gray-haired pussy, man. Every fuck is like their last. They put their whole *life* into it. . . ."

Each time that Bo reached the far end of the room, he would pause for a few seconds to regard himself in the full-length mirror that hung there. He seemed fascinated by what he saw, and spent long seconds rolling his eyes, tweaking his mustache, showing his enormous teeth. It was as if the imaginary Bo, the Kid who came out in his stories, was more vividly real to him than the Bo who stood before him in the flesh. And he always seemed a bit surprised, when he mugged into the mirror, to find confirmation of his existence there. Then on his swing back to the other end of the room he would stop and face his audience on the bed, as if they were another kind of mirror. And he would reach out—to punctuate some point he was trying to make—and touch Merle (never Chris or Val) on the naked toe, the foot, the knee, while his victim watched, more enraged by the second.

The expression on Merle's face, during these long, tense moments, was extraordinary to behold, and brought out all of Chris's most tender and protective instincts: His look was not unlike the one he used to wear around his father, when Gallo was suggesting that Merle was less male than he ought to be. It was the look of a budding patricide.

". . . So it turns out that Uncle Tony is a closet queen, man. They catch him and Sergeant O'Reilly on the floor of a stall in the police horse barn at Precinct 1, wearing ladies' knickers and going sixty-nine, and retire them both from the force on full medical pensions, thanks to the efforts of the Police Benevolent Association. . . ."

"Excuse me, Bo," said Merle, calm, too calm to be true. "You say you tell your stories to illustrate some point. Well, what's the point of this one?"

"Wanna see what you're made out of, boy."

"I'm not made out of that kind of stuff."

"Every man has his breaking point."

"You know that for a fact?"

"Eventually it all comes out," Bo said, reaching out to casually singe the hair on Merle's arm with his lit marijuana cigarette. "You'd be surprised at the studs that crack."

"Come on, Bo," Chris said, not wanting Merle to explode. "Lay off."

"Really," said Val. "What do you want from the poor boy?"

"I want his bod," Bo said, leering, pinching him hard on the cheek. "And if I can't have that, I want him to be my man."

"What kind of man?"

"I want him to be my driver."

"Your what?"

"He don't drive that shit to the border, he don't get his daddy's money back."

Merle got a shifty, trapped look in his eye; and then, glancing around for moral support from Chris and Val, spoke up in his own defense:

"What guarantee have I got that you'll pay me back?"

"My word is my bond."

"That's not good enough."

"You calling me a liar, punk?"

"I'll guarantee it for you, Merle," said Chris. "You trust my word, don't you?"

Reluctantly, Merle agreed.

But Bo couldn't help having the last word.

"Love against nature, that is my meat!" he sang, whirling about the room on the balls of his feet, like an Arthur Murray dancer. "And sooner or later, honcho, your ass will be mine."

At dawn Altamirano came to the door.

"Todo listo," he said. "Get your things on and meet me in the patio."

A few minutes later and they were all out back, peering into the rear of a big old Packard, a Black Maria. It was half-filled with small, tightly wrapped bales of marijuana. FUNERALES ALTAMIRANO, said a sign on the tailgate.

"What do you think, Bo?"

"Looks good."

"Now I think he's going to want to see the money."

"I'll be right back."

"We'll meet you in the courtyard," Chris said. "The maid's going to bring us some coffee and cognac."

Bo went out to the car and returned with the black bag. He laid it on the ground beneath the shade tree, unlocked it and motioned for Altamirano to open it up and have a look inside. Then he sat down to his coffee and cognac.

"Qué es esto, un chiste?—What is this, a joke?"

Bo leaned across, tipped the bag over, and emptied its contents onto the tile. It was filled with reams of paper, *Empresa Carrizo* printed on each one.

"Now you only owe me five," said Merle evenly. But Chris had caught his startled look when Altamirano opened the bag. And she could feel him trembling beside her at the table.

"Smart," said Bo, tossing down his cognac, tipping back his hat.

"I thought so," said Merle, rising, kicking the chair over behind him.

"Qué pasa?" said Altamirano, sensing danger. "Qué pasa?"

"But the joke's on you, honcho," said Bo, smiling. And lunged, losing his hat, gripping Merle by the lapels of his suit jacket. And dragged him hard across the table, upsetting hot coffee, sending the cognac bottle rolling over the edge, shattering on the floor.

"Take your hands off of me!"

"Qué pasa?" said Altamirano, backing away from the table, reaching under his guayabera. "Qué pasa?"

"His dad must've done it, Bo," said Val, touching him on the shoulder. "Honestly, I don't think he knew."

"Liars!" he said, whacking Merle across the chops with the front and back of his hand. "Liars!"

"Stop it, Bo, I'm warning you."

Merle drew the pistol from his back pocket and shoved it in Bo's side.

"I told you to stop, Bo."

But Altamirano had already pulled out a piece of his own, a big black .38 Super. And stuck it in Merle's ear.

"Dejalo caer, cabrón."

Merle wanted to drop that pistol. Chris could see him trying to shake the trigger off his finger.

"He wasn't going to give you the money anyway, Merle," she said. Why she said it, she couldn't imagine. And she would wonder about it the rest of her life.

Merle was still trying to drop that pistol. But it was as if he had some kind of muscle spasm in his finger, and the gun went off. Not very loud, it went off. A kind of small, muffled pop.

Val screamed.

Bo went white. A look of surprise crossed his handsome, saturnine face.

"End of story," he said. "It's all a game."

Val ran to his side, but recoiled in horror when he slid to the ground, coughing and vomiting blood.

Merle let go of the pistol, and it clattered onto the chair where Bo had sat drinking coffee and cognac, a moment before.

Merle had his eyes closed now, waiting for the shot.

Altamirano looked at Chris. Chris shook her head.

"Call the police," he said. "In this town the walls have ears."

An unnatural calm prevailed over the courtyard until the doctor and the chief of police could be summoned by the maid. Val recovered rapidly from her shock, and remarked in a tense but steady tone that the next of kin would have to be notified, and that Morris would have to be called in from Los Angeles, to represent Bo's interests. Chris agreed, but advised her of her rights as a common-law wife under Mexican law: In the absence of a locally filed will, she was the sole executor of her husband's estate within the boundaries of the Republic. Altamirano warned Merle to keep his mouth shut and let him do the talking if he valued his hide. Merle simply smiled and nodded his head; Chris thought he must be suffering from shock. And they all stood there patiently, in more or less the same positions they had occupied at the time of death, while Bo seeped blood and relaxed his bowels and collected flies.

Already Chris found that she had begun to resent his corpse.

The doctor arrived and pronounced Señor Brodsky dead. "Cause of death: gunshot wound; path of bullet: entering 3 cm below left lower rib, exiting 1.5 cm left of right collarbone." Then the chief of police took charge, and proceeded to reconstruct the incident in detail. Coolly, methodically, in a manner that would have met the approval of the deceased himself, he took written depositions from the witnesses, starting with Altamirano and concluding with the maid. He noted the location of the weapon on the chair and tagged it as evidence. He retrieved the cartridge and a spent bullet from the floor of the patio. He outlined the position of the body in chalk, and had it removed to the town icehouse before it began to stink in the heat. He telephoned the examining magistrate in the local administrative center, Coyuco de Benítez, and was directed to hold Merle as a material witness, pending an inquest. Chris and Val were released to seek a lawyer for Merle, and to attend to urgent private business with the president of the Bank of Acapulco. Merle was taken into custody, handcuffed and marched away to the town jail.

His cell was small, hot, damp and smelly, but he didn't really mind, he told Chris. He was relieved to be alone at last, wanted time to sort out his feelings.

Merle spent a week locked up in jail. And, as far as Chris could tell, he spent far more time examining the physical aspects of his cell—the color of light on the adobe walls and the tin ceiling at different times of the day and night, the size, shape and number of pebbles on his dirt floor, the varying textures of the scum on the surface of his slop can, the general nature and individual idiosyncrasies of the flies, mosquitoes, bedbugs and scorpions who kept him company—than he spent examining his own state of mind.

Bo had been such a vivid, overwhelming presence in his life, he said, that he still could not accept the fact that he was dead. He didn't believe that Bo himself would accept it, he said, and he kept expecting him to walk into his cell any moment, or to hear his voice outside in the plaza: ". . . *So the Kid wakes up in an icehouse, man, and just as they're about to fill him up with embalming fluid* . . ."

"Just for the record," Merle said, on the day before the inquest, "I don't think I meant to kill him, but I can't say I'm sorry he's dead."

"He had it coming," Chris said. She was enormously pleased that he chose her, not Val, to confide in. "He was asking for it."

"I suppose the guilt will come later. Right now, the only regret I feel is for myself, for fucking up my life to such an incredible extent."

"The man was like a pall on the planet, Merle," Chris said, recoiling at the notion of Merle's future sense of guilt, worrying that months and years hence he would blame her for putting him into such a position with Bo. "I've talked to Val and she feels the same. He was pure negativity. Wherever he went he spread bad feelings."

"The irony is that my father got even more than he wanted."

"What did he want?"

"He wanted his balls or he wanted his money, and he got both."

"You'll never forgive him for that, will you, Merle?"

"Hey," he said. "What kind of father would use a son like that?"

The inquest was held at the scene of death, with the examining magistrate, Merle, Merle's lawyer, Gallo and Carmen Carrizo, who insisted on attending despite Merle's refusal to speak to his father, Chris, Val, Altamirano, the maid, the doctor, the police chief, and Bo's partner, Morris (accompanied by a bilingual lawyer), in attendance. Morris was as short, pudgy and ordinary-looking as Bo had been tall, slender and imposing. But he had done his homework. He brought evidence of Merle's prior conviction, under suspiciously similar circumstances, in the state of California. He stated his opinion that there was a possibility of foul play in the case, as three of the witnesses had motives for murder. When asked by the magistrate to substantiate his charges, he presented evidence that Merle had recently cohabitated with the common-law wife of the deceased, that Chris held a joint bank account with the deceased and had used the balance as a down payment on the purchase of an Acapulco hotel, and that Val had the obvious motivation of love for Merle and desire to obtain the funds in Bo's secret numbered account at the Bank of Acapulco. Furthermore, he said, he had obtained information that Miss Raymond had already obtained these funds and now intended to assume the deceased's place as co-owner of the hotel, in association with Miss O'Hare. Not to mention the deceased's palomino gold Cadillac, which she had simply appropriated as her own.

While granting that the said individuals did perhaps have potential motives for murder, the magistrate ruled that no evidence existed that they had actually plotted or carried out such a crime. Indeed, he said, according to the sworn testimony of the maid, and of Señor Altamirano, with whom the deceased had been visiting in Aguas Blancas to discuss a possible business venture, the death was purely accidental, a result of the deceased's own volatile and impetuous nature.

Before the magistrate made a final ruling, however, Morris requested and was granted a motion to have an autopsy performed. The autopsy, which was undertaken by the local doctor in the icehouse, among the frozen carcasses of goats, pigs, and chickens, uncovered no evidence that Bo's death had resulted from any action save that described by the witnesses, insomuch as the bullet, on its journey from the left lower rib to the right collarbone, had traveled through the left ventricle and right auricle. Incidentally it was found that the deceased had not long to live in any case, as he suffered from hardening of the arteries in the heart, and cancer of the larynx.

The examining magistrate ruled "justified homicide," and Merle was released from custody. His father and his Aunt Carmen were so overjoyed by the result of the inquest that they felt they had something "in common" with Chris at last. And they approached her with an olive branch. They all agreed that justice had been served in the case, and that the score between them was now even. They even shook hands on it.

Despite all their best efforts, however, neither Chris nor Carmen could convince Merle to bury the hatchet with his father.

"It took me all these years to get free of him," Merle said, a bit self-dramatically, Chris thought. "Why should I sell myself into slavery again?"

Later, when Gallo came around complaining about Merle's "hard-heartedness," Chris just shrugged and said, "Think about it, Gallo. Maybe he's got a legitimate grievance."

"Maybe he has," Gallo said insincerely—he was absolutely incapable of looking one in the eye. "But anyway, dear, I sure do appreciate all your help in that inquest. I really do."

"Don't thank me for that," Chris said. "Thank Altamirano."

"Altamirano? What's he got to do with it?"

"The chief of police is on his payroll," she whispered. "And the examining magistrate is his cousin."

"When'd you find that out?"

"I knew it all along."

"Say, you're one of my own stripe, sweetheart," Gallo lisped, in confidence, just as he and Carmen were leaving to catch their plane. "But lemme tell you something. This guy Altamirano, we heard about him even up in Manzanillo. Now, I know your business with him. But in the state of Guerrero the politicians are very fickle. You never know when they might turn off the protection, on account of heat from above. If you and Altamirano ever find yourselves in a situation where you're in need of a guaranteed supply, under conditions of total official protection, you just lemme know. They got islands out in the delta of the Río Coayuayana, suitable for the growing of crops, where no one ever goes but the Indians. And the Indians are hurting, 'cause the shrimp quit running a couple of seasons back."

"I'll give it some serious thought, Don Gallo," Chris said, and waved goodbye.

After Morris had phoned the next of kin in New York to notify them of the findings of the inquest, Chris was tempted to ask him if the Brodskys and Boggianos corresponded in any way to the grotesque portraits that Bo had painted. But though Morris had spoken to Bo's mother, he apparently knew little more about the family than Chris did. And in any case, Morris was in no mood for small talk. The only scrap of information Chris managed to pry out of him was that, given the remote location of the body in Aguas Blancas, and the primitive conditions prevailing there, Mrs. Brodsky feared it might prove impossible to ship her son's body to the United States for burial.

Chris went immediately to Altamirano and convinced him to offer his services as a friendly mortician, and to ship the body to the border free of charge, in a refrigerated coffin that ran off the generator of his Black Maria. Morris—after only a moment's hesitation—accepted the offer, phoned Mrs. Brodsky yet again and arranged for her and Mr. Brodsky to meet the body in Laredo, Texas, and have it buried there.

What Morris didn't know was that an additional ornate mahogany coffin—lacquered black, stamped and sealed by the Department of Public Health of the State of Guerrero, and officially certified to be carrying the remains of one Benjamin K. Hill of Waco, Texas (but actually filled with contraband)—was to be shipped north alongside that of the deceased. Nor was he informed of the fact that Chris and Val would accompany the body as business friend and bereaved widow. Nor that Merle Carrizo, in gratitude for Chris's support in the inquest, was to go along as driver, under the name of Lytle Mescalero.

They left Aguas Blancas in a record heat wave, all crammed together in the narrow front seat of the Black Maria with the gearshift in the middle. The roadbed was bumpy, the springs were shot, the homemade refrigeration system kept breaking down, and the body began to exude an unpleasant odor. Yet it was silently understood among them that this was something they had to endure, that they would have no peace until the job was done, that in shared adversity a bond had been forged between them. Fortified with heavy doses of cannabis and barbiturates, they fled across Mexico as in a dream—down an endless corridor of century plants and adobe walls, pursued by a long-winded ghost. For four days and three nights they rode, rarely talking, rarely stopping, except for gas and minor repairs, as if Bo might hear them if they spoke, as if his evil odor were a curse.

Reaching Monterrey on the evening of the fourth day, they decided they must have some rest. They deposited the coffins in the local icehouse and drove to the Casa de Piedra, an old garden hotel on the outskirts of town. Only one room remained free for the night, and they took it. They sent for refreshments, bathed, wrung out their underthings, hung them up to dry and sat together naked on the bed drinking cold beer, munching crisp tortillas and guacamole. None of them felt in the least bit self-conscious.

"After what we've been through for the last four days," Chris said, "nothing could shame us."

Val brought out her drugs, they all got high, and soon they were giggling and making irreverent jokes about the corpse. They ridiculed the stories he had told in life, and poked holes in their consistency and veracity. They made fun of his golden dollar sign, and made bets about who he'd been, where he'd come from, and what kind of people his family would turn out to be, when they met them in Laredo, Texas. There was more than a hint of black, Bo-like humor in their speculation on the subject, and by the time they decided to turn out the light it had degenerated into near sacrilege.

"He's our scapegoat."

"He's our own dead Jew."

"He died for our sins."

"I resent him," said Chris, crawling between the sheets, "for managing to intrude himself upon us even in death."

"I resent him," said Merle, beside her, "for being so pathetically mortal, after deceiving me into believing he was bigger than life."

"I don't actually resent him at all," said Val, from the other side of the bed. "But I couldn't help feeling this little wave of euphoria when he first began to stink. Till then I was convinced he might suddenly sit bolt upright in his coffin and start spouting out one of his tales again."

Though they'd been as excited as children while up and about, in bed together in the darkness they were quite circumspect. And slept through the night without touching. At dawn, however, Chris found herself in a state of extreme sexual arousal, and reached out to caress Merle under the sheet. While still asleep he grew hard in her hand. The instant his eyes were open, he was kissing her, crawling atop her.

"I want you to work with me," she whispered into his ear. "I want us all to be partners. But don't touch my clavicle, please. . . ."

At the height of her pleasure she imagined that the mirror on the dressing table at the foot of the bed was two-way, and her mother was standing behind it, watching, laughing at Merle's brown muscular buttocks going up and down, and Chris's slender white legs spread comically apart. Yet when she came, she came so violently—in a fit of great, coughing, thrusting, primal spasms, as if birthing a demon—that she awakened Val, and frightened Merle, and he withdrew from her still hard and wet, as if he'd hurt her.

He hadn't hurt her. She had hurt herself. And already the worms of disappointment and dissatisfaction were gnawing at her.

Val smiled drowsily, and sighed. Instinctively, Chris gave him a little push in her direction, and presently nature took its course. Then she wanted Merle back.

Listening to the lovers beside her, watching them, suffering over them, Chris had a fantasy of dancing on the Kid's grave, fornicating on his coffin. And wondered why she was driven to such extraordinary lengths to defile the corpse of a man for whom she had felt so little in life.

I want everything he wanted, she thought. And more.

At the border crossing the next day the refrigeration broke down in the heat while they were waiting in a two-hour line of house trailers and towed motorboats with Texas license plates, and the corpse began to smell again. Yet thanks to the smell there could be no mistaking the nature of their cargo and they were processed so expeditiously across the international frontier that Chris laughingly considered the possibility of entering into a partnership with Altamirano and "cornering the market on the transshipment of dead gringos."

The nightmare ended in Laredo, Texas, where they parked at a predesignated place in the sagebrush on the outskirts of town and turned over the contraband coffin to a pair of spiffy spade cats in zoot suits and wide-brimmed fedoras who came rolling up in a shiny black Cadillac hearse with an Abyssinian Baptist Funeral Services sign painted on the side panel. "Where's Bo?" they wanted to know. "Oh," they said, and removed their hats, when Chris pointed to the other coffin. Then the late Mr. Brodsky was delivered to the Burger Brothers Mortuary on West 5th Street and Rio Grande Avenue. Later, obeying a macabre impulse, Chris left Merle and Val in the Black Maria and attended a memorial service at the mortuary chapel, where she was introduced to the father and mother of the deceased and confronted a reality far more dreary than she had imagined.

Bo, as it turned out, was a middle-class boy from Great Neck, Long Island. The son of a short, meek Jewish podiatrist and an enormous Italian mama with a thick bleached mustache, he was apparently the victim of his own incurable dreams of romance.

By the time she came out of the funeral parlor, however, Chris found that she had already discounted the mundane facts of Bo's former existence in favor of the lies that he had told. And in memory of those lies, and upon the rock of his dead body, she would build her empire.

She proposed to Merle on the way over the Rio Grande Bridge, while Val lay nodding off in the back of the hearse. She made no mention of love or affection. She had a horror of sentimentality. She laid it out for him like just another business contract.

"I want a kid," she said. "Without one you're terminal. You've got no one to hand things over to when you die, and all of your labor goes for naught."

"All right by me," he said, rather flatly, she thought, but he had doubtless taken his cue from her.

"And I have no intention of becoming any sort of conventional wife or mother, Merle, so you can get that out of your head right now."

"No problem," he agreed. "I don't plan on being any kind of conventional father, either."

They were married in a drive-in matrimonial parlor in Nuevo Laredo, and celebrated by cracking a bottle of Fundador while crossing the fertile green plains of Tamaulipas.

Val slept through the whole thing.

On their return to Acapulco a few days later, however, Chris found herself yearning inexplicably for some kind of church service, some symbolic sign of the sanctity and permanence of their relationship, and she made Merle go through another ceremony, a big traditional Catholic wedding in the Acapulco cathedral, with a white gown, morning clothes, bridesmaids, flower girls, the bishop of Acapulco, and—over Merle's strenuous objections—both families in attendance. Val was the witness. Gallo gave the bride away. Carmen and Maureen, who were not speaking, stood in the audience together crying real tears, and the hired Mexican bridesmaids and flower girls threw rice at the back of Bo's palomino gold Cadillac when they departed on their honeymoon trip to Cuernavaca.

As it was established during their honeymoon, the relationship of Chris and Merle was to be more like that of a pair of rivalrous, rancorous, incestuous siblings—with Chris as the dominant elder—than that of a wedded couple. Yet they agreed that they wouldn't have it any other way, and they couldn't dream of being married to anyone else. It was "fate."

On their return a week later, when Chris discovered that she wasn't pregnant yet, she flew into a panic. She had allowed herself only eleven months to accomplish the whole thing from conception through post-partum depression, and now she was convinced that she must be infertile. Nothing that Merle, Val or her mother told her would dissuade her from the notion, and she went about frantically consulting doctors, religious healers, curanderas and even native witch doctors until suddenly one day she rejected all of their conflicting advice and settled on a strategy of pure unfettered randiness. For a month Chris and Merle lived a life of untempered carnal excess. Then Chris discovered that she was pregnant and instantly cut off the sex entirely, afraid it might cause her to miscarry, or traumatize the embryo. During the next nine months, while Chris was almost totally self-absorbed, taking her own pulse every hour, checking her temperature each morning and night, doing careful prenatal exercises, reading books on genetics, childbirth and childrearing (in order to dispense advice to future nannies), Merle grew into the habit of seeking solace and sexual satisfaction from Val. Chris, who enjoyed sex with Merle but always felt so sullied and guilty afterward, encouraged this development, and from then on the basic structure of their ménage was set: Val was the day-to-day wife (and later mother) and Chris was the sacred cow.

Her daughter, Diana, was born by cesarean section at Nuestra Señora de los Angeles Hospital in Acapulco on the fifth of May, 1955, delivered by old Dr. Weber, with whom Gallo had flown in from Manzanillo.

"Get well soon, dear," Gallo said, when he visited her in the maternity ward. "My Indians are getting anxious."

"Tell them to go ahead and start planting," she said, while Diana slept peacefully at her breast. "I've talked it over with Altamirano. If you can arrange for the delivery, Gallo, we'll be glad to ship the crop to market."

"How do we split the profits?"

"Three ways."

"Half for you, half for me."

"All right, if you can guarantee government protection."

"It's a deal," said Gallo. "But let's keep it under our hat, eh? Your hubby is still not speaking to me over that Aguas Blancas deal. And he can be a bit of a pussy, when it comes to things like this."

After he kissed Chris goodbye, he bent to kiss his infant granddaughter. "No," said Chris, still shrinking from the touch of his lips on her brow. "They're so susceptible to germs."

Diana turned out to be a rather sickly and colicky infant, and for a while they were afraid they might lose her to a kidney ailment. But she responded to the formula that Dr. Weber had prescribed for her, and by her first birthday she was, as her adoring Grandma Maureen phrased it, "the perfect picture of health."

Merle taught her to swim when she was only fourteen months old, while they were still living in the penthouse atop the old Moorish behemoth on La Caletilla Beach where they got their start. The El Morocco, they called it; they opened it just in time for the 5th Annual Acapulco International Film Festival in 1956, and thanks to Val's glamorous aura and her Hollywood connections, Chris's financial and managerial wizardry, and Merle's emerging talents as a publicist—he somehow arranged to have Jayne Mansfield's breasts pop their stays at a crucial moment while Mickey Hargitay was holding her up before the cameras—the place caught on like wildfire. By the end of the year they were turning them away, sending the overflow across the cove to the Tropicana. Chris formed a hotel corporation with herself as president, Merle as vice-president, Maureen as secretary and Val as treasurer and—with a large infusion of cash from her deal with Gallo and Altamirano—bought the Reina del Mar on Tamarindo Beach. And there, in 1958, Merle taught Diana to dive. She was only three years old and he had her doing front flips and twists off the medium-high board. He billed her as "The Water Baby" and got miles of publicity out of her. A plump little redheaded, freckle-faced thing with a cute little button nose and big blue eyes, she was a natural before the cameras. Her picture was in all the papers, they showed her on television, they even put her in an Esther Williams movie that was being shot in Acapulco that year. By the time Diana started school in 1960, all three of the O'Hare-Carrizo hotels were booked solid months in advance.

In June of 1961, Merle and Val were hosting an international charity ball at the Reina del Mar when Merle noticed a tall, distinguished gentleman in his early sixties and recognized him as General Raúl Mondragón. Merle introduced himself, and recalled old times in Manzanillo when they used to promenade together around the gazebo in the Jardín Obregón with Chris and Ramona. But the general professed not to remember the episode, though he admitted that he'd once had a secretary named Ramona Mescalero. "I was so busy at the time, you see." He shrugged. "With the martial law, and all. . . ."

"No matter," said Merle good-naturedly. "It was so long ago." And he introduced the general to Val. Mondragón presented her to several of his fellow officers, political associates and friends from various foreign embassies in Mexico City. A seasoned diplomat from Egypt would not relinquish her for the rest of the evening: Ahmed, a young-looking fifty-five, and in Merle's opinion obscenely handsome, was just emerging from a decent interval of mourning following the death of his English wife, and Val seemed quite taken by his stunning appearance, elegant manners, and his aura of tragedy. In the morning Ahmed sent baskets full of tiny pink orchids and an invitation to dinner. They were inseparable for the remainder of Ahmed's stay in Acapulco, and by the time he left the following week, Val had accepted his proposal of matrimony and was rapturous over the prospect of mothering his three young daughters. A month later they married and Val went to live with him in Mexico City.

Bereft of the buffer that had stood between their warring natures, Chris and Merle were often at each other's throats. And without her Aunt Val, Diana was at first disconsolate, then stoically unhappy, and, finally, to Chris's alarm, more and more dependent on the lavish attentions of her Grandma Maureen.

When Ahmed was called back to Cairo in 1965, Val confided to Merle her unwillingness to follow him. For too long she had struggled against her husband's distinctly Arabic notions of what a wife should be. Besides, she was fed up to the teeth with her three stepdaughters, who were certainly not flowers of Moslem womanhood. Now in various stages of adolescence, and spoiled by the international high life of Mexico City, they smoked dope and—much worse—consumed liquor behind their father's back, sneaked out of the embassy compound in the wee hours and returned home in reprehensible condition, for which Val was ultimately blamed. She longed for Diana with her generous nature and even disposition. Val came back to live in Acapulco. And they all started up again right where they'd left off four years before.

Meanwhile, Chris had purchased the big, modern Excelsior Hotel on La Condesa Beach, started construction on the magnificent Acapulco Intercontinental at Punta Guitarrón, acquired a half mile of prime beachfront property in Puerto Vallarta, and they all had another very powerful reason—aside from their sexual and emotional ties—for maintaining their odd domestic scene: They were getting rich together.

CHAPTER 6

Against the vast arabesque of the delta, amid a swirling, confusing design of brown lagoons and green mangrove islets, Xochitlán posed itself in simple, white contradiction, like a lily upon the flood. It was a village of scores of tiny adobe houses jammed wall to wall around a great circular canal and the edge of the encroaching swamp, crosshatched by four narrower canals that stretched like the spokes of an Aztec wheel of life to the cardinal points. There was not an inch of unused space anywhere on the island. The place had reached the limits of expansion over five hundred years before. Ever since then, its biggest export had been its young people. On reaching the age of marriage in Xochitlán, couples had but two choices: leave and start a new life on the mainland, or stay on in the crowded ancestral adobe. With the blessing of Padre Dau, Rafael and Benicta had chosen the latter course. They moved into the three-room house of Benicta's parents, sharing the ever-diminishing space with her father, Don Pablo Hernández, her mother, Doña Silvia, her little brother, her two married sisters, their husbands and flocks of children. And even though Xochitlán was experiencing an unprecedented prosperity at this time, the financial successes of the extended family were never great enough to keep pace with its natural expansion. One of the sisters or another was always pregnant, and at least one new baby was born every year. Then in 1953 the shrimp quit running. The warm Cocos Current suddenly started flowing stronger, beating back the cold California Current, and the crustaceans retreated to the north, along with most of the fish. Up in Sonora and Baja California the fishermen were striking it rich, but down in Xochitlán they were digging into their stores of cornmeal and beans. The same thing had happened in 1927, the old folks said, yet the next year the fish and shrimp had come back as strong as ever. So, everyone in the village just sat back and waited for luck to change. But the current ran warm all the way through 1953 and 1954, and by January 1955, some of the villagers were starting to go hungry. Then, just when things looked bleakest, a stranger appeared on the island. A large, plump, sensual-looking mestizo with swift conniving eyes, he said his name was Don Rudolfo Muñoz. He came from the governor, Don Gallo Carrizo, he said, and everyone believed him because he had the same sleek, barbered look, and he showed them documents identifying himself as a state undersecretary of the PRI.

"Word of your ill luck, and of your privations, has come to the ears of Don Gallo," he said. "And he has sent me here to see if there is anything he can do for you."

"He could lend us some money at low interest," said Don Pablo, the presidente, "to tide us over till the shrimp run again."

"I wouldn't place all my faith in anything so vague as the ocean currents," the stranger said. "But I did notice on my way over how many of the islands of your delta are fallow and unoccupied, and it gave me an idea. Why don't we go into business together? I'll furnish the seed, the tools to clear the land, and the fertilizer, if needed; you furnish the cropland and farmhands, and we'll grow marijuana for the export trade."

"But jefe," said the presidente, "marijuana is against the law, no?"

"Strictly speaking, yes," said the stranger. "But I'm sure the authorities will be most understanding, in view of your desperate straits, the remoteness of your lands and the fact that you have Don Gallo Carrizo's unqualified support."

"We'll think about it," said the presidente, doubtfully.

"Please do," said the stranger. "And remember, no irrigation is needed. You plant only one crop a year, in May, just before the rainy season. In July the plants are already a meter high. In November they are three and a half meters high and heavy with flowers, and it's time for harvest. You will get a ton of quality mota out of every twenty square meters you plant. And I will give you a thousand pesos a ton."

"A thousand pesos a ton?"

"That is correct."

"But there are countless islands in the delta," said the presidente. "If we plant even a small number of them we'll harvest hundreds of tons every year, and we'll all be rich."

"Well," said the stranger, his eyes glittering like gold, "that's the idea, no?"

"Claro," said the presidente.

"There's only one thing," said the stranger, gripping Don Pablo strongly by the arm. "I must ask you to cut back on the tourist trade. Tell your men to stop ferrying them over from the mainland. Prying eyes, you understand. . . ."

"That should present no problem," said the presidente, and they made a tentative oral contract, pending ratification by the council of elders.

Despite the apparent generosity of the stranger's offer, however, opinion on the island was divided as to whether or not to accept his terms. There were those, among them Padre Dau, who distrusted the stranger and Don Gallo and preferred to place their faith in God and await the return of the shrimp. There were others, including Rafael, who protested that a curtailment of the tourist trade would cause hardship in the village, as a large proportion of its income derived from the selling of trinkets and baskets. Rafael went on to point out that fishing itself was not a trade that one could drop and pick up again very easily. It was, in fact, a vocation that required constant practice, regardless of the size of the catch. Nets, traps and lines rotted quickly in the tropical humidity. Hooks, gaffs and harpoons rusted. And canoes required continuous caulking and painting. Also, fishermen tended to rapidly lose their paddling, net-throwing and harpooning skills, not to mention their knowledge of the tides, the shifting banks and reefs, and the ever-changing fishing grounds. If the marijuana crop ever failed, Rafael said, it would not be easy to take up again where the village had left off.

But the majority of the population agreed with the elders that the stranger's fortuitous arrival was like a sign from heaven, and that Xochitlán had no recourse but to change its basic occupation from fishing and tourism to farming.

Rafael was not happy with this decision, despite his respect for the opinions of the majority, and the prospect of new wealth for his village.

He considered himself first and foremost a man of the sea, and the idea of clearing, plowing and planting mangrove islets under the tropical sun was immensely displeasing to him.

This prospect of an unwanted job change also happened to coincide with a period of family strife in the household of Benicta's father. There were now eight adults and twelve children living in three rooms, and the crowded, unhealthy conditions had resulted in bad feelings. Benicta's sisters and their mates resented the fact that El Niño was served first at dinner, received the largest portion, was deferred to even by the presidente and was allocated the largest and airiest room in the house for himself, Benicta and their two kids, while the remaining sixteen members of the family were crowded into two small windowless rooms.

After several loud arguments had erupted over the issue, Rafael went to Don Pablo and volunteered to share his room with the others. But Don Pablo wouldn't hear of it. It would dishonor his house, he said. And the offer did nothing to endear Rafael to the others. On the contrary, his brothers-in-law sat glowering at him angrily every night at dinner, and went around muttering dire threats at him all day. The time was rapidly approaching, Rafael knew, when he would be forced into a possible machete showdown, and he mourned the fact that he'd brought so much dissension into a hitherto happy family.

He went to visit Padre Dau—so wizened now that he looked as if he might blow away in a strong wind—and sought his advice. But he should have known better: "Que será, será," the padre said, in his oddly compelling voice. "Turn the other cheek, my son. Have faith, have faith. . . ."

He consulted the maestro, and there he had better luck. "You have five years to accept your government scholarship," he said. "And only four years and nine months have elapsed."

"But what about my wife, my children? How will they live?"

"You can take a part of your bursary—perhaps twenty or thirty pesos—and send it to them every month. In the city it isn't much, but here it's enough to get by quite nicely."

Rafael decided that he had little choice but to leave the island, at least for a few years. Then perhaps he could come back as a teacher, and help the maestro expand the school to serve the entire mangrove swamp. With this in mind, he wrote to the Ministry of Education and requested permission to enter the University of Colima in the spring of 1955, under a full national scholarship. The sincerity and erudition of his letter impressed someone at the ministry, and within a week he had received a telegram of approval from the ministro himself, who praised his plan to expand education in the mangrove swamp, and promised to do everything in his power to see that it was implemented upon his graduation from the university. For a week afterward Rafael agonized over whether or not to tell Benicta of his good fortune, but at last he decided to keep it to himself. Physically and emotionally they were marvelously attuned, her buxom, matronly new figure never failed to arouse him, and their passionate and frequent lovemaking was the talk of the house, but they had little in common intellectually—indeed, Benicta could barely read, and had absolutely no notion of the world outside the mangrove swamp—and they rarely spoke of anything beyond the needs of the children or the cares of the household. On the other hand, Benicta had remained in perfect mental concert with her father, Don Pablo, who influenced her in all things. Rafael suspected that she would reveal his secret, if she knew. And a secret it must be, for El Niño would not be able to resist the combined wills of his family, his in-laws, Padre Dau and the pueblo, should they try to make him stay.

Carefully he laid his plans, with only the maestro—who out of boredom had grown huge and fat and dispensed advice to relieve the tedium of his life in Xochitlán—as his counselor and confidant.

At the maestro's suggestion, Rafael refused to participate in the clearing of the marijuana islands, and declared his intention of becoming a shark fisherman instead.

"But we eat no shark!" Don Pablo protested.

"No, but there's a market for it in Manzanillo," Rafael explained. "They grind it up and dry it out and put it into fishmeal and ship it to the gringos as food for their animals."

After only the merest show of symbolic resistance, Don Pablo relented and gave the project his blessing, on the condition that Rafael contribute the total receipts of his enterprise to the communal coffers.

Having won his way so effortlessly, Rafael suddenly found himself wishing that Don Pablo had put up more of an argument. He started feeling shifty-eyed and guilty, and he was afraid that Padre Dau—who had an uncanny knack for ferreting out the secrets of a wayward heart—would uncover his plot. In the end he even began to resent the maestro, for having "pushed" him into this thing.

Nevertheless, nervous and guilty as he felt himself to be, he followed the maestro's suggestion to a tee. He rigged his canoe with a lateen sail, and every morning he would sail through the mouth of the Río Coayuayana and out into the open Pacific, letting everyone in the village get used to the idea. Then, three or four kilometers offshore, he would unfurl his sail, throw out his line and his bait, open a book he'd borrowed from the maestro, and drift for hours, returning home late in the evening, empty-handed, with the light of the maestro's upstairs study as his beacon.

One morning in February he woke up beside Benicta with an empty, aching feeling in the pit of his stomach and realized that already it was time to go. He got up, dressed himself in his fishing clothes, awakened little four-year-old Francisco and sat bouncing him on his knee, ruffling his thatch of shiny black hair. Benicta got up and gave the baby, Octavio, her breast. The room warmed. The sun crept across the clay floor. The mosquitoes fled. The chickens came in from the courtyard to cluck and peck at scraps. Benicta hummed a happy Nahua tune. The baby sucked contentedly. Francisco laughed as he bounced on Papi's knee. And Rafael was hard put to carry out his intention.

At last he roused himself to go. He got his fishing gear, gathered his little family to him, kissed them all goodbye, and went out the door, smiling and waving at them from the pathway outside.

"Better to remember them so," he said aloud, as he paddled off down the canal.

It would be four years before he saw them again, perhaps.

Yet soon Rafael came upon an apparently auspicious omen, which lightened his spirits considerably: In the shallows between the corn island and the cemetery island he spotted a sea turtle. At first he thought it was just a shadow in the murky water. But then it surfaced to breathe, and submerged again to feed on the vegetation at the bottom. Rafael waited patiently, his harpoon at the ready, his canoe drifting in the outgoing tide. Finally the turtle surfaced again, a couple of meters ahead, its nose just barely poking out of the water. Rafael let the canoe drift closer, closer. Now he could see its thick green shell, just beneath the surface. He waited till the turtle was right under his bow, then flung the harpoon straight down, with all the strength in his arm. "Tunk!" the steel sounded, as it pierced the beast's armored back. The turtle started, and tried to swim away. But it was losing much blood, and fading fast. Rafael wound it in closer and closer with his harpoon line. Then he hoisted it aboard, still alive, and tipped it over on its back while its leathery, prehistoric legs kicked feebly. It was a good-sized, "white-meat" turtle, and it would dress out at about thirty kilos.

"Ai ai aaaiiiii!" Rafael cried, in triumph, and rode the strongly ebbing tide toward the mouth of the river. Every time he met a canoeload of marijuana farmers heading toward the islands, he whooped, pointed to the turtle, hollered, "I'm off to Manzanillo!" and awaited their joyous response.

Actually, he'd had so much fun spearing that turtle he almost hated to go. It's clear that I'm a fisherman by nature, he thought. Why do I want to challenge my fate? But he passed out into the open Pacific anyway, and hoisted his sail, and set a course for Manzanillo, in spite of all his misgivings.

And right away his apprehensions were proven out. The wind was dead against him, and very brisk. He had to tack far out to sea to make headway, and by the time he made port two days later, the turtle had already begun to stink in the sun. He got only five pesos out of it in the fish market. And later, when he auctioned off his canoe in a wharfside cantina, the results were equally disappointing: He sold it for a mere eighty pesos. Deeply and personally offended that his canoe—his very life, until now—was apparently worth so little, he hopped an empty banana train for Colima and promptly got bitten by a tarantula. He arrived late that evening, hungry and tired, his pinky finger swollen to twice its normal size, and bought a taco from a vendor in the station, only to find that the meat was full of worms. Then, discomfited by the series of minor calamities that had befallen him since his departure from the delta, and disturbed by the unfamiliar clamor of the city, the mass of humanity, he walked to the outskirts and fell asleep in a cornfield, covered by his sarape.

An hour or so later he awakened again when the air pressure took a sudden drop. A strong, humid north wind sprang up, accompanied by spectacular displays of thunder and lightning. About midnight it started to rain. The wind increased dramatically, and it rained buckets for the rest of the night. Rafael sought shelter in a barranca, under a small, leafy soyate tree. But rest was difficult at best, and when he dozed he had uneasy dreams: It seemed to him, and indeed it had seemed to him ever since he left his home, that he was being watched, and judged, that he was under the observation of Benicta, Francisco, Octavio, Don Pablo, Padre Dau, Pedro and Marta Martínez, and the entire village of Xochitlán.

In the morning, still wearing his soggy sombrero, his dirty turtle-smelling white calzones, muddy huaraches and bloody machete—and quite conscious of the effect that he would create among the student body—he made his way toward the university. By now the rain had stopped, but the air was extraordinarily damp and sticky, and the birds were acting strangely, keeping to their nests long after dawn. A queer purple light shone behind the low, scudding cloud cover, and the gale howled more fiercely than ever, bending the palm trees, rattling the fronds, flattening the corn plants, sending husks and leaves flying high into the air.

He entered the city, passed by the Jardín Libertad, the post office, the police station, the palacio municipal and the cathedral. He dodged street-cars, taco wagons, buses, taxis, and pedestrians rushing off to work. And though this was his first sight of a modern city in the light of day, he found himself accepting it as a matter of course, as if he often did this sort of thing. At the same time, the whole experience was tinged with purple and gold: the colors of unreality. It was like a dream, an uneasy dream that had long ago become familiar. To Rafael the city was like a friend, a friend he'd met in a former life, a friend he could no longer trust.

Warily, therefore, he proceeded past the Seguro Social building and was just starting up the Calle Filomeno Medina toward the university when he heard a newsboy calling out the morning headline. And even before he caught the exact word that he was shouting, or bought a newspaper off him, he knew more or less what it would be, and what it would mean:

"Chubasco! Chubasco! Chubasco!"

A cyclone had struck all along the Colima coast, preceded by a Green Wave of unusual height. Manzanillo, Armería, Boca de Pascuales, and dozens of villages had been devastated. Governor Gallo Carrizo had declared the entire state a disaster area, and requested emergency financial aid from the International Red Cross and the United States. The delta of the Río Cuayuayana had received the brunt of the storm. It was still cut off from the mainland, and damages there had not yet been assessed.

Rafael scanned the story in a few seconds. Then, without another thought, he turned on his heel and headed southward out of town. Loping along in his sturdy huaraches, covering much ground, he reached the outskirts in a few minutes and struck out straight overland toward the coast.

Notwithstanding his sudden about-face, nor his haste, nor his apparent homing instincts, Rafael was not afraid for the lives of his wife and children. As swamp dwellers, they were amphibian by nature: used to periodic inundations, and equipped to weather them safely. In chubasco season there was always a storm watch mounted in the steeple of the church, and an alarm signal would set the entire population of the village running to their canoes, paddling for high ground. Indeed, Rafael was so sure of his family's safety that it seemed to him he could hear their heartbeats coming clean across from the delta, beating just as strongly as his own. No, El Niño had not turned toward his people again out of fear, or anxiety. It was simply that they had sent him a message, and he had heard it loud and clear. It couldn't have been stated more plainly if they'd sent him a telegram: RETURN HOME SOONEST—OR ELSE.

For three days Rafael made his way across country, fording swollen streams, swimming flooded rivers, trudging through deep, black, viscous mud, creeping cautiously along narrow, crumbling, cliffside trails cut hundreds of feet above the jungle, eating stranded rodents and insects that he caught with his hands, sucking sugar cane that he cut with his machete, drinking the muddy floodwaters, sleeping on the wide branches of tacamo trees to avoid the reptiles and scorpions that had been driven from their lairs. When he reached Boca de Pascuales, a wooden town that had been virtually flattened by the storm, he was covered with leeches, and a thousand mosquito bites, and he looked like some kind of creature from the Laguna Negra, but he didn't feel a thing. It had been one long sleepwalk from beginning to end. He would never go back to Colima again. He would never see the university. He would never even find out what it looked like. In his imagination, however, it was a great pink palace made of tezontle stones, set in a vast park full of parrots, monkeys and jacaranda trees.

In the dockside restaurant and cantina of El Chino, the Chinaman—one of the few buildings left standing in town—he ran into his grinning little baldheaded brother, Eusebio. He'd been stranded by the chubasco with a load of white flour and marijuana seed, and he was about to leave for home. He greeted Rafael without apparent surprise, invited him for a beer and welcomed him aboard his canoe, which was tied up under the pilings of El Chino's.

"Que nos vamos, Niño!" Eusebio hollered, cranking over his new Johnson outboard motor. And then they were off at ten miles an hour, shattering the primeval silence of the swamp, setting the herons to flapping out of the wind-stripped mangrove trees.

It was as if his brother had known he was coming. It was as if he'd been waiting for him all along.

"Looks like that chubasco was a blessing in disguise," said Eusebio, as he guided the canoe through the maze of sloughs, logjams and muddy, battered islets. "At least for the marijuana crop."

"Why is that, hermano?"

"Well," he said, "look out there at those islands. The Green Wave came in and tore out everything but the biggest trees. Did half our work for us. Then the flood came down from the mountains, cleaned off all the salt that the ocean laid down, stirred up a load of that good volcanic soil upstream, and sifted it in evenly, a meter deep. We just tear out a few of the fattest mangroves, leave a little fringe of brush around the edge of the islands to keep out prying eyes, and we got ourselves the prettiest little crop of mota you ever seen."

At home in Xochitlán, Benicta had already begun to shovel the mud from their room, and the air was thick and greasy with the smoke of burning coyol nuts, which she used to keep off the clouds of mosquitoes at evening time.

"Hola," she said calmly, when she saw him in the doorway.

"Hola," he said.

"Papi, Papi, Papi!" the children cried, and ran in from the patio, covered with black delta mud.

He kissed the children and set them down. He took the wooden spade from his wife's hand and started shoveling mud. She went to the corner, squatted over her stone metate and began grinding corn for tortillas. The children went back outside to play in the mud.

It was as if he'd never left town. No one even asked where he had gone.

Though El Niño had submitted again to the will of his people, the problem of overcrowding in the presidente's household had not gone away. Nor had the resentment of Rafael's brothers-in-law. Therefore, one of the first things he did after his return was to go before the council of elders and request permission to build a house on the Isleta Chamacua, a three-hectare mangrove islet located about two hundred meters east of town. The elders were shocked by the proposal, as no one had ever asked such a thing before. The Nahua people had a superstitious dread of living alone, away from the tribal walls. Villagers who migrated to the mainland were required by tribal law to return at least twice a year, or else be forever regarded as strangers. The physical unity of the village, and its permanent cohesion, was an article of faith among the swamp dwellers, superseding all individual rights.

As Padre Dau explained it to Rafael in front of the council: "Among the bees, the hive is like a living body. Within the hive, each class of bee has a function that corresponds to some organ of the body, such as the brain, the heart, the liver, the lungs. There are even bees which act as blood, saliva, sweat, semen. Among us it is the same. We are all like an ancient colony of bees, and each of us plays his part in the life of the body, the village. If one of our less important parts is missing, perhaps it is not such a tragedy. But if some vital organ is removed, the body will collapse and die. As the queen is the soul of the hive, so El Niño is the soul of Xochitlán. And without him we shall not long survive."

"Undoubtedly El Niño is a unique and precious asset of our village, essential to our continued health and good fortune," Don Pablo said, in rebuttal to Padre Dau's analogy of the bees. "But he has become restless and unhappy in my home. And if we don't give him his own place," he said, in the only open reference to Rafael's departure that was ever heard in the town, "he will leave us again, and what shall we do then?"

At last, and most reluctantly, the elders decided to approve Rafael's request, on the condition that he maintain an official residence in his family's ancestral home in the barrio of Mexcaltitán, and merely construct a temporary dwelling—a bamboo and palm-thatch jacal—on the Isleta Chamacua.

In order to make El Niño's absence more palatable to the villagers—and to themselves—the council of elders selected the Isleta Chamacua as the first island to be cleared and planted with marijuana, and pretended that his residence there with his family had some ritual significance. Accordingly, they decreed a fiesta on the day that El Niño was to be moved. The villagers decorated their canoes with lilies and went over in a long procession, with the huehuechique and the padre at their head, chanting and waving incense. Once they had landed, and tied up their canoes to the mangrove roots on the bank, Padre Dau stepped ashore and consecrated the island to the use of agriculture, and offered up an extemporaneous but artful little prayer in which he implored the Lord of Miracles to grant the villagers the strength and determination to "throw up a dwelling place for El Niño and his family, so that they may live here in symbolic protection of our new crop."

Singing and swaying, dressed up in their holiday finery, the people responded. The women went down the bank to cut bamboo and cane for the walls. The boys scampered barefoot into the palm trees to cut fronds for the roof. The men drew the dimensions of the house in the dirt, started digging post holes and packing the floor down hard with their huaraches. By nightfall the jacal was finished. El Niño moved in with his family and his belongings, and everyone got drunk on pulque and danced until dawn—even the children.

Next day the men brought over a pair of mules and some tackle, cross saws, axes, hatchets and sharp machetes, and in a week of heavy labor they had cleared the island of mangrove, stacked enough firewood in front of the jacal to last a year, and burned the rest up in a great bonfire that could be seen for miles. Then they put the mules to work again pulling a couple of hand plows, turning over the new topsoil. After that, they left the island to lie fallow until May, and went on to clear and plow the next island, the Isleta Changa, a hundred meters across the channel. There, following El Niño's precedent, they installed another small family to throw up a jacal and act as guardians, and continued on to the next islet, and the next.

In early May, Rafael and Benicta spent a week planting marijuana seeds in the long dark furrows and covering them over with dirt. The rains came a few days later, and the mota began to grow. It grew like a weed, nourished only by the rain, the sun and the rich volcanic soil. And it wasn't until three months later, when the plants were about a meter high, that there was any more work to be done. Then it was necessary to spend a few days cutting down all the male plants and burning them up. Otherwise they would fecundate the females and, it was said, decrease their resin content. From then on, marijuana cultivation was just a matter of trimming and cutting back the less potent "dedo" leaves and making sure that the "colas"—the flowering tips of the plant, where most of the cannabis was concentrated—had plenty of time to grow. When the plants were five and a half months old, and three meters tall, they began to flower, and a week or two later they were ready to harvest. During the harvest many hands were needed, including the entire Hernández and Martínez clans, for it was essential that the entire crop be cut down at the hottest part of the day, when the resin lay thickest on the leaves.

After they had cut all the plants down, they stripped the flowering upper portions and put them into old flour sacks. Then everyone pitched in and carried them to a long, thatch-roofed drying shed that Rafael and Benicta had erected at the edge of the field. There they removed the mota and spread it out on the ground to dry. Every evening Rafael had to gather it up again and put it back into the sacks. Otherwise the dew might dampen it, and cause it to spoil. In two weeks the crop was cured. Rafael and Benicta stuffed it into the sacks for the last time and sewed them up. Rafael paddled into town and sent a telegram to Muñoz. A few days later Muñoz showed up in a big motor launch, with four armed men. He paid Rafael off—subtracting an exorbitant sum for "carrying charges"—and disappeared in the direction of the next marijuana island, trailing a strong scent of cannabis. Rafael paddled into town again, deposited the money in the communal account in his sister's post office savings bank, drew his year's share of the profits from the presidente, had a couple of mugs of pulque at the cantina, and was returning home that night with presents for Benicta and the kids—gold earrings for Benicta, bows and arrows for the boys—when he saw the lights of Muñoz's launch, and decided to play a hunch.

Muñoz had collected all his bags of mota and had set a course in the direction of Boca de Pascuales, the closest mainland town. Rafael cranked up his outboard motor—which he only used in emergencies, on account of the high cost of gasoline—and took a shortcut to Boca de Pascuales, where he hid out at the edge of the riverport, under the overhanging branches of a mangrove tree, waiting for Muñoz to appear. Presently he saw Muñoz's lights on the river, and—hidden in the shadow of the bank—paddled after him to a dock on the other side of town. There, beside a giant cylindrical gas tank owned by the government oil monopoly, PEMEX, five big Packards and Cadillacs were lined up all in a row. Black Marias, they were. On the side panels, Rafael could just make out a small printed sign:

FUNERALES ALTAMIRANO
Capillas Confortables—Translados Internacionales
3, Plaza Miguel Alemán
Aguas Blancas, Guerrero

Rafael had wanted to find out where Muñoz took the mota, and now he knew. To what use he might put the information, he hadn't a clue.

One could not tell the future, and someday it might come in handy, he thought. He had never trusted Muñoz, or Don Gallo, in any case, and he had resented extremely Muñoz's sudden addition of "carrying charges," which had not been a part of their oral contract. Meanwhile, the trip was at least good for a laugh. The sight of the Black Marias being loaded with sacks of mota struck him as funny, and he snickered to himself in the darkness. It looked as if a great battle had been fought in the delta, and men had fallen like marijuana before a sharp machete, and now here were the infernal machines to transport the dead.

The next year Rafael left the cultivation of marijuana to his wife. It was not difficult work, except at harvest time—when he would lend a hand with the others—and he had a yen to go fishing again. He had no intention of spending the rest of his life as a farmer, and he had this very strong visceral need to keep the ancient fishing traditions of Xochitlán alive, and to pass them on to at least one of his sons.

When Francisco was only seven, Rafael began taking him out in his canoe every day, teaching him the trade of fisherman. He showed the boy how to make nets, gaffs, hooks, lines, paddles, fishing poles, harpoons and shrimp traps. As the boy grew, he taught him how to bait his lines and traps, how to throw his net and his harpoon, how to handle the canoe with pole, paddle, sail and outboard motor. He showed him where to look for shrimp—if they ever ran again—where to find turtle, alligator, shark, tuna, bonita, albacore, how to catch freshwater catfish, bluegills, lumpheads, crappie and panfish.

Francisco was a tall, sturdy little fellow, with great manual dexterity. Direct and simple-hearted, with a smile that split his dusky face like a sliver of moon, he worshiped his father, hung on his every word, obeyed him instantly and without question. In the village he was admired for his obedience, and everyone made much of his musculature and physical strength, which were extraordinary for a boy his age. He was a special favorite of his grandfather, Don Pablo, and of Padre Dau, and by the time he was ten they had taken to calling him El Niñito. The other villagers picked it up, and presently they were according him the respect that Rafael had received as a youngster, and it was taken for granted that he would follow in his father's footsteps.

Yet it was clear from the beginning that Francisco had inherited only a part of his father's character, for he was bored in school and manifested little talent for reading or learning. Octavio, who was prettier, frailer, more angular than his brother, and resembled his father more, had inherited the sensitive, thoughtful side of Rafael's nature, and was especially beloved by his uncle, the maestro. But he had a willful, rebellious streak. He would never take his parents' advice without proposing some unique solution of his own, he would not take orders even when threatened with physical violence, he treated his elder brother like a servant, he ordered his mother around as if she were his personal slave, and by the time he was eight he had made life so difficult in the jacal that Rafael let him go live with the maestro during the school year, since that's what they both seemed to want. Soon Octavio's academic exploits were the talk of the village, and everyone spoke of the tribe's good fortune—to have found such a perfect Niño, who had given them such wondrous sons, two sides of the same coin.

When Francisco was fourteen and had passed the rites of puberty with Padre Dau and the huehuechique, Rafael took him to cut down a conacaste tree and make his own canoe. They traveled for three days upriver, far past Boca de Pascuales, searching for exactly the right tree, a good sound one of middling height, growing close enough to the river to be rolled down the bank. But they never found the one they were looking for. The good ones had all been cut down. So they settled for a soft and fragrant little cedro tree, about ten meters tall. If properly caulked and painted, the cedro makes a swift, buoyant little craft, but it will not last anywhere near so long as the conacaste.

Rafael and Francisco chopped the tree down with an ax. They rolled it down to the little river beach where they had tied their canoe and set up camp. The next day, they stripped the tree's limbs and bark with their hatchets and machetes. Then, measuring with his eye, Rafael found the tree's center of balance, and they spent the next two weeks shaping it with adzes. Next they planed it down and smoothed out the bottom of the hull. Then with wedges and levers that they made from scrap wood, they rolled the log over and commenced to hollow it out. For a week they worked on the interior of the canoe, using axes, hatchets, machetes, and carefully controlled charcoal fires, fashioning it according to the shape of the exterior tree. Finally they caulked it, and painted it black with a white and red evil eye on the prow, according to the traditions of their people.

When they were done, Rafael gave Francisco an abrazo and cranked up his outboard motor, leaving the boy to paddle his canoe home alone.

Two days later, when Francisco arrived in Xochitlán, the banks of the circular canal were lined with the entire pueblo, who pelted him with flowers and shouted, "Que viva El Niñito!"

And so the years passed, in peace and prosperity, despite the dearth of shrimp. Rafael was appointed to the now largely ceremonial post of secretary of the fishing cuatequitl, and at his father's death he was elected síndico, just one step down from Don Pablo, the presidente.

Without the influx of tourists, the village became completely insular again, and fell back on its old social and religious traditions. Spanish, which had made great inroads among the population in recent years, retreated again, and the Nahua language made a surprising comeback. The maestro hated the cultural isolation, and complained to Rafael about it all the time. But Padre Dau and the huehuechique were delighted, as participation at their church services had increased dramatically. As for Rafael, he had mixed feelings. On the one hand he enjoyed his life, his sweet-natured, obedient wife, his growing boys, and the little girl babies that followed them every two or three years. On the other hand he had never gotten over his feeling of uneasiness, and he knew in his bones that this life that they led was too good to be true. What concerned him most was the fact that they relied so much on a single crop. Not only had they given up fishing, and the tourist industry, they had even stopped growing corn, beans and chile, and depended on store-bought goods from the mainland.

Then one day in the summer of 1968—the same summer that the Olympics came to Mexico City, and the nation "came of age" as an industrial power, and a great demonstration of four hundred thousand students protesting the "shameful inequalities" of Mexican life took place in the capital (news that only dimly reached the ears of Xochitlán)—word came that the gringos were stirring up trouble along the border, and putting pressure on the Mexican government to stop the flow of mota. Yanqui youth were going wild smoking weed, it was said, they were wearing long hair and beads, marching in the streets, defying the government on the issue of the Vietnam War, and President Nixon had decided to put a stop to it. There was even talk of destroying the marijuana crop on the ground before it could be transported to the north.

At this news, Rafael's anxiety grew even stronger, and he tried to impress upon his fellow elders the need to diversify production, to start growing corn, beans and chile again, and to send the young men out fishing. But the elders had become fat and rich on the mota trade, and they voted to "wait and see" before taking any action on Rafael's suggestion.

In October of that same year—at about the time that news of a great massacre of Mexico City university students by federal troops reached the village—Rudolfo Muñoz came to announce that due to intense pressure from the Yanquis the tacit permission of the governor was to be shortly withdrawn, and after the harvest in November the laws against the growing of marijuana would be strictly enforced.

Convinced that a catastrophe was upon them, the elders dispatched a delegation of villagers to approach Don Gallo in person, at his winter residence in Manzanillo. Rafael was elected leader of the delegation, and it was he who was finally granted—after a week of trying—an audience with the governor's chief aide. The aide was a plump and pretty little woman of about fifty. In fact it was his wife, Doña Carmen. At her desk in the governor's antechamber, flanked by flags of the state and nation and two armed policemen, Doña Carmen held an audience every morning between nine and twelve, and the room was filled with supplicants of every description, from poor mountain Indians seeking water rights to rich mestizos and foreigners seeking beachfront gambling concessions. Rafael waited patiently in the lineup until it was his turn, then he stated his business as briefly and succinctly as possible, without omitting the obligatory show of obeisance and the flowery words of respect.

Bowing humbly, sombrero in hand, he said, "My regards to you, Señora Gobernadora, and I beg you to convey to your illustrious husband, our honored governor, the profound respects and good wishes of the people of Xochitlán, and to implore him in their name, and in memory of our long and mutually profitable association in the export trade, to make an exception to the law against the cultivation of marijuana, and allow us to continue the peaceful production of this crop which is so vital to our communal economy."

Doña Carmen glared at Rafael for a moment, glanced nervously at the crowd of supplicants pressing to meet her, then stood up behind her desk and pointed toward the door.

"Indio," she said, her eyes flashing, "how dare you impute that the governor of the state of Colima would engage in illegal or unsavory activities? Get out of here, before I have you jailed for libel."

Her bodyguards ejected him from the governor's mansion, flinging him down the steps that led to the funicular railway station. He landed in a heap at the bottom, right at the feet of two large state policemen, who had apparently been alerted to his arrival and promptly arrested him for "vagrancy." For an hour they drove him around town in the back of a paddywagon, beating him over the head with their nightsticks and shouting, "Never come back here again, you hear? Never come back here again!" They released him to the custody of the captain of the port, where he rejoined the delegation from Xochitlán: They'd been locked up in a detention facility at the naval base. Then the captain of the port tied on to their canoes with a tugboat and towed them far out to sea. There he confiscated their paddles, sails and outboard motors, and set them adrift.

Paddling with their bare hands, fashioning sails from driftwood and old shirts, eating fish they caught by hand, drinking their own urine and scraping dew off the gunwales to slacken their thirst, they reached Xochitlán a week later, half dead from exposure and dehydration. They barely recovered in time for the marijuana harvest in November, and even then they had a hard time keeping up with the others, as the crop was unusually heavy that year. Afterward a vote was taken among the elders and it was decided that the tribe had little choice but to swallow its pride and send Muñoz a telegram announcing the readiness of the crop.

Muñoz showed up a couple of days later, with a naval patrol boat and a squad of infantry. He started loading the crop on the islands closest to the mainland, working his way outward toward Xochitlán, repeating a little prepared statement at each pickup point to the effect that he was herewith confiscating the entire crop as illegal contraband, on orders of the governor.

Long before Muñoz reached the Isleta Chamacua, therefore, he had a great long train of canoes behind him, each one full of irate, howling Indians, and the entire swamp reverberated with his evil intentions.

Rafael heard the clamor while stalking an alligator with Francisco, on the far side of the isleta. Instantly he gave up all thoughts of the alligator and began to make plans to thwart Muñoz somehow, and recover the crop of marijuana.

His reaction was instinctive, but he knew from the start that this was the moment for which his entire life had been a preparation.

"Francisco, paddle around behind the patrol boat," he said, leaping from the canoe, wading to shore. "Tell the others that we have to stop him. We have no choice. We can't feed ourselves anymore. Tell them that when I give the signal I want them to board the patrol boat and overpower the guards."

"What's the signal, Papá?" Francisco hollered, as he paddled off.

"A single shot!" Rafael shouted after him, proud of the speed and apparent self-possession with which his son had reacted and proud of his smooth brown muscles flashing in the sunlight.

A tall strapping lad of seventeen, Francisco had just been selected by the elders to lead the barrio of Mexcaltitán in the annual Battle of the Saints during the Fiesta of San Martín.

Trotting off across his wife's flat, freshly harvested marijuana field, Rafael hoped that he might live to see it.

At home in the jacal, he armed himself with the old Colt .44 that he'd inherited from his father and stuck it into his calzones, under his tunic.

"Where are you going?" Benicta demanded, clutching their three little girls—Clarita, Albita and Martita—to her breast.

"To have a talk with Muñoz."

"Alone?"

"Why not?" he said, laughing in embarrassment.

"Don't go!" she cried, releasing the children, running after him out the door. "Don't go! Don't go!" she moaned, falling at his feet, catching him round the ankles.

But it was only a symbolic act, and of this they were both aware.

"Take your hands off me, woman," he said. "Go back into the jacal and stay with the children until I come back."

"You will *not* come back," she said bitterly.

And yet she obeyed him without another word.

Rafael went down to the landing and waited, sitting on his stacks of marijuana, smoking a cornhusk cigarette. A few minutes later, Muñoz came chugging up in his patrol boat, with his retinue of canoes. He was standing in the bow, dressed in white pants, white shirt, white Panama hat, flanked by a pair of armed infantrymen in camouflaged jungle fatigues and red berets. The other soldiers were lined up on the opposite side of the wheelhouse, with their M-16 rifles at the ready, warily eyeing the angry Indians who crowded closely around them in their canoes.

A sailor threw out a line. Rafael caught it handily and tied it to a mangrove root. And for a moment there was silence, with only the sound of the wind in the mangrove leaves, and water slapping against the plywood hull of the patrol boat.

"I have come for the bags," Muñoz said finally, lighting a cigar.

"By all means, Don Rudolfo," said Rafael, smiling, bowing, as the cigar smoke wafted by him in the wind. He was only a few meters from Muñoz. He could have leaped on him from where he stood, if he wanted. . . . "This year we have done very well, your excellency. On this one little island we have harvested over two thousand pesos' worth."

"I'm sorry to say that this year there will be no reimbursement," Muñoz said, glancing around at the canoes that clustered to his windward side. Yet there was no fear, or nervousness, in the gesture, and he turned back toward Rafael again without haste, and said flatly, "The crop is being confiscated by the government."

"But where will the government take it, Don Rudolfo?"

"To be burned as contraband."

"How do we know that it will be burned, and not sold on the black market?"

"You have my word on it."

"But what of our labor, señor? How shall we be paid? How shall we live? How shall we feed our children?"

"That is your own affair."

"It's just not right, Don Rudolfo. You know that yourself."

"I have my orders."

"From whom?"

"From Don Gallo himself."

"I am a law-abiding man, Licenciado. I will comply with the orders of the governor, but only under protest."

"Protest all you want, Indio," said Muñoz. "Just hand me up the bags."

"Sí, señor, para servirle," said Rafael. "But one of my boys is out fishing, and the other's at school in the village, and my wife's in the jacal with the little ones. You'll have to send me down some help, if we want to get it loaded before dark."

Muñoz barked an order. Four of the soldiers ran across from the other side, their heavy combat boots clomping loudly on the deck. They stacked their weapons in a clattering, untidy heap against the wall of the wheelhouse, and then two of them vaulted over the railing onto the bank and started hoisting up bags of marijuana to their fellows on deck. They were squat, round-faced, dark little men, Indians from other parts of the Republic, and they made a great racket while they worked, quite incommensurate with their size: "Cuate, mano! Horale pues! Echale, cabrón!"

With four of the soldiers thus disarmed and preoccupied, and only three left to guard the other side of the deck, Rafael figured that he had to make his move now or never. Taking a deep breath, and commending his soul to the alamo tree, he whipped out his revolver, aimed it at Muñoz's heart, and said coolly: "Tell them to lay down their weapons, Don Rudolfo. And no funny business, or you're as good as dead."

Just as coolly, and continuing to puff at his lit cigar, Muñoz measured the seriousness of Rafael's intentions.

"Lay down your arms!" he commanded, and his soldiers obeyed.

"To prove that I'm not fooling . . ." Rafael said, and fired a shot past Muñoz's right ear. Yet even then, the mestizo stood unblinking. For a fat man, he had astonishing cojones.

Francisco heard his father's signal, and boarded from the other side with a contingent of villagers. Fanning out across the deck, retrieving the M-16s as they went, they herded the soldiers and the two sailors onto the stern.

"Now, Francisco, let's put them all to work," Rafael said.

And they made them unload the entire crop of marijuana onto the bank.

After confiscating all the weapons on board and sending the patrol boat on its way back to the mainland, Rafael and his men reloaded the marijuana into their canoes and hid it in remote parts of the delta, in shallow sloughs and lagoons where the navy could never go, on heavily wooded mangrove islets that were home only to white herons and spawning turtles. There were over three thousand islands in the mangrove swamp, just a handful of which had ever been touched by the plow, and it would take Muñoz a hundred years to search them all.

Then Rafael demanded and was granted by the council of elders a commission as war leader, until the current troubles were over. His first order as leader was to mount a twenty-four-hour watch in the church tower, in case Muñoz came back with reinforcements.

Two weeks later Muñoz showed up as expected, this time with two patrol boats—one of them with a .50 caliber machine gun mounted on its deck—and a platoon of naval infantry. But by the time he reached Xochitlán, Rafael and his men had faded into the maze of the delta.

Muñoz spent several days searching for them, but he never found them. Every time he got close, they slid their canoes into caves under the muddy banks of the islands, between the mangrove roots, chased out the crabs and alligators, and resided in amphibian tranquillity until

Muñoz departed the area. Later, when Muñoz decided to give up the chase entirely and return to the mainland, El Niño and his muchachos paddled back home to Xochitlán and blended in with the population.

That winter the villagers kept themselves busy by preparing their old marijuana fields for the planting of corn, beans and chile, in order to signify their compliance with official government policy, and to satisfy the demands of their war leader, who insisted that they become self-sufficient in food production. Meanwhile Rafael sent out another large crew of men to secretly clear and prepare a number of the remotest islets in the delta for the planting of marijuana.

Muñoz came back three times that winter, but he never found the mota, the weapons or the "guerrillas" that he was looking for. Shortly before he departed for the last time, he took into custody three innocent old men of the village. He interrogated them on the deck of his patrol boat for twenty-four hours, without food or water. He tortured them with lit cigarettes, electric cattle prods and lengthy dunkings in the river. But he got nothing out of them because they knew nothing.

Rafael had made sure of that. His men were forbidden on pain of death to reveal even to their wives and mothers the locations of their hiding places, or where the marijuana island lay. Rafael himself was the only person who knew the precise location of all the hiding places, all the marijuana islands, and he had vowed that he would never allow himself to be captured alive.

Meanwhile he was aware of reliving his mother's life in a way he would not have chosen, and he prayed to her nightly for guidance as if she had been a saint in heaven.

In May the villagers sowed their new crop of mota. The rains came, and the plants began to grow. At this time another council of elders was convened, as several of the members had voiced concern that last year's crop might rot in the rainy-season damp, if it was not quickly disposed of.

"What we need is a new buyer," said the presidente. "Someone who's not connected with Don Gallo or Muñoz."

"Or someone who's *no longer* connected," Rafael said.

"But where shall we find such a person?" the padre wanted to know.

"I have an idea about that," Rafael said. "But it will mean a journey to the state of Guerrero to find out."

CHAPTER 7

In a dramatic setting, high on a green hillside above Punta Guitarrón, surrounded by two hundred tastefully decorated private units, a hundred and fifty acres of lovely terraced grounds, six swimming pools, five tennis courts, a nine-hole golf course, a driving range, a private dock, and a secluded white sand beach, the deluxe, forty-two-story Acapulco Intercontinental, gem of the O'Hare-Carrizo chain, rose triumphantly to meet the wide and empty Mexican sky.

On a particularly sunny and pleasant early morning in late 1969, one of the principal shareholders in the hotel corporation was seated at a table by the private penthouse pool, with his feet upon a chair. A sleek, well-tanned, rather *soigné*-looking chap of about forty, Merle Carrizo, executive vice-president for public relations, was taking his café con leche while puffing at a long cigarillo and watching his daughter work out on the high dive. In keeping with the times he wore white shell beads, a white embroidered Hindu tunic, a black bikini and a pair of Madrasi sandals, and he sported a heavy black mustache, luxuriant side-whiskers and nearly shoulder-length hair.

Diana, his daughter, was a tall, big-boned, ginger-haired girl with a large, intense, darkly freckled face just on the verge of prettiness. Barely fourteen, she was very mature and well developed for her age, and took the sport of diving quite seriously. In a black maillot swim suit and white bathing cap, she marched up the ladder with a stately measured pace, eyes straight ahead. At the top of the platform she rose on her toes, lifted her long strong arms as if about to take flight—head up, shoulders back, fanny tucked in—and glided to the end of the board. There she pivoted gracefully on her right foot and, never breaking her remarkable concentration, bounced once, launched herself backward into space—body arched, arms wide, legs together, toes pointed—in a nearly flawless backflip in swan-dive form. She broke the shady green surface of the pool with barely a ripple.

"Incredible, baby, a nine if I ever saw one!"

"The only thing is, Daddy," she said, swimming for the ladder, "I felt my right knee leading my left."

"You bent it just as you went in," he said, as she emerged, streaming water, from the pool. "Just a smidgeon. Try it again."

Jesus, they grow so fast, he thought, watching her tread carefully across the tiles, past the potted bougainvillea and the open-air bar, remembering just a couple of years back when she'd have run slipping and sliding for the board and he'd have to yell at her to slow down. And then they're gone.

Merle had been especially conscious of this painful fact of nature ever since one morning last week when he received a complaint about Diana from a hotel guest. Apparently, she had been going around the lobby the night before, soliciting money on behalf of a squatters' organization called the Second of October Movement.

At first, he couldn't believe that she would do such a thing.

"Why, you must be mistaken, sir," he said. "My daughter has no interest in politics."

"I assure you it's true," said the guest, a rich Texan who'd been coming to the O'Hare-Carrizo hotels for years and had dropped thousands in their private casino. "My wife, my son and my secretary saw it too. She went around shaking a can in people's faces, saying, 'Help us feed the hungry, help us feed the hungry.' "

"I'm so sorry, Mr. Grant," Merle said. "I promise you, I'll put a stop to this at once."

What made the whole thing doubly embarrassing was the fact that a month before, several dozen members of the Second of October Movement had occupied property on the outskirts of Acapulco belonging to the O'Hare-Carrizo Corporation. There they had built themselves some cardboard shacks and dug some latrines, and were now squatting in defiance of several court orders. It was widely known that Chris and a few of her politician friends had plans to develop the land as a golf course and recreational complex for tourists, and Merle had recently had the devil's own time fending off inquisitive reporters while trying to maintain the excellent public relations he'd always enjoyed in the past:

"Are you aware that there's been an invasion of your property, señor?"

"We only know what we read in the newspapers."

"The leader of the squatters, Padre Morán, has asserted that the property was meant to be a communal ejido, that it was acquired illegally and in defiance of local ordinances, with the active collusion of certain corrupt officials."

"He has made no such statement to us."

"Does Señora O'Hare intend to . . . ?"

"I'm sorry, but Señora O'Hare is in Paris at the moment, concluding an agreement to bring a new Club Méditerranée to Acapulco. She will be happy to acquaint you with her views on the subject on her return. . . ."

And the worst of it was that the local authorities, worried that the flow of bribery money to their pockets might be impeded by the squatters' intransigence, had taken the matter into their own hands. Already there had been shootings, bombings, "disappearances," raids of the encampment by "right-wing death squads" composed of off-duty policemen.

Merle had not forgotten that he had spent a year or two of his own young life in a similar encampment. He sympathized with the plight of the squatters, and he was not happy in his present role as defender of an oppressive status quo. Yet he felt compelled by loyalty to his wife and his family business to continue to do the best job of public relations that he could.

He racked his brain, trying to figure out who could have put Diana up to such a stupid trick. He remembered that a Padre Morán had been her retreat master at the Dominican school a couple of years back, and that Padre Morán was close to Sister María Magdalena, Diana's homeroom teacher. So, that afternoon, shortly before classes let out, Merle took the hotel limousine to the Dominican school and had a talk with Mother Francisca.

"I want my daughter moved out of Sister María Magdalena's class immediately," he said. "And I want this involvement with the Second of October Movement to cease."

"I will place your daughter in another class, Señor Carrizo," said Mother Francisca, as they concluded their interview, "but I must remind you that all my sisters are followers of Christ, and all share His special love for the weak, the poor and the oppressed. . . ."

Afterward, Merle went out and sat in the limousine with the motor running, the air conditioning going, and the driver dozing in front, waiting for his daughter's classes to let out, silently cursing the Mexican Catholic Church: Goddam, it's just one fucking extreme after another in this country. A few years ago the bastards were the bulwark of the right. Now they're in the vanguard of the social reform movement. And I call myself a liberal. But when I think of my daughter, wasting her time in a cause as hopeless as the poor people of Mexico . . .

And was reminded of his Aunt Ramona, whom he had loved so dearly, and of her devotion to the unfortunate, and of her terrible end.

Diana came down the steps of her school building in a throng of chattering fourteen- and fifteen-year-old mestiza girls surrounding a pretty creole nun in a knee-length white dress and head scarf that made her look like some kind of nurse. It was Sister María Magdalena. He had met her once with Chris at a school Christmas party.

Diana, blue-eyed, freckle-faced, her short frizzy hair shining red in the sunlight, towered above the white nun and her dark little entourage. She looked like an overgrown Little Orphan Annie in her plaid school uniform, quintessentially North American. Yet he knew that in her soul she was more Mexican than he himself. And the sight of her there nearly broke his heart, for there was something in Diana that Mexican men would not like. She was on the verge of prettiness, but she would never cross over the fine line. She would grow too tall and too large, and she would loom over them. They would hate her and ridicule her for precisely her best qualities: Her frankness, her self-confidence, her maturity, her fundamental goodness. They would want to abuse her, to sully her, to cut her down to their size. When they discovered her inner strength, and found that they could not diminish her, they would try to destroy her, in one way or another. "La chingar!" as they would express it to themselves. And she was infinitely dear to her father for that, for what she was, and what she was not, and what they might do to her.

He called to her from the limousine window.

"Diana, let's go home!"

"Oh, Daddy," she said, approaching the car. "What're you doing here?"

And it was clear from her aggrieved tone that she already knew of his interview with Mother Francisca, and was mortified by it.

"Get in," he insisted, trying to look stern.

"Adiós, Monja! Adiós, chicas!" she called, and entered the limousine obediently.

"Now tell me, Daddy, why did you want to go and do a thing like that?" she asked him, more wounded than angry, as they drove away. "Why did you go to Mother Francisca without talking to me first?"

"I . . . I was angry," he lied. "I was overexcited. I mean, is it true what I heard, baby, that you've been soliciting guests for money?"

"Yes, of course it's true."

"You know your mother doesn't permit anyone to bother the guests. They come down here to have a good time. They don't want to know about our national problems."

"When people are hungry, Daddy, they must be fed."

"That money isn't just for food, Diana. Did you know that? It's to stir up trouble, to agitate, to defy the law."

"We're not obliged to obey unjust laws," she said, as if by rote. "We should go out of our way to disobey them."

"On some ideal plane, Diana, that may be right. But here in Mexico it's an extremely dangerous proposition."

"Land and Liberty," she said very gravely. "That's why the Revolution was fought."

And Merle had to catch himself from laughing then, for such gravity coming from a fourteen-year-old was surely preposterous.

"Where do you get that stuff, baby? The Revolution was dead before you were born. All we've done is exchange one set of incompetent rulers for another."

"The Revolution lives on," Diana said, repeating the words as he remembered her repeating the words of the Catechism as a tiny girl. "It lives on in the hearts of the people, en el corazón de la raza."

Merle's mind had wandered. He had missed Diana's latest plunge.

"Fabulous, Diana!" he hollered anyway, as her head broke the surface. "A perfect ten."

And thought of how he had followed her the next day, on a hunch, and discovered that she was stealing food from the hotel kitchen and delivering it in person to the Second of October encampment on her bicycle. Creeping along behind her in a battered, anonymous taxi, watching her pedal along beside the white dirt roads, the broken-down adobe walls, the open sewage canals, the scraggly cactus trees, the cardboard shacks, the filthy potbellied children, the pariah dogs, the uncollected garbage of non-tourist-recommended Acapulco, her large intelligent face intent on the road ahead of her, her wiry red hair plastered against her head by the wind, her plaid skirt billowing up to show her strong, freckled, swimmer's thighs, Merle felt at once overwhelmed with pride and love for his daughter, and terrified for her life.

Even so, he allowed her to carry on down that white dirt road to the squatters' camp and to make her delivery there, preferring to tag along behind her like some kind of furtive guardian angel. And when he confronted her later, on the way home, leaving his taxi and wending his way through a traffic jam and catching her at a stoplight on the Malecón, his protest was muted—"I'm worried about what you're doing, baby"—and half drowned out by the blaring of horns in any case, and he admitted to her with only the merest prodding that she did have "justice and common decency" on her side.

After he had managed to extricate her bike from the traffic jam, however, and they were sitting in a little thatch-roofed open bar by the side of the road, drinking Dos Equis and Fanta out of the bottle, he felt compelled to remind her of the bombings, the shootings, the "disappearances" and the threats by "right-wing death squads" to which the Second of October encampment was prone.

"Will you promise me, Diana, that you'll never go out there again?" he asked.

"But someone has to go," she said. "Will you take my place?"

"It's a deal," he said, without thinking. "I'll do even better than that, if you'll agree to go to school in the States next year."

"Why do you want me to go to school up there?"

"It's dangerous for you here, Diana. I worry about you. Things are changing so fast. Every day you read about kids, from some of the best families, going into radical politics, joining peasant revolts, urban guerrilla gangs. . . ."

"Well, you don't have to worry about me, Daddy. I'm not the type."

"I know, I know, Diana, but listen. If you promise me you'll go to school in the States, I tell you what I'll do. When your mother gets back from her business trip, I'll do everything in my power to get her to change her plans for that land where those people are squatting. I'll do more than that. I'll set up a foundation for the squatters and people like them.

I'll convince your mother that it's time for a little corporate philanthropy, that it's good for public relations. I'll encourage other corporations to contribute funds. I'll raise millions of pesos."

"You don't have to bribe me, Daddy," she said, laughing. "I'm not one of Mama's politicians."

"But let's keep this to ourselves, okay?" he said, thinking of her tendency to confide in Val, and Val's tendency to favor Chris—and even to snitch, on occasion—whenever family disputes arose. "I'd like to take this up with your mother in my own time, and in my own way."

And so now every afternoon after work he loaded up on food that Diana had pinched from the hotel kitchen and money that he'd withdrawn from his own bank account and he climbed into an anonymous taxi and rode out to the Second of October encampment and delivered the gifts to the organizing committee and got back into the taxi and rode back to the hotel laughing like a fiend.

For of course they must have thought him perfectly mad, since his wife was the author of all their troubles.

Nor apparently had his peculiar behavior escaped the attention of the municipal authorities. On the second day of his little errand he discovered that he was being followed by an unmarked police car, and realized that even if Diana kept her mouth shut the news might reach Chris before he got a chance to broach the subject delicately. And delicate it must be, for Chris could be vindictive, if she felt that her authority was being challenged.

So . . . in search of an ally, someone he could rely on in the coming confrontation with Chris, he turned to Maureen. At eighty-five years old, Maureen was still tall and straight and clear-eyed, a remarkably commanding woman, and a terrible adversary when roused. Granted that she dyed her hair red and had a face lift every few years, she still looked a decade younger than her true age, and she had the energy and vitality of someone in the prime of life.

"Anything for my boy," she said, when he visited her for supper at the Tropicana. "We'll deal with Chris as soon as she gets back. There can be no question of 'business as usual,' when her daughter's life's involved. As for Diana, you leave her to me. I'll have her to lunch tomorrow and we'll have a little heart-to-heart talk. Believe me, I'll make her *listen*. I don't know why she hasn't been packed off to school in the States long ago."

"Chris didn't want her to go," Merle said. "She wanted her at home."

"Well, this time," Maureen said, "Chris is just going to have to see it our way."

At first Merle was much relieved by his conversation with Maureen. She sounded so sane, so sensible, and she took charge so thoroughly. But when he got back home it occurred to him that he had probably committed a grave strategic error. Chris would consider his consultation with Maureen as a betrayal: Though mother and daughter had remained close, their relationship was incurably fractious, riven with jealousy and mistrust.

Chris would be furious. No telling what she might do.

He wondered why he had chosen to provoke her in this way. And finally he understood that on some level he actually wanted to force the issue between them, for he was sick to death of Chris's imperious ways, and he was willing to do almost anything to destroy her tyrannical hold over his life.

Diana was on the diving platform again. She moved to the end of the board, pivoted, bounced once, reached for her ankles, and executed a beautiful open cutaway one and a half, missing the board by inches, slicing the water without a splash.

"Wonderful, Diana, wonderful!" Merle shouted.

"Bravo!" someone yelled, coming up behind him. It was Val Raymond, treasurer and social director of the O'Hare-Carrizo hotel chain, wearing a pink bikini and a white terry-cloth robe open at the front. In fifteen years the Mexican sun had weathered Val considerably about the eyes and mouth, and it had bleached her hair to the color of platinum. But her body was just as sensational as ever.

"Thanks," Diana said, emerging from the water to bestow a wet good-morning kiss upon her Aunt Val's perspiring brow. "But don't watch the next few dives, okay? It's something new I'm working on. I want to warm up a bit, and then I'll let you know when I'm ready."

"She's really something, isn't she?" said Val, flinging her pack of cigarettes on the table, sliding into the seat across from Merle.

"I don't know what we'd do without her," Merle said, wondering if all households were like this, everyone just repeating the same stock phrases over and over.

"I worry about this religious stage, though," Val said, lighting a cigarette, beckoning to the Indian maid who stood by the retaining wall. "Don't you, love?"

"Well, Diana's always been kind of devout," he parried, wondering how much she knew. And if she did know, had she phoned Chris in Paris?

"Oh, it's gone farther than that now," Val said, ordering a cappuccino from the maid. "You know what she does every morning before school? She spends an hour on her knees in the school chapel, imploring the Blessed Virgin to forgive her for all her advantages in life."

"It'll all blow over, Val. Remember that other stage she went through, when she was seven and eight, traipsing into the hotel with an endless assortment of broken-winged seagulls, one-eyed alley cats, one-legged pariah dogs, setting them up comfortably in her room, coaxing them back to health? And then when she was nine and ten, graduating to homeless street urchins, bringing them in and hiding them in out-of-the-way corners of the basement and the laundry room. . . ."

"Like little stowaways," Val said, smiling fondly at the memory. "You're right, darling. She'll probably be over this thing in a flash. Maybe it's just some kind of adolescent revolt."

"Revolt against what?" Merle said distractedly, sneaking a peek at Diana's latest dive.

"Are you kidding?" Val said. "Our whole life-style here."

"Oh, I see what you mean," Merle said, locking eyes with her. And then they both smiled at once. Val's eyes were far more expressive than in the days when she was with Bo, and her smile was somewhat less professional. After Diana was born she'd given up drugs entirely, and though she'd taken up the slack with liquor, to a certain extent, she'd become a much more lively and responsive companion. "Yes," Merle said, remembering what they'd done together in bed last night and planning to do it again with her after work this afternoon, or after the reception for the International Transactional Analysis Association convention crowd that they were giving this evening . . . unless Chris showed up from Paris, in which case he would beg off and try to talk *her* into something. . . . God, what a life I lead! he was thinking. And yet another part of him felt trapped, used, stifled by his job, guilty over the luxurious life he led while surrounded by so much poverty, bored with Val, exasperated with Chris's eccentricities. "Yes, Val," Merle said again. "But I thought Diana'd come to terms with our life-style ages ago."

"Well, last night she came to me, love, and she said it right out. 'Aunt

Val,' she said, 'I don't want to be like you and Mama and Daddy. I want to be like other people.' "

"Sounds pretty healthy to me," Merle said, reaching out to run his hand over Val's bronzed fingers. He had a compulsion to touch them all, all of his women, constantly—Val, Chris, Diana, even old Maureen—as if to confirm that they were indeed real and solid and worth everything he appeared to have given up for them. Surrounded by women, petted and pampered and mothered and ruled by them, Merle felt like a captive drone in a community of Amazons, and he'd not written a thing of value since the day of his marriage. This was not something that Merle kept to himself. He complained about it all the time. But they just laughed every time he brought it up, as if it were some kind of joke.

". . . Yes," Val was saying. "I suppose it is rather healthy, at that."

"I mean, when you think of it, Val," Merle said, picking up where he'd left off, "we are a bit bizarre, aren't we?"

"Weird," she said, giggling, squeezing his hand.

And it struck Merle, not for the first time, that they were all a good deal weirder than she imagined. They lived in a world of Chris's devising. As such, it was at once very complicated and very seductive and very deeply flawed. It was a cracked and wobbly world, a world off its poles, yet its atmosphere was thick and heady and its gravity was amazingly strong and it was almost impossible to break its hold. It was a little like being in a room full of trained rats presided over by a mad lady scientist who, convinced that she had some vitally important experiment to perform, tilted the floor a little more each day. There was no sense of balance, no point of reference, no ethical norm, no rationale by which to judge one's own actions. Yet everything was hermetically sealed and tightly controlled, leading to frequent episodes of sterile, rodentlike panic.

"All right, you can watch now!" Diana called, and made her approach, bounced high—knees locked, toes pointed—and did a spectacular one and a half with a full twist, striking the water cleanly but with tremendous force, plunging all the way to the bottom, floating slowly to the surface, keeping her form.

"Absolute perfection, Diana!" Val yelled.

"Next year we go for the Olympic team!" Merle hollered.

"Oh," Val said, when Diana had padded off around the pool again, "I wouldn't count on that, Merle."

"Why not?"

"She doesn't enjoy competition, she tells me. Prefers to do it for pleasure."

"What I'd like to know," Merle replied irritably, "is how come she tells these things to you and not me."

"I'm a woman," Val said. "She tells me all kinds of things, things you only want to tell another female."

"You don't want Chris to hear you say that."

"Chris has got no right to mind," Val replied. "No right at all."

And yet there was nothing indignant in her tone. It was a simple statement of fact: Chris was gone most of the time, off to Puerto Vallarta, Zihuatenejo, Cabo San Lucas, Cancún, Cozumel in a chartered plane with the windows blacked out on account of her acrophobia, buying up property right and left, putting together fabulous deals with rich foreign investors and shrewd native entrepreneurs, riding the tourist boom for all it was worth.

"The truth is, love, Chris couldn't get along without me," Val said. "I'm an essential convenience. Without me she'd probably end up repeating her mother's sad maternal performance."

"I wouldn't want her to hear that either," Merle said, sitting up, glancing over his shoulder, as if Chris might suddenly materialize behind him.

And in no time at all, it seemed, she did just that.

A pretty, sharp-featured little woman in her early forties, she appeared in the doorway to the penthouse, wearing a long green sundress, espadrilles, a wide straw hat, and a pair of wire-rimmed granny glasses perched on her nose.

"Hello you two," she said, crossing the tiles, glancing brightly from one of them to the other.

To Merle, her high birdlike voice seemed unusually brittle and intense, and he knew that someone had phoned her and told her what he was up to.

"Hello, darling," Val said. And her tone, coolly guarded rather than startled, struck him as exceedingly odd, and confirmed his suspicion that she was the culprit.

"What a surprise," Merle said, rising to kiss his wife.

"Well," Chris said breathlessly, throwing herself down in a chair beside Val, "I'd just closed the deal with Club Méditerranée and I had another appointment with World Holidays in London when suddenly it occurred to me, 'My God, I've missed Mama's birthday again!' So I hopped the first flight back. Stopped off at the Tropicana on the way in from the airport. And here we are, absolutely intent upon celebrating!"

"In my case not so intent," said Maureen, crossing the patio from the penthouse, wearing her usual festive china poblana, "as ensnared. And my birthday, as you all know well, passed unnoticed by Chris over a month ago."

". . . I've arranged everything," Chris was saying. "We'll have a late lunch by the pool. We'll have a cake. I've even got a mariachi band coming up to play 'Las Mañanitas.' "

"I'd like to know what's wrong with plain old 'Happy Birthday,' " Maureen said, as Merle seated her by his side.

"After sixty-five years south of the border," Chris said, "my mother still refuses to acknowledge the fact that she's in Mexico."

"I loathe mariachis, and Chris knows it."

"Maureen has always been the soul of tact."

Incurable as ever, mother and daughter sat there verbally flagellating each other for several moments, thoroughly enjoying themselves. And then abruptly, as if by mutual consent, they broke it off and went on to speak of other things.

"Hey, gorgeous!" Chris called out, as Diana stepped out on the diving platform. "Come down here and give us a kiss!"

"Mama!" Diana cried, and promptly made her worst dive of the day. She nearly fell off the board in her excitement, and failed to pull out of her full gainer in time to prevent herself from flopping comically on her back.

And yet Merle was sure that Diana had seen her mother appear many minutes before, and had merely pretended not to notice her; and her whole performance now was just a kind of childish show, a nervous reaction. Chris affected a lot of people like that.

"Mama!" Diana said, running to her, slipping and sliding, across the tiles.

"Now don't get me wet, dear," Chris said. "Just kiss me on the cheek. Then go give your grandma a big hug and climb right back up on the board. I want to see that full gainer again. You can certainly do better than the last one."

The birthday party was the disaster that both Chris and her mother seemed to require. Though such scenes were not uncommon between them, this one seemed unusually harsh, with vast undercurrents of mutual suspicion and animosity. Neither of them mentioned Merle or Diana, except in the most passing way, but it was clear that they were the real bones of contention between them, and that they had already had words on the issue, probably in the limousine on the way over from the Tropicana.

The climax of their inverse celebration came shortly after the cake—an implausible volcano-shaped concoction of chocolate and coconut implanted with eighty-five candles—was wheeled in, and Chris presented her mother with a magnificent diamond brooch in the form of a tree-of-life that must have set her back a fortune.

"What are these, dear?"

"Why, they're diamonds, Mother. What do they look like?"

"Well, I couldn't believe they were diamonds, Chris, because you've known for years that I cannot abide diamonds. I find them tawdry. I've never worn them in my life."

"Oh, really, Mama? I thought you'd like them," Chris said. "Well, never mind, you've never liked anything I've given you anyway."

And suddenly Merle remembered another party, a lifetime ago, on Mother's Day, as he recalled, when he'd heard the same uncertain tone, suspended somewhere between insolence and self-pity, and his heart had gone out to little Chris, as it did now.

And he began to regret that he had provoked this scene. For under it all, he thought, Chris meant everything to him.

"Diana," Maureen said, calmly rising to her feet, "why don't you see me to the limousine, my precious? Your mother isn't feeling well. Besides," she said, throwing Merle a sympathetic look, "I think she's got something pressing on her mind at the moment. There's something she wants to talk over with your father."

Merle was not particularly surprised, therefore, when immediately after their departure Val excused herself and abruptly left the table. Nor was he surprised, a moment later, when Chris dismissed the servants, fixed him with a malevolent stare and lunged out at him, "You've had a free ride too long, Merle. From now on you're going to have to start paying your dues."

What surprised him was the fact that she did not immediately take him to task for his conspiracy with Maureen, or his rash promise to Diana, or his dealings at the Second of October encampment. And he pressed his temporary advantage quickly, for even a moment's hesitation could have the most serious consequences, when Chris was in a mood like this.

He said, "What makes you think I haven't been paying my dues all along?"

"I'd like to know how. I mean, you don't call public relations *work,* do you?"

"By letting you run my life for fifteen years, by putting up with all your silly fears and phobias, and your insane competition with your mother, and never saying a word about it."

"You were too lazy to say anything about it, Merle. It's your nature as a Mexican."

"You always roll out the heavy artillery, don't you, Chris? Even in the most minor disputes."

"Don't think I can't see through your little plot with my mother," she said. "Sending Diana off to school in the States and then discreetly following her in a couple of years, leaving me behind. And don't think I'm sending you off to manage one of my cushy hotels," she said. "The place I have in mind is not for a young girl."

"Chris, this whole thing started because I was out of my head with worry over Diana. I helped her with the Second of October people because it was the only way I could stop her from going out there herself. I thought you'd be as worried as I am, that you'd want to send her out of harm's way, that . . ."

"All right, all right, all right!" she said, holding up her hand for him to stop. Then she broke into one of her brightest, most untrustworthy smiles. "All right, honey," she sighed. "Let's just say it never happened. Let's just say I'm in a very tight spot right now and I need your help."

Merle laughed.

"What's so funny?"

"You never give anything away, do you?" he said. "Not even your forgiveness."

"What?"

"Sure, Chris, I'd be glad to help."

It was an old game with them, one that Merle always let himself lose, because it was often the preliminary to one of their rare amorous interludes, for which he was willing to pay just about anything.

"Sure," he said again, rising to his feet, leading her toward the penthouse. "Let's go to your room, and you can lay it out for me there."

"No," she said. "Let's go to your room. I want to see what you've been writing lately."

"Lately," he said, "not too much."

"Sometimes I suspect you're writing about me."

"Sometimes I am."

They crossed their living room—a large anonymous room with heavy red-and-yellow drapery, overstuffed furniture, glass coffee tables, wall-to-wall carpeting and Bernard Buffet reproductions that were standard issue at the hotel—and made their way down the corridor to Merle's room. It was sparsely furnished, to suit his own taste. There was a bed, a desk, a chair, a draftsman's lamp, a bookshelf, a fridge, a typewriter and a small colorful Mexican rug. The walls were bare and white.

Two or three evenings a week for the past decade or so, he had come into this room—or one very much like it at another of their hotels—and he had tried to write. Now there were stacks of manuscripts, reams of plot outlines, piles of notes all over the floor and shelves. In all those years, however, he had not completed a single project. But the thing of it was . . . he had so many wonderful ideas for stories. Stories about his cunning, Snopesian old man. Stories he'd heard Chris's mother tell, dating back before Chris was born. Tragic-romantic tales like that of Brian and Ramona. Stories of initiation like Crazy Eddie and the Delts. Macabre tales like Bo Brodsky's. Smutty stories about his *ménage à trois* with Chris and Val. And one long and overly complex story about his obsessive, self-destructive, lifelong fascination with Chris . . . "his sibling, his rival, his wife, his ward, his ruler. . . ."

It was Chris, in fact, who inspired all his works. And she existed in each of them, disguised in her many forms and fragments. In a sense, she *was* his work. The very heart of it. Its very deepest core.

Merle showed Chris into his room and got them each a canned margarita from the fridge.

"All right," he said, pouring their drinks onto the ice at the bottom of a couple of plastic hotel cups. "What's the deal?"

"It all boils down to this," she said, accepting the drink, smiling thanks. But then she handed it back to him with a small shrug of apology.

He tasted it for her and gave it back.

Their intimacy was total now, as when they were kids. Locked in his room together, with the blinds drawn and the air conditioner droning in the background, it was as if they inhabited the same brain.

"Years ago," she said, starting to pace up and down the room, rattling the ice in her cup, "I made this deal with your dad. . . ."

"You've made lots of deals with my dad," Merle said. "And there wasn't one I liked, or trusted."

"This was different," she said. "Altamirano was in on this one. Gallo had these Indians out in the delta growing pot. He bought it off them for a song, handed it over to me and Altamirano, and we shipped it to the border. . . ."

For years, apparently, everything had gone along smoothly for the partners until a few months back when the U.S. government decided to declare war on the drug trade and started offering millions of dollars to the Mexican government to stop the flow of drugs. Most of the money found its way into the pockets of big-shot politicians like Gallo. And people like Chris and Altamirano got nothing. The worst part of it, Chris discovered, was that she'd been relying on the dope money far more than she'd realized. She found that she was actually "very seriously overextended financially." Without that considerable untaxed income every year, she would not be able to keep up on all the mortgage loans she'd taken out to finance her expansion.

"Then quite recently," she said, "just when it was starting to look like I might default, this Indian shows up at Altamirano's. Says he represents the marijuana growers of the delta, and he's looking for a new buyer, since he no longer has a deal with the governor. He's got tons of the stuff, he says, where no one can ever find it. Altamirano gives me a buzz, and right away we decide to strike a deal. But what we need now, Merle, is someone we can trust absolutely, someone who's dark enough to pass for an Indian, if need be, someone to go back with the guy to the delta, establish some trust there with the growers and the powers-that-be, inspect the situation, figure out how much dope we can count on, and the best method of shipping it."

"Very interesting," he said, concealing a welter of emotions that began with distaste for the dope trafficking itself, escalated upward in intensity to revulsion over Chris's continued involvement with his father, and reached a pinnacle at the discovery that his wife could have excluded him from her confidence for so long over a matter of such crucial importance. "But what I want to know is this. Why, after all these years, do you suddenly want to bring me into the business end?"

"Oh, I don't know," she said, pausing at the window, staring at the closed blinds as if she could see a magnificent vista spreading out before her eyes. "I thought you might be in a rut, in need of a change. You're always complaining. You're unhappy. You feel like a 'drone.' You can't write. Who knows? You might even turn up some new literary material, local color, or something."

"Chris, do you love me at all?"

"I've known you so long, Merle, it's like you're really a part of me," she said, still staring intently at the geometric Aztec pattern on the blind. "Sometimes I look in the mirror and I swear I don't see me. I see you. And then there are other times," she said, smiling, turning suddenly to meet his eyes, "when I wish you were—"

"What?" he asked. Her madness, he found, was still as luminous and beguiling as ever, and he had rarely shirked to follow where she led. Breathless, he repeated, "What?"

"There are other times when I . . . oh, nothing. When I wish you were growing. I wish you were working at something really challenging. Listen, Merle, this operation needs a strong hand."

"So now it comes out."

"What?"

"There's danger."

"Well, it's against the law to grow the stuff. And the military has given the Indians some trouble over it. But not recently. Actually, I don't think there's much to worry about, at least not in your case. You're the governor's son, Merle."

"I'd forgotten."

"The army wouldn't dare lay a hand on you. But for God's sake don't tell those Indians your real name. Gallo's the enemy now, out there in the mangrove swamp."

"Is he?" said Merle. "Well, at least I'll be fighting on the right side."

"So you'll do it?"

"What'll you give me, Chris, if I do?"

"Anything you want."

"I want Diana out of here."

Chris hesitated for a moment, and Merle wondered. . . .

"All right, no problem," she said. "We'll send her to school in the States next year."

"And I want you," he said. "I want you now; and I want you more often."

"Oh, Merle," she said, sighing, joining him on the bed. "I always feel so . . . like my mother might come in and catch us at it, or something.

And then afterward we always feel so spent, both of us, so turned inside out."

"I never get enough of you," he murmured, trembling, cupping her hard little breast. "I want to crawl up inside of you and . . ."

"You leave me no rest," she said, lying stiff and taut beneath him. "I dream of you when I'm away. But when I'm with you, my love, I wish every time were the last."

CHAPTER 8

Put an Indian into European clothes, and you've got a mestizo. Put a mestizo into Indian clothes, and you've got an Indian. Rafael trimmed the stranger's hair and sidewhiskers, bought him a sombrero, calzones and huaraches; they caught a third-class bus for Zihuatenejo, and nobody gave him a second glance, in spite of his blue eyes.

"It's almost uncanny," the stranger said, "the way one reverts to the ways of one's ancestors."

All the way up the coast of Guerrero State the army was out in force, with jeeps, trucks, armored cars, machine guns, even helicopters. The peasants of the Sierra Madre del Sur were resisting the government campaign to destroy their marijuana crops, and a schoolteacher named Lucio Cabanas had led several villages in open revolt.

Rafael was cheered and encouraged by the sight. If the resistance became generalized in the mountains, the military would have little time to spare for the delta.

In Zihuatenejo they wandered out to the end of the jetty, where Rafael had arranged to meet Francisco. But they were early, and there was no canoe in sight, so they went back to shore, curled up in the shade of a beached tuna boat beside a couple of local fishermen and had themselves a little siesta. When they awakened at sunset they were just in time to see the black canoe come sailing through the mouth of the little bay, its lateen sail billowing in the wind.

They walked out to the end of the jetty again and waved their sombreros. Francisco saw them and brought the canoe swiftly alongside, cutting sharply at the last instant, swinging his tail around deftly, riding his own backwash till he bumped gently against the concrete.

"Quite a tillerman you've got there," the stranger remarked.

"He's my son," Rafael proudly replied. "I taught him myself."

The instant they were aboard, Francisco swung her around into the wind and headed out to sea again, tacking easily across the little bay till he made a skillful exit through the narrow rocky inlet.

Rafael and the stranger had not been formally introduced in Aguas Blancas. "It's probably better to avoid all mention of names," Altamirano had said. But now that they were under way, sailing up the coast through a feathery white sea, with a brisk, humid south wind behind them, Rafael could see no harm in getting better acquainted.

"Señor," he said gravely, "I would like to present my eldest son, Francisco."

"Con mucho gusto."

"And I am Rafael Martínez, síndico of Xochitlán."

"Encantado."

"And your name, señor?"

"Lytle."

"Lytle?"

"My mother had an affinity for gringos, it seems."

"As did mine," said Rafael. "She was with one when she died, I'm afraid."

"I see."

"And your surname, señor?"

"Mescalero."

"Pardon me?"

"Mescalero."

"Can it be that you are some relation to Ramona Mescalero?"

"There are so many Mescaleros. . . ."

"She used to live in Manzanillo, later in the Islas Tres Marías, where I was born."

"Oh?" said the stranger suspiciously. "What relation is she to you?"

"She was my mother."

"Your mother?"

"Pues claro que sí, señor."

"Where did she live in Manzanillo?"

"In Manzanillo she lived in a hotel, I think. She took care of some children there, and worked in the dining room."

"When did she die?"

"Many years ago, señor. When I was only a baby."

"Then how is it that you know so much about her?"

"It's all in her diary, señor. I've kept it all these years, in a watertight packet."

"I'd like to see it sometime, if I could."

"My house is your house, señor."

"But the name Ramona Mescalero just doesn't ring a bell."

"No matter," Rafael said, yet when they reached the village, he introduced him everywhere as Mescalero, and hinted at some distant family relationship between him and his mother, and made sure that all doors were open to him, even those of the presidente, the régido, the maestro, and the huehuechique. Why he went to so much trouble for the stranger, he could not say. "For business reasons," he told Benicta. But that was not strictly true. In fact he had always been secretly insecure as an orphan, with no blood relatives but his children. And he was proud to be associated with this educated mestizo from the city, who bore the same name as his mother: Here was the man that Rafael himself might have become, had the chips fallen differently.

El Niño admired the stranger so much that he was tempted to bring him out to live with him and his family on the Isleta Chamacua, but then he decided that he would probably be uncomfortable in the jacal, sleeping on the ground, relieving himself in the marijuana field, so he took the trouble to find him lodgings with the maestro, with whom he obviously had more in common.

Later Rafael presented the stranger to the council of elders, and secured their permission to take him on a guided tour of the mangrove swamp, including the cemetery island where the sacred alamo tree grew, the secret islands where the marijuana grew, and the drying sheds where last year's crop was stored.

Everywhere Mescalero went, he took notes. And by the end of the tour he had filled a whole ledger with numbers and facts. He sent a telegram to his partners in code confirming that the crop was still dry and potent and well stored. But speed was of the essence, he told them, because of the danger of rainy-season mold. In order to avoid unpleasant complications on the mainland during the shipment of the crop, Mescalero recommended to his partners that the entire operation be conducted by sea. A mother ship could anchor in international waters just off the delta. The villagers could carry the crop out at night in their swift canoes, and the mother ship could steam off for the United States, where it could anchor again in international waters, and off-load onto fast speedboats at night.

Mescalero received an immediate affirmative response, which he showed to Rafael. Rafael submitted the entire plan to the council of elders, where it was endorsed unanimously. A week later Mescalero was notified by coded telegram that his partners had chartered a coastal motorship of Panamanian registry. The telegram also specified the hour, the date and place of its arrival: "0010, 27 M. 1 K W St P Rock, PW Chiriquí," which translated as "1 A.M., May 27, one kilometer west of St. Paul Rock, password 'Chiriquí.'" On the appointed day, Mescalero supervised the loading of the crop, while Rafael was responsible for its transportation to the rendezvous point. The operation went off without a hitch, and that night—which was happily cloudy and moonless—the flotilla of heavily laden canoes was in position off St. Paul Rock, awaiting the arrival of the motorship. They waited an hour, two hours, and they were just about to give up for the night and head for home when they heard the chug-chug, chug-chug of a marine diesel engine coming up slowly from the south.

"Vamonos," Mescalero said. Rafael cranked up his outboard and sped toward the sound. Presently, a large shadow loomed out of the darkness. It was the *Balboa Enterprise,* running without lights, and flying a Panamanian flag.

"Chiriquí!" Mescalero hollered.

"Chiriquí!" someone hollered back.

The motorship cut her engines and Rafael swung alongside.

"Stand clear! Stand clear!" the captain yelled, waving a sawed-off shotgun. "No one comes near till I talk to Señor Mescalero!"

"Take it easy, cabrón," Mescalero said. "I'm right here. Just let down the ladder for me, will you?"

Mescalero went aboard, shook hands with the captain, and with another, taller mestizo in a white linen suit, and then he turned around and gave the order to load.

"One at a time, now, one at a time!" he hollered, as the canoes crowded around. "Rafael, you load first. All right? Then please get back there and try to keep them in line."

"De acuerdo!" Rafael said, hoisting a big burlap sack onto his back while he fastened a brace band around his forehead. Then he climbed barefoot up the ladder, swung the bag onto the deck, and clambered nimbly back down the ladder for another.

"This is going too slow, Niño," Mescalero said, when Rafael had finished loading. "Let's bring them in two in line, and load from both sides at once."

After that, the loading went much more smoothly, and they were done by first light. The captain handed Mescalero a small black suitcase. Mescalero handed it to Rafael. Rafael opened it, checked it out, and then ran to the side of the ship and raised it high above his head.

"Ai ai ai aiiiiiiii!" he cried, waving it at the canoes that clustered around the mother ship.

"Ai ai ai aiiiiiiiii!" they shrieked back at him.

There was a hundred thousand pesos in the suitcase, enough to feed and clothe the village for an entire year, enough to buy more weapons to resist the military, should they ever come snooping around again.

After the dope transaction, Rafael and everyone else expected the stranger to return to his family in Acapulco, at least until harvest time in November. Instead, he sent them his love and regrets, and explained to his partners that he was staying on to "expedite the growth phase as well as the shipping phase of the operation."

Rafael protested that he and his men were perfectly competent to handle the entire operation by themselves. Mescalero agreed, but excused himself on the grounds that he had become "enchanted" with Xochitlán, and could not tear himself away. "There's a righteousness, an indigenous purity in your struggle, Rafael," he said, "that appeals to my imagination. I mean, what right have the gringos to tell the Indians of Mexico that they can no longer grow a weed which they've cultivated for two thousand years?"

But it seemed Mescalero was not clear in his own mind why he was staying, as he had a different explanation for everyone. To Rafael's younger son, Octavio, with whom he shared a room at the maestro's, he said, "For the first time in my life I feel free." To the maestro one night over a bottle of tequila he said, "I have finally gained a perspective on my life; till now I have been almost completely parasitical and dependent."

But the truth of the matter was perhaps even more complicated than this, for Mescalero's note-taking had led him into literary pursuits, and he spent much of his time now wandering around Xochitlán asking the natives questions about themselves, their families, their customs, the history of their village, and noting the answers in his journal. He talked to Rafael, to his wife, Benicta, to his sons, Francisco and Octavio, and to each of the little Martínez girls. He talked to the presidente, the régido, the huehuechique, and to the maestro at florid length. "I'm writing the history of your village," he told everyone. "It will have an important place in a much larger work that I'm writing, about the whole of Mexico, and for that reason I don't want to leave anything out." Except for Rafael, Octavio and the maestro, the people seemed to have no idea what he was talking about, but no one held anything back from him. Aside from the fact that he was now universally considered to be "related" to El Niño, and that the villagers were indebted to him for saving their marijuana crop, there was something about him—the careful and attentive way he listened and took notes, perhaps—that made them feel honored and important, inspired their confidence, and encouraged them to make confessions despite their instinctive taciturnity and secretiveness. The only holdout was Padre Dau. He refused to have anything to do with Mescalero, even when Rafael appealed to him personally. And he barred the door of his garden cottage whenever Mescalero came around. This was a bitter disappointment, not only to Mescalero, but to everyone else in the village, as the padre was by far the most mysterious character in Xochitlán. He was a foreigner, after all, a white man. Yet no one knew where he came from, and his life before his arrival in the delta was a complete enigma. Most people couldn't even remember how he got to the village or when.

Then one Saturday afternoon, on a visit to Rafael's jacal, Mescalero was reading in Ramona's diary and he turned abruptly to Rafael and said, "Your mother wrote of people called Chris, Merle, Brian, Maureen. . . ."

"So?"

"Nothing. I guess I would wonder who they were if I were you," said Mescalero. "Has the padre ever read this?"

"I don't think so. He told me it was only for my eyes."

Mescalero nodded with a kind of satisfaction. A moment later he said, "You're allowing me to read it."

Rafael shrugged, for it seemed natural to him that someone with his own mother's name should read it. He thought no more about it. It seemed clear to him, too, from Mescalero's ill-concealed passion for the diary, that he knew some of the people Ramona had known. Rafael thought no more about that either. The people his mother had known were as remote from him as was his brief, long-ago journey to the mainland to attend the university.

Some weeks later, as Rafael and Mescalero were leaving Sunday Mass, Mescalero managed to accost the padre point-blank. In answer to the questions that Mescalero posed about the padre's past, Dau merely responded in religious parables and non sequiturs.

"Where were you born, padre?"

"I came alive when I reached this island of peace."

"What is your nationality?"

"I am a subject of the crown."

"What crown?"

"The crown of the king."

"What king?"

"Christ the King."

"How did you come to Xochitlán?"

"By the grace of God."

"Where is your family?"

"My people are here."

"Who was your father?"

"My Father is in heaven."

"Who was your mother?"

"My mother is Mary, the Queen of Heaven."

After the padre drifted away from them, Mescalero looked at Rafael and laughed. The ancient, shrunken foreigner had lived so long in Xochitlán, he said, that he probably had no recollection of his previous life. And he told Rafael the story of B. Traven, the mysterious and reclusive author who had died in Mexico City the year before, taking the secret of his history, his parentage and nationality along with him. "But in the padre's case," Mescalero added, "I'm sure there will be somebody left behind who knows his story."

By late October the marijuana plants were three meters high, covered with flowers, thick with resin, and all the signs pointed to an exceptional harvest. Then one day when Rafael was out fishing with Francisco and Mescalero they heard a curious flapping noise in the sky and looked up to see a small military helicopter flying over from the mainland. It passed over the village and flew on toward the outer edge of the swamp. A half hour later it came flying back, passing overhead again in the direction of the mainland.

Rafael, fearing the worst, cranked over his outboard motor and raced to the village. There he collected two more canoes and eleven men and sped off in the direction the helicopter had taken. Two hours later, when they reached the most remote of the marijuana islets, they found its crop completely destroyed.

"He sprayed it with something," the caretaker said. "It burned the leaves and wilted the flowers and killed the plants within an hour."

"If he comes back again, we'll shoot him down," Rafael said, and issued everyone an M-16 rifle from a secret store he'd cached in a mangrove cave.

When Mescalero received his rifle, he thought it over for a minute, and then he came to speak with Rafael.

"Niño, I don't want to get involved in the fighting," he said. "I only want to watch, and to record what happens."

"Here we are all warriors," Rafael said. Suddenly he felt he had no more time for Mescalero's "objective" approach. "You must stay and fight, or hide in the cave with the women."

"Bueno, bueno, Niño," he said, capitulating, and deciding his own fate, with a quick and easy little bow of his head. "I'll stay with you."

And it occurred to Rafael that perhaps the stranger had come to the delta seeking just this kind of test, just this kind of leader, just this kind of struggle . . . in replacement of the others he had known.

The next day, early in the morning, the helicopter came back again. He made a quick pass over the island that he'd wasted the day before, and then came across to spray the next planted island. But on this island, El Niño and his men lay in wait, with their M-16s at the ready. There was even an old .30 caliber Maxim gun, Mexican army issue, which Rafael had managed to pick up on the black market, shortly after the sale of last year's mota crop.

"Aim for the pilot," he said. "And don't fire till I give the order."

The helicopter came in very low, and very slow, like a crop-dusting plane, methodically flying up one row and down another, spraying poison out its tail end, with an army machine gunner in a steel helmet manning an M-60 in the open side door.

"Remember, only the pilot," El Niño repeated, as the copter clattered near the thicket where they all lay hidden. Then, "Fuego!" he cried, and they let loose with everything they had from a distance of only fifty meters. The machine gunner returned fire immediately, and his aim was good, for soon little puffs of dust came marching across the field toward the ambushers.

Mescalero apparently lost all of his scruples as quickly as he discovered that he was being shot at. And he fired on the helicopter with Niño and the others, who were scoring hits on the canopy and fuselage all around the pilot, making the Plexiglas just fly. Abruptly the chopper swerved up and off to the left, heading out across the channel. But the pilot was flying erratically now. Spinning, chasing his own tail, he lost altitude rapidly. He skimmed over the lily pads for a second, then his nose dipped, he struck a floating log, somersaulted in the air, and landed upside down in the water. There was no fire, and the aircraft sank almost immediately, leaving only an oil slick, a couple of floating ammunition boxes, and one bobbing human head behind on the surface.

Awed by their incredible victory, El Niño and his men remained perfectly still. You could hear the little waves lapping at the mangrove roots, and the bees buzzing in the lilies.

Then Rafael let out a bloodcurdling war cry, and they ran to their canoes, launched them, and paddled toward the scene of the crash, chanting: "Amoato-rili-rili-rón, amoato-rili-rili-rón . . ." By the time they got there, the bobbing head had already vanished beneath the lily pads. But the helicopter itself was showing just under the surface. "When the tide goes out, it will be exposed to view," El Niño said, and ordered his men to tie on to the tail with manila rope. Then, after sending a diver down to remove the M-60 machine gun from its mount in the helicopter's doorway and hauling it up to the surface, they opened up their outboard motors full throttle and dragged the aircraft to a deep hole in the channel, where they cut it loose.

"Sure hope he didn't have time to radio home," Mescalero said, as the chopper sank from sight.

"Let's just assume he didn't," Rafael said. But he was not so sanguine as he pretended. In his euphoria, perhaps, thoughts of possible aerial retaliation, in the form of napalm or fragmentation bombs, had slipped his mind. The slip was significant, and extremely disquieting, for it reminded El Niño that he was perhaps fatally unequipped for the battle ahead of him.

Apparently, however, the pilot had not had time to radio home, because late that same afternoon the military returned in two helicopters and a light artillery spotter plane, scouring the delta for their fallen comrade.

El Niño and his men stayed in hiding, and after an hour or so the aircraft went away.

"For the moment," Rafael said, "they probably don't believe we shot down their machine. But they're angry as hornets. One of those copters costs more than our whole crop of marijuana. So tomorrow, not only will the aviation return, the army and the navy will come as well. They will take prisoners. They will torture them. And someone will break. If they find out the truth, it will go hard on the village. So we must swear ourselves to secrecy, and stay hidden in the swamp."

"Excuse me, Niño," said Mescalero. His eyes were bright with fear. "But does that include me as well?"

"I don't know why not," said Rafael. "You're just as liable to crack under torture as any of the rest of us. . . ."

That night before they went back into hiding, they visited another caretaker and his family, a couple of islands away.

"Qué pasó, Niño?" the caretaker asked, when they landed. But it was clear from his guilty expression that he knew very well what had passed.

"You saw nothing strange today?"

"Nothing."

"You're not holding anything back from us?"

"Nada, nada, nada. . . ."

By then his wife and kids had come out. They were a family of seven, including five children ranging from six to sixteen. El Niño took the youngest aside and gave her a lump of chocolate from his pocket.

"What's your name, bonita?"

"Naná."

"You like that chocolate?"

"Sí, señor."

"You saw that helicopter today?"

"Sí."

"And what happened?"

"A man came out of the water," she said, smiling, nodding her dark little head. "He was bleeding. We threw things at him, but he wouldn't go away. Then he died."

El Niño took her back to her family and addressed them sternly.

"You have lied," he said. "And for this you must be punished."

"Spare us, Niño," the caretaker said, falling to his knees. "He wanted to kill our plants."

"I will forgive you on one condition. That you show us where you've put him, and come with us into hiding in the swamp, until the military has gone."

"All of us?"

"All."

"It will be hard on the little ones."

"If the military hears of this, they will have no mercy on even the smallest."

"The piloto is buried over there," said the caretaker, pointing across the marijuana field.

They dug up the pilot and examined him. He was a young, blond, city-bred creole with extremely refined features. He was so obviously the enemy that it made everything easier. He had received a flesh wound in the head, and a more serious bullet wound in the chest. He had managed somehow to swim around two islands, drag himself to shore, stagger up to the jacal and ask for help. The children, who had witnessed the crash of the helicopter, were horrified by his appearance and thought he might have come back from the dead to haunt them.

"Fuera, fuera!" they had said. "Away, away!" And when he refused, and became angry and threatening, they had begun to pelt him with sticks and stones. The mother and father and two elder sons, who had been working in the marijuana field, heard the commotion and came running. On recognizing the man as an army pilot, and seeing the children in conflict with him, a primitive rage, a kind of bloodlust, had overcome them, and they had joined the children, hitting him with sticks, stones, hoes and rakes, until at last he died.

"*Amoato-rili-rili-rón, amoato-rili-rili-rón*," they had chanted, dancing around his body. Then they had urinated on him, slit his throat with a machete, and mutilated his body according to the ancient rituals of warfare. They tore out his eyes and his tongue and fed them to the dog, so that he might not bear witness against them from the grave. They cut his Achilles tendons so that he might not come back to haunt them. And they sliced off his genitals and stuffed them into his mouth so that he might appear ridiculous before the gods. . . .

At this point in the caretaker's confession Mescalero appeared to blank out, and he walked around for the rest of the night as if in a trance.

Rafael weighted the corpse with stones and had one of his men sink it alongside the downed helicopter. Then he loaded the caretaker and his family into the canoes along with his men and set out for a mangrove cave where he had laid in a supply of food, water and ammunition. All told, he had twenty-five men, women and children with him now in three canoes. But the cave, four kilometers away across the swamp, was spacious and adequately ventilated through gaps in the clay and intertwined mangrove roots that formed the roof.

When they reached the mouth of the cave, which was obscured by foliage, Rafael had the men slide all three canoes up inside, one behind the other. This was not difficult, as it was ebb tide and the floor of the cave was still slick and wet. Once they were all safely inside, Rafael ordered his people to remain in their canoes, for the principal hazards of the place were its oppressive dampness, the hordes of insects that were stirred up from the mud floor by unnecessary movement, and the small carnivorous fish—relatives of the piranha—which swam inside at high tide.

That night they tried to sleep, each with his head on his neighbor's shoulder, but conditions were very cramped, the children whimpered, the mosquitoes buzzed and bit, and no one got much rest.

Mescalero was seated just behind Rafael, and in the middle of the night El Niño could feel him begin to shake with dry sobs.

"Niño, what am I doing here? What am I doing here?" he said. "I'm in this thing way over my head."

"You want to cross the bridge, you got to pay the toll."

"I don't want to pay, not this way."

"Oh, but you will pay, compañero, you will pay. . . ."

And then later Mescalero dozed off and began mumbling incoherently and disconsolately in his sleep.

And Rafael found himself suddenly quite angry, for he knew it was the bloody actions of the caretaker and his family that had unstrung Mescalero so, and Rafael found their actions quite understandable, if not justifiable, under the circumstances.

In the morning they heard a number of large helicopters clatter overhead. The choppers descended onto several islands at once, spent about a quarter of an hour on each, and then flew off to land on several more.

Later, Rafael began to hear small-arms fire and explosions, and he sent Francisco up to reconnoiter. Rafael feared for his son, and because he was ashamed of being afraid at a time like this, he forced himself to think of his other children one by one. And Francisco returned in a couple of hours with news that the army was conducting a systematic search-and-destroy mission over this entire section of the delta, with five big troop-carrying helicopters and five platoons of infantry. After searching each island, blowing up any human habitation located there, and firing the marijuana crop, they always left a two-man guard behind to prevent reinfiltration. The navy was also involved in the operation, he reported. Armed with Uzi machine pistols and hand grenades, they had commandeered a dozen or more outboard motor-powered Indian canoes in Xochitlán, and they were practicing "reconnaissance-by-fire," spraying the banks of the islets with their Uzis and lobbing hand grenades into every mangrove cave they came across.

"The way I figure it, Papá," Francisco said, "they found out some way what happened. No?"

"But how?"

"Hey," said Mescalero impatiently. "This is modern warfare, Niño. They've got radar, sonar, metal detectors, underwater listening devices, things that you and I have never even dreamed of."

"All right then, compañeros," Rafael said, with a self-confidence he didn't feel, "we just stay hunkered down right here until they leave. There are thousands of islands, and thousands of caves, and they can't cover them all. The odds are still in our favor."

That afternoon the weather turned extraordinarily hot and humid, and the tide came up unusually high. When it flowed into the cave, it rose up to nearly a meter and a half. The gunwales of the canoes were riding up near the roof of the cave, and everyone had to get out and stand in the mud. The water reached the armpits of the adults, and it was over the heads of the little ones. As breathing space diminished, the cave grew even hotter and more humid. Leeches dropped from the twisted mangrove roots on the roof. Flying insects seemed to multiply dramatically in the limited airspace. Fleas, gnats, flies and mosquitoes devoured the exposed portions of the skin, attacking even the scalp, the eyelids and the nostrils. While from beneath the scummy surface of the water the legs and feet were attacked by crabs, sea snakes and carnivorous fish. An alligator came nosing his way in, causing the children to scream in fright, but El Niño managed to beat him off with the butt of his automatic rifle.

By the time the tide went out in the evening, everyone was covered with multiple insect bites and open running sores. Flies collected in the sores, and laid eggs there, and by late the next day everyone was crawling with maggots. The children suffered especially. Four of them were below the age of ten. The youngest was Naná, the caretaker's daughter. Already she was a mass of bloody sores, her hands had turned yellow, her eyes were shut with insect bites, she could not hold up her head unassisted, and she had to be passed from one adult to another to prevent her from drowning. When Mescalero's turn came, and he was holding the tiny whimpering creature in his arms, he said he remembered his own daughter Diana at the same age—so plump and healthy—and she broke his heart. And he clung to her with his life, plucking the maggots from her little eyes and nostrils, rocking her and crooning to her and kissing her painful sores and smoothing her salt-encrusted hair.

"I'll keep her!" he said, when Rafael tried to make him pass her on. And clutched her to himself.

After that, even her mother dared not protest.

Later he whispered, "In the child you find the race."

And though he seemed utterly demented, he recalled to Rafael's mind something that his mother had written in her diary.

"We must save the children," Rafael said aloud.

And yet the machine-gun fire rattled across the mangrove swamp, hour after hour, day after day, and the hand grenades exploded and the helicopters clattered back and forth overhead.

In their extremity—after their fifth inundation—Rafael and Mescalero grew closer, as close as lovers, and Rafael told him what he had told no one, not even his sons, about paddling by canoe to the mainland as a young man, taking the train to Colima, and starting up the Calle Filomeno Medina toward the university but never quite getting there; and Mescalero babbled confessions into Rafael's ear.

One time he told him that he had shot to death a man with the odd name of Bo, and then with a very sane, very wry laugh, he added, "A marijuana importer."

Another time he told him that Padre Dau was grandfather to his daughter, but that time Rafael did not find his laughter so sane, and he dismissed the remark.

And near the end, he said, "Niño, listen to me. There were once two little girls in Michoacán. One was named Ramona, the other Carmen. Their mother was dead, their father, too, so they walked all the way to Manzanillo to find their sister, María. María was my mother. When she died, my father married her youngest sister, Carmen. My father is Don Gallo Carrizo, the governor of this state. My name is Merle Carrizo, and your mother, Ramona, was my aunt, and you are of my blood. You must send someone up to negotiate a surrender, and tell the commander who I am. It's our only chance. As you say, we must save the children."

But in the morning, before Rafael had a chance to send anyone out, the navy came around the island doing their recon-by-fire. They blew up one cave, then another, and another, and finally they blew up the one right next door.

The detonation, though muffled by the walls of the cave, knocked them all off their feet, and caused debris to fall from the ceiling, half filling the cave. Rafael was thrown down into the water, and then covered with dirt. Panic-stricken, he clawed his way out, gasping for breath, only to find it nearly impossible to breathe because of the thick black cloud of cordite-smelling smoke that issued from the cracks and passageways that led to the other cave. Though his ears were still ringing from the shock wave that had accompanied the explosion, Rafael was dimly aware that children were screaming somewhere around him, women were crying, the wounded were moaning in pain, and that Merle and Naná were no longer near him.

It was then that he heard Merle start to yell.

"Don't shoot! Don't shoot! I'm Merle Carrizo, the son of Don Gallo Carrizo. We've got children in here, and we're coming out!"

They tied up all the adult survivors with their hands behind their backs and loaded them onto canoes and carried them across to the cultivated island and lined them up on a burned-out marijuana field. There were only nine of them left alive, and Francisco was not among them. The only child was Naná, and she was near death.

The captain in charge would not believe that Merle was the governor's son, and asked him to furnish proof. He pulled forth his rotting wallet and out fell a laminated voter's registration card with the names of his parents listed just under "Party Affiliation: PRI," and "Spouse: Christopher O'Hare."

The officer took the card, examined it closely, shook his head slowly, and said, "If you're the governor's son, what the hell you doing in a place like this?"

"It's a long story," Merle said. "But this child needs immediate medical attention. Have you a medical corpsman with you?"

The young captain, a mild-looking mestizo, perhaps the father of a child this age, contemplated Naná for a moment. Then he pointed toward the helicopter and directed a lance corporal to carry her there. When Merle stepped back into line, the captain said, "No, you go along with them, too."

After the helicopter had departed, the captain told them they could all sit down. He even gave them cigarettes. And they sat there waiting, smoking silently, for a long, long time. So long, in fact, that two of them expired of their wounds. The captain, who had wandered off to confer with some of his men, seemed to have forgotten them entirely.

Rafael, exhausted, beyond grief, beyond what would pass for thought, ticked off the names of his surviving children, like the sacred names in the litany of saints—Octavio, Clarita, Albita, Martita, and the one in Benicta's belly, Ramón, Ramona, as God willed it.

When the captain finally came back to them, he wore a decisive and reasonable smile. His frank dark eyes seemed to be exhorting them all to be as sensible as he. No less so when he drew his sidearm and marched them all ahead of him single-file and lined them up on the riverbank.

"Bueno," he said. He was still smiling as he said it, and all the prisoners smiled back, unsteadily, and in unsteady voices said, "Bueno, mi capitán."

"So," he said, "you've got yourselves into quite a pickle here, haven't you?"

"Sí, sí, mi capitán," they responded. "Claro que sí."

"And you got one of our helicopters, didn't you?" he said, his smile wilting. He ran his hand absently along his brow, indicating distress and fatigue of his own. "But you had your genuine grievances, didn't you? And you're tired to death, aren't you?"

"Sí, sí, mi capitán," they all said. "Usted tiene razón."

"All you want is to get back to your families," he said, in a voice extraordinarily weary and mournful. "As I want to get back to mine."

"Sí, sí, mi capitán, entendido," they all said.

"And as my dead comrades wanted to get back to theirs."

They were silent then. They searched his face and found reason again, reason all too perfect.

"Turn," he commanded. "On your knees!"

And they turned around together and fell onto their knees all in a row and closed their eyes, and the captain proceeded to place a neat hole in the base of each of their skulls with his 8mm Beretta.

Rafael was last in line, and by the time he felt the steel against his neck, he had already begun to dream. His mother came to him across the years, and he could remember her face at last. It was the face of the Dark Virgin, Guadalupe. She was bending over him. Her tears were falling on him. She put him in a basket and set him on the water. She kissed him and let him go. He was alone. He cried. He was carried away on the tide. And it seemed to him then that his whole life had been little more than the dream of a drowning child, and he congratulated himself for having outwitted one destiny for so long, while fulfilling yet another, and managing at the same time to leave his own small imprint on a small world:

DELTA GUERRILLAS
ANNIHILATED IN
FIREFIGHT WITH MILITARY

CHAPTER 9

Naná died in Merle's arms in the helicopter, a thousand feet above the delta.

"What do they want us to do with her?" the medical corpsman asked the pilot.

The pilot radioed headquarters for instructions.

"Throw her out," he said, after a while.

"No," Merle said, holding her tight. "No."

"You want to go with her?" the corpsman asked, and Merle let her loose.

She fluttered down toward the muddy water like a little rag doll.

They flew him to a military field in Colima, put him into a Red Cross ambulance with an armed guard, and carried him to the Colonia Militar, an old gray-walled former convent on the Calle Ahumada, overlooking a deep barranca called the Arroyo del Manrique. They cleaned his wounds, locked him in a private room in the infirmary and posted a guard outside the door.

An hour later a squat, tough-looking little mestizo colonel in a starched jungle fatigue uniform stepped inside. He wore wire-rimmed, opaque sunglasses and a short bristly black crew cut under which his scalp showed shiny white.

Gallo Carrizo followed closely behind him.

Merle was struck by the appearance of his father, whom he hadn't seen since Diana's Confirmation ceremony three years before: He had not changed in the least. In his tan tropical-weight slacks and white embroidered guayabera, his black toupée that he wore to hide the dent in his head, his pore-minimizer makeup and his pencil-thin mustache, he looked as if he'd been embalmed at the age of forty.

"Can you identify this person, Governor?" the colonel asked.

Gallo peered deeply into Merle's face, as if trying to make out his features under the suppurating insect bites.

"Well yes," he admitted at last, with the look of a defendant in a paternity suit.

"Who is he?"

"He is . . . he is . . ." Gallo lisped, doing a rapid little two-step beside the bed. "He is my son."

"I see," said the colonel, with some satisfaction. "What do you think we ought to do with him, sir?" And in his insinuating tone Merle detected the possibility of hope, or at least what passes in Mexico for hope: la mordida, the little bite.

"How many people know about this, Colonel?"

"Nearly everyone who took part in the operation."

Gallo hesitated, his eyes shifting quickly from Merle to the colonel. "My son was captured by the guerrillas and taken hostage," he said. "I thank you from the bottom of my heart for saving his life. I don't know how I can ever repay you."

And something in his wheedling tone, and in the tacit, unseemly understanding that he'd silently established with the colonel, made Merle recoil. He thought of El Niño and the others, and he had a vision of what had happened to them after he'd been led away, and he said, "That's not true, Papá. I joined the Indians voluntarily."

"My son is unbalanced from his ordeal," Gallo said instantly, talking fast. "A few hours' rest, a bite to eat, and he'll be as good as new."

"What was your son doing in the delta region, Governor?"

"I was . . ."

"He was on a secret fact-finding mission for me."

"What was the purpose of the mission?"

"To . . . to ascertain the origin of the unrest among the Indians," Gallo said. "And now if you'll be good enough to accompany us to the governor's mansion, mi coronel, perhaps we could discuss the matter in privacy."

"In view of your son's infirmity and his . . . uncertainty, mi gobernador, perhaps it would be better if he were left here while we discussed the matter in my office."

"I must insist."

"No, no, it is I who must insist."

"As you wish," said Gallo, throwing Merle a look that said, "Now see what you've done," as he went out the door with the colonel.

A half-hour later he came back, alone.

"All right, Merle, goddammit," he said, pacing up and down the room, sweating, breathing in short unhealthy gasps. "I'm not gonna waste my time or yours, telling you how much I resent that damn trick you just pulled, or what you and Chris did to me—going out there and stirring up those crazy fucking Indians when we'd already pulled out safe and sound—'cause it's all water under the bridge now. But if you want me to get you outa here, then you're gonna have to cooperate. Now here's the deal. The colonel is gonna be giving a press conference tomorrow explaining that operation in the delta. You'll show up for a minute or two and say that you were taken hostage by the Indians and rescued when the army stormed in and killed 'em all."

"I won't do it."

"What's that you say?"

"I refuse to cooperate with the people who murdered them."

Through painful, swollen, half-closed eyes, Merle looked up at his father, and it seemed to him that Gallo would strike him. He raised his little yellow fist, its fat diamond rings glowing in the fluorescent light, and let it hover for a moment over Merle's aching head like the hand of God. And then something quite unexampled, something almost akin to admiration, flickered across Gallo's sharp, gray, ferretlike little face, and he said, "Hell, they're dead and gone now, Merle. They ain't gonna know the difference."

"But *I* will," Merle said, and his father's look of admiration quickly changed to disgust.

"You're not gonna start that nobility shit again, are you?" Gallo scoffed. "This is no movie we're running here, kid. This is reality. You know what the colonel is gonna do to you, if you don't play ball? He's gonna turn you over to the federal prosecutor. And that prosecutor is gonna bring in some

Indians and have 'em testify against you. You'll do thirty years in prison, Merle. And while he's at it, he'll drag out that whole can of worms in the delta. He'll get the Indians to testify that a certain Rudolfo Muñoz had a deal with them for years. Muñoz is a snake. He's for sale to the highest bidder. So he'll turn state's evidence and bring me and Altamirano into it. Altamirano will blow the whistle on Chris, and the whole house of cards will come tumbling down. So you better think twice about what you're doing, son."

"Let the chips fall where they may."

"You're sick, boy, you know that?" Gallo said. "This is your own family we're talking about."

"I refuse to go on with business as usual," Merle said. "I reject my life, and everything it stands for."

"You know what?" Gallo said, banging on the door to be let out. "You're cold, Merle. You're like a fuckin' gringo."

A few minutes later the colonel came in, flanked by two big, mean-looking paratroopers carrying Uzi machine pistols, and delivered Merle a little lecture on the Ley de Fuga, or Law of Flight.

"In Mexico we have no death penalty," he said, as if Merle were unacquainted with the fact. "Instead we have the Law of Flight, which stipulates that deadly force shall be employed only against dangerous prisoners caught in the act of escape. In practice it is a discretionary death penalty, used against enemies of the state who have proved intractable to reason, or habitual criminals who might receive lenient sentences from liberal or subversive judges. Now, if you don't agree to attend my little press conference tomorrow, Señor Carrizo, I can promise you that the Ley de Fuga will be applied against you with all due haste."

"I refuse to attend your press conference, colonel," Merle said, gathering strength from his own unprecedented obduracy. "And if you force me to, I'll tell the truth about what happened to those prisoners out in the delta."

The colonel left without another word, trailing his paratroopers behind him, and a few minutes later Gallo showed up again.

"All right, get out of bed and come with me," he said. "If you knew what it's gonna cost me to get you out of this . . ."

"Where're we going?" Merle demanded, clutching the iron bedstead as if he might suddenly be taken out and shot.

"You're going into exile," Gallo said. "If you promise to keep your mouth shut."

Merle couldn't believe his ears at first, and he regarded his father for a moment without speaking. Then, once he'd assured himself that his stand on principle had actually succeeded, he decided immediately to up the ante.

"I'm not going anywhere," he said, "without my wife and daughter."

"You shoulda thought of them when the press conference was proposed."

"Dad, I've got to let them know."

"No, goddammit. Not one word to them, Merle. Once the newspapers get ahold of this thing, all hell is gonna break loose. The police could trace you through letters and phone calls. They could have you extradited."

"Okay, let's go," he said, climbing out of bed.

"You swear to keep your mouth shut?"

"Yeah," he said, following him out the door and down the corridor in his stinking rags, his bare, bleeding feet, down the stairs and out onto the gravel driveway where the colonel was waiting in the governor's limousine.

Merle and Gallo got in, and they all sat in back behind tinted glass. But Gallo made Merle pull down the jump seat and sit apart.

"Frankly, you stink," he said, and the colonel laughed unpleasantly.

They spoke not at all in the limousine, and when they reached the governor's mansion—a modest, flat-topped, modern structure across from the university, on the Calle Filomeno Medina—they pulled around in back to the servants' entrance.

"Go on inside, Merle," Gallo said, giving him a little shove. "While I tend to business with the colonel."

Carmen—looking a bit plumper and fuller in the face than Merle remembered her—was waiting just inside the door.

"Follow me," she said sternly, after a perfunctory abrazito and a buss on the cheek.

She led him into a small white-tiled bathroom just off the service porch.

"I want you to shower quickly and change into these," she said, pointing to a stack of clean, folded old clothes resting on a straw hamper: a pair of Levi's, a denim shirt and jacket, a pair of work boots; he recognized them instantly as the clothes he'd left behind on a visit to his father's Manzanillo home in 1954, when he and Val were running from Bo Brodsky.

And he was touched that his aunt had chosen to keep them all these years.

Carmen stood right there in the bathroom while Merle removed his filthy, bloody delta clothes and dropped them onto the floor. "My God, you are a sight!" she said, as he climbed into the shower. "And you don't look much better now," she said, when he got out.

She threw him a towel and watched while he gingerly patted himself dry. She watched him fondly, almost sorrowfully, he thought.

Merle gazed down at his fat little overdressed, overpainted, fifty-eight-year-old aunt and he remembered a time when she was young and beautiful, squatting by the river with her skirts hiked up to her thighs, beating her washing on a rock, while her sister Ramona squatted beside her and her little three-year-old nephew Merle played nearby in the sand; and he recalled how proud she was of him when a stranger came down to ask his name: "His name is Merle. He was born in a whirlwind. He really is amazing. . . ."

She was all he had that would pass for a mother, and she'd never failed him yet.

It occurred to him also that she was the sister of El Niño's mother. And the death of his cousin El Niño seemed to him then as terrible as the death of a wife or a daughter. Until meeting Rafael, Merle had never loved a man.

Carmen cleaned and dressed his wounds and stood watching him dress and groom himself until his father appeared.

"I sure hope you appreciate this, boy," Gallo said, frowning, slapping his hands to indicate that his business with the colonel was concluded, and that a great deal of money had passed between them. "Now go on out to the airport with Carmen. And I don't wanna hear another peep outa you till this thing blows over."

Again Merle was in the hands of a woman, and he let her handle him as she liked. She took him to meet a friend at the United States Consulate, and obtained travel documents and a residency permit for him, under the name of Hilario Fuentes. She bought him an airline ticket to San Francisco and drove him to the airport in her own car. She offered him five thousand dollars in cash, "to make a fresh start," but he turned it down.

"Don't worry, Aunt Carmen," he said, trying to form a smile with his scabby, swollen mouth. "I'll do all right."

"Make something of yourself, boy," she said, kissing him goodbye. "Hell, you're gonna be forty years old next month."

Only when he got on the plane did he realize that it had fallen dark outside, and that—incredible as it seemed—he had spent the previous night trapped in a tidal cave with El Niño and the Indians.

In San Francisco, Merle started where he'd left off fifteen years before, sleeping under newspapers in the cable-car stops, scrounging for food. But things were different now: He'd lost his pride. Or perhaps he'd replaced it with another kind.

He got a job washing dishes at the Café Sport, a Sicilian pasta parlor on Green Street in North Beach, and a room in a flophouse around the corner on Grant Avenue. From dishwasher, he graduated to busboy, from the Café Sport to the Washington Square Bar & Grill, a chic literary watering hole on the corner of Union and Powell.

Meanwhile he was following developments in Colima by reading press reports in the Guadalajara papers, which were available at a kiosk in the lobby of the Mark Hopkins Hotel.

Apparently Gallo and the colonel had put out the hostage story after all, and they held off the press for several days by claiming that Merle was in seclusion recovering from his wounds. Then they claimed that he had flown to Switzerland to seek medical treatment. When it became apparent that the "hostage" had flown the coop, the press grew suspicious of the whole story and descended on Xochitlán en masse. They interviewed the maestro, the régido, the presidente and several private soldiers who had participated in the campaign against El Niño, and quickly discovered the salient facts: The governor of Colima State had been involved in the drug trade in the delta for many years, through a surrogate named Rudolfo Muñoz. After the government's clampdown on narcotics, Muñoz's place had been taken by the governor's son, Merle Carrizo, alias Lytle Mescalero, who was certainly no hostage, but had actively participated in the insurrection.

The story caused a sensation in Mexico, and the public clamored for an investigation. The federal prosecutor for Colima—an old friend and political ally of Gallo's—reluctantly initiated an inquiry. He subpoenaed Merle Carrizo and Rudolfo Muñoz, who'd been named by the Indians as co-conspirators with the governor, but neither of them could be found. Carrizo had last been seen boarding a plane for the United States, and Muñoz had last been seen with a group of heavily armed men in a Ford Falcon, who had approached him at his home and asked him to come for a ride. Without witnesses to corroborate the Indians' testimony, Gallo's involvement was considered mere hearsay, and the prosecutor closed the case for lack of evidence. The headlines continued for a few weeks longer, then the story got lost in the back pages.

Though it pained Merle to think that the people of Xochitlán had become embittered toward him because of his connection with the governor, he would not have been human had he not breathed a deep sigh of relief when the story disappeared from the Guadalajara newspapers altogether.

Six months after his employment at the Washington Square Bar & Grill, Merle was promoted to waiter, and in a year he was made host. He got himself an apartment on Mason Street, a secondhand car and a typewriter. He worked nights by choice and spent his days writing the novel he'd been waiting to write all his life. In a way it made up for the letters he could not write his daughter. The book, though inspired by Chris, was dedicated to Diana.

For the first time in his life, he found that his enthusiasm for the pursuit of women had waned. It was as if in long hours of wondering about his wife and daughter, he spent all his masculine energy. He wondered if they'd been harmed in any way by the fiasco in the delta. He wondered about Chris's tenuous hold on sanity now that she had only Val to support her. He wondered about old Maureen and how Chris was getting on with her. He wondered if perhaps Chris had found a new man. And if she had, was he good to Diana? And had Diana broken off her involvement with the Second of October Movement? Or had Chris kept her promise and sent her to school in the States?

Merle phoned St. Anne's Academy in San Francisco and asked if there was a Diana Carrizo enrolled there. But they said they didn't give out that kind of information. He started hanging around the school, at the corner of Gough and Sacramento, watching the fifteen- and sixteen-year-old girls in their plaid uniforms as they formed two straight lines and walked down to gym class every morning, and he imagined Chris doing the same thing in the thirties, and her mother before the turn of the century. He loitered there for several weeks until the cop on the beat grew suspicious and swore he'd haul him off for "lewd vagrancy" if he didn't move on. But by that time Merle had ascertained beyond a shadow of a doubt that Diana could not possibly be enrolled there.

Then, two years after his return to California, while he was sitting in a laundromat on Columbus Avenue waiting for his clothes to dry, Merle made the acquaintance of a precocious six-year-old named Jill Rosado. He had noticed her and her mother and her big sister Kim around the neighborhood for nearly a year, and had been struck by how very attractive they all were, especially the mommy, and by the fact that there was no daddy in evidence.

"Stop bothering the man, Jill," the mother said.

She was very tall for a Chicana and very pale, with full lips, high cheekbones, thick straight black hair and slanting green eyes that betrayed her mixed Indian and Spanish ancestry.

"Oh, she's no bother at all," Merle said, smiling. "She reminds me of my daughter at that age."

"How old is your daughter now?"

"She just turned sixteen," Merle said. "I'd give anything to see her."

"She's not with you?"

"No, she's in Acapulco. Her mother and I are separated."

"I see," said Jill's mother, looking as if she might be willing to carry on with the conversation. But just then her washing was ready and she had to go put her clothes in the dryer, and Merle couldn't bring himself to push things.

Next Sunday he showed up at the same time, and was delighted to see her sitting in the same place, reading a book, while her daughters squatted in the corner, playing jacks.

She looked up as Merle approached, and smiled at him. He noticed that she was reading a textbook, *Theories of Personality*.

"You go to college?"

She nodded.

"How do you manage with the kids?"

"I go while they're in school," she said. "Why do you smile? Do you think I'm too old for college?"

"Old?" Merle said, laughing, sitting down beside her. "You couldn't be over twenty-five years old."

"I'm twenty-seven," she said.

For the first time he noticed her faint Southwestern accent.

"I had a very beautiful aunt," he blurted out. "And you remind me very much of her."

And with a whirring chorus of washers and dryers backing him up, he told her Ramona's whole story from the hacienda in Michoacán to the years in Texas to the Barbarian Colony and the Three Marías to the final shipwreck in the delta of the Río Coayuayana.

He told it well, with great expression and feeling, for he'd just been working on Ramona's section in his novel, and the words were still fresh in his mind.

"My God," she said, when he was done. "What a tragic life."

"Yes," he said, "but you've had your share as well, haven't you?"

"What makes you say that?"

"I don't know, something. . . ."

"My husband was killed in a mining accident two years ago," she said, and with only a little encouragement from Merle she began to relate the story of her life:

Her name was Anita Rosado, neé Talamante. She had been born in Fort Bayard, New Mexico, in the Mimbres Mountains. Her father was a copper miner, and she grew up in a company house down the hill from the mine. She hated the town and the mine and she didn't get along with her father and dreamed of running off to a new life in California. But when she was seventeen she started going steady with a boy named Teddy Rosado and one thing led to another and she got pregnant. They married and he went to work in the mine and she was stuck. She spent all her time cleaning their new company house, changing diapers, watching daytime TV and gossiping with the neighbors. She thought she was happy enough. And she loved her husband dearly. But she had this kind of vague yearning that would never go away. Then, when her husband was killed in a mine explosion, she had to guiltily admit to herself that she was immensely relieved. She collected his insurance, packed the kids in the car and set out for the Coast. She got herself an apartment in San Francisco, put the kids in school and enrolled in City College with the intention of eventually becoming a teacher of the deaf and blind.

"Why the deaf and blind?" he asked.

"I don't know," she said, flustered, looking away from him. "I mean I know why, but I can't explain."

Why was it, Merle wondered, that a response like that should sweep him off his feet? And in the weeks to come, as he began to see Anita and her girls with increasing regularity, he became more and more captivated by her inexpressible sense of self. When he tried to lend her a favorite novel, she said, "I know it sounds silly, but I have to read other things first." When he tried to treat her and the kids to dinner, she said, "It's better if I cook for us." She was firm in her decisions, but when he challenged them, she could not explain them, and occasionally burst into tears and protested that she was "not good with words," and would never be equal to Merle, and wasn't his type.

And it was true, Merle thought. She was not his type. And he was falling desperately in love with her.

With Anita, he moved more slowly than he had with any other woman. He took her and the girls to Golden Gate Park and the Fleishhacker Zoo, to the aquarium and the Cliff House and Fisherman's Wharf and the Renaissance Faire, and spent hours sitting by their television set drinking beer and watching her feeding and bathing the children and putting them to bed. He was totally assimilated into family life, intoxicated by it, before he ever actually made love to Anita.

And after he made love to her, he drew away from her for days, not out of disappointment, but out of an overwhelming sense that he was losing his real wife and daughter, Chris and Diana, once and for all.

Then Anita came to him one evening at work, her jaw squarely set, her eyes burning with conviction. She waited patiently until he had seated a party of Argentine tourists, grabbed him by the lapels and said, "I can't explain it, Merle, but I know I'm the right woman for you."

When he moved his things into her apartment, the girls seemed to take it for granted. By the end of the year, they were calling him Daddy, and they could barely remember living any other way.

Merle thought of Chris and Diana no less than before, but he thought of Anita and her daughters at least as often.

In June of 1974, Anita got pregnant and they decided to have the baby. Merle risked writing a long letter to Chris suggesting—in the most delicate way possible—that perhaps she ought to file for divorce. Immediately after writing the letter, he began agonizing over his motives.

CHAPTER 10

Before leaving her suite in the Stanford Court, Chris felt very much as her mother must have felt in 1933, just as she was setting out to meet Brian in the Manzanillo railroad tower. Over and over she rehearsed the lines that she would deliver to Merle, changing them, perfecting them as she went along. She examined herself in the mirror, making adjustment after adjustment, cursing herself for not coming as soon as she received his letter. Even then, five weeks ago, she would have looked better than she looked now, she thought. Before her last hairdo had gone awry. Before the loss of another four or five pounds of badly needed weight. Before the final blow in a long litany of blows which had—she felt sure—destroyed the last vestiges of her youth. "Some women go on looking the same for fifteen or twenty years," her mother had said recently, "and then all of a sudden they crumble overnight." Leave it to Maureen to find the softest place between the ribs to slide the knife: Chris had just turned forty-six years old.

She added a plummy layer of lipstick to distract his eye from the fine vertical lines above her lip. Then she tissued the color off completely and applied a much paler shade to achieve a more vulnerable effect. Even with the costliest array of cosmetics and the pick of designer clothes, she looked a mess. With her fortune soon gone, she thought, she would look like the living dead.

She brushed her little cap of graying hair straight back, but instead of creating the chic effect which Merle used to admire, she transformed herself into a skeleton. She tousled her hair and proceeded to assess her clothing for the fifth time. Within her little oatmeal-colored dress of wool crepe, she seemed to fade away altogether. She should have stuck with the navy-blue suit, but her hands were too unsteady to make another change. . . . She looked at her hands and they seemed now like topographical maps of the west coast of Mexico: a web of raised blue ranges and deep-creased barrancas. She could not bear to contemplate her hands. She longed for the little white gloves that her mother had made her wear for the first five years of life, until Dr. Weber had cut off her batlike webs and transformed her appearance into that of a normal girl. But gloves, of course, were long out of fashion.

In the taxi on the way to Merle's place, she began to silently mouth her sorrows like the little prayers she used to say between each decade of the rosary to Our Lady of Mercy. Even as a child in prayer, she had been cunning, psyching out the Holy Virgin, appealing to her bleeding heart first on the most poignant level, then on the most theatrical. When she bared her soul to Merle, she would begin with Diana's recent—fateful—decision and end with Altamirano's delayed downfall, which was leading swiftly to her own.

As the taxi stopped in front of a two-story pink stucco house on Russian Hill, she fell to calculating what sort of man Merle might have become in the last four years. She really had no idea. And she was terrified of strangers.

"Ain't this the address you give me, ma'am?" the driver asked.

"No," she said firmly. And then, flustered, "Yes. Yes, it is."

It happened so quickly once she had climbed the stairs and glanced through the beveled-glass door. Across a small Victorian parlor, in a half-circular dining room with huge bow windows through which the afternoon sun streamed, Merle was standing above an oval dining table cutting a cake as two little girls in pigtails and oversized sweatshirts squirmed in their seats, greedy for the biggest piece. Across from Merle sat a woman with very long black hair whose face she could not see. But the Merle she saw was trim and young and agreeable-looking, really no different from the Merle who had sat at her mother's birthday party four years ago being a good sport. And Chris could have killed him for it. It was as if no time had passed, as if he had been living a double life with her in Acapulco and with this woman in San Francisco and he deserved to die for his treachery. They all deserved to die.

Then suddenly she had a vision of herself and Merle and Val and Maureen on Diana's fifth birthday. They were sitting on the terrace at the Reina del Mar and Merle was cutting the cake and they were all laughing about something silly that Diana had said—something that Chris couldn't even remember anymore—and it seemed to her then, and it seemed to her still, that she had never been happier in her life. . . .

Chris was on the verge of turning around and leaving Merle to his happiness when the smaller girl glanced around and saw her peeking through the glass, and the whole picture came into frame. The little girl looked as helpless and blameless as Diana had at the same age. Suddenly the black-haired woman turned around to see what her daughter was staring at and revealed an artless face, distinctly Mexican, almost familiar.

Merle spun around and glanced uncertainly at Chris. For an instant he seemed not to know her. Then he mouthed her name and rushed forward, sliding across the hardwood floor in his stocking feet.

"Well," he said, smiling, as he opened the door.

"I would've come as soon as I got your letter, Merle, but I had business I couldn't set aside," she said, when actually she'd been brooding over his letter for weeks, and had flown north only when several fresh blows—Diana's insistence on entering the novitiate at the Dominican convent, Val's announcement of her coming marriage, and a message from Gallo explaining that Altamirano had been arrested on a narcotics charge in Tijuana and was offering to testify about the dormant El Niño case in return for immunity from prosecution—gave her pause to reflect on her own mortality and the ephemeral nature of worldly success, and convinced her that she'd better get Merle back or soon she'd have nothing left to call her own.

"Yeah, business, yeah," Merle said stupidly, standing there as if he were nailed to a cross. Then he seemed to recover slightly, and said, "Come in, please, come meet . . . everyone."

Leading her into the dining room, he said, "Anita, this is Chris, who I've told you so much about," in the most casual way, as if Chris were some long-lost fraternity brother. But Chris hadn't known him all his life for nothing. She knew he was desperate. She knew it from the way he began hitching up his Levi's, pulling at the sleeves of his tattered fisherman's sweater, playing with his curly hair.

"The place is a wreck," the woman, Anita, began saying. "Nice to meet you, Mrs. . . . Chris. Kim, clear the table! Jill, don't play with your food! Go wash that icing out of your hair! I told you ten minutes ago. I . . . excuse me, I have to put these kids to bed."

"Please stay. It isn't even dark yet," Chris said, feeling sorry for this woman, with no maid or nanny to help her with the kids. Her pity quickly encompassed herself. It was more than likely that she would soon flee to exile and live out her life in some god-awful place, a place without extradition treaties, a woman without means. . . . "Please," Chris added, with the perfect measure of compassion, "don't let me make you uncomfortable, Anita."

"Oh, you're not making her uncomfortable, Chris," Merle said, shifting from foot to foot.

"Yes, she is," Anita said, staring at the untouched cake in her plate. She looked up abruptly and met Chris's eyes. She was rather pretty in a common Latin mold, and she had that beatific flush of early pregnancy that turned a man's head. "I know you don't mean to, but you're making me very uncomfortable. I want to bathe the kids and put them to bed."

"Anita . . ." Merle began.

"I want to," she said, already on her feet, marshaling her two silent, staring little daughters around her, leading them out of the room. "It's okay, really. You two go ahead and have your talk."

Merle shrugged apologetically at Chris and pulled out a chair for her. "God, Chris, how are you?" he said, strolling over to an antique washing stand where liquor was displayed in sparkling cut-glass decanters.

Chris looked out through hanging coleus plants and potted ferns at Alcatraz Island and Tiburón. For the moment she could not recall a single line she had rehearsed. She could barely remember the topics, or the order in which she was supposed to deliver them. And she was just at the point of letting it all hang out, of confessing what had happened this morning at the state capitol building in Colima, when the oldest girl raced back into the room, squealing, "Daddy, you promised you'd read us to sleep!"

"I did not, and you know it, Kim." He laughed. "It's your mommy's turn tonight." But he escorted the child from the room anyway.

How would she describe to Merle her meeting with his father this morning? In comic, ironic terms, she thought, as if it were something that had happened to someone else. She would describe the black suit and black tie and patent-leather shoes that Gallo had chosen to wear—like a pallbearer—and the bluish tinge that his most recent dye job had imparted to his pencil-thin mustache, and his obscene everlasting lisp, and the elaborate Latin courtesies that he never forgot, even when his world was about to crumble.

"Glad you came, dear," Gallo had said, ushering her into his spacious wood-paneled office. "Been trying to get ahold of you all morning. I got some news on the Altamirano thing."

"Yes?" she said, holding her breath.

"Here, Chris, sit down," he said, motioning her toward a brown leather couch in the corner, with a view of the smoking Volcano of Colima. "Can I get you anything? A drink? Cigarettes? Something to eat?"

"No thanks, I had breakfast on the plane," she said. "And I'd just as soon take this one standing up, if you don't mind."

"They gave him the deal he wanted, Chris, and he sang his guts out."

"That man should have been eliminated a long time ago," she said, relieved to find some outlet for the fear and anger and nervous anticipation that had consumed her for the past few weeks.

"Don't think I didn't try," Gallo said. "But he got antsy when he heard about Muñoz, and I couldn't get anyone near him."

"What I don't understand is this," Chris said. "Why do they want us now, after all this time?"

"It's politics, dear. I spent all my coin with the Party getting Merle out of his jam. They been trying to ease me out ever since, on account of the scandal. They got a new technocratic image they're trying to cultivate, and I don't fit in."

"Now what's the next move, Gallo?"

"They don't want this thing to come to trial. I doubt if they're even particularly after you, Chris. You just got swept up in the net. But you see, once they get the ball rolling, it's hell getting it to stop. So, what they'd really like us to do is just sort of disappear. Preferably to some place where there's no extradition treaty, so they don't have to go through all the trouble of bringing us back."

"I'm sorry I got you into this, Gallo."

"Hey, you were only doing what comes natural, girl. I would've done the same. We're two of a kind."

"So what happens now?"

"The jig is up, honey. The federal prosecutor's already preparing the indictments. I'm gonna hand in my resignation tomorrow, and I hope to be out of here with Carmen by the end of the week."

"Where you going, Gallo?"

"Paraguay," he said.

"Paraguay?"

"Sure, I got friends there," he said. "In the cement-block business. They offered me a franchise."

Chris burst out laughing.

"What's so funny? They're building the biggest dam in the world down there. There's a lot of money to be made."

"I see what you mean," she said. And then, feeling the floor suddenly start to give way beneath her feet: "If you were me, Gallo, what would you do now?"

"Get out while you can," he said. "And sign everything over to your mother or they'll confiscate it for sure."

Merle returned in a couple of minutes with a shrug of apology.

"Kids," he said.

"Oh, don't be so grim," Chris said, thinking of Merle in comparison to his father, wondering how two people of the same family could be so different. It was almost as if they belonged to separate species.

"I'm not grim," he said, bringing her a drink and one for himself.

"Of course you are," she said, clucking at him in a way that her mother had often done. "But I find it all rather touching."

He fell serious all at once. "Tell me about Diana. Please."

"She's . . . fine," Chris said, hesitating. "I mean she's happy, genuinely happy, though it's all beyond me. She's entered the Novitiate of St. Dominic, just to . . ."

She stopped, wondering at herself for the way she was trying to soften the blow. He was gazing at her in an expressionless way that she remembered from Altamirano's patio in 1954 and recognized instantly as the first stage of shock.

"Come on, Merle, I've been all through that myself," she went on, "and it's not worth it. I raised hell with her, and, I swear to God, all I did was make her feel persecuted in her faith, like a little martyr of the Church."

"I should talk to her," he said, barely listening. "I should find a way to talk to her."

This was just what Chris had intended to suggest, and yet she felt that Merle was moving too quickly, and she said, "After the novice year, a lot of them change their minds, you know."

"If I had been there . . ." he began.

"Don't blame yourself, darling," she said. "It's more my fault than anyone's. I could have sent her to school in the States, but after she lost you, I just didn't have the heart."

He shook his head, blaming her, exonerating her, she couldn't tell.

"She talks about being a missionary, working with the Indians in Chiapas. It makes me sick, but with your concern for the downtrodden," she said, unable to resist a barbed reference to his inexplicable and foolhardy impulse to join El Niño's last stand, "you ought to be delighted."

He shook his head more violently this time, as if coming to a decision.

"And tell me about your mother," he said.

"Maureen? Oh, Maureen's the same as ever. Does she ever change? But Val's getting married again. A Venezuelan banker she met through me. A bit of a fairy, frankly. But he's kind, and rich as Croesus. They'll be living in Caracas."

Merle smiled and raised his glass as if to toast Val in her happiness, and Chris raised hers in return, but could not bring herself to drink.

"Would you prefer mine?" Merle asked, after taking a sip from it.

She accepted his glass, swallowed a bit, and they both started giggling, just as they had when they were kids together in the nursery at the old Hotel O'Hare.

"You're okay," she said. "You're happy, aren't you?"

He seemed to be thinking it over.

"I've thought so lately," he said. "But how can you measure happiness?"

"You're happy," she said decisively. She had already settled it with herself. She would tell him nothing of Gallo or Altamirano. She would leave him as she had found him. Indeed, she probably had no choice in the matter.

And yet just then he looked anything but happy, and she wanted to slap him for indulging himself in this momentary uncertainty, for tempting her yet again. She rose, unable to bear his uncertainty an instant longer, nor the common voice of the young mother coming from a distant room coaxing the children to bed, nor their confident yelps of protest.

"I just wanted to see you one last time and make sure," she said, starting ahead of him in the direction of the door. "I had some business in San Francisco, anyway. A couple of investors."

"How is business?" he asked, stopping with her at the door.

"Everything I touch turns to gold," she said, brushing his cheek with her lips. "And your writing?"

"I'm just about to finish something."

She rested her head against his shoulder. He still smelled the same, she thought. He smelled like a Mexican, of tortillas and beans. But he'd bite her head off if she said that. And she would love his anger. She would love anything he gave her.

His arms closed around her. He said, "Chris?"

"Yes, of course I'll file for divorce."

"I wasn't going to ask that."

She pulled gently away, squeezing his hand, "I know you weren't."

As she started down the stairs, he called, "Tell Diana how much I love her."

"I'll write her," she called back. "Visits aren't allowed for the first six months."

He started after her down the stairs. "I'll find a taxi for you, Chris."

But just then, mercifully, a cab squealed to a stop at the curb and she let it swallow her up.

At the Stanford Court there was a message from Val: *"Don't bother phoning. No need to return home. Uncle Harry was here. See you soon in Kathmandu. Will offer every assistance."* Which Chris translated in the elevator to the ninth floor as: *"Don't phone because the line may be tapped. Don't come home to Mexico because there's a warrant out for your arrest. Meet me in Caracas where my banker boyfriend will help you sort out your financial problems and find you a safe haven from the law."*

As soon as she got to her room, she dropped the message on the nightstand and threw open all the windows, for she felt as if she might suffocate. She removed all her clothes, folded them neatly on a chair with her shoes underneath, set her panties and panty hose to soak in Woolite in the bathroom sink, and slipped on a white dressing gown. Then she poured herself a drink and sat down cross-legged on the bed to think. But she couldn't think. And soon she found herself cataloguing the details of her room.

It was a tiny room that cost a great price. But it was tastefully decorated. Everything was about three-quarter size. The walls were painted a fresh off-white. The curtains, counterpane, armchair and love seat were royal blue. The closets and bathroom were also very small, built into the south wall and concealed behind identical little doors. One had to think twice before heading into the bathroom, Chris observed, or one might find oneself in a closet. The effect of all this miniaturizing was charmingly precarious, like a doll's house: One had the feeling that it might all fall apart with only the gentlest push. There were no pictures on the walls. Instead, there were lovely little gilt-frame mirrors everywhere, and red and blue anemones in blue and white china vases. In her present state of mind, Chris did not find the room particularly comforting. It took her back to a Corpus Christi fiesta in 1934 or 1935, when she and Merle had visited the miniature marketplace in the Jardín Obregón and fought viciously over the affections of little Delia Nieves. Delia, who had been moldering in the grave for the past forty years.

Chris got up and poured herself another whiskey. For some reason she felt not in the least bit fastidious about it. She had suddenly lost her fear of poisoning. It was as if—life had dealt her so many low blows lately, what else could it do to her now? It was an exhilarating feeling, and she filled her glass to the top.

"Now sit yourself down, Christopher," she said to herself, "and go over your options."

But when she sat down again she could think of none. She couldn't stay in San Francisco. She couldn't go back to Acapulco. She had no desire to go to Caracas with Val and become a ward of Val's fiancé. And the worst of it was, she kept thinking about what Diana would feel when she learned of her disgrace. She would almost rather die, she thought, than have the girl find out that her mother had traded in dope. She kept imagining remote corners of the world where she could hide and perhaps start over again: Hong Kong, Singapore, Montevideo, New Zealand, South Africa. . . . But no matter what place she contemplated, she kept seeing Mexico, the place where she had invested all of her energy and love, the place where she had been born and raised, her home.

She remembered leaving Gallo's office in the Colima State capitol building this morning and ordering her driver to stop at the old Moorish-looking hotel on the Plaza Libertad where her mother had gotten her start back in 1911. The place had been replastered, repainted pastel gray, and the name had been changed, but it looked as good as new. She recalled getting out of the car, crossing the shady portico and going inside to have a look around. The tiled inner courtyard, full of potted orange trees, banana trees and tropical flowers, was cool and refreshing as ever, and the little fountain in the middle splashed water out of the dolphin's mouth, just as it had when she was a little girl. She was delighted to find that the door to her little room on the second floor was still painted red. It was open, as all the doors were, to allow for cross-ventilation. Chris peeked inside. The floor was still tile, alternating red and white squares. The windows had the same old green wooden shutters. Most of the same pale oak colonial-style furniture remained. The large matrimonio bed was different, of course, for the room was no longer a nursery. Chris recalled that over there by the window her nanny, Manola, had slept on a straw pallet. And over there by the whitewashed western wall had been her own little fanciful pink-and-white bed, cluttered with heart-shaped pillows and lacy counterpanes. And she wondered how she could have been so desperately unhappy, so hateful and tortured and haunted in such a pleasant little room as this.

But she had puzzled over such questions often in her life, and the answer was still the same: There's something wrong with me. I'm not like other people.

Chris did not visit her mother's old room, but as she passed it on the arcade she found its door closed and locked, and remembered herself as a little thing of three and four, hovering outside for hours listening to the endless tapping sound of her mother's antique typewriter, yearning to knock on the door and be let in.

A hotel maid came along then and asked if there was anything Chris wanted.

"I'm just having a look around," she said. "My mother used to own this place."

And gave her a five-peso coin to show her the little attic room where—Maureen once confessed—Chris had been conceived.

It was empty now, full of cobwebs and mice droppings, which she thought somehow appropriate.

"Gracias," she said to the maid, and returned to her limousine, wondering what it must have been like in 1927, in the middle of the Cristero Rebellion, finding a priest in a muddy field and bringing him home and hiding him in the attic and nursing him back to health and then ruthlessly seducing him. It seemed such a wildly, improbably romantic tale—like any one of a dozen of Maureen's unpublished stories—that Chris wondered if the whole thing hadn't been made up.

Yet on the way to the Colima airport her heart had stilled, her bittersweet nostalgia waned, and she indulged herself in a delicious little daydream: She would make the driver turn around and take her back to the hotel. She would book herself into her mother's old room, which she would find unchanged, right down to the bed where she had been born. She would walk across the plaza to the grocery store, buy a half-liter bottle of lye-based cleaning solution and a package of single-edged razor blades. She would return to her room, remove her clothes, climb into the bathtub, slit her wrists and drink the entire bottle of cleaning solution. She would even remember to leave a little note: *"I was only a transient here. I've spent all my life in hotels."*

But now as Chris poured herself yet another drink, she found that the fantasy no longer appealed to her, because under everything else, she thought, she was born to suffer, she deserved to suffer, and death would be too sweet.

And she felt a crazy little thrill of pleasure that she had nothing left, not her husband, not her daughter, not her mother, not her country or her business, not even her looks.

And decided to follow Gallo to Paraguay, which she had heard was a hell on earth.

Pleased with her decision, and excited by the prospect of adventure, she went to the window to look out at the lights of Nob Hill, the Embarcadero, the Bay Bridge, Treasure Island and Berkeley, and suddenly found herself outside on the ledge above California Street with her drink still in her hand and her white dressing gown billowing in the wind and the cable cars going by underneath and she said to herself, "No, it's impossible, I'm going home," and jumped.

"Mama!" she cried, as she fell.